BELKA,

Why Don't You Bark?

Hideo Furukawa

BELKA,
Why Don't You Bark?

by
Hideo Furukawa

Translated by
Michael Emmerich

**HAIKA
SORU**

SAN FRANCISCO

Belka, Why Don't You Bark?

Beruka, hoenainoka? © Hideo Furukawa, 2005
Originally published in Japan by Bungei Shunju in 2005 (hardcover) and 2008 (paperback).
English translation Copyright © Michael Emmerich 2012

Cover design by Sam Elzway

This book has been selected by the Japanese Literature Publishing Project (JLPP), an initiative of the Agency for Cultural Affairs of Japan.

HAIKASORU
Published by VIZ Media, LLC
295 Bay Street
San Francisco, CA 94133

www.haikasoru.com

Furukawa, Hideo, 1966-
  [Beruka, hoenainoka? English]
 Belka, why don't you bark? / by Hideo Furukawa ; translated by Michael Emmerich.
    p. cm.
 ISBN 978-1-4215-4937-8
 I. Emmerich, Michael. II. Title.
 PL870.R85B4713 2012
 895.6'36--dc23
                        2012028981

Printed in the U.S.A.
First printing, October 2012

This book is dedicated to Boris Yeltsin:

Hey, Boris, I know your secret.

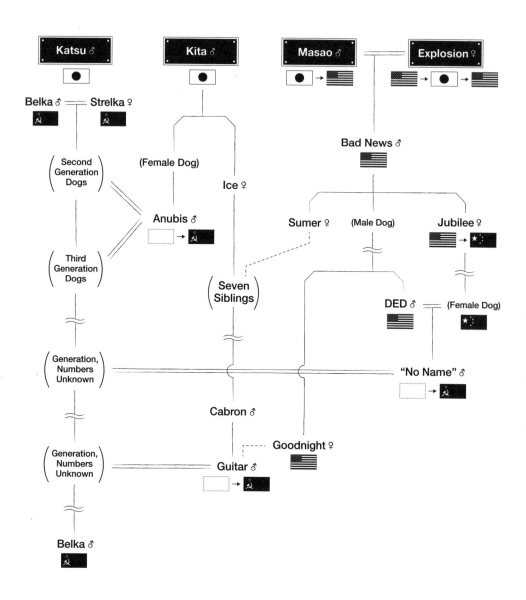

Canine Family Tree

1943–1990

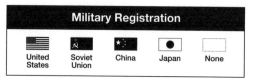

Military Registration

| United States | Soviet Union | China | Japan | None |

TABLE OF CONTENTS

You'll say this is fiction.
Sure, I'll admit that. But
then what isn't a fiction?

"I want to set them loose."

—*Siberia (the sleeping land)*, 199X

The snow had let up, but the temperature remained below zero. The road was hemmed in on each side by a forest of white birches. The young man trudged onward, bundled from head to toe against the cold, snow crunching underfoot. He had been walking an hour already. Then, at last, he saw a house. A cabin—made of logs, rough-hewn. Clearly inhabited. The smoking chimney proved that.

The young man's face brightened.

The place looked as if it belonged to a hunter. The man noted the four skis propped against the wall. Two inhabitants, maybe? Or was one pair an extra? You'd think there'd be a guard dog, but there wasn't. Instead, the owner himself pushed the door open, stepped outdoors. Must have heard the footsteps in the snow. Realized he had an unanticipated visitor.

He was old. An old man. His expression softened in response to the young man's greeting. "What are you doing way out here?" he said. "So deep in the hills, this time of year, in this no man's land? There is not a *dacha* for miles. Lost your way?"

"Does the road lead to a village?" the young man asked.

The old man nodded. "It does, but it is a five-hour walk."

"The back wheels of our car got stuck in a stream," the young man said. "We couldn't push the car out, so I left my friend and came on alone to ask for help in the village."

"Come in for a bit," the old man said. "You had better warm up."

The young man thanked him and stepped inside. The temperature was easily seventy degrees. Which made it at least seventy degrees warmer than outside. The young man removed his mink *shapka*, his heavy gloves, his coat. He scanned the room, not even trying to conceal his curiosity. Just inside the door was a hunting knife, a hatchet. Farther back in the room was a rifle. A shelf lined with bottles of vodka, a globe. A map of the world on the wall. It was old, though. The Soviet Union carpeted the Eurasian supercontinent. Tacked up around the map, several family photographs, portraits of the old "founding fathers." *It's been ages*, the young man mused, *since I last saw that profile of Vladimir Lenin.*

"Never seen how a hunter lives, I take it? Here, take a chair."

"Thanks."

"I was just getting some lunch together," the old man said. "I have stewed venison. Will you join me?"

"That would be great, thank you."

Vodka appeared. They toasted.

"It is too quiet out here," the old man said. "You have made my day, turning up like this. It is a delight to host you."

"You live alone here?" the young man asked.

"Never liked hunting with others. Not my style."

"No hunting dogs either?"

"No," the old man said. "I do not keep any."

The young man observed his host across the table. It was hard to gauge his exact age. He was in his sixties, maybe seventies. His hair and beard were white. The young man could tell what color it had been. It had never been black. This old man had been blond in his youth. His features were pure Slav.

The young man was Central Asian.

"Have another glass." The old man poured more vodka.

A woodpecker called outside.

The young man kept looking around. "You shot this deer yourself?" he asked. He kept talking, scanning the room. Beside the table was a shelf crammed with jars of pickles and preserved foods. Mushrooms, cucumbers. The old man was complaining about his pension. The whole system would be bankrupt soon, he said. His tone was calm, measured; these financial issues didn't appear to be causing him any real trouble. "Worked my whole life in the Ministry of Railroads, you know. Who would think times would get so bad?" he said. "They were always screwing with us."

There was a radio by the wall.

"You get your news from that?" the young man asked.

"Yes, though I try not to run the batteries down," the old man said with a chuckle. "Still, I know what is happening in the world. Even here in the woods, miles from anywhere."

"Do you really?" the young man said.

"You know what? I have fish too—let me get some. Smoked salmon, how could I have forgotten. Getting old, I guess, not offering you anything with your vodka." The old man tossed back a glass and stood up. He wandered off toward the cooking area.

The young man rose too. "Please don't bother," he said. *Please come back to the table. Please. Too many dangerous things over there. That rifle, the axe.*

"Stop," the young man said. "Archbishop."

His right hand held an Austrian pistol with a polymer frame.

The old man froze in his tracks.

"Hands up," the young man ordered. "Turn around."

The old man did as the young man said. His face betrayed no hint of fear; he hadn't even paled. Though he wasn't smiling either.

The young man walked over. He grinned.

And then something happened. The young man was no amateur. He had kept his distance, taking care not to get too close. He had held his elbow out to one side, kept the pistol trained on the old man. He hadn't let down his guard, he was still in his safety zone. Or so he thought. But then, all of a sudden, he couldn't see. He was stunned. *What's happening?!* He smelled alcohol. *Vodka. He spat vodka at me. He had it in his mouth.*

The young man pulled the trigger.

But by then his knee was broken. His left kneecap had been kicked, bashed in, his leg snapped backward. He felt his body crumbling. One second his right leg was there, perfectly straight, the next it too had been kicked out from under him. His body hung in midair for a split second, then crashed to the floor. A motion so clean it was beautiful. Zero gravity. Then his weight returned. He felt the old man bring his heel down on his spine, then kick his skull. The other foot ground into his palm. The pistol was gone, kicked away.

He felt a pressure on his back.

He felt something knobby slam against his spinal cord.

The old man's elbow.

He couldn't move. There was an arm around his neck, his head spun.

And there was a crack. A crack, however, that he didn't hear.

The young man was dead.

"*Sheesh,*" the old man sighed, hoisting himself off the body he was straddling, clambering to his feet. "So you found this hideaway. Finally caught the scent," he crooned. "You have some nose."

Dogs, he thought. *Just like dogs.*

But what do you know about real *dogs?*

The old man crossed the room. Went over to a shelf on the wall where the map of the world was hung, the family pictures, the "founding fathers." He took the globe in his arms.

"Impostors. You do not know shit about real dogs," he said. "Never will."

Suddenly the globe was split in two, top and bottom. He lifted the metal lid from its base. A skull sat inside it. An animal skull. The skull of a medium-sized dog. It was charred, but here and there patches of skin remained. The interior of the globe had been fitted out with protective supports and foam. The globe was a case. The old man gazed tenderly at the skull.

He said he had a friend back in the car. Guess I need to take care of him too.

"It is true, I admit it," he announced, evidently to the dog's skull. "I have lost my mind. I *want* to set them loose. More than anything. All the old powers, before I die. Before my...before *our* old world disappears forever."

Is that not right, my darling?

You, you great Soviet hero, the greatest dog ever to live, the only one who deserves this globe.

By then the old man was no longer talking aloud.

Already it had begun.

1943

It was forgotten.

People forgot, for instance, that a foreign power had, in fact, seized American territory during the course of the twentieth century. In an entire century, it happened only once. In the North Pacific, Japanese forces occupied two of the Aleutian Islands. The first was Attu, at the westernmost tip of the archipelago; the second was Kiska, farther to the east. The Japanese army raised the Rising Sun over the islands in June 1942 and gave each a new Japanese name. Henceforth Attu would be called Atsuta; Kiska would be known as Narukami.

The occupation of the two islands was part of a broader strategy to divert American attention from the Japanese offensive on Midway Atoll, in the Central Pacific. On June 4, air attacks were launched against Dutch Harbor on Unalaska Island, in the heart of the Aleutians; the Battle of Midway began the next day. Japanese forces conducted surprise landings on Attu and Kiska from the night of June 7 to the morning of June 8.

The islands fell easily. America lost land to the enemy.

The Japanese had no intention of holding the islands indefinitely, however. The Aleutian campaign had originally been devised as a diversion, and it was far from clear that the islands offered any strategic value. The military planned to hold them for the short term, until winter, then consider how to proceed. This plan was revised when surveys conducted in the wake of the occupation revealed that the islands would remain habitable through the winter; toward the end of June, it was decided to hold them for the long term.

Habitable the islands were, but the climate was extraordinarily harsh. The Aleutian chain as a whole was often said to have the worst weather in the world. The frigid waters of the Bering Sea ran up against the warmer waters of the Pacific along the archipelago's length, leaving its islands shrouded in fog that never lifted. Only rarely did the sun peek out. Ferocious winds whipped the rocks; torrential rains battered the earth. And then, of course, there was the snow.

Soon the bitter winter set in.

Things were bad on the islands in 1942, but true disaster had yet to strike. The Japanese lost air superiority, enabling the Americans to pound the islands from the skies, and there were delays in establishing ground defenses. And the worst was still to come. The full-blown tragedy would not occur until the following year.

May 1943. The garrison on Atsuta/Attu was wiped out.

As eleven thousand American soldiers rushed ashore under cover of naval bombardment, the twenty-five hundred Japanese troops stationed on the island charged into a hopeless battle, ready to meet their deaths. It was a so-called banzai attack. Not a single soldier was taken. Every last man among their number died for the Emperor.

Kiska Island.

Or now that it was Japanese territory, Narukami.

Kiska/Narukami was occupied by a force twice as large as the force on Attu/Atsuta. Some way had to be found to avoid a second tragedy. And so, though the Japanese had effectively already lost naval superiority, it was suggested that the entire force be evacuated in a plan called the "Ke-gō Operation." The first stage, involving the evacuation by submarine of sick and injured soldiers and civilian contractors, concluded in June. The second stage, in which a naval fleet was dispatched to collect the remaining units, was carried out in July, on "Zero day." Z-Day had first been set for July 11 but had to be postponed repeatedly owing to inclement weather. Then at last, on July 29, a rescue fleet consisting of two light cruisers and nine destroyers sailed into Kiska/Narukami Harbor and safely evacuated the island's entire fifty-two-hundred-man garrison.

The Ke-gō Operation was a success. A heavy fog kept the Americans from noticing what they were doing.

Everyone on the island escaped. Or rather: every *human*.

The Japanese army abandoned the rest.

They left the military dogs. Four dogs in all. Each came from a different line. One was a Hokkaido dog—or an Ainu dog, as they were once called—a breed known for its musculature and its ability to withstand the cold. His name was Kita, and he belonged to the navy. His job was to show which of the wild plants on the island were edible: he was a taster. The second and third dogs, both German shepherds, belonged to the army. One was named Masao, the other Katsu. The fourth, also a German shepherd, was neither a navy nor an army dog; she was a bitch and had been taken from an American prisoner. Her name was Explosion.

Prior to the invasion the previous year, ten men had been operating a wireless telegraph and aerological station on the island under the aegis of the US Navy. When the Japanese military landed, eight of these soldiers escaped; the other two were taken prisoner. Explosion had been captured along with them.

The United States was deploying vast numbers of highly trained military dogs all around the world in those days, dispatching them to the front lines. It had established its first training center in 1935 at Camp Lejeune, North Carolina, the Marine Corps main base, and the next decade saw the creation of an additional five centers. By the end of World War II, some forty thousand dogs had been raised in these facilities. Explosion was one of these. After June 1942, however, she was no longer an American. Now she belonged to the Japanese.

Japan, as it happened, had a three-decade lead on America in military dog combat. The first time Japanese dogs ever took to the field of battle was in 1904, during the Russo-Japanese War. Japanese breeds were used, but they were trained in Germany. Eventually the military began importing German shepherds, and a research institute at an infantry school in Chiba launched Japan's first serious effort to breed military dogs. Following the Manchurian Incident in 1931, the army ministry helped oversee the creation of a civilian-run Imperial Military Dog Society, and the Independent Garrison Unit's War Dog Platoon began conducting experimental canine maneuvers in Manchukuo.

Not surprisingly, Germany had led the way in world military dog history. Systematic efforts to train German shepherds commenced in 1899 with the establishment of the German Shepherd Society. As early as the Great War (otherwise known as World War I), Germany was already deploying large numbers of *modern* military dogs. Indeed, the figure had climbed as high as twenty thousand by the time hostilities ended. And the dogs had performed incredibly well.

Germany's success was a revelation to other nations. *We can let dogs fight our wars!*

Two catastrophic wars were fought during the twentieth century. The twentieth century was, it is often said, a century of war. It was also the century of military dogs.

Hundreds of thousands of dogs were sent into battle.

In July 1943, four such dogs were abandoned on an island. A certain island.

The island no longer had a name. The Japanese forces had retreated, taking the Rising Sun flags and the rest of their paraphernalia with them. The island wasn't called Narukami anymore. As far as the Americans knew, though, it was still occupied by Japan, and until it was reclaimed it would remain an illegitimate Japanese territory. So the island was no longer Narukami, but neither had it gone back to being the American territory known as Kiska Island.

It was a nameless place, owned by four abandoned dogs.

The island was about half the size of Tokyo. A dense fog hung over it and the surrounding waters, never clearing, isolating it from the mainland and its tundra. It was an island of white. But not the white of snow, which lingered only on the peaks. Clear springs burbled through the valleys. Grasses covered the land, their blades glistened with dew that never dried. EVERYONE'S GONE, the dogs thought. THERE'S NO ONE LEFT. They knew the Japanese had gone, that they had been forsaken. Kita, Masao, Katsu, Explosion. Yes. They understood.

It was all over.

Each dealt differently with this new reality.

The nameless island had been set adrift in zero time. It was like the end of the world, or the cradle of the world's imminent creation. Ferocious downpours daily spattered the earth. The howling wind never let up, and yet the fog never dispersed. Yellow flowers blooming among the grasses were the only flecks of brightness. The Japanese had left enough food for the dogs to last a few weeks. During squalls, the dogs hid in the trenches. On the white island.

On the foggy island.

Reddish-purple thistles bloomed.

Bouts of heavy shelling seemed to proclaim that the world had ended. Day in and day out the Americans persevered in their pointless raids, unaware that the Japanese were already gone. The flying corps showered the island with leaflets urging surrender. In all, one hundred thousand of these scraps of paper were dropped. The dogs raised their heads to watch as they rained from the sky.

Rain, leaflets, bombs. Slicing through fog.

Bombs dropped, blasted the earth.

And in the midst of it all, the world was beginning. A new world hatching from the egg of zero time. *This world.* Some of the dogs sensed its coming. They had no human keepers now—they had their liberty. Four muscular dogs with exceptionally keen senses, trained to withstand the cold, living on a nameless island. Free.

Explosion was a bitch. Kita, Masao, and Katsu were male. Explosion and Masao mated. Ordinarily military dogs' reproductive activities were rigorously controlled, but here they were unsupervised. Explosion acquiesced to Masao's advances, let him straddle her. They were both purebred German shepherds—perhaps that sparked their romance. Kita, the Hokkaido, often romped with Explosion and Masao, but he never approached Explosion.

The other German shepherd, Katsu, kept to himself. He didn't relish his freedom. He realized that he had been abandoned on the island, that his masters would never return, but still he stayed close to the antiaircraft guns his army unit had operated, making the area his home and spending the better part of every day there.

He knew it was all over, but he refused to accept it.

Explosion, Masao, and Kita ran wild through the fields.

Frolicking, barking.

Finally the Americans decided to stage a large-scale offensive. They stopped this zero time. The island was to be given its old name back: Kiska. Their forces landed on August 15, 1943. Some fifty-three hundred Canadian troops joined the operation, forming a combined force of thirty-five thousand men. Soldiers entered the Japanese camp. There was no one there. From August 18 to 22, as many as thirty-five thousand troops combed the island in search of the enemy.

They captured three dogs.

Explosion understood. For the first time in more than a year, the soldiers she saw walking toward her were her old masters—Americans! "C'mon, boy!" someone yelled, and she dashed off ecstatically in his direction. Masao and Kita followed. They replied to the American soldiers' calls with wagging tails. True, these were the very men they had been warned to be cautious of, trained to attack. Battle targets. But they had been released from these notions. What did they care? The men were beckoning to them, why not go? The dogs knew their days on the nameless island were over. This was Kiska again. And apparently they were going to be taken in.

They had been abandoned, freed from time. Now they were being welcomed back.

Three dogs, together, whimpered at the troops. FINALLY, they said. YOU'VE RETURNED.

The fourth dog, too, was ecstatic in his own way. Katsu lay in wait for the landing forces in his den. His masters might not have returned, but the enemy had come. He was overjoyed. He waited for the Americans by the antiaircraft guns, where he belonged, and counterattacked. NO REASON TO LOSE HOPE! I STILL HAVE WORK TO DO! When one of the Americans wandered obliviously into range, Katsu sank his teeth into his leg, then ran into a clearing that had been sewn with land mines. A few soldiers gave chase, determined to "grab that Japanese dog," and triggered the mines. Katsu, too, had carried out a banzai attack. Katsu, like the Japanese soldiers who were his masters, sacrificed his life for the cause.

Explosion, Masao, and Kita, however, didn't die.

They were fed, cared for. All three were American dogs now. They belonged to the American military. And their numbers increased. After nine weeks' gestation, Explosion gave birth. It was October on Kiska Island. As a rule dogs give birth easily, but the harshness of the environment made this birth unexpectedly difficult. The soldiers called in a military surgeon to operate, and the mother and several of her pups were saved. Of nine puppies, five lived.

There were eight dogs in 1943, including Explosion's puppies.

Eight dogs, still on Kiska Island.

"Nighty-Night, Vor."

The mansion was surrounded by a wall. The wall itself was perhaps two and a half meters high, but it was topped by loops of wire. The wire wasn't barbed. It was electrified. Security cameras had been installed at intervals, approximately eight meters apart. They were aimed outward, naturally. Out over the wall.

One of the lenses had been shattered.

The compound lay under a thick silence. It seemed, somehow, unnaturally still, as though something that should have been there wasn't.

Patches of snow dotted the garden, and there was a drift in the corner where two walls met, blown higher by the wind, untouched. Here and there small footprints scarred the mud. No, not footprints: paw prints. Four or five pads. Animal tracks. Traces.

It was twilight now, but the compound was bathed in light. Lamps glared high overhead, carefully positioned to eliminate all shadows. The darkness lay beyond the walls. There were a few lit windows in the high-rise apartment buildings off to the left, if you were facing the compound's main entrance to the northeast. Those buildings, the "projects," had gone up in the 1970s. The buildings to the right of the compound were mere silhouettes. Rooflines. They had once housed factories. Once upon a time, those factories had operated late into the night. But that was years ago, back when this was still the USSR. The factories filled orders from the Ministry of Defense, churning out tanks and automatic rifles—not that anyone had known. It wasn't public information. Mechanical plants whirring at full capacity, amassing huge stockpiles of munitions. There was no demand for that stuff anymore. The new Russian capitalism had not been good for this sector.

It favored a different sort of market.

The black market.

Money poured in *here*, for instance. Inside these walls, into this compound.

The owner of the mansion was coming home after sunset. His two cars drew up outside the front gate. A Volvo and a BMW. The BMW had tinted windows. The man in the guardhouse glanced at the cars, then pushed a button. The gate lurched into motion.

When it had opened all the way, the two cars entered. The gate glided closed.

The cars rolled slowly up the cobblestone drive toward the roundabout and the front door. After twenty seconds one of the Volvo's front wheels hit something. Something that stuck up from the drive. A clank. The device had been planted right out in the open, disguised so that it looked like just another cobblestone. Very bold. It had been tripped. The driver of the Volvo felt it. It felt like he had driven full speed onto a road full of potholes or… maybe he'd run up against—

That was the end of the thought. The driver was blown up, straight up into the air, still in his seat. The hood of the car, flying.

The BMW slammed to a halt.

Three men sprang from the car: one from the front passenger seat, two from the back. Kicking open the doors, they jumped out, dispersing. One wore a *shapka* with the earflaps raised, the others were bareheaded and had crew cuts. The first wore a fur coat; the other two had on expensive dark suits. Neither the coat nor the suit jackets were buttoned. They never were. The men had their hands thrust under their lapels. The fur coat took out a submachine gun, the suits whipped their pistols from their holsters, and they stood still, ready to fire.

Two men tumbled out of the Volvo's unexploded back seat, alive. Bloody, screaming. They crawled away from the car.

The BMW's driver seemed to have come to his senses, because all of a sudden he threw the car into reverse. He had to get the hell out of here, to get his boss, sitting there in the back seat, in the middle, away from this vision of hell in the mansion's front garden.

Suddenly, all the lights in the building crashed.

As if a fuse had blown. The building, visible a second ago, was gone.

There had been a small pop inside, but it wasn't audible out front.

The darkness unnerved the men even more.

One of the men from the BMW broke into a run, though he had no idea whom he ought to be attacking. It was just a reflex. He jumped off the drive, zigzagging as he ran, heading for the porch, searching for an assailant. His left foot felt something. He had been a wrestler and had an impressive physique—that's how he ended up in this job, working as a bodyguard. Shit, it's a feint, he thought, recalling the single worst blunder he had made as a wrestler. His hair stood on end. Just then, his left ankle was pulling the wire. About ten centimeters above the ground. A booby trap. The wire had tripped it. Something flew at him from one side. Searing pain.

Not just in one place. Everywhere on his body.

The submachine gun in his hand fired at random, senselessly, as his muscles contracted. He was in agony. An agonizing death.

One of the men crawling on the driveway took a bullet.

The BMW reached the gate, backward. The driver lowered his window, yelled at the guard, "Open up! Open the fuck up!" But the guard didn't answer. He was prostrate on the floor of the guardhouse. A line drawn across his throat.

One clean horizontal line.

It looked to the driver as if the guard wasn't there. He considered getting out and opening the gate himself, but at the sound of gunfire he instinctively hit the gas. He rammed the bumper back into the gate, then shifted gears and screeched forward.

The lamps illuminating the garden were going out now, one after another. Each time one went out, there was a crash. Somehow they were being smashed. The rest of the compound joined the mansion in its darkened invisibility. There was hardly light at all, anywhere.

A single, precise gunshot.

A second.

A third. A fourth…a seventh.

The sound of a new magazine snapping into place. Someone tossing aside the old magazine, even though it still had a few bullets left, swapping it out for another. A fresh, full cartridge. The BMW swerved wildly, searching for a way out. The gunman watched the car go, then sprang into action. He was fast, yes. But he was also a step ahead of them. He saw where things were going.

Another series of gunshots. One bullet shattered the BMW's windshield and lodged itself in the driver's forehead; another buried itself in the hip of the man who tumbled out of the car's back seat as it hit a tree. Soon after, a third bullet entered his head.

Silence.

Only one man moving. A pistol in each hand. The BMW's headlights were still burning, and their faint light revealed his face. His profile. His hair was pure white. White the way an old man's hair is white, when it has lost its color. Two weeks ago, he had been holed up deep in the forest. Living in a hunter's shack like a hermit. The guns in his gloved hands weren't hunting rifles, though. They were army weapons: 9mm machine pistols.

The old man strode over to the body.

The body of the last man he killed. The body of the owner of the mansion. He worked the shirt down over the corpse's shoulders, exposing its chest. He inspected each shoulder. The large cross tattooed on the left, the skull on the right.

The locations of the designs showed that he was indeed a Russian mafia kingpin, that he had been acknowledged as a leader by his fellows.

He was a boss. The tattoos proved that. Not in one of the new organizations, however. He belonged to the old mafia; he was a product of the Soviet system.

Having found the proof he wanted, the old man let slip a smile. A smile so subtle his face remained all but expressionless. "Nighty-night, Vor," he murmured.

The old man wasted no time. A minute later, he was inside. Not a light in the entire building. Two buff corpses sprawled in the parlor, shot dead in the middle of a card game; on the sofa behind them, the body of a carefully made-up young woman in a flashy dress. These bodies had been there for an hour or so.

Another body in the hall.

The old man stepped into the half-hidden security room behind the parlor.

A young man was waiting inside. Alive. Terrified. Drenched in sweat. Drops fell periodically from his face, his neck. He was sitting on a chair, his posture oddly strained, straight as a rod.

"If you are hot, why not take off your sweater?" the old man said.

"I can't move," the young man replied.

"Sure you can, just take it off," the old man repeated.

Desperation in his eyes, the young man nodded and stiffly, tensely, stripped the sweater off. Underneath the sweater he had on a paratrooper shirt with horizontal blue stripes.

The wall behind the young man was completely taken up by ten television monitors. Images from the security cameras were projected on their screens. Or not. Some were blank. From where he sat, the young man could operate the recorder, and he had a microphone that let him respond to communications from outside.

"You give them the all-clear, like I said?" the old man said.

"I did exactly as you told me to," the young man said. "Everything."

"Good job," the old man replied. "You did well."

"Don't kill me!" the young man pleaded. He was perched oddly on his chair. Sort of. There was an object between his butt and the seat, like a little pillow. It was a hand grenade. The pin had been pulled. The young man's butt was holding the safety lever down. If he shifted his body the slightest bit, if the grenade happened to slip out from under him, it would explode.

The old man turned to the monitors. He spent a few moments checking the screens, or their blankness. The young man was still sweating. The old man was right beside him, but the young man couldn't turn to face him. There was a sound by the recorder, like duct tape coming off.

"Look at all this crap," the old man muttered. "With all this, you would think…"

With all this, you would think…what? the young man wondered, terrified.

"…you could do better." The old man answered the boy's unspoken question, his tone crisp. "Amateurs. That is what you are. A bunch of amateurs."

A sound the young man had heard once before: a pin being drawn.

It came again, then a third time.

Huh? he thought.

The old man left the security room. On his way out he turned and fired a 9mm bullet into the young man's head, just like that. The young man jerked backwards, then fell, causing the grenade he was sitting on to explode. A second later the three grenades on the video recorder were going off, one after the next, destroying all evidence.

Two minutes later, the old man was in the back garden.

He stood before a low, gray, concrete enclosure. A row of cages with chain-link doors, some open, some closed. He had passed four dead Doberman pinschers on his way here. They had been poisoned. He himself had carefully stirred the poison into their food. There were still some dogs in the kennels, though, alive. He had killed the adults, but not the puppies.

They were barking. Their young voices. The old man stared at them through the chain-link doors.

He watched them for half a minute, then nodded to himself, opened a door, stepped inside. He scooped up an armful of puppies.

The attack on the mansion was all over the media the next day. The first reports were vague, mere repetitions of statements issued by the government. That weekend, a fringe newspaper ran a sensational version of the story on its front page. The provocative headline announced OPPOSITION GROUP RESPONSIBLE. The article said an organization "specializing in bomb attacks" had targeted the residence of a "Vor," the head of a major criminal organization that operated two banks, three hotel chains, and numerous restaurants. The article commented provocatively on the group, which, it said, had sold weapons pilfered from army warehouses. It continued with a lengthy profile of the criminals who were presumed to have killed the Vor, who had, by and large, taken control of this city in the Russian Far East. The article concluded: "At last, the epic battle has arrived on our doorstep, here at the edge of Siberia—a war between the two great forces of the underworld, old and new: the Russian mafia and the Chechen mafia."

1944-1947

Dogs, dogs, where are you now?

For the first forty days of 1944, they remained on Kiska. There were only seven of them now. On January 2, one dog died. Explosion. This female German shepherd had been too weak, after the surgically aided birth she had undergone, to survive the brutal Aleutian winter. During the first six or seven weeks, while the five puppies born alive were still suckling, she tried her best to raise them. But when the time came to wean them, she lost strength. Finally, shortly before dawn on the second day of the new year, she died.

The Americans had already figured out who she was. The previous year, when the Japanese military launched the second stage of its Ke-gō Operation, evacuating its forces *en masse* from Kiska/Narukami, it had blown up the factories, garages, ammunition, and other munitions that had to be left on the island. But they hadn't gotten everything. They ran out of time. More than fifty-two hundred members of the island's garrison had to be loaded into the rescue fleet's ships in just fifty-five minutes. The troops could take only the most essential personal belongings, so any number of notebooks, diaries, and other papers remained in the camps. Important classified documents were burned, of course, but they couldn't dispose of the rest.

As soon as the Americans had retaken the island, they had the landing force's intelligence officers translate what they found. Several documents indicated that Explosion had originally been an American military dog until she was captured by the Japanese on Kiska. "We seized a dog from a US Navy private (a prisoner) at the wireless station," one reference explained. "Her name is Explosion." The Alaska Defense Command conducted an inquiry into her provenance under the jurisdiction of the Navy Flotilla 13.

And so, once again, Explosion was an American.

What about the others? They all *belonged* to the Americans, of course. They were fed by the Americans, cared for by the Americans. But in the end, they hadn't actually become American military dogs. The five puppies were treated as pets by the garrisoned forces, not as fighters, and since the two adults—the German shepherd Masao and the Hokkaido Kita—were military dogs, the Americans considered them Japanese, and prisoners.

Not that this was a bad thing.

The dogs weren't overly concerned with the instructions war minister Tōjō Hideki had laid down in the *Field Army Service Code*: "Do not live to endure the prisoner's humiliation." Neither Masao nor Kita felt particularly humiliated. They saw how Explosion responded to commands in English, and within a week or two they had learned to answer the commands the American troops garrisoned on Kiska issued. They were almost perfect. The soldiers adored them. The two dogs weren't humiliated, they were treated like kings.

February 10, 1944. Seven dogs. Having been stationed for approximately six months on the island, the troops were ordered on to their next field of battle. As they boarded the transport ships that had pulled into Kiska Harbor, the seven dogs went with them.

The twentieth century: a century of war, a century of war dogs. These dogs did more than simply die on the battlefields. They took prisoners and were taken. It happened all the time on the front lines. Dogs were captured. Trained in battle, bred in all sorts of ways, developed, perfected, the dogs were crucial, secret weapons. In the second decade of the twentieth century, Germany seized mastiffs from all over Belgium, which it had conquered, and inducted them into their military, where they were used to pull guns and carts—tasks German dogs were unable to perform. All along the Eastern and

Western Fronts, Europe's great powers busied themselves snatching whatever types of dogs their own armies lacked. The situation was the same during the Second World War. Germany, for instance, still the most advanced nation in terms of its dogs, had compelled almost every dog in the French military to turn on its homeland by the time Germany conquered France.

The seven dogs on Kiska would be sent to the mainland. Two as "prisoners" captured on the front lines, the remaining five to be trained as "candidate military dogs." The dog-training unit of the Marine Corps was especially interested in the puppies. They couldn't wait to see how good these animals would be—a new generation born of two purebred German shepherds, the first (Explosion) American and the second (Masao) a sample of the sort of dog that Japan, with its admittedly greater experience in this area, was sending into the field. The order had been issued for the dogs to be shipped to the mainland precisely for this reason.

If things went well, all seven dogs would be retrained at a Marine Corps camp and emerge from the experience as American military dogs.

Not prisoners, not candidates. Full-fledged military dogs.

The seven dogs had been brought onto one of the transport ships, but no kennels or beds had been prepared. For the time being, they were simply chained to the bridge. The puppies, less than four months old, were terrified. Not that this mattered, of course; the fleet departed anyway. The ship's first stop would be Dutch Harbor, on Unalaska Island, over four hundred miles away.

Three miles brought it outside Kiska Harbor.

The seven dogs would never return.

And they were seasick.

Violently seasick. Tracing the arc of the Aleutian Islands, the boat pushed relentlessly eastward through the North Pacific Ocean. The body of the boat itself, however, rocked in all directions: not just east but west, south, and north. The Aleutians' unique climate played with it, preyed upon it. Clouds hung a mere ten meters or so above the waves; fierce gusts of wind dashed snow across the deck. And the weather kept changing suddenly, then suddenly changing again. First the puppies felt it. They vomited, shivered; their eyes were blank. What terrible punishment was this? Incapable of comprehending what was happening, what it meant to be seasick, the five puppies succumbed. Kita, the Hokkaido, was the next to go. He was the only non–German shepherd, and his symptoms were even worse. Masao, meanwhile, was fine. He remembered having made this crossing to the Aleutians once before. Boarding a similar ship, a transport ship or a destroyer or whatever it was, part of the Northern Command's Hokkai Task Force—he remembered that experience, the long passage from Mutsu Bay. That knowledge kept him from getting sick. Kita remembered too, of course, but it didn't help him.

Kita's nerves were shot.

The men on the bridge assumed, as they made for Unalaska, that he had succumbed to the depression that sometimes comes over dogs in harsh environments.

Depression. Once it hits, a dog loses all will to live.

Still, at root it was just a different form of seasickness. So the humans told themselves. And why shouldn't they? After all, several of the soldiers on board, some among the troops heading home and some being transferred, were vomiting, groaning, lying spattered by their own puke, and by that of their comrades. But their diagnosis was wrong. Yes, Kita was seasick. But this was more than ordinary seasickness. The true cause was the rabies vaccine he had been given before they left Kiska. The vaccination had become obligatory as soon as their relocation to the mainland was decided upon. The Army Air Corps supply unit delivered the vaccinations in the course of their usual duties. There was nothing wrong with the vaccine itself. The problem was that this was Kita's third vaccination, and not enough time had elapsed since his previous shot when he first shipped off with the navy for Kiska/Narukami.

Kita was having a reaction. He had absorbed too much of the vaccine. He grew feverish, lethargic, incapable of controlling his appetite—he was in agony. And so he became depressed, and they misunderstood.

When the ship arrived at Unalaska, Kita was unloaded with the other six dogs, but unlike them he wasn't passed on to the Aleutians' permanent garrison.

"This one's no good," someone said, "don't bother with him."

And so he was separated from the rest.

He remained on Unalaska Island, unable even to watch when, after spending a few days at the Dutch Harbor Naval Operations Facility, the other six dogs were sent off to Camp Lejeune, in North Carolina.

Left behind.

Kita, all alone, on the Aleutian archipelago.

He didn't recover. People still interpreted his symptoms as signs of depression. He showed no desire to live. But they didn't put him to sleep. He was just a dog, so why bother killing him? They tied him up like a guard dog outside a warehouse on a wharf the military used.

Kita, Kita, what are you feeling?

He was a military dog from a lineage of acknowledged superiority. He was strong. A dog among dogs, selected with the utmost care from among his peers. He had been trained to carry out an array of tasks: to be a watchdog, to attack, to search out and rescue wounded soldiers. And then he had been sent to the battlefield. But once he was there, what job was he assigned? On Kiska/Narukami, he had been made to work as a taster, demonstrating to his masters that the island's plants weren't poisonous. He would eat them, show them with his body that they weren't poisonous. That was all. Naturally, it was a very important job. It was only because he served that role that the forces on Kiska/Narukami managed to remain free from scurvy when even basic food supplies were not reliably available in these far-flung occupied areas. But how much did people appreciate his work? His masters, the men to whom he remained so loyal, had left him behind during the Ke-gō Operation. They abandoned him and the other three dogs. And then there were those days spent in the company of others of his kind. Days of freedom on a nameless, uninhabited island. Timeless days. And then his new masters had appeared. They brought food, and when Kita learned English commands, they adored him. Kita trusted them.

Kita was a dog.

So he trusted them.

And now he was sick, and here he was. And once again his masters were gone. Not a single man he recognized. They had shunned him again. Abandoned him again. And the other dogs, from the island...he had been separated from them too. Why? he keened. Shivering from the chills that wracked his body, he keened as though he had contracted a case of pseudo-rabies. Why must I suffer like this? Masters appeared, disappeared. They taught him loyalty, then heartlessly cast him aside. What had been the point of all that training? He had been the cream of the crop, an elite among military dogs. There was no point. No value. And now he was sick and depressed.

What sense is there in living?

Utter, irresistible apathy. There by the harbor, Kita acknowledged hardly anything. He was living in a nightmare. Reality itself was a dream.

But he had food. He wouldn't be allowed to starve.

Though Kita didn't realize it, there was a young man taking care of him. He was twenty-two, a land-based member of the air corps. He had been conscripted in 1942. He loved dogs, so he looked after Kita. He was fascinated by Kita—by his appearance. He had never seen a dog like this back home. It was totally unlike other northern breeds he was familiar with, like Samoyeds or malamutes. This was only to be expected, since the young man had never seen a Japanese dog—or rather, a dog of Japanese origins. The Hokkaido is like a Spitz, with upright ears and a tail that curves up over its back, so courageous and ferocious that it was long used to hunt brown bears. There is an unmistakable aura of wildness in its appearance. *What kind of dog is this?* the young man wondered.

His curiosity piqued, he made a practice of visiting Kita twice every day.

Kita wouldn't die.

He got his strength back, but still he continued to wander in a dream world, as if his spirit had yet to heal. His consciousness was trapped in its nightmare state.

One day in April 1944, two men came and stood before Kita. One was the young man, the other was a mail pilot. The pilot was thirty years old. "Incredible," he muttered. "I've never seen anything like him either." He checked the dog over.

The young man stood off to one side. "I felt bad for him, you know?" he said. "They just sorta left him here, no doghouse or anything, like those two blankets were enough. This is the Aleutians, for Chrissake."

Then: "You can really take him?"

The pilot glanced up. "Sure I can."

"You like him?"

"Absolutely. I'll put him in the post office kennel. It's sort of a hobby— I've got all kinds of dogs. A rare animal like him will give me bragging rights, that's for sure."

"Good news, huh?" the young man said to Kita. "You'll have friends. Mail dogs."

Three days later, the pilot was back. He had taken care of the minimal paperwork necessary for him to take charge of Kita, over at the facility's central office. It was a matter of signing a form, that was all. And then Kita was on a plane. Loaded into the space where the mail had been before it was delivered. Now Kita was an airborne dog.

The weight of a Hokkaido dog on a plane, in place of a few hundred items of mail.

Still Kita hadn't returned from dreamland. He had no idea what was happening—that now, two months after being sick on that boat, he was flying along the eastern tip of the Aleutian arc. He felt only an unfamiliar pull on his body, an unmistakably mechanical shaking.

The nose of the airplane pointed toward Alaska. Toward Anchorage.

In 1944, Alaska wasn't yet a state of the United States. It was no more than a peripheral territory. A territory that nonetheless occupied fully a fifth the area of the United States. In the summer, the sun rose in the north northeast and sank in the north northwest; in the winter it rose in the south southeast and sank in the south southwest.

At first, the pilot kept Kita in the post office kennel. There was a lot going on there. The same pen held a setter, a borzoi, a malamute, a Siberian husky, a Greenland dog, and a bull mastiff. Other dogs were constantly threatening him, sniffing him. Little by little, Kita began to notice the world. Still, during the next three months he didn't make much progress.

On July 22, in Fairbanks, the pilot was shot dead by a robber.

The night before he was shot, the pilot had been at a bar with an old friend, urging him to come see his dogs. "You gotta come and see these boys," he said. "C'mon, make a trip up to Anchorage! You'd understand what they're worth." The friend's father was a legend in Alaskan mail circles, a pioneer in dog-sled mail delivery. For forty years, ever since the gold rush had turned this land into a madhouse, he had been carrying mail to isolated villages scattered in the interior, so remote that neither trains nor any other motored vehicle could possibly reach them. The pilot had gone to pay his respects to this living legend several times and got to know his son, who was about the same age he was. The son had grown up watching his father ride off with his dogs, he had played on sleds and cuddled up with the dogs in their kennel—he *knew* dogs. It seemed only natural that he become a musher himself when he got older, and he had taken first prize in a few local races. He lived off prize money and by trapping.

A week after the pilot's death, this musher friend came to Anchorage as he had promised. He visited the post office kennel. The pilot's prize collection was, truth be told, more than his colleagues could handle. Two or three dogs were all they could use, either at work or as pets. That was how things stood when this close friend of the deceased, a musher, turned up. They asked for his help.

"Sure thing," he told them. "I'll take any dogs that can pull a sled."

In August, Kita was taken, as part of the pilot's "estate," to a place far from any other human habitation, a few dozen miles northwest of Fairbanks.

Six months had passed since Kita left Kiska. The latitude here was even higher. The Arctic Circle was near. Kita, Kita, what are you feeling? You're living in the north now, in the real north, as though your name marked your destiny. Kita. North. The musher trained you. Taught you how a sled dog was supposed to run, how to pull the flat practice sled known as a *pulk*. THIS IS TRAINING—I HAVEN'T DONE THIS IN A WHILE, you thought. I'M BEING TAUGHT, I'M LEARNING TO DO MY DUTY. Somewhere inside you, a switch was flipped. The mail dogs your master had brought back couldn't keep up, but you didn't stop. You felt no pain. No, not you. The strictness of this training agreed with you.

And then it happened. Winter came. You were harnessed and you ran. Before your master's sled, perfectly in sync with the other dogs, your stride the same as theirs…you ran. You had gone from being a sled dog in training to a real, bona fide sled dog. You grasped the hierarchy that structured the team, followed the lead dog, ran. This, this was your duty. You felt it.

The musher had his sights set on first place in the next race. There was a war on, but the government wasn't dumb enough to cancel an event with such a long tradition in Alaska. It wasn't going to risk alienating the populace. If the musher was going to win, he had to practice like it was the real thing. He never took a day off. And so neither did his dogs. He was running them as hard as he could by February 1945. The master and his dogs were hardly ever at home. They must have covered half of Alaska—half a universe of white. Kita was on the move. He devoured the colorless scenery. The spruce trees, his own white breath and that of the other dogs, the great rivers now frozen solid—everything was perfect. An ideal sled route.

On February 17 there was an incident. The whole area was buried in snow. Suddenly the sled capsized. The dogs were baying. Something had scared them out of their wits. A moose. It hadn't eaten in ages because of the snow. It had lunged wildly at the dogs. From their flank. The dogs were harnessed, of course. The moose was a female; she weighed more than seventeen hundred pounds. She was a beast, starved to the limit, aggressive. The lead dog was killed, then another two. All of a sudden, somewhere inside Kita, another switch was flipped. Just like that. While the other dogs darted back and forth in terror, Kita awoke.

Attack!

His instincts called to him. Now, now, he remembered the lessons that had been beaten into him when he belonged to the military—he remembered how to attack. THIS IS IT, he realized in this midst of his extreme agitation. THIS IS WHAT I WAS SUPPOSED TO DO ON THAT ISLAND, THIS IS MY DUTY! Kita tensed, then barked. NOW IS THE TIME. I'LL LIVE. YES, I'M LIVING!

Finally snapping back into reality, Kita sprang into action. His harness was loose, almost falling off. He leapt. He wasn't intimidated by the enemy, despite the tremendous difference in their weight. The fight was on. Slipping through the moose's hooves, he sank his teeth into its windpipe. The moose bled. The moose bellowed. The struggle continued for thirty minutes, until at last Kita emerged victorious, practically unscathed.

The team had lost three dogs. Six more were wounded. One had tried to flee. The sled was halfway destroyed.

Then a blizzard blew up. The musher was almost dead, and Kita warmed his body with his own. Gave his master his own warmth to keep him from freezing. The surviving dogs gathered around him.

Dogs, you other dogs from Kiska, where are you now?

By the end of the war, Kita had won himself a position as a sled dog on the snowfields of Alaska. But what happened to the dogs that had parted with Kita at Dutch Harbor? They continued to serve as military dogs. During the war, of course, and even after it. Except that only one of them was still alive when it ended. The others fell in action, here and there, across the Pacific. On the Marianas, in the Philippines, on Iwo Jima, on Okinawa.

From February 1944, the six dogs who had been sent to the American mainland via Dutch Harbor—Masao as a "prisoner" dog and the five four-month-old purebred German shepherds as "candidate" military dogs—were housed in the spacious training center at Camp Lejeune. All six went on to become American military dogs—following, as it were, the script that had been written for them. Explosion's unplanned union with a Japanese dog (Masao) had, as it happened, yielded an outstanding litter. It was hardly a surprise that the pups exhibited all the usual traits of the breed and were free from imperfections. Indeed, the superiority of their bloodline had come to an even fuller fruition in them. They seemed to have inherited only the best aspects of the latest breeding as it was practiced by the Japanese and American militaries. Having been tested in any number of areas, all five placed in the A class. Masao, too, exceeded expectations. The pups' father adapted immediately to the commands his new American masters taught him. He made it abundantly clear how much he could do, almost as though he knew that this was an inspection, to see if he was fit to be admitted as an immigrant, to become an American. Within two months, the father and his pups were reunited, allowed to live together.

In order to be recognized as a full-fledged military dog, a pup must have reached a certain age. Military dogs can't be too young. So it wasn't until the fall, when the five pups were about a year old, that they were finally shipped off to the front lines. By then they had been thoroughly trained. They had learned how to carry out various tasks: guarding, reconnaissance, attacking, transport. They were sent onto mock battlefields where they were inured to bomb blasts, smoke, flames. They learned to crawl under barbed wire. All five were certified as A-class dogs and sent to various islands in the Pacific. Masao had gone off to war months earlier. He no longer felt any compunction about attacking the Japanese.

During the latter half of 1943, American forces were engaged in a vast campaign across the Pacific Ocean. On November 1, troops landed on Bougainville Island, at the northern edge of the Solomon Islands; shortly thereafter they took Rabaul on New Britain, the site of a Japanese naval and air base, and the fighting shifted north of the equator. February 1944 saw the inauguration of a fierce campaign against the Marshall and the Chuuk island group; on June 15, the Americans landed on Saipan; two months later they had captured the Marianas. And then they advanced on the Philippines. The Japanese sustained a disastrous defeat in a land battle on Leyte. A war of attrition was being fought on Luzon. And then it was 1945. A land battle of incredible scale broke out on Iwo Jima, and the fighting moved to Okinawa.

How many people died in all?

And how many dogs?

Tens of thousands. Literally tens of thousands, all across the Pacific. And those dogs were among the casualties. One after another, they were killed in battle. Only one of their number was still alive when, in August 1945, two atom bombs—one made of uranium that was called Little Boy, one made of plutonium that was called Fat Man—flashed within the space of a few days over the Japanese islands of Honshū and Kyūshū.

That dog wasn't Masao. It was one of Masao's children. Four puppies in that litter of nine, four of the little ones that had come into this world alive after Masao and Explosion mated, were dead now. Only one returned unscathed.

Returned to the American mainland. From the west side of the Pacific to the east. A German shepherd named Bad News. A male.

America, having emerged victorious, continued to expand its military dog population. The kennels were maintained. Because the dogs remained useful. Their numbers had to be increased in preparation *for the next war*. Stronger dogs, better dogs. Some of the active dogs were selected for breeding. Bad News, an A-class male, was given the right to mate.

The right to straddle beautiful female dogs.

And then there was Kita, in Alaska.

In 1945, Kita became a lead dog. His authority in the team could not be challenged. The musher who was his master treated him as his best friend, trusted him implicitly. After all, Kita had saved his life. They were bound now by a powerful tie; each understood what the other was thinking. Kita's master had always been a talented and energetic musher, but now that he had Kita as his lead dog he began winning even more races. Kita wasn't a standard breed for a sled dog, of course. But he was *strong*. Four times a day, before and after practice, his master rubbed his body down with alcohol; his energy was never exhausted, and he poured it all into doing his duty. That winter, and the next, Kita led his team to more than one record-breaking victory. His master was a star, and Kita came to be known as *the* dog, not only in Alaska but across the entire Arctic. Kita was the most famous sled dog there was.

Naturally, his master encouraged him to sire as many children as he could. The pups in his bloodline, inheriting his traits, became a sought-after breed of their own. The bitches all came from fine stock too. Only they weren't the same breed as Kita. They were Siberian huskies, malamutes. Mushers had been selectively breeding sled dogs for some time, and they knew the power of guided mongrelization. Eventually, Alaska would produce its own breed of Alaskan husky, bred specially for racing. It was only natural that Kita became a breeding dog.

Puppies from famous dogs weren't cheap. Sewing his seed, Kita earned his master a living. And the other dogs too. He became their benefactor.

Sled racing continued to develop as a sport in Alaska in the wake of the Second World War. The establishment in 1948 of the Alaska Dog Mushers Association was followed in 1949 by the creation of the Alaska Sled Dog and Racing Association, and races began to be held on an unprecedented scale.

The number of applicants increased and with it the demand for pedigree sled dogs.

Already by 1949, Kita had sired 124 puppies.

And the other dog?

By the same year, Bad News had fathered 277 puppies. He had long since retired from life as an active military dog, but he went on planting his seed.

"Russians are better off dead."

"That was an interesting article you ran."

"That one last week, you mean? 'The Chechen Train of Death'? *Ha ha ha!* Yes, indeed—that drew quite a response."

"Yes. It was truly…truly *masterfully* done."

"Of course. It was the truth."

"The truth of the situation."

"Those Chechens have been springing one surprise after another on us, since before the establishment of the Soviet system. Such ardent separatists! Such fierce anti-Russian sentiment! Yes—that, in short, is the *situation*. The North Caucasus is in turmoil. Our dear president has cut off all funding from the Russian Federation, recalled the engineers who were teaching them to drill and refine their oil. They've been left with no means of preserving their identity as a so-called 'independent state'—apart, that is, from illegitimate business activities. And, *voilà!* The bloody Train of Death, set upon out of the blue by a band of robbers! *Ha ha ha!*"

"You seem pleased."

"I'm just a regular Russian, same as everyone else."

"Hence your popular appeal. I see…just what an editor needs."

"You said it!"

"It's a glorious age we live in."

"Yes, a glorious age—for me, at least. I'm flabbergasted by these heretical Chechens, with their unyielding moral vision. And our readers love it when I'm flabbergasted! They love how 'true' it is!"

"So it seems."

"It's astonishing. I'm overwhelmed with gratitude. The numbers talk. Yes, this, my friend, is what capitalism is all about! And liberalism, the market economy! *Numbers!*"

"Anticommunism."

"Precisely. And anti-'red totalitarianism' too. While we're on the topic of heretics, though…You've heard about the Islamic prophet being killed? Guy with tattoos, quite high up?"

"Is that true?"

"It's true."

"Then I guess I've just heard about it."

"He was part of the inner circle of the Chechen mafia's boss in the Far East. The boss's right-hand man. What I wouldn't give to run a photo of the scene…ideally with the body."

"In your paper?"

"That's right."

"In *Freedom Daily?* The tabloid?"

"Right smack on the front page."

"In place of the usual satirical cartoon, occult scoop, or alien corpse?"

"Our new readership doesn't go for that stuff."

"That's encouraging."

"Isn't it?"

"A photo would boost sales," the old man said.

"On another note, this restaurant…rather loud, isn't it?"

"Very. I like it loud."

"Salted herring in oil! Smoked eel! Cow tongue in sea salt! These appetizers are as good as it gets. You like it…because there's no fear of being overheard?"

"Not, at any rate, so long as we're just talking. Take a look at us, my friend. We look like an elderly uncle and his nephew, dining together for the first time in ages. The nephew has made it big in the great capitalist city. And here I am, straight out of the forest, being treated to a magnificent meal."

"Straight out of the forest?"

"Yes. Your old uncle used to be…a hunter, shall we say. Deep in the forest."

"Splendid. A *hunter*! Cheers, then! Once again—to us!"

"Cheers."

"*Mmmnnnmm*. Paper-thin slices of salted fatback! Exquisite!"

"A nephew I can be proud of. Taking me to such a classy restaurant."

"*Ha ha ha!* Hats off to the restaurant! But to continue *just talking*…last month, a guy with an eagle tattoo was murdered. The month before, someone else. A cat tattoo. A nasty cat."

"Russians."

"Yes, the Russian mafia. Members of the Vor. For seven months now, the tension has been escalating, the fighting growing steadily worse and worse."

"Tension sparked by a certain newspaper. A scoop."

"Yes, indeed! A tabloid exposé. It must be said, however, that no lies were printed in that article. Speculation, yes, but the evidence itself, advanced in support of the conclusion—that was pure *truth*! How else could it have been so persuasive?"

"No doubt."

"None whatsoever. Hence the public's enthusiasm for our current investigative series on the Chechens. It's been like this from the start, you know. From the first installment."

"It was that immediate?"

"How can gangsters emerge as 'hometown heroes'—or rather, as they'd put it, 'homeland heroes'? How can one account for this peculiarly Chechen structure? See here, just look at me. I get all flabbergasted just thinking about it. Glorious, glorious! Another glass!"

"Here, drink up."

"Thank you, dear Uncle! *Ha ha ha!* The point is, it was their *homeland*, you see. As long as the funds furthered the movement—independence, separation from the Russian Federation!—no one cared where they came from. Kill the outsiders, take their wealth! That was good, that was heroism. Anyone in the Chechen mafia was a righteous bandit struggling to liberate his people. It didn't matter where—in Moscow, St. Petersburg, Yekaterinburg. Flawless 'homeland heroes' of the North Caucasus, one and all! What a moral sense! What a vision!"

"Flabbergasted again?"

"Stunned. Absolutely. These people…leaping, just like that, beyond our comprehension. That's what made them such a potent force, here in our Russia—that's how they made waves in the criminal world. And in just a decade! The Chechen mafia enters Moscow, they set up in…damn, it's on the tip of my tongue. That port, on the Moscow River. Yuzhny Port, that's it. They come in, and in a decade they've captured the market for stolen cars in Yuzhny Port. Just ten short years! Even less!"

"It's impressive. I give them that."

"Do you?"

"I do," says the old man.

"They brought down the old system, after all. The Soviet underworld. Impressive indeed. Not only to me, but to you—even you, Uncle. The old system was very solid, of course. It had lasted since the 1930s. Vors running everything from the slammer. There they were in prison, in camps. Precisely where all the political criminals wind up. The state used them to keep an eye on anti-Soviet elements, it actually *relied* on the mafia's organizational capabilities!"

"On the traditional Russian criminal organizations, that is."

"Precisely! From then on, the Communist Party and the Russian mafia became subtly and inextricably entwined. And that's how the Soviet social structure was preserved. Front and back. Witness the birth of a bureaucratic mafia rife with corruption. *Ha ha ha!* Sturdy as a prison—no exit! Naturally, back then—I was young then, working as a reporter for *Trud*, the labor union newspaper—I assumed that the Russian mafia would control the underground economy forever."

"As did I."

"You too? Well, then! Another drink! *Na zdorovye!*"

"Cheers."

"Ah, the rich flavor of aged liquor! Delicious! But...where was I? Don't tell me, I know! The emergence of the Chechen mafia. With extraordinary speed—no more than a decade or so. They were a veritable army with all that equipment. Right from the beginning. Marching into Moscow with grenades, bazookas. And armed, moreover, with the ferocity of their loathing for Russia! How do you deal with that? How, that is to say, were the Vors supposed to deal with that? Shock waves ran through the old mafia world. Conventional underworld ways, notions of benevolence and justice, meant nothing to them! The headaches they caused, these fighters! And then... Act II. In Moscow, in St. Petersburg—Leningrad, just given its old name back—the Vors started hunting down the Chechen mafia bosses. Just like that, they drove the Chechens from their turf. But wait! It's not over! *Not yet!* Because the Chechens have their ways. Their customs. *Krovnaya mest*—blood revenge. Oh, the horror! One by one, the leaders of the Russian mafia began to be assassinated...sprayed full of holes with machine guns, blown to bits with bombs...and then, at last—the incident."

"The incident?"

"Twelve dead, in one fell swoop."

"Twelve...?"

"Twelve Vors, all prominent figures in the current Russian Federation, had gathered for a conference. When the Soviet system collapsed, the Federation was split up into twelve regions. The mafia divvied up its turf. Each of these twelve Vors controlled a region. They'd gathered to brainstorm strategies for dealing with the Chechens. Someone attacked the conference, and all twelve Vors were killed. *Ha ha ha!* A remarkably *efficient* massacre! The attacker was a professional, obviously. And of course the Chechens must have hired him. I wasn't much of a reporter at the time, just a kid with a pen and a pad of paper, but I managed to learn, not his name, no—but his nickname. They called him *the Archbishop.*"

"The...Archbishop?"

"Yes. Somehow just hearing that makes you sober up a bit, doesn't it?

I don't know why. I wonder why. *Ha ha ha!* What next? Things get interesting—as soon as he killed the twelve Vors, he immediately betrayed the Chechens. The two groups were decapitated, and their struggle, this feud between the Russian and the Chechen mafia, grew messier, more ferocious. All these little Vors trying to fight their way to the top, all sorts of people like that—and to make it worse, you've got these ethnic groups, Ukrainians and Kazakhs and so on, now they're joining the fray too. They've turned the western regions of our great Russia into a bloodbath. It's gone on this way for years, groups competing for profits that swell day by day, week after week, month after month. And now, at last, this year, the struggle between the two main forces has spread, leaping like a spark, to the Far East."

"So the *Freedom Daily* reported. Seven months ago."

"So we reported. It was a tremendous scoop. And what fun we've had since! Of course, it was unfortunate that a hundred blameless civilians had to get mixed up in it all. That was too bad. But it's a fact—it is the *truth*—that the Chechen mafia has started moving into the Far East, hoping to further its business interests in used cars, gasoline, and firearms. They're serving themselves nice fat pieces from the Russian mafia's pie. That, too, is the *truth*. So you see, Uncle, I never wrote any lies! I never asked my reporters to lie! I don't publish lies!"

"Just speculation," the old man said.

"Yes, speculation. We do that."

"And that created this situation. This world we're in. Gangsters all over the place, riding around in heavily armored cars—not that this keeps the gangsters from being blown sky-high, along with their bodyguards."

"We'll keep the speculations coming. *Ha ha ha!*"

"Not long ago *Freedom Daily* reported that they've started targeting rigs?"

"The Chechen mafia? Trying to get control of the rigs? Hell yes! Of course! That seems to have irritated the Russians. Still, it's not a lie. The information may not have come from you, Uncle, but even so. On another note..."

"What is it, Nephew?"

"You don't belong to either side."

"Let us drink a fourth time."

"Na zdorovye!"

"Delicious."

"Delicious indeed."

"It's best not to probe too deeply, wouldn't you say? I'm helping you, yes, but only because you're valuable to me. Those articles you print stir things up. I would advise you, for instance, not to call me inappropriate nicknames. That would be dangerous. You mustn't ask me what sort of nickname I have in mind. You understand? Take care. I'm warning you. I've bought you. Don't ever forget that."

"I wouldn't dream of it."

"And why not?"

"Because I value my life."

"And?"

"And?"

"It boosts sales."

"It certainly does! Good ol' capitalism! *Ha ha ha!*"

"You have a charming smile."

"And this is a marvelous restaurant, isn't it?"

"Nice and loud?"

"Conveniently loud. So conveniently."

"Sometimes it's quiet."

"Quiet? Is it?"

"A rumor for you."

"Yes?"

"People have seen *yakuza* here."

"Yakuza? The Japanese mafia?"

"Yes. They're here to foster international cooperation. The Russian mafia is stronger at the moment, right? This month they're pushing back at the Chechens. What do you make of that? Balance is more important than anything, right? And then—this is simply a rumor, of course—the yakuza turn up. What happens next? Here's a prophecy for you. I wouldn't be surprised if the whole Far East turns into an enormous powder keg."

"If you're right, we'll change the name of our newspaper."

"Change it? No more *Freedom Daily?*"

"That's right…to *Terror Daily. Na zdorovye!*"

Three days later. Same restaurant. Unusual sounds mixed in with the Russian. A conversation in Japanese. Jeering, tongue-clicking, raucous laughter, a ribald exchange. *Hey, dick, is this the best champagne they got? What the fuck's up with this sweet shit? It's from Moldova, Boss. Mol…what? Where the fuck is that? Whatever, forget it. Is it me or does this shit taste exactly the fucking fuck like those vitamin drinks back home? Am I right or what?*

Everyone in the circle laughs.

Zoom in on the man at the head of the circle.

The Boss, they call him. Long black hair swept back over his head, a mustache, a double-breasted suit, pot belly. Can't be more than forty. His eyes roam restlessly, like a reptile's.

Boss, here's something new.

Ah. Cognac?

From Armenia.

This is better. Get some caviar too. Good stuff, from the Caspian. Enough for everyone.

The Boss pauses, then continues. *Not a bad place, huh? Officially recognized casino and everything. Not bad. Got one up on us in that respect, here. These Russians.*

All at once, he gets a different sort of look in his eyes. He turns to the next table.

"So what'd you do today?" he asks.

The person sitting there looks completely out of place. She's a Japanese girl, not yet in her teens. Eleven, maybe twelve. On the verge of puberty. "Rode the tram," she says coldly.

"I took her around," adds the handsome young Slavic woman seated beside her, speaking in Japanese.

"Have a nice time?"

"Yeah, great," the girl tells her father, her tone even icier.

She is peculiarly plump. Certain areas of her body seem bloated out of proportion. She isn't obese, but her face and her chin are flabby. Her hands too. She gives the impression, somehow, of an infant who was inflated, some days ago, to this enormous size.

The table where the girl and the Russian woman sit is littered with an odd chaos of dishes: pineapple cake, apple kudzu tea, reindeer steaks, piroshki… Everything, from the desserts to the meat dishes, has been picked at and left unfinished.

"Ah," her father says. "Anyway, have Sonya take you around again tomorrow."

With that, this Japanese mafioso, hefty like his daughter, turns his gaze toward the entrance, his eyes assuming their former steeliness. Two Georgian guards stand just inside. They're built like professional athletes. The Russians furnished these two men as protection for the group of "businessmen." Georgians had always blended perfectly into the Russian mafia, ever since the early days of the Russian Federation. They seemed perfectly at home in this world, with its peculiar customs and the Vors as its unquestioned leaders.

Nice outfits, huh? says the girl's father, The Boss, as they call him. *They're raking it in, you can see that. Every one of those fucking guys we saw today, they all had on Italian suits. You notice that?*

Gold necklaces, gold rings. Gold bracelets.

No gold nose rings, though, huh? one of the men in the circle says.

The Boss erupts into laughter. Then he looks back at the table. *So you got three kinds of caviar. The price depends on the size, see? Look at these fuckers. Fucking big, aren't they? You gotta love seafood. The treasures of the sea, right? The Caspian's sort of a sea too, you know. And we're gonna make a business out of this shit, these treasures of the sea.* The Boss runs through it all again. Lectures them. They'll import poached seafood from Russia—shrimp, crab, sea urchin—and export stolen cars from Japan. *It's a fucking two-way Russo-Japanese venture! And we make it all look legal! Man, how fucking lucky are we that Nippon and Russia are neighbors like this, fucking linked up by the fucking Japan Sea! We get a foothold here, and you know what? You know what, you dickheads? It's not just the little tip of Siberia, is it!*

No, because there's Sakhalin too.

And don't forget the Kamchatka Peninsula! Feel like I'm gonna bite my tongue every time I fucking try to say that word. You know what I'm talking about, right? Kamchatka, huge peninsula sticking out into the Sea of Okhotsk. Fucking huge.

The Russians are there too?

They got organization. They got a boss. You know. A Vor.

It's great, getting into this stuff. All in support of Japanese-Russian friendly relations.

The Boss laughs uproariously. He guffaws again. *The future is fucking rosy. Think big, you dicks! Think big!* he says. He gives them another little lecture, this time about how easy it is to launder dirty money in the new Russia. *Japanese-Russian friendship*, he says a few times, borrowing the phrase from his underling. *Russian mafia and Japanese yakuza unite! How about that, you dicks! Solidarity!*

Once again he's in stitches.

Anyway, he says, losing the grin, *we've got our first fucking deal.*

The main house is gonna like that, huh? one of the men says.

Except, the Boss says, *that from now on, this Russian link is ours.*

His voice is lower now. Secretive.

He continues: *We're brothers, now, these Russians and us. So we can make this shit happen, we can go fucking illegal all the way, go for the gold. This country's the world's armory!* he says. *You have any idea how cheap an old 9mm Tokarev pistol is? You know how incredibly fucking easy it is to get your hands on a new model Kalashnikov machine gun with a folding butt?* It all sells, he explains, for about a tenth of the going international rate. *This shit is fucking gold!*

Absolute fucking gold, the men say.

And sooner or later, we're gonna use this to take over the Hokuriku group.

Nice, nice. The men are now whispering.

The only fucking problem is the Chechens, the Boss says. *The Chechen mafia. As far as the Russians are concerned, right, these Chechens are something else. Black eyes, black hair. Black as in blacks. And now these black guys are intruding on their territory. Selling cars in Moscow and out west, making overtures in the Japan Sea, right? You get what I'm fucking saying? Just imagine what'd happen if these Chechen blackies got together with those idiot Chinese in the Triad and exchanged a fucking toast to their joint future…Forget your fucking Russian-Japanese friend-ship, we're talking Chechen-Chinese lovefest. CheChi. And what happens to our business interests, huh? Bam. Out the window. You get what I'm saying? The point is, you gotta fucking be prepared. Be ready to drive the fucking Chechens out of this whole region—*

Just then, the Japanese businessmen notice that something is wrong. That it's too quiet. All of a sudden they realize that the kitchen is empty. All the other customers are gone, as are the waiters who have been serving them. A few of them glance simultaneously at the door. They're looking for the two Georgian guards. One of them is stretched out on the ground. Blood. His larynx has been slashed, or maybe his jugular. The other guy is gone. Missing. Probably dead too, somewhere. Two or three of the younger yakuza spring to their feet, stunned. They've whipped out their guns, of course. Brand-new Makarovs, bought at great bargain prices. Suddenly they are distracted by a shrill, piercing noise in the kitchen—a timer has gone off. And now there's a man in a ski mask standing right behind their table. In his left hand he holds a submachine gun with a silencer; in his right, a knife with a curved blade smeared with blood. In less than a second, the man has shot every man in the ring through the back of his head. The gun makes hardly any sound: *pssssht, pssssht, pssssht.* The massacre is over almost before it has begun; it's so simple and quiet it's beautiful. And now only the Boss—the man they called the Boss—is left at the table. And, at the next table, the girl and the young Russian woman who serves as her translator. The ski-masked attacker walks around, takes up a position directly in front of the Boss's table. The tip of the silencer is pointed at the Boss's forehead. It's about three feet from the gun to the Boss's head.

The Boss sits very still.

He can't move.

The young woman, the Russian, is going to move. She's rising from her chair.

The attacker does something with the knife in his right hand, gives it an odd sort of flick, sends it flying. It buries itself with a soft thud in the woman's chest. It doesn't hit her heart. So she doesn't die—not yet. She is skewered, pinned to the back of her chair. *Unh…unh…unh…*she says. But she can't even really say that much. *Unh…unh…*

Unh.

The submachine gun never wavers. The attacker turns his face—just his face—toward the woman. He looks her over.

And then his eyes land on the girl.

The Japanese girl.

The attacker has on a ski mask, but his eyes are clearly trained on her. The oddly plump girl, decked out from head to toe in famous brands, her hair cut in the very latest fashion, looking too expensively attired for her age, somehow unsettlingly wrong. He stares.

He keeps staring.

And then he turns back to the Boss and lays a card on the table.

A playing card with something written on it in Russian.

It says RUSSIANS ARE BETTER OFF DEAD.

The Boss can't read it.

Obviously.

"Can't read that, can you?" the ski-masked attacker says, speaking in Russian even though he knows the yakuza won't understand. "You don't even hear what I'm saying, do you? That's fine. I can't read Japanese, can't speak it. We're even. In a second, I'll have that woman with the knife interpret for me. We've got a while yet before she bleeds to death. I can calculate that much."

The Boss doesn't know what to say.

Obviously.

The woman with the knife in her groans. *Unh…unh…*

"I have to tell you, though," the attacker says. "You're really stupid. You're a yakuza boss, right? What the hell are you thinking, bringing family on a business trip? What the hell were you thinking even having a family? Don't you consider the dangers that come with being yakuza? Are you Japanese that naïve? In Russia, it's the rule in the underworld that Vors and combatants don't take wives or have children. Because, obviously, they make you *vulnerable.* You understand what I'm saying? Do you not see that? As a yakuza boss, someone in the same business as the Vors? If you don't get it now, you will.

You'll see what it means to have a hostage taken. You see what I'm saying? I'm not going to kill you, not now. Not ever, maybe. But this *vulnerability* of yours…your family. It's gone. I'm taking it with me."

The attacker turns his gaze once more to the next table. To the girl.

She stares straight back at him.

Ferociously.

"I'll fucking take one of your fingers, you dick," she says.

To the man responsible for the noiseless massacre. In Japanese.

In the voice of an eleven- or twelve-year-old.

1950-1956

Dogs, dogs, where are you now?

There were seventeen on the Korean Peninsula. They had landed together in September 1950. American dogs, sent in as reinforcements with the UN "security operations," members of an elite corps eager to achieve distinction on the battlefield. They were Bad News's children, siblings by different mothers. Some bore names that marked their paternal lineage, some did not. There was Big News and Hard News. Hot News and Gospel. One named Speculation. Another named Listener. Jubilee, Argonaut, Gehenna. One had "E Venture" written on his collar, with a circle around the E, but was on the books as News News. The other seven were Natural Killer, Fear, Atmosphere, Ogre, Bonaparte, Raisin, and finally News News News. The last went by the nickname Mentallo, also written on his collar.

Obviously the peninsula needed help maintaining security. From the American perspective, that is. And so, without any declaration of war, a war began. On June 25, 1950, the army of the Democratic People's Republic of Korea, aka North Korea, rolled into the peninsula's southern half in Soviet tanks, launching an invasion of the Republic of Korea, aka South Korea, whose goal was to "reunify the homeland" forcibly and to spread communism throughout the peninsula.

Back in 1945, the Korean Peninsula had supposedly been liberated from Japan, which had ruled it since 1910. But the country split in two. No, that's not right—it didn't split, it had *been* split. Divided into two separate states along a temporary buffer at the 38th parallel north. The American military was stationed in the south; Soviet forces occupied the north, where they were working toward the establishment of a communist system. And so, through a mindlessly geometric process, the peninsula was divvied up between America and the USSR. The Republic of Korea came into being first, in 1948, with the proclamation of a liberalistic government in the south, and the US and other capitalist countries promptly recognized it as a legitimate state. Less than a month later, the Democratic People's Republic of Korea was established as a communist regime in the north, and it was soon recognized as an independent state by various communist countries, with the USSR at the lead. And within two years, the war to liberate the homeland broke out.

The dogs entered the picture right before UN forces retook Seoul. Most of the UN forces were American, and their commander-in-chief was Douglas MacArthur, the same man who, as the supreme commander of the Allied Forces, had headed GHQ in Japan. The dogs came under MacArthur's command as part of what was known as Operation Chromite, in the Battle of Inchon.

The surprise attack was a success. Seoul was returned to Korea, whose capital it became. But things didn't end there. The Americans got greedy. All of a sudden, they changed their strategy, decided that now *they* were going to pursue the military reunification of the peninsula—the same "reunification of the homeland" that the north had wanted, only under a liberalistic government. UN forces crossed the 38th parallel, invading North Korea, and immediately took Pyongyang, its capital. Indeed, they kept going north, rapidly approaching the border with China.

But here they made a miscalculation. In October 1950, the Chinese People's Volunteer Army joined the fight in support of North Korea with 180,000 troops. Their slogan was *Kang Mei Yuan Chao*: "Resist the US, Aid Korea!"

The People's Republic of China, popularly known as China, had come into being just one year earlier. It hadn't simply sprouted up overnight in the wake of Japan's defeat in 1945. The nationalist Kuomintang and the

Communist Party, led by Chiang Kai-shek and Mao Zedong respectively, had fought together during the Second Sino-Japanese War, but the moment they achieved their goal the alliance collapsed. In July 1946, after a year of sporadic fighting during which each side struggled frantically to secure the support of the Americans and the Russians, they plunged into an all-out civil war. In three years, three million people died. Early on, America lent its full support to the Kuomintang, and yet its army still found itself losing. Then, in 1949, the Nationalists finally retreated to Taiwan. Taiwan, by the way, had been a Japanese colony from 1895 until 1943, when the United Kingdom, the United States, and China decided at the so-called Cairo Conference that it would be returned to China. Chiang Kai-shek had participated in the Cairo Conference as China's representative.

In October 1949, Mao Zedong announced the birth of the People's Republic of China.

The communist countries immediately recognized it as a state.

America declined to have diplomatic relations with China. Instead, it continued to recognize the Kuomintang government Chiang Kai-shek had reestablished in Taiwan.

In February 1950, Mao Zedong and Joseph Stalin signed the Sino-Soviet Treaty of Friendship, Alliance, and Mutual Assistance.

Four months later, the Korean War broke out. Another four months and China joined the fray. Five years after the conclusion of World War II, along the western edge of the Pacific Ocean, the tug-of-war continued. And everything that was happening had its roots in a single dynamic: the tension between the US and the USSR. Harry S. Truman, who was in favor of combating the communist menace with force, was president at the time. Truman detested Stalin. Stalin detested Truman. Who knows, perhaps ultimately the intense *personal* dislike these two men had for each other was wreaking havoc with...

The Pacific Ocean.

History.

And the dogs.

Yes, even the dogs.

Seventeen dogs with no sense of how they were being used. Their fates might intersect in the most mysterious ways, there on the Korean Peninsula, on the site of a proxy war between East and West, part of the broader Cold War, but they would never know. It was the season for war. The twentieth century, a century of war dogs. The dogs were played with, toyed with, exploited. As the fighting intensified, dragged on, devolved into a quagmire, UN forces began procuring dogs from closer by. In January 1952, America's Far East Air Force purchased its first dogs from Japan: sixty German shepherds. They had been selected from a group of more than two hundred dogs brought to Ueno Park from throughout the Kantō region. More than a third had passed the first battery of inspections and tests, which included height and overall physical condition, the ability to remain calm in the presence of close-range gunfire, the willingness to attack people clad in protective gear, and the absence of filariasis. Both the commissioned officer in charge of the Far East Air Force's dogs and the veterinarian were surprised that so many animals passed the test, but given their ancestry it shouldn't have been a surprise. These were the descendants of war dogs that had not only lived *during* but also *through* the Fifteen Years' War, which included both the Second Sino-Japanese War and the Pacific War. And, of course, they were purebred German shepherds. Purebred *Japanese* German shepherds.

There were no dogs left in Tokyo in the immediate wake of the defeat. There were no dogs in Osaka either. Or in Hakata, Nagoya, Kanazawa—zero. In the two years leading up to the surrender, dogs had disappeared from Japan's cities. There was nothing to feed them. With the food situation as dire as it was for humans, fretting over dogs was out of the picture. War dogs were the only exception—they had rations. But they were destined for the battlefield. And then, toward the end of the war, citizens were ordered to turn in their dogs. These weren't war dogs, just ordinary pets. They weren't deployed as reinforcements. They were procured as military *supplies*. They were valued, now, for their fur. Dogs from all across Japan were offered up for the Japanese military to kill and skin. Between ten and twenty percent of Japan's civilian dogs survived. These lucky dogs lived in rural areas where their owners could feed them.

As for the war dogs, only those strong enough, fierce enough, lucky enough to escape death on the battlefield, not just once but time after time, survived.

By and large, the dogs that gathered in Ueno Park in January 1952 were descended from the second of these two groups.

Something rather amazing happened as a result. American dogs ended up fighting on the front lines and living in the camps with these formerly Japanese dogs, newly incorporated into the UN forces. And among the Japanese dogs were some that, if you traced their lineage, had as their great-great-grandfather the same German shepherd who had sired Katsu. Katsu, the dog that had served in the army garrison manning the Kiska/Narukami antiaircraft battery. The same German shepherd that had kept his distance from the three other dogs left behind on the island, that had ultimately sacrificed himself in a banzai attack, leading the American soldiers into a minefield. And that wasn't all. There were, in addition, a few dogs descended on their mother's side from Masao. Yes, that same Masao—Bad News's father, the grandfather of those seventeen dogs sent into South Korea. But so what? Brought together in this unexpected place by the purest of coincidences, the dogs themselves remained oblivious.

The dogs' owners kept breed registries, but the dogs didn't. They knew nothing about their pedigrees, their history.

The very uneventfulness of the dogs' reunion marked their subjection to their destiny.

To the tense dynamic playing out between the US and the Soviet Union. Or, perhaps, to Truman's and Stalin's intense *personal* hatred of each other.

The hand of fate played in its fickle way with Bad News's children elsewhere too, not only on the Korean Peninsula.

In autumn 1951, in the suburbs of Chicago, Illinois, a female dog started giving birth to puppies that would have a shot at the top. Her name was Sumer, and she was a sister by the same mother of Gospel and Jubilee, then fighting on the Korean Peninsula. Sumer had never been sent to the front. She wasn't an elite dog—in fact, she wasn't even a war dog. She was tested when she was six months old, and she had failed. Naturally each puppy in a litter has its own character and abilities, even though it and its siblings are born of the same seed. By the close of 1949, Bad News had fathered some 277 puppies; of that total no more than 150 were judged appropriate for military use—though among those who were, a good half proved to be extraordinarily capable on the battlefield. Most of the pups that were rejected—on the grounds that they were too friendly, say, or too excitable—were given away for free to ordinary households, or sometimes sold for a small sum. And there were buyers. These were purebred German shepherds, after all. They might not have been suited for war, but they were certified purebreds. And they were pups, and they were adorable.

So that's how it was. The puppies scattered. They left the training center kennels behind and went out into the great wide world to live their lives as ordinary pets.

Sumer, however, ended up in another large kennel like the one she had left. Caged.

Her owner was a young woman who maintained the kennel at her own expense. She was a breeder, though more often she referred to herself as a handler. She brought her dogs to shows, walked them around the ring. Held their leashes, handled them. The "shows" were, of course, dog shows. She was a regular at venues all across the United States, an up-and-coming breeder whose dogs took, and continued to take, prize after prize.

She had first become interested in the puppies that didn't make the grade as war dogs—second-generation rejects, so to speak—two years earlier, and by now she had acquired twenty-four by this route. She treasured them. These *rejects* might not have had what it took to succeed as war dogs, but they came from an extremely attractive lineage; they might have been tossed out as failures in the world of military breeding, but they were ideally suited to dog shows that were focused, above all, on bodily form. When the military breeders branded these dogs as "standard but useless," they were in fact certifying that they possessed the fine external appearance that was most valued in the dog shows, and that was, more than anything, what it took to make a dog a king.

Unmistakably pure, perfectly proportioned.

Unadulterated formal beauty.

Of the twenty-four puppies the woman acquired, half were Bad News's children. Sumer was by far the most beautiful. She was hopeless as a war dog, true, but she was outstanding as a plaything, a pet. *Such a gorgeous coat*, the handler murmured. *Just look at how perfect her bite is.* At the same time, the handler had also spotted her weaknesses. She had been doing this ever since she graduated from high school, an up-and-coming breeder, a twenty-five-year-old pro. She entered Sumer in several local shows, to see how she would do, but the best she ever placed was third in her group. *No surprise there*, the handler thought. *She needs a bit more pizzazz, a sort of a sensuousness, something to catch the judge's eyes.* If only the handler could bring that out, she would have a perfect champion dog.

She would have, that is, a brand.

Just one more step.

In order to bring out what she needed, the handler started breeding Sumer. If only this last step could be achieved with this bitch, the next generation would be able to take the grand prize at any dog show in the land. And so Sumer began giving birth to litter after litter by different fathers, twice every year. She was given all the care she needed so she could focus on raising her children.

The dogs who straddled Sumer over the next five years were all certified purebred German shepherds. She had intercourse with seven different dogs, but every one of the puppies that emerged from her womb belonged to the same breed.

The purity of her blood was preserved.

The German shepherd line continued unadulterated. But what of the other dogs?

Dogs, you dogs in Kita's line, where are you now?

Most of your number—124 by the end of 1949—remained in Far North Alaska. You were pulling sleds. Half the blood coursing through your veins derived from the Hokkaido breed; half came from other Northern breeds. You were mongrels, every one of you. But you were a mongrel aristocracy—the sons and daughters of Kita, the greatest sled-racing hero of the late 1940s—and as such everyone in the region associated in any way with sled racing knew of your existence. You were nobility, and you were priced accordingly. You might fetch two hundred, five hundred, even a thousand dollars. And you found buyers, every one of you. A few dozen ambitious mushers, new faces in the evolving world of dog sledding, shelled out the cash and bought you. One day you would be their lead dogs.

You were dispersed. Mostly around Alaska and the Arctic Circle.

And you mongrelized your line even further.

One dog left the territory behind and descended far to the south. Her name was Ice. Her mother, a Siberian husky, had given her a foxlike face and blue eyes. Her maternal grandmother had a touch of Samoyed blood in her, however, and from her Ice had inherited a snow-white coat of long hair, light and fluffy, especially from the ridge between her shoulders down along her spine. She looked a little like a wild beast you might find roaming the snowfields.

Ice had left the territory over which Kita's children ruled, it was true, but not by accident—it wasn't as if she had gotten lost. Though in the end, she might as well have been lost. That, more or less, was her fate...but that wasn't how it began. The musher who bought her realized it would be foolish for someone so inexperienced—and his new team of sled dogs, with Ice at its head—to commit to an endurance race without adequate preparation, so he made the wise decision to enter his team in shorter competitions. That, at any rate, was what he did the first two winters. And they did impressively well. Ice was the master of her team, she took pride in her leadership, skillfully kept the other dogs in line. And so they moved on to the next stage. In January 1953, Ice went south—or, rather, was taken south—to participate in a competition in Minnesota. Her master always picked races he was convinced they could win, but he had never actually taken the prize. The competition was too stiff in Alaska, in both the American and the Canadian regions. Ice had far too many worthy opponents. There was no guarantee that she would emerge supreme. But her master wanted that, he wanted it so badly...He wanted her to be recognized as a winner in a short- to mid-distance race, and then, if possible, to make a dazzling debut in the world of long-distance racing. Consumed with ambition, Ice's master searched for just the right race. And he found it. In the snowy Minnesota highlands, where dog sledding was just catching on as a winter sport. Just below the border with Canada.

Who would ever take a real team that far?

No one.

No one but me.

So he rented a truck and drove his twelve dogs down.

In January, Ice and her team attempted the three-hundred-mile Minnesota Dog Sled Marathon. The dogs were in mint physical condition and they encountered no particular difficulties along the way, but still they came in second, losing by fifteen minutes. Ice and the other dogs expected their master to shower them with praise, since second place was still awfully good, but he was clearly disappointed; his shoulders drooped. They got no medal, no prize money—he couldn't even cover the cost of transporting the dogs. He had screwed up. He was overcome by despair. And then, two days later, he was over it. He had met the woman he was destined for. She was twenty-eight years old and single and lived eighteen miles south of Minneapolis. She didn't have any dogs. She had, instead, twenty cats that lived with her in a house on land inherited from an aunt. They exchanged glances, for no particular reason, and they realized in a flash that they had been in love in some previous life, and that was that. They got married. The musher moved in with her, bringing his twelve sled dogs, and he put down big, thick roots in Minnesota. He didn't care about racing anymore. Winning, losing. So what? Love was all that mattered. Medals and prize money? *Pshaw*—all you need is love. No more of this dog sledding shit for him.

Early in February 1953, Ice and her eleven teammates settled in the low-lying plains of Minnesota, reduced to the status of pets. They were in America now, the home front of the Korean War, in an age when the mood of the country was tense from red-baiting. Everyone was watching *I Love Lucy* on TV—such a riot. Everything went slow and easy here in the lazy, lukewarm heartland. Totally different from life up in Far North Alaska. Down here in the *south*.

It got stressful.

There were no ice floes. No vast expanses of snow. You couldn't run. Not only couldn't you run, you were ordered *not* to run. WHAT'S GOING ON HERE?

Ice wondered. WHERE THE HELL ARE WE? One member of the team, overcome by the same feelings, fell sick, grew progressively weaker. The depression spread. Still the sled dogs remained obedient to the musher. Except he was no longer a musher. Their master had abandoned his sled, he was no musher. He was their owner, plain and simple. And he knew this, and he felt a little bad. The former musher thought he knew what had made his dogs so disconsolate—it was because he no longer had them pull the sled. But, hey, love wins out in the end! The new wife trumps the dogs. When four dogs finally died, the former musher actually found himself thinking dogs could be kind of a pain.

The sled dogs were no longer loved. But Ice and the other seven loved their master.

The cats were worst of all. Time and again, the twenty housecats attacked the chained-up dogs. There was a malamute with a shredded ear, a husky who had lost an eye. Retaliation was impossible. Because their master's wife was cat crazy. She was the problem. Their master was still the leader of their pack, of course. Ice, as lead dog, was number two. But now their master made it clear he wanted them to obey his wife. So where did that leave Ice? Number three? And what about the cats, basking in the wife's affection? *Just you try and touch us*, they seemed to be saying, leering at the dogs. *You'll catch it from the master's wife*.

So in this world, the dogs…were they all the way at the bottom?

Unwilling to accept this, two more dogs died. Fell sick and died.

A year passed. In winter, a sparkling white blanket of snow allowed the survivors to feel a modicum of their former happiness. But their master was even more overjoyed. He had gotten it on with a nineteen-year-old waitress in town, and he was up to his ears in love. "In the end, love is all that matters," he told his still new wife, and scrammed, leaving her behind. Leaving the dogs behind too, of course. Ice and the other five.

The dogs no longer had a master.

They couldn't stand being below the cats.

Finally, in February 1954, Ice directed them to make their escape. She barked and barked until the woman (now a twenty-nine-year-old divorcée) felt she had no choice but to take them for a walk, and when she testily unhooked their chains and led them outside, Ice suddenly leapt at her. RUN! she ordered the others. WE'RE ESCAPING! There was authority in Ice's barking. The six dogs fell naturally into line and dashed gallantly off across the asphalt-paved road that wound through the housing development.

Hope!

At last, the dogs set out.

And so six "wild dogs" began their struggle to survive. Basically, they yearned to return to nature. The town was a little too hot. They had all been bred, these "wild dogs"—both as breeds and as individuals—to withstand the cold. So they aimed for the highlands. They didn't make it anywhere as cold as Alaska, but they got used to it. Ice was clever. She led the pack, found food. She took advantage of the town. Sometimes they snuck quietly into residential neighborhoods, like American black bears in the hungry season. They lived along the edge of human territory, though of course they spent most of their time in the mountains. When their hormones stirred, Ice and the other five dogs obeyed their instincts. They mated with each other, yes, but they also pursued dogs in town. People's dogs. Pets. Whenever Ice caught the scent of a dog she liked, she leapt the fence. She stood outside the doghouse, drawing him to her.

Naturally, she became pregnant.

One spring passed, another came. She had given birth twice. Ice, the second generation in Kita's line, was spawning a third generation, more mongrelized than the second. Dogs, you dogs who care nothing for the purity of your blood, what turbulent lives you lead! You have become "wild dogs," and over time the townspeople have come to despise you. They grow wary. Ice, just look at you, how gorgeous. Your foxlike face, your white mane— your appearance strikes fear into people's hearts. *Look at that ferocious animal!* people cry, shuddering, at the sight of you. You are almost a wolf.

The mountain dogs had begun attacking the town.

And so it was decided. You were to be eliminated. You were dangerous "wild dogs," rumored to have bred with wolves.

They came after you with rifles. You kept fighting.

Wolves. Of course, the dogs in Ice's pack had no way of knowing, but in fact by 1952 the blood of a bona fide wolf had indeed entered Kita's line. One of the dogs who inherited it had found his way into the northernmost regions of Far North Alaska, as if he were living out the fate suggested by his grandfather's name. Here's how it happened. Many of the new mushers, inspired to dreams of glory by Kita's fame, bought dogs belonging to the second generation—Ice's siblings, some by the same mother, others by different mothers—but not all had substantial financial resources to draw upon. One musher, having found a way to do a favor for Kita's owner, managed to buy a dog with her noble blood at the bargain basement price of twenty dollars. Unfortunately the rest of the team he had put together was, in a word, worthless. So this new musher hit upon a method by which he might increase his stock of the noble blood without spending a penny—a breeding program that would instantly turn the game in his favor. First, after congratulating himself on the fact that the puppy he had acquired was a bitch, he waited until she was nine or ten months old. Then he hiked into the forest and set up camp, preparing to stay for as long as it took, intentionally leaving the young bitch tied up outside the tent. He was going to get her pregnant by a wolf. This rather primitive and violent mating technique had a venerable history in Alaska and Greenland as a means of boosting sled dogs' speed and endurance, and this poor new musher had decided to give it a try. He had blown just about all he had buying just one of Kita's children, but that wasn't enough for him—the dreamer had bigger dreams. He could do it. One day he would be a top musher.

Dogs, you dogs in Kita's line, look at you—mongrelized almost beyond belief, with wolf seed part of the mix. The story keeps unfolding: seven wolf-dogs join the family tree.

These seven dogs, he told himself, would be his redemption. *Imagine the team I can put together now! At the head a child of Kita's, the hero, followed by seven dogs who are not only Kita's grandchildren, but are the strongest possible hybrid.* He was delirious with excitement. *How strong,* he wondered, *are these seven puppies? What miracle of heredity is theirs?* He was their master now, and he was dying to put them to the test. And so, incredibly, when they were still only three-and-a-half-months old, he harnessed them up and began their training. The puppies endured it; they had no other choice. Then, when the seven dogs were ten months old, the dreamer became obsessed by a new and glorious notion. The time had come to try them out for real.

He didn't enter them in a race.

The dreamer decided to test his team's true strength by taking them, Kita's child and the seven wolfdogs, on a legendary route. Half a century earlier, a brilliant musher had run his dogs as far as the islands of the Canadian Arctic and made it back alive. *I'll duplicate that run*, he thought. That's what this man was like—he loved to try out old customs, see how he measured up to legends. He couldn't restrain himself. Dazzled by dreams of glory and adventure, he often lost his sense of what was completely stupid and what was not.

By the time we return from this trip, I'll have one of the best teams around!

The dogs were in trouble. Seven ten-month-old puppies following the lead of their mother, joined by four more completely worthless dogs, bound for the ice floes of the Arctic Ocean. This was an adventure, yes—the same adventure a brilliant musher had set out on fifty years earlier, in full knowledge that he was risking his life. The dreamer, of course, had no sense at this point that he was seriously gambling with his life. He and his twelve dogs crossed the Brooks Range and set out across the Arctic Ocean. And then came forty days of hell. One of the dogs put a leg through a patch of thin ice and drowned. Another ended up alone on a large chunk of ice while the team was sleeping one night and drifted off. One tumbled down a crevice in the ice and dragged several down with it as it fell. The tangled harness strangled another dog. Of the seven wolfdogs, only two lived to see their eleventh month. The survivors were utterly fatigued. Their master had started drilling them at three and a half months. It was too early. And too intense. He had pushed them too hard.

The two surviving puppies lost their mother.

The sled was hardly moving. Some days the dogs' bodies would be frozen stiff, each hair on their bodies like an icicle. A fierce blizzard gusted down over them, and the dogs' master, the dreamer, came down with bronchitis. *Fuck, I'm done for*, he thought. *Whiteout. I can't see anything, I don't know where I am.*

I'm dying.

He died. It was their fortieth day on the Arctic Ocean. Only one of the wolfdogs was still alive. His name was Anubis; he was now almost a year old. Amazingly enough, three of the worthless dogs had survived. These four surviving dogs lay in a circle around their master's corpse. They couldn't have run away if they wanted to—they were still tied to the harness. They survived for four days on their master's flesh.

And then they were saved.

They were hunters, members of one of the tribes of Arctic natives that would later come to be known collectively as the Inuit. Residents of these regions had no government. They weren't Canadians, they weren't Americans. Neither were they citizens of the Soviet Union. Until 1960, they had no fixed abode. During the winter—what they considered winter—they traversed the frozen sea from camp to camp hunting ringed seals and polar bears, setting out on an occasional trip to kill musk oxen. They traveled by dogsled. Eventually they would switch to snowmobiles, but at this point, when the hunters saved Anubis and the three others, dogs were still their only means of transport. They could see what had happened. Some stupid white guy had died. An adventurer who fell victim to his own incompetence. Leaving the dogs behind. Four of them!

Hilarious.

The dogs were teetering on the verge of starvation. The hunters fed them just a little, took possession of them.

Two years passed. Anubis was still alive. The other team members, too, were alive, with the exception of one dog that had died in an accident. The hunters, their new masters, directed their sleds with whips. It stung, but the dogs got used to it. Anubis learned to read the weather. He could pull a sled to the hunting grounds and back, but he also showed himself to be a capable hunter, able to find game, chase it down, attack. He noticed that when he helped his masters hunt, they treated him somewhat better, so he tried even harder. He exhibited a special ability to sense various impending dangers. This, the hunters realized, was no ordinary dog. He was made of different stuff from the other three they had found him with—they were worthless. There was something in this animal, hidden deep inside…a rare talent for doing exactly what he was told. Not only that—faithful as he was to his human masters, he also had a wild animal's instinct for battle.

This was how they saw Anubis two years later.

In November 1955, an unusual man visited the camp where Anubis's masters were living at the time—one of several they moved between. Anubis's masters were citizens of no country; this man was a citizen of the USSR. He was a researcher at the Arctic and Antarctic Research Institute in Leningrad, commonly known as AARI. The Soviet Union was gathering secret data about the Arctic Ocean for military purposes. The Soviet Union wasn't alone—its greatest enemy, the US, was using its intelligence agencies and military to collect the same sort of information. Both countries acted covertly. The Soviet Union had erected numerous observation stations in the Arctic, building them on the ice floes. "Drifting ice stations," they were called. They were constantly moving. It was a dangerous business. The AARI researchers were having problems with the polar bears that turned up at their bases from time to time. Hence the visit to the camp where Anubis's masters lived. The man drove up in a snow tractor. The camp and the observation station were adjacent to each other then—a mere twenty miles apart, which made them neighbors by Arctic standards—but this was purely a coincidence, owing to the drifting of the station and the movement of the camp.

The AARI researcher said he wanted to buy a dog to keep the bears away.

They negotiated a deal. In exchange for supplies that had been brought in on a transport plane the previous week, the researcher got the best dog for the purpose.

Anubis was three years and one month old.

He spent the next year or so drifting on the Arctic Ocean, between 73 degrees and 84 degrees north latitude, and between 120 degrees east and 160 degrees west longitude. Early in December 1956, they were to the east of Wrangel Island, on the Chukchi Sea. The Bering Strait lay somewhere way off to the south, and beyond it the Bering Sea. The Bering Sea came to an end at a line of islands. The Aleutians. But Anubis felt no longing for home.

I'M AN ARCTIC OCEAN DOG, he thought.

He lost that sense of himself. The researchers completed their surveys, and the ice stations were dismantled. They took Anubis on the icebreaker with them. But that was the end. They sold him at a small harbor town at the eastern edge of Siberia. The town's inhabitants were all dressed in reindeer hides. They used reindeer bones to beat the snow from the hides they wore. These people became Anubis's new masters. For the fourth time.

He was in the middle of nowhere, but still he had made it to the mainland, the great Soviet continent. He was walking, now, on Eurasian soil.

But tell me, dogs, you other dogs—what has become of you?

Three other dogs ended up in the communist sphere. Jubilee, News News (known as E Venture), and Ogre were captured on the Korean Peninsula by the People's Liberation Army. The pure German shepherds changed their nationality. In 1953, the situation was totally different. Truman was no longer president of the United States. Stalin, former general secretary of the Communist Party of the Soviet Union, had died of a brain hemorrhage on March 5. The two men no longer had a personal relationship. In the confusion that accompanied the UN forces' retreat, these three dogs were left behind on the "other side" of the 38th parallel. They would never return. An armistice was signed in July, but the dogs were not handed over like other prisoners.

Come 1956, all three dogs were still among the dogs of the People's Liberation Army War Dog Battalion. The two males, News News (E Venture) and Ogre, had been castrated; the bitch, Jubilee, remained as she had been born. She had not yet given birth.

And what of the capitalist sphere?

Two lines of dogs lived in its center, on the American mainland.

Sumer and Ice.

"What, are those fucking dog names?"

It's winter, the girl muttered, *winter winter winter winter.* Over and over again, ferociously annoyed. Once more. In Japanese, monotonal. How could she not be annoyed? She flung herself down on the narrow bed, not even fifty centimeters wide, and screamed. She noticed a coat lying on the floor. *Look at that fucking dipshit coat,* she hissed, *the kind of thing middle-class fucks wear, fucking assholes! If you're gonna kidnap someone, treat 'em a bit fucking better, fucking dicks. Gimme Louis Vuitton!*

Her shouting drew no response.

Winter winter, the girl repeated, *winter winter winter.*

Fucking cold.

Her once carefully arranged hair was a mess. Not having a blow dryer had been one of the first things to piss her off. *Fucking Russia, it's like the fucking Stone Age.* Forget blow dryers, there wasn't even a bath! They'd ordered her into some fucked-up little hut full of steam a few times, but that was it. The girl was not familiar with saunas. She assumed it was some kind of torture.

Fucking assholes, dicking around with me.

The girl hadn't lost any weight. She remained as fat as ever, radiating a sense of precarious imbalance in every direction. She bellowed some more. In Japanese. They never understood, not a word. She knew they wouldn't understand her now either.

She turned to the window. There had been a blizzard in the morning, but by now the snow had largely stopped. Fine flakes pirouetted through the air. An image of a decadent, delicious dessert rose up in her mind's eye, then fizzled. *Something light, sweet, melting…*Gone. What the fuckity fuck had she been thinking of, anyway? This was intolerable. Just wait. She would *crush* those assholes.

She was on the second floor. Outside, a vista of white extended off into the distance, directly in front of the building, and to the right and left. That was all there was, in other words. Just the ground. The grounds. Exercise grounds. How did she know? Because they exercised there. They were *born* to exercise. Even when it snowed, in the midst of a blizzard. They hadn't started barking yet this morning.

This place was huge. There was a whole town inside, if a small one. Closed in. Concrete walls separated the inside from whatever lay outside. Beyond the walls, all sorts of enormous structures massed together. Inside, in the corner, a stand of dead trees.

The town was out there somewhere, to the right. Several white buildings, a very tall observation tower, a paved road pockmarked with holes. The depressions were filled with snow. At the end of the road, way down, past even the concrete wall that marked the compound's boundary, was a small clearing. There, in that direction only.

The town looked dead, shrouded in snow. To her eyes, at least.

It was being engulfed on three sides, it seemed, by the *taiga*.

At the same time, the sight of that concrete wall shutting out whatever was beyond it called to mind a familiar word. That land out there, excluded, was *shaba*. The outside world, the world where the ordinary fucks lived—or, from the perspective of an unlucky member of the gang, the world past the prison walls. And here she was, doing time. Prison, that was the closest thing to this fucked-up "dead town." She could feel it in her skin.

That was as much as she knew. Maybe they had explained the situation to her, but if they had, they'd done it in Russian. It meant nothing. *Fucking assholes, fucking around*, she muttered at least twenty times a day. *Fucking Russia, it's always always ALWAYS winter here, for like a million fucking years or a billion years or something this fucking cold.*

Still cursing monotonally, the girl moved to the room with the fireplace.

She could move about freely inside the building. The door to her bedroom wasn't locked. There was no chain shutting her in. No iron balls chained to her legs. This freedom pissed her off too. Obviously they didn't take her seriously. But what was she supposed to do? Break out?

Fucking pain in the ass.

She went down to the first floor. She had more or less gotten a handle on the layout of the building. The others were probably pretty similar. They looked like dorms, capable of housing dozens at once. Dorms for stupid fucks who spent their days doing nothing but exercise. Her instincts weren't far off. She wasn't entirely right, but she wasn't far off. The Dead Town had been created in the 1950s, and until 1991 it had been known by a number. It was one of many such towns whose presence was never marked on any map. One of any number of such spaces that served as bases or military cities. Not only were people outside the party and the military rarely allowed into these areas, but also ordinary people—ordinary Soviets—didn't even know they existed. That held even for the residents of nearby cities. They were kept secret, and they stayed that way for almost forty years.

Until they lost their strategic value and were abandoned.

The girl was living in the barracks.

The old man who had kidnapped her had always known about this Dead Town. This town whose location, even now, was not marked on maps.

The old man lived in the Dead Town with the girl. It wasn't clear whether or not he lived in the same building, but they often sat down together to eat. Perhaps once a week, he came to her room with a video camera. He filmed her. The tape would be used, no doubt, as proof that the hostage was alive and well. This was part of the extortion. Every time the old man turned the camera on the girl, she would spit out, "Hurry up and fucking save me, old man." "What the fuck's taking so long, you senile dick." "So you gotta give 'em a million. I'm worth it, right? Fucking rob the bank if you have to. You're a yakuza, right?"

Fucking asshole, fucking around like this. Save your princess.

At the end, after the old man had finished his filming, he always talked to her. For instance, he might say: *Japanese "soldiers" are killing Russians, everyone is talking about it.*

In Russian, of course.

Seems like your dad really loves you, he says.

Whatever…there's more money in it if you stay here.

The filming took place once a week or so, probably. She wasn't exactly counting the days. She never thought she'd be here this long. So after her fourth or fifth day as a hostage, she stopped paying attention—who cared whether it was the fourth or fifth, or even the third day, it didn't fucking matter. Later on, she came to find this infuriating. Because she had no way of knowing when her birthday came. She was pretty sure she must be twelve by now, but maybe not. She probably wasn't eleven anymore, but maybe she was. Or maybe…she was neither?

Maybe…maybe she was caught in between? In a hole without age, without time?

Some things she could count. The old man sat at the same table with her for roughly two out of every three meals. And not just him. There were others living in this Dead Town too, and most of the time they came for the meals. First there was the old lady who worked in the kitchen. She was a grandmotherly type with broad shoulders, big ass, thick glasses. She made all three meals and looked after the girl's needs. Then there were two middle-aged women with almost identical faces, most likely the old lady's daughters. And then there was a middle-aged guy, probably the old lady's son, whose head was completely bald. None of these four seemed to be related to the old man. Not by blood anyway. Neither did the old lady and the old man appear to be married.

Still, here in the Dead Town, they sat down to take their meals together. Not just them, but the girl too. She was just old enough to be the old man's granddaughter, except that she wasn't related to him. She didn't even belong to the same race.

Still, the pseudo family ate together. All six. All the time.

Ukha, smoked salmon, borscht, some kind of boiled dumpling things.
Sour bread.

Pickled mushrooms, again and again. Always these fucking pickles.

The girl glared across the table at the four or five others.

No one glared back. They were unfazed.

The old man even smiled.

"You all creep me out," the girl said. "What are you, fucking ghosts?"

Speaking, of course, in Japanese.

Would you like some more? the old lady asked in Russian.

The old lady didn't only cook for the girl, and she didn't only cook for the
pseudo family. The old lady spent her time in the kitchen preparing large quantities of food not meant for human consumption. Dog food. This Dead Town,
which had been left empty ever since the Russian Federation abandoned it,
was now home to a few people and an even larger nonhuman population.

A few dozen dogs.

Kept in special kennels outside.

Left exposed to the atmosphere, in this region of bitter winters, to keep
them wild. So that their fighting instincts wouldn't dull. Often the old lady
cooked mutton for the dogs. She had a store of it that she bought in large
quantities and kept in an underground freezer. Every other day she would
take some out and cook it. Mutton legs, mutton heads, mutton skin, mutton
fat. She used just a few spices. Enough to give a slight Central Asian flavor.
This, too, was supposed to keep the dogs wild. To keep them from forgetting
the odor of flesh.

This way, they wouldn't hesitate to attack a living person.

The old lady's "Russian dog food" recipe had been carefully thought out.

The dogs also drank milk, sheep's milk.

The girl watched from the spacious first-floor room with the fireplace as
the dogs wolfed down their meal. Stared at them across a distance of a few
dozen meters. The windowpanes were clouded from the heat inside, but she
had swept three fingers down the glass and peered out through those three

lines. She had used her right hand, moving it in a furious sweep…her fingers held together, a single motion. After that, she stared out without moving, absolutely still. She had known it was time because she heard the dogs barking. She knew the others were feeding the dogs because there was no one in the room. *Woof woof.* A few dogs started barking. The girl watched them. The middle-aged women were carrying over a giant pot of milk, together. An enormous silver pot that reminded her of school lunch. *Fucking lunch ladies,* she thought, *for the fucking dogs.* That's why they had to take the pot to the kennel. It would say MILK on the calendar.

The dogs were barking wildly. GIVE IT TO US! they seemed to be saying. GIVE IT TO US! GIVE US MILK!

Released from their cages, the dogs devoured the milk. Clouds of white breath rose from their mouths, drops of white milk dribbled down. *Fucking Russians,* the girl thought. *Fucking eat anything as long as it's got fucking nutrients. Middle-class shit dogs.*

Too much white. Your breath. Your slobber.

Assholes.

Such a fucking cold color!

But she went on watching them through the glass. She kept cursing them in her thoughts, but she was a hostage, what else could she do? She had to watch the dogs. She would watch as they ate, and then she would watch them exercise in the exercise grounds. Exercise. A field day for dogs. *Or maybe… they're practicing for doggie field day,* she thought. Their exercise—or maybe their practicing—went on for two hours every morning. And that was just the morning.

The dogs were being trained.

In different ways. They were given different tasks. There were also various breeds of dogs. The only two the girl had seen before were Doberman pinschers and German shepherds. She didn't recognize most of them. They weren't like the Western dogs she knew. They looked sort of odd, somehow—their bodies. Most were mid-sized with ears that stood straight up, pretty long hair, muscular hind legs. Their coats were all different colors, and yet they seemed, overall, to make sense together. Ten to twenty of them probably had the same blood running in their veins.

…blood?

The girl began to sense something, a sort of authoritative aura, in the ten to twenty similar dogs. *I bet you cost a lot, you shits*, she thought, getting angry. *I bet you've got good parents.*

The dogs barked, and the training got under way. The girl stared fixedly at them, unmoving, as they ran around. Caught somewhere between the dogs' dynamism and the girl's stasis was a man, or rather two men, exposed to the same minus-twenty-degree air as the dogs. Two men out there with the dogs on the exercise grounds, directing their movements.

They called constantly to the animals.

The old man most of all.

The old man led. He was training the dogs to fight, to attack. The dogs were fast. When he gave the sign, they dashed off at about forty miles an hour. Ran as hard as they could toward their target and leapt at him, hit him, took him down. The second man was the target. He stood some distance away, dressed in protective gear. The bald man, the old lady's son. Not that his face was visible. He had a helmet on that covered his entire head. His throat, too, was wrapped in two or three protective layers. That was what the dogs aimed for. Biting, twisting, dragging him down. Ordinarily, such protective outfits only covered the arms and trunk. Because as a rule, war and police dogs are trained to go for the wrists. Their primary goal is to disarm, to "kill" only the target's wrists. That wasn't how the old man trained his dogs. His aim was different. He didn't want his dogs to kill the target's wrists, he wanted them to kill the target. To lunge at his face, his throat. To maul. To kill.

Again and again, they repeated the simple exercise.

Learning to kill. That was it. As quickly and precisely as possible.

Clearly when one of those dogs got up its speed, it had all the momentum it needed to hurl itself at its target and take him down, rolling and twisting, biting clear through his neck. Those dogs had the force they needed to detach a head from its body.

They were just getting warmed up.

Next they were paired in two-dog attack formations. One dog would aim for the thighs and stop the target; the other would kill it. The dogs were assigned roles in accordance with their personalities. The old man assessed their characters and paired them in shifting teams. A and B. C and D. E and F. C and B. A and F. The dogs were trained in the more sophisticated technique of firearm recovery as well, both singly and in pairs. The old man taught them to recognize the scent of gunpowder. He trained each dog to lunge first at a target's wrists, as in a standard disarmament, and then, when the gun fell to the ground, to pick it up and carry it straight back to its master in its mouth.

Instinctively, the dogs tended to progress in a straight line toward their targets, or by the shortest possible route. This was an unimpeachable method, at least as far as orthodox attacks were concerned. Hardly a man alive would have the presence of mind to shoot a mid-sized dog barreling straight at him at forty miles an hour—to calmly raise his gun, train his sights on the animal…forget it. And yet sometimes the old man forced them to go against this instinct. At a sign from him, the dogs abandoned their straight lines, progressed instead in a series of Zs. They would bound off to one side, then dash at an angle, then dart sideways again, all the while moving in on the target. This unorthodox attack made it reasonably likely that they would survive even in the face of an enemy armed with a machine gun trying to spray them with bullets.

And all this effort aimed at taking out a single target—a single person, the prey—was only basic training. It was just an energetic warm-up.

Half an hour into training, the old man had the dogs put their training to use.

This was the real stuff.

Ten dogs were assigned a four-story building, one of the many in this deserted Dead Town, and the command was given. *Take it.* The dogs scattered in all directions, rehearsed the motions of herding people into the building, cornering them. The dogs scaled the stairs, sprang through doors and windows, in and out, all the while barking. They moved in a sort of formation, in collaboration, like three sheepdogs guiding a herd of several dozen sheep. They acquired the ability to "cleanse" a building within a set time frame.

They practiced jumping. The old man had them wait at attention along one of the roads that crisscrossed the Dead Town. A car came driving along, and they jumped on top, jumped over. Or they ran around it. They forced the driver to slow down, jumped onto the hood. This, ultimately, was their goal. To block the windshield, obscure the driver's view, make the driver lose control.

To cause havoc in urban environments.

To do battle in the cities.

Here in the Dead Town, they were learning. Little by little.

The old man handled the dogs so masterfully it seemed, looking on, as though he were not merely training the dogs, but honing their intellect. Little by little. Gradually each dog came to understand its particular specialty. If a ladder stood leaning against a wall, the dogs darted up it. They also learned to climb trees. They would wait in the foliage, keeping still, biding their time, until their prey came along, until a person walked directly underneath, and then they would pounce, they would attack.

This morning, they were learning to carry burning branches, torches. For seven days now they had been engaged in this task. Learning to be arsonists.

The dogs learned "subversive activities."

All at once, the twenty-some-odd dogs froze. They turned and faced the same direction, growling. In warning. An intruder had appeared on the field. The old man commanded them, with a single clipped word, stop. Don't attack. A few of the dogs kept growling, so the old man called them by name.

"Asha, down! Ptashko, down! Ponka, down!"

Each dog obeyed instantly as its name was called.

"Aldebaran!"

One last dog, scolded, fell silent.

Now all the dogs were crouching on the ground, staring at the intruder, at the girl who had put on her coat and come outside. She stood seven or eight meters away from the old man.

"What, are those fucking dog names? Call 'em Pooch or something," she spat.

In Japanese.

Easy, stay there, the man ordered the dogs in Russian.

They understood.

What the fuck are you doing? I came to watch you, asshole. Playing around with your dogs. Don't fucking stop, she said in Japanese.

Well, well, this is a surprise, the old man said, walking over. What is it, little girl? Are you interested in my dogs?

Don't fucking come near me, gramps, said the girl.

If you like dogs, the old man continued, maybe later I'll show you the doghouse.

It's fucking winter out, you senile dick.

There are puppies.

I fucking told you not to come near me. Don't fuck with me.

But the girl made no move to leave. The old man was right in front of her now, standing still, ready to talk. To have a conversation, in Japanese and Russian, that would communicate nothing. The girl glared up at the old man. The difference between their heights was about the size of an adult dog, foot to shoulder.

You're quite an interesting little girl, the old man said.

Yeah, fuck you too. You're probably calling me a brat in Russian, I know. Whatever, senile old dick, the girl replied. Someday I'm gonna fucking kill you.

The old man grinned. Smiled. For real.

"Huh?" the old man exclaimed suddenly. He wasn't talking to the girl. He had looked away, sensing something. His face was turned up now, he was gazing up into the air, just as the girl was gazing up at him. The four-story building. The deserted building where the ten dogs had been training, learning to herd, to corner. A silhouette on the roof. A dog in outline.

The dog stepped quietly, calmly to the edge.

He was gazing down, it seemed, at the old man and the girl.

Slightly larger than the other dogs, he lacked their youthfulness. That much was clear even at a distance. But he had something else in its place. Authority, a commanding presence. That, too, was clear even at this distance.

"Belka," the old man said.

The dog didn't respond.

He's old, really old, the old man told the girl. Same as me. But he's not deaf.

Once again, the old man called to the dog, somewhat louder. "Belka, why don't you bark?"

This time the dog replied. *Uuoof.* Just once, quietly. To the old man and the girl.

By then the girl was looking up at the roof too. All of a sudden, she was pissed. She felt as if the old man had ordered the fucking dog to bark at her, and it had. She was furious.

"Hey, gramps," she said, ignoring the dog. The old man sensed the forcefulness of her tone. He turned to face her. She looked him straight in the eye and continued, "I fucking hate you more than anything. Fucking Roosky. Drop dead."

Drop dead, she said. In Japanese. *Shi-ne.*

The old man paused, as if he were reflecting on what she had said. And then he repeated the sounds of the Japanese word she had spoken.

"SHE-neh."

"Senile dick. Don't fucking converse with me."

1957

Dogs, dogs, where are you now?

Mainland USA, 1957. Fate unites two lineages. On the one hand, the purebred Sumer; on the other, the mongrel Ice. Both were bitches, each having borne more than one litter.

Sumer was gorgeous. Her skull and muzzle were of equal length, et cetera, et cetera—she was the perfect embodiment of the purebred German shepherd standard. She hadn't lost her looks, even now that she was getting old. There she was, in a cage, in a kennel, in the suburbs of Chicago, Illinois.

Ice was frightening. Her father had been a Hokkaido dog, her mother a Siberian husky, and one of her grandmothers was a Samoyed. She had a face like a fox's with brilliant blue eyes, a sturdy bone structure, hair on her back that the wind whipped like a mane. She looked odd, even eerie, resembling the standard image of no breed. No one owned her. She roamed freely across a wide swath of Minnesota, bound by nothing. Until they came after her with rifles.

Sumer bore puppies who were contenders to the throne. Any number of them, blessed creatures with everything going for them, expected by dint of their distinguished lineage to dominate the dog shows. She was getting on in age, but the planned mating continued; she got pregnant and gave birth again and again and raised her pups until they were four or five months old. She was, in short, a mother.

Ice obeyed her instincts, mating with pet dogs in residential developments when she was in heat, absorbing into her own bloodline the strengths of dogs whose looks and personalities suited hers. The puppies she gave birth to were another step away from purity. Their looks were unclassifiable; they had a dangerous, untamed strength. Ice led her children, and she led those of the other dogs in her pack. Five dogs from the team that had once pulled a sled in Far North Alaska and their children. They were all "wild dogs" now, regarded with unease by the humans, and she was the top dog. The leader of the pack.

A beautiful German shepherd who was, above all, a mother.

A freakish mongrel who was a mother, yes, but also a queen.

Queen of the freaks, of the monsters.

Ice, Ice—they came after you with rifles. The townspeople despised you. They hated you, and they hated your pack. Human society could not countenance your existence. You were evil. Monsters stalking the towns. Dogs unleashed were beasts, natural that they be destroyed. But you were not destroyed. You were too clever. Sometimes you retreated into the mountains, sometimes you set upon the towns. You never rested for long. Because to do so was dangerous. Because you felt how dangerous it could be. Though you had no knowledge of this—of course you didn't—the blood that coursed through your father's veins was the blood of a victor. You were descended from a long line of Hokkaido dogs who kept to this side of the line. Survivors. For thousands of years, the Ainu, the natives of Hokkaido, had used your ancestors to hunt large game. Your ancestors were the hunters. Hokkaido dogs who fought with bears and *lived*. These were your ancestors. Hokkaido dogs who brought down mighty deer. These were your ancestors. Every one of them survived the process of unnatural selection that hunting became. They had made it, they abided on this side of the line. And so you understood. You understood what it was to be on the side of the hunters, and you made sense of it all. You could almost tell what people were going to do before they did it. There was no way they would ever eliminate you.

Every bullet the rifles fired was another wasted bullet.

IDIOTS, you said. And you told the pack you led, WE WILL NOT BE CAUGHT. WE WILL KEEP RUNNING.

Yes, you kept running. You "wild dogs" ran and ran, dashed ahead the way you had in Far North Alaska, over the land, over the fields of snow, over the ice floes. Minneapolis was far behind you now. You roamed through Minnesota, but you did not go north. The situation—their attempts to eradicate you, and your evasions—led you in an altogether different direction. You headed south. Yes, south. Do you grasp what that means? You, Ice, and you, former sled dogs, members of Ice's pack, you were banished from the land of your birth, sent far, far to the south, and now, of necessity, you moved further south.

Do you understand what that means? It means this: destiny.

The pack had swelled to a few dozen. A pack of monsters, "wild dogs," growing ever more mongrelized, following the dictates of Ice's wisdom, her instinct, obeying the queen as they ran up and down, hither and yon, across a region that spanned four states, southern Minnesota, Wisconsin, Iowa, and Illinois.

You galloped.

You lived. You ran like lightning. You weren't going to die.

But in America, in 1957, the gun barrels were always there, tracking you.

Ice ran. Sumer did not. Sumer busied herself caring for her children in a clean and spacious cage that had been specially made for her. She moved lethargically, offering her pups her teats. She helped her newborns eliminate their waste. She was dignified, relaxed. She had the majesty of an earth goddess, the confident glow that was the sign of her productivity, her fertility. And this was the perfect environment for raising her pups, it was kept utterly clean, uncontaminated, and every last one of her children was pure as well. Perfect German shepherds, every one.

In the world Sumer inhabited, of course, mongrels were abhorred.

There was no reason, in its value system, for a mongrel to be born.

You, Sumer, do not run. You are waited upon. The owner of the kennel you live in—its owner as well as yours—lavishes attention upon you because you are the mother of her future champions. She places enormous value in your existence. You are cared for. You care for your children, and the woman who ought to be your master but is instead your breeder and handler, she cares for you.

Because you give birth to a beautiful elite.

Because you give birth to dogs of the highest quality, a second generation that is gorgeous above all else, possessed from birth of the qualities necessary to meet even the most stringent dog show standards and to remain unfazed by the judges' stern, appraising gazes.

The puppies milled around your teats.

And then, when they had drunk their fill, they frolicked and tangled in the shadow of your protective aura.

Until 1957, when at last fate began playing its tricks with you.

What happened? Your master did something she shouldn't have. Your master and the master of your fellow dogs, and of your children, the owner of your spotlessly clean kennel, she did something unclean, morally contaminated. Her patience had finally reached its limit. She wasn't taking the trophy. She had been breeding all these dogs with the sole aim of winning the highest title, and here she was, her aspirations still unfulfilled. Her dogs always took second, not first, place. Yes, they had won repeatedly in group judging, totally overwhelming the other dogs. But none had ever been Best in Show. Not one had managed to ascend to the pinnacle, to become the Number One Doggie in the United States. Your master had once been described as "the queen of the postwar American dog show universe" for her utterly masterful handling, her ability to become one with her dogs. But she didn't have the crown. She was a celebrity who appeared regularly in dog magazines. But without the crown. Each time she became the focus of attention as "a young—and beautiful!—woman handler," her self-esteem soared; each time the Best in Show ribbon slipped from her grasp, she was more spectacularly wounded. And now, to make matters worse, she was losing her youth. And so your master tried to bribe the judges. It didn't work. Well then, what if she spread her legs for one of the bigwigs who ran the show? She tried, but she wasn't young enough; the association chairman couldn't get it up. I'm way too old, she thought. I'm running out of time. And once she had convinced herself of this, she got so overwrought that she began to lose it. Take your age, Sumer, for instance. Before long you would be too old to give birth, past the age when so-called "late pregnancy" was possible, and all of a sudden that came to seem, in her mind, like some sort of sign—a revelation. It was now or never. And so your master tried a third trick: she went into the paddock and slipped poison to all the other candidates for Best in Show—a Doberman pinscher, a cocker spaniel, a Scottish terrier, a boxer, an Afghan hound, a toy poodle—and then, just to be absolutely sure that everything was all right, put poison in their owners' lunches too. Four dogs died and two of the owners were hospitalized. Her transgression was discovered with almost hilarious ease, and she was immediately found guilty and shipped off to prison.

Now, Sumer, there was no one to maintain your kennel.

The woman who cared for you had been banished from society.

It was late summer 1957.

And what had Ice been doing that summer? What had become of our mongrel Queen of the Monsters, leader of a pack that roamed back and forth across the borders of four states?

She had puppies. She had given birth again. She was an active mother, suckling her young. How many times had you given birth, Ice? You had no idea. You never counted. Only idiots bother to count each little digit like that, crooking the five fingers on their two hands. Counting is a cross borne by the people of civilized communities, saddled with their decimals. You, Ice, had feet, not hands, and pads on your toes, because your feet were meant for running. They were the engines of your speed. You, Ice—you do not count. You don't skitter from number to number, you live by instinct. You heed your blood…you are swayed by the intuitions you inherited from a line of victors.

It was, probably, your fourth birth, though you didn't know that.

And so, Ice, as summer drew to a close, you and your pack ceased your roving.

You were in your nest. You hated summer. The blood coursing through your veins derived, every drop, from northern breeds. Summer was your enemy. Truth be told, the south itself was your enemy. But it was your destiny to move southward, and destiny is not something you can shake. Your mane, which had evolved to help you endure the bitter cold, was no more now than a soft brush. Each time you birthed a litter, you caressed the puppies with your mane. It was a sign of your motherly love. You and your pack stayed close to the nest. Seven pups were born over seven hours in that gray area at the end of August and the beginning of September, before and after midnight on August 31—you could say the puppies had been born in one month or the other, depending on the time zone—and for the next week you didn't have a free moment. Another week went by and still you had no time to yourself, but you could at least begin teaching your pups to walk. And other things too. THIS WORLD IS HOT, you told them. IT'S BRUTALLY HOT, AND SO YOU'LL HAVE TO LEARN TO ADAPT AS YOU LIVE YOUR LIVES. This was your command to them: *Mongrelize.* This was the sacred law of mongrelization: *Mix. Be contaminated. Refute the notion of the standard.*

Because people are the ones who tried to keep dogs pure.

You and your pack ceased your roving, Ice, if only for a time, and that was very dangerous indeed. True, you had given birth several times before, but this was not then, this was America in 1957. You were public enemies. You, Ice, were Public Enemy Number One. You assumed it would be safe to stay put for two or three weeks, that it would be enough, but you were wrong. You miscalculated. You didn't even calculate. Because you didn't count.

People were idiots, yes, with five fingers on their two hands. But they did more with those fingers than count to ten. They also gripped their guns and pulled the triggers.

What happened?

You were surrounded. You and your pack were no longer roving freely. Your territory, and your hunting, began to center on a single point. A single point on the broad map of America. A place one could have pointed to on the mainland—*there.* A place with clearly identifiable coordinates. You were beasts, it was fitting that you be eliminated, and now at last they had tracked you down. Little by little, they closed in on you. They had you by your tail. These idiots, with their ten fingers…these *humans*, Ice, had the highest respect for your intelligence. The amateur hunters had all given up. Now only professionals were left on the side of the hunters, and they were hunting you.

National Guard.

Past developments, years of repeated failure, had led to their dispatch.

It was 1957 in America. The governor gave the local members of the National Guard the go-ahead, and they took up their guns—their military guns. Gripped them with their ten fingers. The National Guard was a reserve corps, of course, but they were professionals. Equipped as professionals, with the authority of professionals.

You were fine, Ice, you and the pack of "wild dogs" you led, as long as you could run. You were safe, you didn't die. But now you didn't run. You couldn't run. And so it happened. One of the squads at the western edge of Wisconsin closed the border and came in pursuit. They used every trick in the book. You could hardly move. You were stuck in the nest with your puppies, not yet three weeks old, and so you couldn't rely on your intuition to anticipate what was coming, to lead the other dogs. You couldn't run at the head of the pack. No longer could you assure them, WE WILL NOT BE CAUGHT. No longer could you say, WE WILL KEEP RUNNING.

And so it happened.

Panicked, terrorized, the pack dispersed.

Ice was still a mother then. Not the queen, not the leader of her pack; she was the mother of seven little pups. What's happening? Ice responds slug-gishly. The other dogs are fast, fleeing. Their speed attracts attention. The leaderless pack, dissolving, yet incapable of dissolving fully, winding up some-how in town, in groups of three and two and four. They are discovered, they are shot. The call goes out and they are shot. The dogs are shot, and so quickly too, in no time at all—the guard have accomplished their mission! And so Ice and her children, a bitch and seven pups, are left alive.

They survived until the very end.

They left the nest. Of course. WALK, she told them. WE WILL ESCAPE, STEP BY STEP. WE WILL SURVIVE. The mother and her children stumbled forward. Ice was growling softly. *Rrrrrrr.* Searching for a path that would save them from extermination, a path to deliverance.

Searching.

They came to the state highway. They could hide their scents by crossing here. Hide their tracks. WAIT HERE A MOMENT, Ice told her children. I'LL INVESTIGATE, YOU WAIT HERE. With that, she darted out onto the highway. She was crossing. There was nothing at all difficult about this. She had crossed any number of these nameless rivers, "human roads." A moment later, she had crossed to the middle. This river was heavily trafficked, yes, but not so much that it could not be forded. And then…Ice stopped. There in the middle of the river, she paused, turned, looked back. Stood still, looking back. One of her pups had barked. Yelped for its mother. It was about to run out into the road. No! STAY THERE! YOU MUSTN'T FOLLOW! Ice commanded. She watched until the puppy had retreated. And then—

She was hit.

A pickup truck traveling at seventy-five miles per hour threw her nine feet into the air.

She hit the ground. She died instantly. Countless cars ran over her, and in fifteen minutes she was flat. Cars, cars, cars. Ice, of course, would never have even tried to count them.

And so, Ice, you are dead. Utterly and completely dead.

You are dead, and Sumer is still alive.

Sumer: the other mother. The earth goddess, whose whole life was centered on the shows, who lived in her clean cage and gave birth to one litter after the next, spawning a beautiful elite. Except that no one looked after her cage anymore. The woman who had cared for her had been locked up herself now, in a much bigger cage. So your kennel was no longer maintained. Not that it had been completely abandoned. True, the first two days after the arrest, no one had fed the dogs, but then the authorities noticed. Something had to be done.

The situation was taken care of within a single day.

The kennel was auctioned off. The dogs too. Most of the dogs found new homes right away. They had belonged to the queen (now deposed) of the American dog show universe, after all, and their breeding was impeccable. Over a dozen bids were placed for some of the newborn pups in Sumer's newest litter. There was much maneuvering. Sumer's former owner had plotted to take down her rivals; now the other dog-show regulars were eager to take what they could from her. The owner was a celebrity—a queen, even if she had lost her throne.

The dogs fetched prices incomprehensible to anyone outside the dog-show loop.

It happened very quickly. Less than twenty-four hours after the authorities decided to hold the auction, almost all the problems had been solved. An agent had taken control. On the face of it, the dogs seemed to have been sold off in a manner that was completely fair; in reality all sorts of secret, backroom deals were struck. The agent made a tidy profit. Not only the dogs, but all the equipment, too, was disposed of. The kennel was dismantled.

And you, Sumer, where are you?

No answer, not a bark. Why not? Because you were dazed. Because you had been separated. From your children, your kin. They had still been suckling, but they were taken from you, your pups, every one. Gone. Snatched from your protection, from the range of your loving gaze. And what about you? What happened to you? No one wanted you. Not one of your children's buyers wanted you. Zero, zip. They had their eyes on the future champions, not on the aging bitch who seemed unlikely to bear any more children. You were still very beautiful, Sumer, but you were too old to be entered in dog shows. So you had no value in that world, and everyone who saw you reached the same conclusion: you weren't worth the trouble and expense. Your old master might not have been so quick to give up. But she was locked up, and the authorities no longer recognized her as your master.

Where are you?

Late summer 1957. The agent had to get rid of you somehow. A few other dogs remained unsold. But he told the authorities he had sold you. To avoid complications. He would have to dispose of you. You and the others. He would kill you.

He herded you all into a trailer.

To take you to another state and kill you. Secretly.

All around you, the other dogs were trembling. They sensed what was happening. But you were still dazed. You had frozen. You were by the window,

Sumer. The agent had tied you all up in one corner so that you wouldn't soil the floor. He had put down a rubber mat. The trailer lurched. Pulled by the car in front of it. You were moving.

Toward death.

And then it happened.

You were on the highway. You had crossed from Illinois into Wisconsin. It was 1957. Late summer, verging on early autumn. You were dazed, staring out the window with empty eyes. You didn't notice when the trailer's wheels rolled over the body of an animal. The body of a dog on the road, run over, flattened. And then, suddenly—you are seeing something. You are gripped by what you see, this scene. Puppies, abandoned on the roadside. Seven puppies, huddled together, shivering. WE'RE WAITING. WE'RE WAITING, JUST LIKE YOU TOLD US TO. WE'RE STILL WAITING, they seem to be saying. And you hear them. You recognize this scene. Something seizes you, moves you. Seven hungry puppies, waiting for their mother's ghost.

It speaks to you. Go, it says. *Wake up.*

Suddenly, you understand. Those puppies have lost their mother. And so—

At last, Sumer, your blood stirred within you. You were never just a pretty dog. Your father was Bad News: one of the greatest war dogs ever to fight in the Second World War, one of the few who returned unscathed from the battlegrounds of the Pacific. Explosion was your grandmother, and Masao was your grandfather. Two war dogs, one American, one Japanese, who had survived those timeless days at the westernmost tip of the Aleutians. Slumbering deep within you was the power to attack. Sleeping within you. And now it had awoken. Your teeth were meant to chew through ropes tying you down. Your muscular legs were built to hurl you against the wall of this trailer, shaking it, tilting it. Your agitation roused the other dogs, tied up around you, destined for death—it was infectious, and one after the next they rose, joined in your rebellion. Still tied up, they flung themselves against the walls, over and over. The trailer skidded, rocked. The dogs were barking. The trailer's driver noticed, hit the brakes, and the agent got out of the cab, opened the door, and stuck his head in. And then, Sumer, you leapt. You attacked. GET BACK, you said. GET OUT OF MY WAY. DON'T INTERFERE. I'LL KILL YOU.

Yes, Sumer, you were awake. You left the agent badly wounded, and you ran. You fled.

Yes, Sumer, you made a break for it.

You were running.

At last, seven puppies waiting by the roadside found their phantom mother.

She didn't look at all like Ice, but she had come to protect them, and they gathered around her, keening.

Their mother had come.

With her full teats, milk enough for seven. With her love.

Sumer: earth goddess and, her father's blood awakened within her, destroyer.

The seven pups raised their heads, gazing up at you. And you told them.

GO ON, you said. SUCK. DRINK MY MILK. GATHER AT MY TEATS.

You suckled them, Sumer.

Starting that very night, you were on the run. You were a mother again, and they were your children. You crossed the highway, all but empty now that night had come. Crossed to the far side, forded that river. And so Ice's final wishes were carried out. Beyond all expectation, a second mother realized the intentions of the first. You made an odd group, of course. The mother, a German shepherd enlisted in the pursuit of pureblooded beauty; her children, seven puppies who looked nothing alike, offspring of a belief in monstrosity and the power of mongrelization. One puppy had the smile of a Samoyed; another had a mane the color of sesame seeds; another had the face of a Labrador retriever, the chest of a Siberian husky, and the high shoulder joints and thick curl of the tail of a Hokkaido dog.

When you joined them, you united two different worlds with different values.

Your mutual love obliterated every meaning that had been invested in you.

The destinies of two bloodlines crossed, and you were a family.

You lived as a family in a "nest" that Sumer found. In a railroad switch-yard, at the edge of the classification yard, where the freight trains stood as though abandoned. Almost no one came here behind the arrival tracks. Sumer settled on a boxcar. She led the children in through the cracked-open door. HIDE HERE IN THE DARKNESS, GET USED TO THE DARKNESS, she told them. THIS IS OUR NEST. She knew they would be well protected in this place. And she was right: it was as sturdy as a fortress. Steel walls surrounded them, raised off the ground. It wasn't very clean, but it reminded Sumer of her cage at the kennel. This was a good place to raise her children. Her old cage had been brightly lit; here there was only darkness. That was fine. Sumer cared for the puppies. For *her own* mongrel puppies. No one cared for Sumer now. She hunted for food. For the whole family. The puppies were ready to be weaned. Late at night, Sumer poked through garbage around the station. In the late 1950s, people loved the wholesomeness of their American lifestyle, their way was the best, and food left over was emerging as a symbol of their victory, a validation of capitalism. Frozen vegetables had come to seem natural; they were always available, there was always more. This culture of excess was what allowed Sumer to care for her family, her nest. Sumer didn't look like a "wild dog," and she didn't rove in a pack, so humans didn't pursue her. She lived quietly. She kept going, quietly. The puppies kept growing. In the nest in the boxcar, they frolicked and tangled in the shadow of Sumer's protective aura.

Sumer, destiny's toy, you were the mother of seven puppies.

For a month.

But destiny wasn't finished with you.

This was 1957. A year that will remain etched in dog history.

One day, you returned from an excursion in search of food to find the door to the boxcar pushed wide open. A man sat on the ledge, his feet dangling in pointy-toed cowboy boots, smoking a cigarette and reading a book. He had a mustache and wore an oddly shaped hat. He was obviously a drifter, probably in his mid-thirties. Not that you, Sumer, had any notion of his age. The thing that got your attention, stunned you, was your children, who were clustered around him. Frisking, frolicking, around him. The man looked up. He stared at you, cocked his head.

What're you doing here? he asked, speaking your thoughts. You're a shepherd. You can't be related to these kids.

YES, I AM, you barked. Was it best to threaten him? The puppies were within reach, and he didn't seem to have harmed them. And that smell—the foul odor of his cigarettes. That same smell clung to the walls of your nest. Your sensitive nose noticed that instantly.

The puppies saw you and started barking: MOM, MOM, MOM!

You're kidding me, the man said. You're their mother? He grinned.

THEY'RE MY CHILDREN, you barked.

Looks that way, the man said, answering his own question with a nod. All right, then. C'mon over. I got food.

THEY'RE MY CHILDREN, you barked.

Listen here, dog, the man said clearly, shutting his book and looking you straight in the eye. This is my train.

On October 22, 1957, the boxcar you had chosen as your nest was coupled to an electric engine and became a link in a very, very, very long chain. You were inside. Your children were with you: they were still too young to make it on their own, of course, and since they were less than two months old it would have been dangerous to try and leave the nest. The man adored them, he loved their mixed-up mongrel appearance, and he treated you with respect. He saw you for what you were: the elegance of your comportment, your physical beauty as a purebred, a perfect German shepherd, and at the same time, the terrible violence your beauty concealed, the instincts that ran, invisible, in your blood. The man fed you. He made all eight of you, the whole family, his pets.

He said you would make a good guard dog.

You didn't yet understand what that meant. But you acknowledged him, just as he did you. And so you became his pet. You felt no hesitation about being a pet. It was only natural: your nest belonged to him.

You slid along the iron rails. Traversed the continent without ever leaving home.

Heading south.

The man who claimed ownership of the train belonged to the transport underworld: he ran a smuggling operation, bribing conductors and overseeing a vast network of migrant laborers. He shipped goods brought in from across the continent south of the border. The operation was much larger than he could have managed on his own. He had a sponsor: a prominent Mexican-

American who lived in Texas. His family had been living on the same land since before the Mexican-American War; they were Catholics, and they ran an orchard of orange and lemon trees, the product of sophisticated irrigation techniques. The orchard was harvested by gringo laborers the man in the train provided, and by illegal workers brought up over the border from Mexico. Since at the time United States law didn't prohibit the employment of illegal immigrants, the Texan had no need to conceal what he was doing, hiring men and women who would have been his compatriots in the last century—until the 1840s, at any rate. The illegality lay, not in employing the immigrants, but in "shipping" them into the country in the first place, and this task was left to the man in the train. That was how he had developed his underworld transport network.

The man hadn't been lying: the train was *his*. Usually, it carried products destined to be sold. Sometimes it carried people. Even now, the other cars in the train were full. Only this boxcar was different: there was nothing here but a family of dogs, lying in the corner.

On October 26, the nest stopped moving. The man, Sumer, and the puppies were close to the border now. Listen here, the man said to Sumer. I'm going to see you live a good life, okay? You're not like other dogs, you're smart—I can see that. So here's what I'm going to do. You listening? I'm going to give you to the Don and you'll be his guard dog, watch his orchard. The puppies too, of course. You'll do a good job, right? You can do it? You do that, and he'll be grateful to me, see, and that'll be your repayment. You can do that, right?

You won't let me down, will you?

When the man, Sumer, and the seven puppies descended from the nest at the station, the Don's men were waiting, rifles in their hands. And after that, Sumer, you took your children and went to work at the orchard. You understood what was being asked of you. You spent a day on the orchard, a second day, a third day, and gradually you got used to it. A fourth day, a fifth day, a sixth day. Your children were growing. They were doing fine. All seven survived to the end of their second month.

November. November 1957.

Horses whinnied. Frogs croaked. Roosters crowed in the mornings. A dozen ducks swam in the pond in the mansion's courtyard. There were times when the orchard misted over, and you were struck by its beauty. Your children too, with the high concentration of northern blood in their veins, loved these moments. THE MIST IS GOOD, they thought. COOL AND GOOD.

The beauty of an orchard in November.

In 1957—a year that would go down in the history of a race of dogs that first came into being here, on this earth, more than ten thousand years ago.

It was night. There was a television in the Don's mansion, and the whole family was inside staring at its screen. They were in the living room, gasping in wonder. In awe, in disbelief. The servants were in the garden, gazing up at the sky. Their expressions focused, intent, as if they were hoping, somewhere up there, to find the truth. Is that it? No, no. How about that, over there? Hey, we're not looking for a falling star, okay?

And you, Sumer, and your children—you felt it.

A kind of buzzing in your hearts that made you lift your heads to the clear, starry sky.

A man-made satellite flew overhead. It took about 103 minutes for it to orbit the earth. The previous month, the Soviet Union had beaten America in the Space Race. The Soviet Union, having poured astonishing amounts of money into the program, had succeeded in launching into orbit the very first man-made satellite: Sputnik 1. Now, less than a month later, in an effort to demonstrate the overwhelming superiority of Communism to the entire world, it had done something even more extraordinary. Sputnik 2 had been outfitted with an airtight chamber, and a living creature had been loaded inside. The first Earthling to experience space flight. The creature was not human. It was a dog. A bitch.

The airtight chamber had a window.

The bitch looked down at the earth.

She was a Russian laika. In the initial reports of her flight, conflicting information was given regarding her name. She was said to be named Damka, Limonchik, and Kudryavka, but within a few days Laika had stuck. She was Laika, the laika. Laika the space dog. One of the USSR's top-secret national projects. A dog.

She orbited the globe, alive.

Gazing out, down, in zero gravity.

You felt her gaze.

You, Sumer, and your children: you felt it. And so, there on the Mexican-American border, you raised your heads to look up at the sky. You and several thousand others. On November 3, 1957, all at once, 3,733 descendants of a Hokkaido dog named Kita and 2,928 descendants of a German shepherd named Bad News, scattered across the surface of the globe, unaware of the lines that separated communist and capitalist spheres, all those dogs raised their heads to peer into the vastness of the sky.

"Don't mess with a yakuza girl."

Who the fucking hell do you think I am?

The girl ponders the question she asks. Age X, stranded between eleven and twelve, trapped in this fucking cold Stone-Age country, Russia. Fucking dicks, fucking around with me like this.

Are you planning to keep me hostage forever?

What am I, fucking invisible?

Something had changed, ever since that day when she went out onto the grounds to watch the old man train the dogs. Somehow, suddenly and inexplicably, the situation had shifted in that moment when she told the old man to drop dead, and he handed her the word right back: *Shi-ne*. SHE-neh. She often put on her coat and went outside. She left the building that contained her little room—her cell, at least in theory—and the kitchen and dining room and other rooms and went out to wander through the Dead Town. She did this every day. This, the girl thought, was her job, the daily grind. Until then she had spent the better part of every day lying on her bed, shouting, cursing, making a show of her rage. During meals she would hurl imprecations at the Russians who sat around the table with her, spit her hatred at their faces. No longer. She went out now, all the time. On her own, of her own free will, she wandered the Dead Town, inspecting it and the concrete walls that enclosed it. One by one she walked the paved roads that segmented the expanse of land within the walls. She left footprints in the snow that filled the potholes. This was her routine, now, and no one objected.

Hey, I'm a fucking hostage, right? You *need* me.

Fucking around with me.

Why don't you guard me, you dicks? What am I, the invisible girl?

And so she decided to fight back. All right then, she thought. If I'm invisible, let's see what it's like to be invisible. I'll do the seeing. She began following the other inhabitants of the Dead Town, observing them at close range. She gave all five of them names. The old man was "Old Fuck," of course. The old lady with the glasses who managed the kitchen was "Old Bag." Or, alternatively, "Russian Hag." She came to think of the two middle-aged women who looked so alike and were always with the Old Bag as Woman One and Woman Two, because they had no distinguishing characteristics. Soon these were shortened to WO and WT. The last of the five, the bald middle-aged man, was Opera. Because he sometimes hummed to himself. He favored old workers' songs, revolutionary marches—melodies the girl found unnerving. He could belt them out at considerable volume. *What the fuck, go to a karaoke place if you want to sing. You creep me out.* So that was his name: Opera.

Old Fuck, Old Bag, WO, WT, and Opera. And me.

These were the residents of the Dead Town.

This was how she catalogued them.

And these were the people she observed.

On some level, she was actively engaging with them. But at the same time, she made zero effort to communicate—to convey anything at all, feelings or intentions. She simply put herself in the same spaces and watched their every move. She stared at the five Russians.

And then there were the dogs.

A few dozen dogs, the *other* residents of this Dead Town unmarked on any map from the time it was built and now forgotten by history.

There was time in her schedule for observing the dogs.

Every day, she watched the old man train them. Once in the morning, once in the afternoon. He was teaching them more advanced techniques now, fighting and attacking, on a field that gradually came to encompass the whole of Dead Town. The dogs moved frequently from place to place, covering an enormous territory, rehearsing their destructive maneuvers; and the girl followed. Rehearsing—yes, because this was only a *rehearsal*. A dry run for some sort of field day of the dogs, a fucking preview of the Great Doggie Festival. She understood, more or less, what was happening. That they were practicing. That one day they would take to the streets.

She kept her distance. She always stayed a few yards away, watching. Watching the dogs do their exercises. I don't go in for this fucking gym class shit, thanks, I'd rather sit out. Look at these shitheads, fucking scampering around like maniacs. *Woof--woof-woof-woof-woof-woof!* Don't you ever get tired? Actually, the dogs seldom barked. For the most part, they darted off and sprang at their simulated targets in total silence. They'd had it pounded into their heads that this was the way to do it: covert attacks. The old man, their trainer—the Old Fuck—had made this clear. And yet there was such ferocity in their movements that you almost seemed to hear them barking, baying, their voices rich and loud.

If one actually heard a sound, it was more likely to be a gunshot.

The bullets weren't real, they were blanks. But they accustomed the dogs to the sound.

The dogs no longer regarded the girl as an intruder, no longer growled. Because the old man scolded them that first time. The dogs remembered. And so they kept quiet. A few had barked at her the second time, when she came to watch, to *study* them, and she herself had told them off.

"Shut the fuck up," she said, glaring. "You're annoying me."

She stared straight at them as she spoke, and they shut up.

The old man laughed when he saw this.

Upwards of forty dogs would participate in these exercises, learning specialized techniques. Honing their abilities. Seven or eight would take the day off. The old man let them rest before they got too worn out. He took stock of each dog's condition individually and based his decision on his assessment, though for the most part he followed a fixed order. The dogs he released from training spent the day in their cages.

In the doghouse.

Outside, exposed to the air.

The girl went by the cages too. It was only natural that she incorporated a visit to this area, given over entirely to the dogs' use, into her daily schedule. Every so often, a new dog would join the ranks. The newcomers tended to be young; they must have been captured outside. The new dogs stayed for some time in the cages with the dogs that had been released from training, all day every day. And there were puppies too. Little dogs, natives of the Dead Town, who had only just been removed from the cage they had shared with their mother, where they had sucked at her teats.

Now the whole litter was kept in a large cage of its own.

During the day, at least, it was *theirs*.

Only six or seven weeks old, these puppies had not yet learned caution. The girl watched them through the chain-link fence. The first time she saw the little bastards in their cage, she had a thought. There were old dogs here, and little ones. She remembered the old dog that had appeared on the roof and barked at her that time when the Old Fuck spoke in Japanese, "SHE-neh," *drop dead*—that dog, she thought, was a senile old fuck himself. The thing is, she sensed, whether they're dogs or people, I fucking hate old fucks.

"Don't get any ideas, though," she told the puppies, speaking through the chain-link fence. "That doesn't mean I think you're cute."

This too, she said in Japanese.

After that, she came every day to grumble outside the puppies' cage. Objectively speaking, they were adorable. Roly-poly with ears that poked out from their round heads, bodies covered with light, soft hair. That wasn't how the girl saw it. "Morons. Idiots. Fuckheads. Fucking little doggie-shits," she said. She twined her fingers around the chain-link fence. "Look at you. So fucking tame. Some fuck feeds you and you're his." Each puppy had a tag. She couldn't read the names, of course, because they were written in the Cyrillic alphabet, but she could read the numbers. Arabic numerals were okay: 44, 45, 46, 47, 48, and then 113, 114. Seven in all. As far as she was concerned the numbers might as well have been names, and so she added them to her list.

She recognized the puppies through the numbers they had been assigned.

This, in part, was what allowed her to focus so intently on them. This, in part, was why she sometimes looked so enchanted as she stood before their cage. Though at the same time, there was something in the unpredictability of their actions that fascinated her, kept her from getting tired of standing there *looking*.

So she went on visiting the cage, grumbling to the puppies.

"Look at you, tripping like that," she said. "Can't even walk right."

"Little doggie-shits, fucking gnawing on each other," she said.

"Think you're so grown up, huh?" she said. "Fucking think again."

"Assholes," she said.

There was something good about this part of her schedule. She felt better.

One day, she decided to see how dumb the puppies were. She searched the kitchen and the stores of dog food. She knew what they were fed. *Obviously. I watch the Old Bag preparing the shit.* She had a hypothesis she wanted to test. "All people have to do is feed you and you're theirs, right? You fucks. Yeah, I'm talking to you Forty-four. And Forty-five, Forty-six, Forty-seven, Forty-eight, One hundred thirteen, and One hundred fourteen, all of you. Fuckers. I bet you'll let me feed you too."

This was her hypothesis.

The result was a chorus of yelping.

Number 44: FEED ME!

Number 114: FEED ME!

Number 45, number 46, number 47, number 48, and number 113: FEED ME! FEED ME! FEED ME! FEED ME! FEED ME!

The second she pushed the food through the fence, they gathered around and began going for it, snapping at it, not even bothering to sniff it and see what it was.

No, they hadn't yet learned to be wary—not at all. And since they had already been weaned from their mother's milk, they had no problem eating the sort of "Russian dog food" the girl gave them. She gave them sheep hooves. Leftovers. But they chewed them all the same, licked them all over.

There was a bit of meat and gelatin left, if only a little.

"Happy?" the girl asked. "You like that?"

They looked happy.

"You like stinky crap like that?"

WE'RE HAPPY, the dogs replied. WE LIKE IT.

"See, I knew it," the girl said, the pride in her words not entirely matched by the unusual stiffness and, simultaneously, the slight relaxation of her expression. "I can make you mine as easily as they can. Look at you, wagging your fucking tails. Fucking morons. Fucking shitheads. That's Russia for you. Eating this foul-smelling mutton crap because you'll take any nutrition you can get."

From that day on, she worked to prove her hypothesis. Each time she visited the puppies' cage, she took food—stolen food. And she fed them. The seven puppies were always overjoyed to see her. They started wagging their tails the second they saw her. *Woof woof, woof woof,* they said. And the girl, watching them tear into the food, kept grumbling. In Japanese. Monotone. "Sometimes they feed me mutton too. Disgusting crap. Tastes so fucking strong. You seem to like it though, huh? Sure looks that way. But not me... fucking ass. It's winter food, this crap. It makes your body feel toasty when you eat it, right? You know? That's something I learned. Shit. I'm learning all kinds of fucking shit. Hey, c'mere," she said, sticking her hand into the cage near the bottom of the chain-link fence.

Four or five puppies gathered around.

Licking her hand.

The girl gave one of their heads a rough pat.

"See how hot you are? Right, One hundred fourteen?"

One or two of the others rubbed their heads and bodies against her, evidently eager to be petted too. Rubbed up against her hand. Her fingers.

You're hot, right?

YES.

Right?

FEED ME.

That was the end of the girl's schedule. With this—for the time being at least—her *job* was over. Watch the tagged puppies, secretly feed them, fill their ears with Japanese. Lots of Japanese, complaining in Japanese. Monotonal Japanese. She had to accustom the puppies to the sound and rhythms of her speech.

The daily grind continued. And then one day, it ended.

Dramatically. It was unclear how many days...or weeks the new monotony of her routine had continued by then, in the Dead Town, from the beginning to the moment when it ended. She herself couldn't have said. She wasn't counting the days. What day was this? The question didn't exist. *I'm X years old. I don't fucking need time.*

So the day it happened was just another day.

They had finished lunch. The old lady was in the kitchen making jam. The girl observed her from behind. She was the invisible girl, monitoring the Old Bag. Reverse monitoring. You get what that means, Old Bag? Maybe, just fucking maybe, you're *my* hostage. The girl hadn't said anything. She spoke the words to herself. Silent Japanese. She snuck food from the kitchen all the time, for the puppies—she knew what went on in the kitchen was important. So she monitored the kitchen. She planted herself there in the same space as the old lady, day after day, and regarded her. Long and hard. Taking it all in. The old lady's trunk, shaped like a barrel. Her thick glasses. Ingredients. Vegetables, herbs. Beets. Dill. Scallions. Heaped in baskets. Not the dill: it was in a glass. A bouquet. Buckwheat seeds, flour. Oil...sunflower seed oil. The girl could tell because of the enormous yellow flower on the label. And then the kitchen supplies. Pots, of course. Some with handles on both sides. Frying pans. Bowls. Ladles. Carving knives.

The old lady didn't use any of this when she made jam.

She had masses of gooseberries and strawberries. She dropped them into wide-mouthed jars with an equal amount of sugar. And that was it. A very simple task.

Strawberries, the girl thought.

Is it the season for strawberries?

The girl had explored large swaths of the Dead Town on her walks, but she hadn't seen a garden anywhere. Maybe the Old Bag gathered them in the forest? Was there a market nearby? She had no idea. When the fuck do you make jam anyway? What season? Before winter? This is fucking Russia, though. It's fucking endless winter here.

There are no seasons, asshole. I'm X years old.

She kept thinking about the strawberries.

Needless to say, she and the old lady didn't speak. A few minutes later, the girl was outside. She had left the kitchen to wander around the Dead Town as she always did. Two blocks away from the building was a concrete wall. One of the walls that cut this place off from the outside world. One of the barriers that made it all too apparent that this place was her prison. As she walked, she happened to catch sight of WO and WT. They were wheeling a motorcycle out of a garage. This was unexpected. It looked like they were going to ride it together, sitting in its tandem seat. One of them, either WO or WT, was going to drive that thing. They were going to buy food. She knew, she could sense it. And so she started *observing* them, the way she always did. Except that this time she took a different approach—this time, she didn't act as though she were invisible. Without even thinking, she concealed herself behind a building. *Strawberries*, she thought. Shadowing people had become part of her daily routine, but this time she wanted to go further: she wanted to see where they went. Did they pick the strawberries themselves? Or buy them? And where? The two middle-aged women, WO and WT, opened the gate to the outside world. One of the exits from the Dead Town, an iron gate that opened out to both sides. One of the *exits*. The girl had never considered trying to escape. If this were her prison, she might have struggled to scale the walls, tried to find some way out into the world beyond, the *shaba*, but she never had, not once. Because it would be a total fucking pain in the ass. What the fuck would she do once she was out? Gather fucking mushrooms in the forest, wrestle with bears? Like hell she was going to do that shit. But now she found herself wanting to see outside. WO and WT straddled the motorcycle. She was sneaking toward them. Keeping in their blind spot, creeping down the street, hugging the wall. She poked her head out from behind the wall of the building closest to them, low down. *Strawberries*, she thought.

Can I run after the motorcycle?

The door. There was no click.

There was no lock.

So she decided to try and see where WO and WT went. To get a good look, see what direction they went, and where they were going.

A forest? A garden? A market?

She rested her hand on the door. She was almost beyond the concrete wall. Half her foot was past the edge.

Just then, there was a tremendous explosion behind her. A gunshot. Not a blank this time. It was an actual bullet. A sliver of concrete burst from the wall. Blasted off. A deep hole appeared. Not that the girl noticed. She couldn't have. The bullet had whizzed by so close she could have reached out and touched it. The air had trembled as the bullet passed; she could still feel it under her skin.

She was quaking.

…was he aiming for me?

She stiffened. All over her skin, her hair was standing on end.

Her face began to flush. She was still shaking, and her face kept turning redder and redder, the redness moving quietly, ever so quietly up and up, like water rising, until it reached her ears. At the same time, a new expression appeared on her face. She was biting her bottom lip. Biting down. Hard. Very slowly, she turned around and looked behind her.

Straight behind her.

Just three meters away, the old lady who she had thought was in the kitchen stood holding a pistol with both hands. Her apron covered with juice from the berries.

"Old Bag," the girl said.

The old lady didn't reply.

"So you were watching me, huh? I'm not the invisible girl after all."

The old lady's thick-lensed glasses made it hard to read her expression. Her true feelings.

And those same lenses were watching her. Observing. Like a machine.

"Pleased with yourself, aren't you, Old Bag? Firing your fucking pistol at me. You fucking asshole, dicking around with me. I'm used to this kind of shit, you know. Even more than the dogs. You think a fucking gunshot can scare me? Don't mess with a yakuza girl."

She spat this out. These words.

And yet she had wet herself.

The stain was spreading even now across the crotch of her jeans. She could feel it. And she suspected the old lady could see it too. So she said what she had to say. To the old lady standing there with the pistol, posed just as she had been when she fired that warning shot.

"Shit…I swear I'm going to stab you one day. You and the rest of the world."

Ten minutes later, the girl was back in the room she had been given, changing her clothes. She put on new underwear. She threw away the pissed-on jeans. She put her feet through into a pair of pants she had been given as a spare—the old lady had provided these too. The girl had never worn them before. Look at these cheap-ass shitty pants, she thought, resenting them, hating them. Are you fucking making fun of me? Don't try to fucking make me wear little kid's clothes. Those jeans I just tossed aren't for fucking middle class losers, you know. Those were Gucci. Those were brand-name jeans, you assholes. That's why I kept wearing them, even if I never washed them. Those were my favorite fucking jeans. Fucking Gucci washed denim.

And now they've got piss on 'em.

The girl felt it. A feeling she couldn't name. Humiliation.

She put on her coat. She put on her hat. She dressed herself against the cold as if she were donning some sort of armor, shielding her raging emotions from view, disguising herself as an ordinary Russian child. She could have been a member of some mongoloid Siberian minority. Except that the words brimming inside her were Japanese. Japanese imprecations. Expressions of boundless rage. She could no longer contain it. She needed to let it out, and in order to do that, she needed the puppies.

Those puppies.

Number 44, 45, 46, 47, 48, 113, and 114.

That cage. The time she spent, day after day, standing before it.

But the puppies weren't in the cage that afternoon. The girl knew why. Three or four days earlier, things had changed. Already, the dramatic new developments that would take place in her daily routine had been hinted at, foreshadowed. The puppies weren't being trained to fight and attack like the other dogs, not really. They had been taken out to the grounds, leaving the cage empty, for only a short time. During that period, the old man checked them out. Checked to see whether they were naturally inclined to fight. To see how they reacted to gunfire. How they responded to smoke. They were being tested, in other words. They had moved on from playing with balls to the next stage. One stage before he began training them in earnest.

Would these puppies imitate the "finished" dogs, the adults the old man had already trained? Or rather, would they one day learn to imitate their seniors?

Did they listen to human commands? Would they eventually?

These were the questions the old man had to answer.

Already, then, in a small way, their training had begun.

And already the results were in. All seven were suitable. Of course. The old man had known to expect this. Considering their breeding, their lineage. So naturally he increased the difficulty of the tests. Two or three days earlier, he had started testing their ability to respond to basic commands like "Go," "Stop," and "Down," and having them play, for instance, at attacking a target.

Of course, out here on the grounds they had models to follow. They could imitate the adult dogs. They had to catch their scent, grasp the mood. What was it like to attack? What precisely was required of them? The puppies' every movement radiated youth, but that was okay, that was only natural. It was all a game. Indeed, the fact that they were only playing made it more clear how well, or how poorly, they were suited to the task that awaited them.

And so she knew.

She understood the situation. There was no point going to stand before the cage. Because the puppies weren't there. They were on the grounds. Fucking asshole, after all the time I spent taming them, now that I've finally succeeded, you drag the fuckers out to train them? Don't fucking steal them. Don't fucking steal my doggies, you dick. She knew they would be back in the cage soon, in a half hour, maybe an hour. But she didn't feel like waiting. She understood the situation, and so she headed out to the exercise grounds.

Directly.

Her coat buttoned up all the way, her hat pulled down low over her eyes, her head full of hatred, taking form in Japanese.

The girl saw what was happening. The old man gave the word, and the puppies responded. I fucking showered them with Japanese, fucking shit-ass Japanese. And now the Old Fuck is teaching the little doggie-shits Russian. What's the fucking idea? He doesn't want them to hear my voice, is that it? She listened. She focused on each command as it was given. Disgusted, annoyed, she nevertheless let the words soak into her brain. As sounds. Just sounds. Soon she found herself unable just to stand there watching as he trained the puppies. She couldn't hang back, observing from several yards off. She went up right behind the old man, not hesitating at all, not at all afraid of the dogs. She was confrontational. She was filled with raw, real hatred. She saw Opera off in the distance. The Old Fuck's buddy, Opera. He was playing the role of the target, his torso and arms swaddled in protective padding, but without the helmet. He was the target in this game the puppies were playing. You're training them, the girl thought, I know. Training them to kill. I realize what you're fucking doing, assholes. She was feeling emotions she couldn't have expressed in words. Destruction. That's what they were doing. She wanted it to happen. *Yeah, do it! Bring it all down!* The old man paid no attention to her. He wasn't exactly ignoring her, but he was focused on the puppies, on seeing how well they suited his needs. He spoke only to them. Gave them commands in Russian. The girl was able to remember them. That Old Fuck spoke to me. I never asked to have a conversation with him, he just did it. SHE-neh, he said. Drop dead. Yeah, well two can play that game. I'll fucking get in your way. This time, it's my turn, right?

The seven puppies were waiting for the next command.

All of a sudden, she shouted. Imitating the sounds of Russian.

Sic him! She was thinking. Attack that asshole!

And those were the words she yelled: "Go! Sic him!" In Russian. The accent wasn't perfect, but she had absorbed the sounds well enough.

There were the seven puppies. They had been doing these tests for days, they were used to the commands. They had a vague understanding of the concept—that these words the people spoke were instructions. And they were used to the girl's voice. She had come and talked to them every day, after all. That had been part of her routine. And so.

The smartest puppy responded to her command.

One puppy started running.

It was number 47. He sprinted off at full speed. His little hind legs bending, their joints creaking. He ran faster. Heading for the target. Because a voice he knew had ordered him to attack. He was supposed to do something, he knew. THROW YOURSELF AT THE TARGET, that was it, maybe. Or maybe it was, RUN AT HIM. And then, BITE HIM, KILL HIM.

Number 47 understood the girl's words.

He leapt at Opera.

He sprang at him and kept attacking until Opera pushed him down, and when the old man shouted "Down," he turned and looked first at the girl.

The girl stared, dumbstruck, at number 47.

"I did it, right?" the puppy was asking.

Number 47 was a boy.

And then the girl...nodded. She nodded at number 47.

It had started. She'd had a conversation. For the first time since she had been brought here as a prisoner to the Dead Town, she had willingly communicated with another living creature. Not with a person, with a dog. But still, it had happened. This Japanese girl had spoken to a dog, and the dog had understood. True, the medium had been a monkey-see-monkey-do imitation of Russian, but that didn't matter: the linguistic gap between the original Russian and her fake Russian was no more than a few millimeters.

A minute later, ten minutes later, an hour later, the shock was still sinking in.

Sinking in.

Night fell. At the dinner table, the girl had an announcement to make. The Old Fuck, the Old Bag, Opera, WO, and WT were all sitting there around the table when she made it. "That dog is mine," she told them, speaking very clearly, in Japanese. Naturally no one understood. None of them had the slightest idea what she had said, at least not at this stage. But she didn't care.

"You heard me, right? I asked for permission, and I got it," she declared.

The old man sensed something. *You made some kind of announcement, didn't you?* he asked.

In Russian. And that was it. He didn't pursue the matter.

The rest of the meal was like any other. A salad with beets in it, cold kidney beans, borscht, some sort of sour bread.

Already her routine was disrupted. After dinner, the girl left the building. This was the first time since her arrival that she had been out after dark. She headed straight for the area with the kennels. She had no trouble finding her way. She carried something in her hand: the remains of a mutton rib roast that she had walked off with without even trying to hide what she was doing, as the old lady watched, while she was cleaning up the kitchen and getting things ready for the following day. The girl had taken what was left after the meat was carved, the extras.

She came to the puppies' cage.

The seven puppies welcomed her, yelping. One was half asleep, but the smell of the meat woke it up. In the other cages, the adult dogs began making noise as well, attracted by the odor. The girl ignored them, gave all the meat to the puppies.

The mutton rib roast.

She waited for her eyes to get completely used to the dark. She didn't have a flashlight, of course. She waited until she could recognize the puppies gathered around the roast.

"Hey," she said. In Japanese, as always. "That's mutton. I told you before, right? When you gnaw on mutton, your body gets hot. So how the fuck is it, huh? That's why I brought it."

The girl rested her hands on the cage door. A rectangle of iron pipes covered with chain-link. The lock was just a latch. All that mattered was that the dogs couldn't open it and run out. The girl raised the latch. She stepped into the cage, gingerly scooped up one of the puppies. She cradled number 47 in her arms.

"Hey, fucker. Come keep me warm," she said.

Number 47 didn't struggle.

"You're okay coming to my room? Being my heater?"

Number 47 didn't struggle.

That night, the bed in the girl's cell became a double bed for one girl and one puppy. Her cell was now a cell for two. She hugged number 47 tightly in the narrow bed, five feet wide at most, petting him roughly but with profound emotion. She couldn't have put her feelings into words. Number 47 didn't struggle. Far from it, he jumped at her. Burrowed under her squishy stomach.

One girl and one dog slept.

Nice and warm.

She got up right away when she woke the next morning. Already her new routine had been established. The old schedule had fallen apart, she knew that. Everything was just beginning. Something was just beginning. She was no longer the invisible girl, and she no longer had to observe the Old Fuck, the Old Bag, WO, WT, and Opera. She had realized that they were, in fact, observing her. And so...what?

She, along with her dogs, would find a third position.

Making adjustments along the way.

So she got up the next morning and went outside with number 47. They went to the bathroom. It was a good thirty feet away from the building, and she went there every morning to wash her face. She peed, as she always did. Number 47 found a place to pee too. After that, they headed over to the kennels. This time the girl didn't pick number 47 up; she let him walk, and they made their way together toward the cages. They stopped before the puppies' cage. Number 47's siblings looked out, puzzled, through the chain-link fence. WHAT ARE YOU DOING OUT THERE? they asked number 47. "I picked him," the girl said. "He's the one I chose." YOU DID? the six puppies asked. "He's my guard, this guy. Forty-seven," the girl said. Number 47 confirmed her statement with a silent yelp. SO THAT'S WHY YOU WEREN'T AROUND LAST NIGHT? IS THAT TRUE, BROTHER? the six puppies asked. "Listen to me. He's going to stay here in the cage with you in the morning and during the day and stuff. I'll bring Forty-seven back every morning. He'll stay here and play with you, and he'll train with you too. You got that? So I'm telling you, don't you fucking ignore him. You do that, and I'll fucking kick the shit out of you. I'll get a bat and I'll fucking pulverize you. I mean it. Because he's going to be my guard..." The girl turned to number 47. "I'm gonna make you top dog, you hear? I'm gonna turn you into a real fucking dog. You got that, Forty-seven? You hear what I'm saying? But when you're with the other dogs, you'll just be a dog. A little doggie-shit. That's how you're gonna live."

Live, the girl said.

Number 47, standing right next to her, replied with a silent yelp.

And the girl returned him to the cage.

His six siblings obediently welcomed him back. Though they did sniff him.

That morning, number 47 ate the same dog food he always had. And the girl ate the breakfast the old lady prepared. Number 47 devoured the "Russian dog food" that WO and WT left in the cage, while the girl had rye bread and some sort of sour drink. Already the new routine had begun. The girl struck a dauntless figure at the breakfast table. No more watching for her, no more being watched. If you want to try, go the fuck ahead. Her attitude made it clear she wouldn't take questions from anyone at the table.

Number 47 frolicked all morning with his siblings in the large cage. Playing at fighting, at attacking. Running around. Rolling on the ground.

The girl stood before the cage as usual, observing them.

Everything was okay. She could feel it.

Lunchtime.

The afternoon. The girl joined in the training. She made it clear she was participating. This, above all, was the core of her new routine. The test period had essentially ended now, and the puppies were being given the early training appropriate for dogs in their first four months. They did their best to learn the basics. The girl was right there on the grounds with the old man and Opera. She didn't interfere. She did, however, help number 47 learn his lessons. She made sure he didn't slack off, came up with little tricks to keep him from losing interest, taught him commands: Good, no, roll left, roll right.

The commands were in Russian.

The girl was now making a conscious effort to learn the Russian words.

The puppies' training didn't last very long.

After an hour or two, they were put back in their cage.

I guess the Old Fuck doesn't want to wear them out, the girl thought.

"Are you tired?" the girl asked number 47.

The dog looked fine. But she let him rest. Him and the other puppies, his siblings.

That was the right thing to do. She could feel it.

That night, she took number 47 out of the cage again. To have him sleep with her in her room. One person and one dog, bonding, enveloped in each other's warmth. "Tired?" she asked him again. I'M BEAT, the dog said—not in words, of course, but with his body—and buried himself in the folds of her flesh, the odd fatness that was hers and no one else's.

At night, the dog was not a dog.

At night, the girl was no longer just a human girl.

The dog and the girl became, here in the Dead Town, a third being.

And stayed that way until morning.

Morning came. Once again, the girl repeated the new routine. Making adjustments as she went along. Essentially, though, the content stayed the same. The essential elements remained unchanged. The girl had planned her schedule well. On the first day, the first morning, she had set it all out in her mind. Now she just had to push ahead, uncompromising, and make it happen. Night fell. Morning came. Night fell. Morning came. Days passed, some number of days passed, untallied. The girl, X years old, never counted them.

During the day, number 47 recognized the girl as his master. He obeyed her commands unfailingly. The girl could now control his moods, stirring him to excitement or bringing him to his senses. She had the words to do that. She had mastered the Russian she needed to issue her commands. Though she had made no particular effort to encourage number 47's six siblings to respond to her orders on the grounds, they did. The puppies were now large enough to be considered adolescent and were on their way to becoming young dogs. One day, the old man stood and watched the girl for some time. He tracked her movements as she skillfully handled the dogs, number 47 and his six siblings. It was clear: she was their master.

What are you looking at? the girl asked.

You're doing great, the old man said.

Don't you dare take number 47 from me, the girl said.

Some little girl you are, the old man said. You're a trainer already.

Just you try and take him, the girl said. I'll fucking kill you.

Or maybe you're a dog? Is that it? the old man asked.

"Anyway, you Old Fuck, it's you're fault—you and the Old Bag. Fucking shooting at me and shit. With a fucking pistol...scared the shit out of me. So this is fucking self-defense. You hear me, asshole? I'm gonna train number 47 to be my guard. Just you try and fuck with me again, see what happens. I'll fucking sic him on you."

Is that it? Are you a dog too? the old man asked again in Russian. He cocked his head. Are you, is it possible...*her*?

Self-defense. The girl's own dog, dedicated to her protection. Hovering nearby, ready to be of assistance. Night fell. Morning came. Night fell. Morning came. The young number 47 acquired a new technique—to attack a person in silence. Without barking, darting out from behind a building, for instance, in a flash—the power to kill in a second, noiselessly. Still he had learned only the very basics. He had to be faster, had to use all five senses for the purpose for which they were meant. To attack. All the while, he watched the other dogs putting their knowledge to use. He was there on the grounds, a young dog, looking on as the adults practiced what they had learned. Subversive activities. He was there, observing. Always. Night fell. Morning came. Slight adjustments were made in the routine. One day, one afternoon after the young dogs had finished their training, number 47's siblings were taken back to their cage but number 47 was not. A person and a dog, "off duty," as it were. It was like an outgrowth of the night. The girl took number 47 with her as she traipsed through the Dead Town, now a stage for simulated bouts of street fighting. They ran together through a white, four-story building. Climbed the stairs. Ran back down. Up. Down. They climbed to the top of a tall observation tower. A person and a dog, looking down over the Dead Town. Hey, number 47, the girl said, as she gazed out over the landscape. Sometime...someday, we're going to kill the world. Number 47 stood perfectly still, listening to the girl's voice. To her muttering in Japanese. These words weren't Russian, they weren't commands. A person and a dog went back down. On the paved road, number 47 scrambled up alone onto the roof of a burnt-out car. He hadn't yet learned to jump a moving car. To spring toward it as it approached, to leap over it, spring onto the hood—it was too early for that. But he could imitate the others. He knew to watch the adult dogs, engaged in their subversive activities, and he could grasp the essence of what they were doing, instantly. He could copy them.

Eventually, a young dog grows up.

Eventually, number 47 would mature.

One day, while they were off duty, the girl found herself in a room. A room in one of the other buildings, not the one that served as their base, where she had her bedroom and where the kitchen and the dining room were—a different building. She had known about this place, she knew the old man and Opera were always going in and out of it. But it didn't interest her. She assumed it was just a place for storing the paraphernalia they used to train the dogs. And in fact it was. But that wasn't all it was. There was more than one room in there. More than one kind of room.

Number 47 was the first to become curious. He had caught some sort of scent, and it had led him to the door. The sound of singing came from inside. As the voice echoed off the concrete walls, it acquired a sort of vibrato. Opera. The melody was catchy. The girl, however, found it as eerie as ever. *Loouu, loooouuuuoo! Loooooouuuuuuoo!* Number 47 ignored the singing. He kept sniffing the ground, the lingering traces of whatever it had been. "I thought they just kept their shit in here. Is there something else?" the girl asked. "Hey, Forty-seven, have other dogs come by here? Is that it?"

Not just people? she asked in Japanese. Dogs too?

Number 47 answered in dogspeech: ANOTHER DOG HAS BEEN HERE.

"It smells like a fucking dead Hawaii in here," the girl muttered as she stepped through the door into the building. Of course, this was Russia—that made sense. An eternal summer killed forever. Actually, it smelled like a locker room. The smell called up a memory of the time before she turned X years old. Fucking shit...now I've got those fucking moneyless assholes in my head, the fucking *world*....Shit. A person and a dog, off duty, striding rapidly through the dim interior. The building was laid out along the same pattern as the one they used as their base, so there was no fear of getting lost. She went into the main hall.

127

The room was at the end of the hall. And now here she was, inside it.

It's like a yakuza office, one of the branches. The thought hit her immediately. And then she was putting it into words, muttering to herself. It reminded her of the wide-open office her dad's organization rented, one whole floor of a building shared by various other companies and groups. Only this place had none of the bold, forceful calligraphy hanging on the walls, characters reading "Spirit" and "Kill One to Save Many" and that sort of shit. Instead, there was a map. A really, really old map of the world. Her dad's office had a little Shinto shrine on one wall, up close to the ceiling, but there was nothing like that here. No Russian Orthodox icons. Instead, there was a television. The first television she had seen in the Dead Town. It wasn't on. The screen was blank. Of course, there was no one in the room. And yet, somehow, she felt something. A strong sense of *something*. "I bet there's a fucking dead body under the floor or something. Can you smell it, Forty-seven?" The dog didn't answer. The sound of Opera singing echoed down the corridor at the other end of the main hall. As it had before. There was no leather sofa like the one in her dad's office, but there was a table and some seats. There was a mound of money on the table. Rows and rows of bundled banknotes that seemed, at first sight, to be neatly stacked but weren't really. No rubles as far as she could see. Look at all this cash, the girl thought, glancing it over. That's fucking American money, isn't it? Dollars or whatever?

Yeah, she thought. It is like Dad's office after all.

Just then, she caught sight of a shrine. Something, at any rate, that felt like a shrine in the context of this room. There were no paper lanterns, and there was no Japanese sword resting on its stands, but it had the same aura. That was it. The source of whatever it was she was feeling. The globe.

It was on a shelf. Displayed. Set out to be seen, regarded. Revered.

That, the girl sensed, was the most important thing in the room.

She knew it right away.

So she went to take it in her hands.

She walked around the table, reached out. She picked it up. She had expected it to be fairly heavy, but it was surprisingly light. It felt like metal, though. It felt old. She had assumed it would be hollow like other globes, but it didn't seem to be. She turned it in her palms. Rotated the earth. It was bigger than her head.

She sensed it. This isn't empty.

She sensed it. There's something here.

She sensed it. Something *alive*.

But what?

Is it…inside?

She turned it in her palms, looking for a seam. The northern and southern hemispheres looked like they might crack apart. That was the line. Ever so carefully, she opened it. And out it came. Bone. An animal's skull. It looked like it had been burned…bits of skin or something clinging to it, hanging. Skin like a mummy's, desiccated.

…what the hell?

Are you kidding me?

Number 47 was trying to communicate something. Trying to tell her something. It had nothing to do, however, with the skull in the globe. He was trying to draw her attention to the figure now standing in the doorway. No, not the figure—the figures. Like the girl and number 47, they were two: a person and a dog.

A person and a dog, both old.

At number 47's urging, the girl turned around.

"You have opened the coffin, have you?" the old man said.

"What…the hell?" the girl said.

"You wanted to hold it? Is that it, girl?"

The dog standing beside the old man was very old. The girl remembered him, of course—she had seen him before. He was fairly large, stately. This was the same dog that had barked down at her once before, from the roof.

"You wanted to touch the very first dog?" the old man said in Russian. Then, "But it is not Belka, you know."

"I didn't break it," the girl said in Japanese. "I just opened it." Then, suddenly realizing what was inside, she continued. "Fuck, you asshole, keeping a fucking creepy skull like this, hidden in this thing. What is it…a fucking dog? Is that what this is, you Old Fuck?"

"That is the first great Soviet hero. A dog who did not make it back to the earth alive. Those are her remains. That is not Belka."

"What the fuck are you saying?" the girl asked.

The old man pointed to the old dog beside him. He looked the girl in the eye.

"This is Belka," he said.

"It's a dog, isn't it…a fucking dog's skull."

"You understand, little girl? He is the one dog I did not kill, the year before the Soviet Union, the Homeland, disappeared. I let him go. *This* Belka. I could not bear to destroy the bloodline I helped to create with my own hands. And yet that was what they ordered me to do."

"Why do you have a dog's skull in a shrine? Like some dog religion…"

"That was what Russia ordered me to do. Russian history. I betrayed history. I entrusted *this* Belka to her, the woman who looks after you, your nurse. I wanted to let him live out his life, nothing more. I had no intention of reviving his line. I did not. I had retired. I was serious about my retirement."

The old man advanced two or three steps into the room.

This time he pointed down at number 47.

The girl stepped closer to her dog, as if to protect him. Without thinking about what she was doing, she lifted the skull up and rested it on her head.

She was holding it in both hands. Over her head.

"See," the girl said. "Kind of spiritual, right? Kind of religious?"

"Very amusing." The old man chuckled.

Number 47 sat like a good dog.

"You are going to put that on, are you?" the old man said in Russian.

"What were you saying about Forty-seven?" the girl shot back in Japanese.

"As it happens, number forty-seven is the child of *this* Belka. Is that not right, old boy?"

The old man turned to look at Belka. The old dog barked in reply.

"He is old, but he still had what it took, luckily. We made it just in time."

"Forty-seven is related to that old shit? Is that it?"

"I have the feeling we are getting through to each other. You understand me, little girl? You, with the skull of that great dog over your head, like a dog-clan shaman. Do you understand what I am saying? Seven puppies were born. A new generation. One of them will be our Belka. Or Strelka, if it is a bitch. That will be the name of the leader. Once they graduate from number to name. And number forty-seven may be the one, the next Belka, it looks to me. The possibility is there. There is a good chance."

"He does look like him, come to think of it. Are you saying that old shit is his dad?"

"He is Belka," the old man said, nodding at the old dog, to the girl.

And right away, the girl replied, "BEL-kah."

"That is right. And you know what? I had a feeling. In this new litter there is no bitch who is fit to be the next Strelka. Number forty-seven might be the next Belka, but there is no Strelka—not, at any rate, among the dogs. None of them will take that name. And you know why not? Because—" For the third time he pointed, this time at the girl. "Because I am giving that name to you."

Hey, dick, the girl, X years old, barked. She glared at the old man. Don't fucking point your finger at me.

"Because you are Strelka," the old man said, chuckling.

He had given the girl a dog name.

1958-1962
(Year 5 Anno Canis)

Dogs, dogs, where are you now?

1958. Still the world was divided along the same lines. Every patch of ground across the surface of the earth had been categorized as belonging to one of two ideologies. Either you were communist or you were capitalist. Or else you wanted to be one or the other. Except for you, dogs—you belonged to both sides.

First of all, four dogs entered communist territory. Three became Chinese. Originally American, these purebred German shepherds were captured on the Korean Peninsula by the People's Liberation Army. They had been the pride of the US Army, part of the military dog elite: Jubilee, News News (aka E Venture), and Ogre, siblings by different mothers. They had been fathered by Bad News, which meant that their grandparents, on their father's side, were Masao and Explosion. That was their lineage. And now they were Chinese. The last of the four dogs belonged to Kita's line. But while his lineage could be traced back to Kita, a Hokkaido dog, his blood was far from pure; he was an Arctic mongrel, a "hybrid breed." A wolfdog. And so far, he belonged to no nation. He was on Soviet land and was destined eventually to become a Soviet dog, but for now, in 1958, he still had no experience of the thing we call a nation.

Anubis, there you were on the Eurasian continent.

On that vast expanse of land, in Soviet territory.

But this was the Arctic. You hadn't yet left Far East Siberia, though it was only a matter of weeks before you would. Already you had moved away from the coast of the East Siberian Sea, crossing the Kolyma River. You, Anubis, were pulling a dogsled. And in a little more than a year—between December 1956 and the beginning of 1958—you had passed from your fourth master to your fifth, and from your fifth to your sixth. Why? Because there was something wrong with you. It had nothing to do with your abilities; you were extraordinarily capable. Your senses were more acute than those of any ordinary dog, and you could anticipate all kinds of danger before they appeared. You identified passable routes faster than your masters, dashed easily over the most arduous terrain. You were a magnificent sled dog. The problem, Anubis, was that the dogs you ran with feared you. Most of the dogs in Far East Siberia were Russian Laikas. You weren't at home in that environment. Or rather, you were—but only at first. In the beginning, things went smoothly. Because people trusted you and you communicated well with them. Because you always tried to do your duty. The problem was that face of yours…your mien. You were nothing like the others. You were no ordinary dog. Something in you was decidedly different.

You were, it almost seemed, half beast.

Because you were.

And so, for no apparent reason, the other dogs were struck with fear. WHAT'S GOING ON? they asked. WHY IS THIS ENEMY AMONG US? He smelled like a wild wolf, and their master had ordered them to watch out for wolves. He smelled just like the members of those *other* packs, the ones that lived on the outskirts of human territories, watching for a chance to slip in and take down a reindeer or some domesticated animal. His features were half wolf. And so—WHAT'S GOING ON? Eventually, hard as they tried to keep in line as they pulled the sled, they lost the rhythm. They fell out of sync, and the sled capsized. Other times, they might get so spooked that they would ignore their master and his whip and start running on their own. Because they were afraid, every one of them. Of him. Of you.

Anubis. It was your fault.

But you didn't let it bother you.

As the dogs scrambled for food, you bit them, ever so calmly. You bit them as if you were their leader. You liked dried fish. You liked reindeer meat that had been boiled with barley and allowed to cool. You ate seal meat. You devoured…the peace.

That, Anubis, was your problem.

So your masters let you go. They made the trip from one town to the next, and when they headed back, you were no longer hitched to the sled. They traveled from a town to a village, and left you—only you—behind. They would never abandon you; they passed you on to a new master. "He's a good dog," they all said. "He just doesn't get along with my team. I don't know what it is. So you can have him," they said.

You kept moving.

You crossed Far East Siberia, from one village to the next, from a village to a town, from a town to a town, from a town to a village.

Heading west.

To a village further west.

To a town further west.

Purely by chance, you kept tracing a path west across the Eurasian continent, skirting the mountains that marked the southern border of the Arctic Circle. You crossed from Chukchi lands to Koryak lands, then on into Evenk territory. You had a fifth master, and then a sixth, and after that you didn't count. Neither, Anubis, did you care at all what ethnicity (what "traditional ethnic minority") your successive masters belonged to.

THERE'S THE ARCTIC OCEAN AGAIN, you thought. Yes, because you had once been a dog of the Arctic Ocean. You had lived on the ice, on one of those "drifting" observation stations. For about a year, from the time you were three to sometime after your fourth birthday, you had been carried by the tides across the Arctic Sea.

I HAVEN'T LEFT THE ARCTIC OCEAN, you thought. And it was true—you were still within the Arctic Circle, still following the shore. Limning the ocean's edge. Circling.

Circling west.

You had set out from the shores of the East Siberian Sea, which is part of the larger Arctic Ocean. Though in that season, there was no border between water and land. You had traveled for a little over a year, until you found yourself gazing out at another sea, also part of the Arctic Ocean, but with a different name. The Laptev Sea, to the west of the Novosibirsk Islands.

Then, Anubis, sometime in 1958, you left Far East Siberia.

Anubis, Anubis, where are you now? You were on the Lena Delta, in the port town of Tiksi. There, around you, the waters of the Lena River flowed. The second largest river in the USSR, 2,650 miles long—it ended in this port, fanning out into an enormous delta as it streamed into the Laptev Sea. And what, Anubis, were you doing here?

Pulling a sled, of course.

Only now you were pulling it in a different direction. You were no longer heading west. You moved along a north-south axis. It was winter, and the Lena was frozen over—a perfect way to travel. The river had been transformed into a well-equipped sledding route. That's where you were running. That's where you were made to run. The thick pads on your feet hit the frozen river, forelegs and hind legs, crossing the ice. The Lena River had two sources: one in the Baikal Range, the other in the Stanovoy Range. Both lay south of the Laptev Sea, the Lena Delta, and the port town Tiksi. In the interior of the Eurasian continent. And so you could tell, Anubis—you could sense it. Sometimes, I move away from the Arctic Ocean. You moved for a time along a north-south axis. Up and down the frozen Lena, up and down, with Tiksi as your base.

Midway along the Lena was the town of Yakutsk, capital of the Yakutia Republic, one of the members of the Russian Soviet Federative Socialist Republic within the Soviet Union. Half the town's inhabitants were Yakuts. Your new master was one of them. Not that you, Anubis, cared who your master was. In the beginning, in Tiksi, you had a different master. Then one day your master changed; he was someone else now, only with the same face.

These two men were twins. In their late thirties. The younger brother lived just outside Yakutsk and worked as a fur hunter, using supplies provided by the kolkhoz. He could never fulfill his quota, however, and so he lived in wretched poverty. The older brother had been granted a transport license that made it possible, in an age when ordinary people, ordinary Soviets, were forbidden to travel from town to town or region to region without an "internal passport," for him to run his dogsled up and down the Lena, from the lower reaches to the middle. He carried goods. Only specialists could do this kind of work, and the pay was good. Needless to say this was before snowmobiles became common in Siberia, when it was hard to move things fast, and he did such consistently excellent work that he had been officially recognized for his service. In short, the older brother succeeded. And his younger brother seethed with envy. So one day, when they met in Yakutsk after months apart, the younger brother secretly killed the older brother. Clubbed him to death. He buried the body in the forest, near the hut he stayed in when he went hunting. And he became his brother. He made the older brother's privileges his own and went back to the port town Tiksi.

No one noticed.

People's comings and goings were strictly monitored in Tiksi, which was home to a base, but the evil younger brother was easily mistaken for his good older brother; they let him right in without subjecting him to a security check or anything.

The dogs didn't know what was what. It was precisely on occasions like this, however, that you showed your mettle. You, Anubis, helped the younger brother. You were *too* skilled a dog. Your new master was an amateur—though as a member of a tribe of nomadic horse riders he was used to driving horse-drawn sleighs, and he had ridden in dogsleds a few times—but you could divine his intentions, you knew in advance what it was he wanted you, your team, to do. You subjugated yourself to his will. And you led. The other dogs feared you, and because they recognized a crisis, they obeyed you. You appraised the situation, Anubis, and they fell in line.

Rather than let your stupid master's flimsy orders play havoc with them, they recognized your authority.

The pack cohered.

The team functioned as a team.

You terrified the other dogs because you were a wolfdog. But still, a dog is a dog. Once the hierarchy was established, terror bred obedience. You inspired fear in the other dogs, not as a wolfdog, but as the leader of the pack. That, at any rate, was how they themselves, subject to their fear, understood the situation.

You ruled them, Anubis.

You brought the team into harmony.

The sled. Traveling down the Lena.

You ran. You were made to run. You were no longer pawned off on anyone else. Your new master—strictly speaking he was your fake master, the evil younger brother with the same face as the good older brother—had no intention of giving you away. "Good dog," he said. "You get along great with the other dogs, you keep them in line so well," he said. "I wouldn't give this dog to anyone," he said, "no matter how many thousand rubles I was offered." And he ran the hell out of you. He pushed you and the other sled dogs to the limit. Show me what you can do! Show me what you can do! Move these goods! Move it! Move it! You ran. You were made to run. You understood the intentions behind your amateur master's ambiguous commands, and you communicated them to the rest of the dogs, led the team back and forth across the frozen waters. Again and again, dozens of times, along a north-south axis.

"I'm in transport!" your idiot master howled. "It takes a specialist to do this kind of work, and I'm that specialist! I'm a transporter, the pride of the Soviet Union!"

The winter was endless. The Lena remained covered with a thick layer of ice. And then, all of a sudden, it was spring.

Just like that, the thaw had come.

The amateur "transporter" didn't recognize the signs. In certain regions, the thawing of the Lena breeds natural catastrophes. It etches an enormous, awful hymn to the power of nature, there in the landscape itself. In Yakutsk, for instance, it often causes massive flooding.

You, Anubis, were the first to notice. You heard the spring of 1958 coming. To the Lena. It was a sort of cracking sound. Something snapped. You were running. You had left the port and were headed somewhere upriver.

Headed south. As you ran, you sensed something. I'm MOVING FARTHER FROM THE ARCTIC OCEAN, FARTHER AND FARTHER. You pulled the sled, you made sure the other dogs did their part. And then it happened. Your ears caught the sound, and the pads of your feet, forelegs, hind legs—they *heard* it too. Crick. Crick. Crack. Craaack.

You tried to stop.

You felt instinctively that WE HAVE TO STOP!

You whined in warning.

"Shut up!" your master said.

The harness and your place at the head of the team made it impossible for you to stop on your own. If you tried to stop anyway, you would be dragged along, tangled in the ropes. In the worst case you might suffocate and lose your legs, and the team would be thrown instantly out of line. But you had noticed what was happening. IT'S BREAKING, IT'S BREAKING, IT'S BREAKING. You whined a warning to the other dogs. But how could you convey the force of the vision that rose before you?

You wanted to tell them: THIS PATH IS BREAKING UP!

"Hey! Don't stop!" your master commanded, cracking his whip violently in the air. "Keep running! Run until you die!"

Little did he realize what these ominous words foretold.

A second or two later, the frozen Lena was roiling. It had happened. In a sudden, dramatic burst, the thaw had begun. The route snapped apart into countless chunks of ice that heaved and churned, creaked and snapped and strained. The earth was sliding, roaring. Rolling. Flipping. Fissures crisscrossed the river's surface. No—the river's surface *was* a mass of fissures. The ice that had stretched off into the distance before them had vanished. Their destination was gone. A few dogs tumbled in and sank. The icy water gurgled around them as they drowned. They kept moving their legs even in the water, as if they were still running. "Run until you die!" indeed. The ropes dragged the sled toward the hole. *Sink!* The ropes intoned. *Drown! Submit to your death!* The man with the whip seemed to be blowing bubbles. Anubis, your master was an idiot. Your master didn't know anything. But you, Anubis, you knew.

Woof! you barked.

As fiercely as you could.

Your master stared at you.

You opened your mouth wide, bared your fangs. You were a wolfdog, and they were sharp.

That was the sign. You were telling him what to do. CUT THE ROPE! you were saying. CUT THE ROPE THAT BINDS US!

IF YOU WANT TO LIVE, CUT IT!

Woof! you barked.

You had given your master an order.

You had bared your fangs. And he reacted instantly. He responded automatically, as if inspired by mental association. He leapt from the sled, whipped out the knife on his belt, and ran toward you, wheezing. He slashed through the rope he had tied to you, and then threw himself around you, tried to hang on. *Woof!* you barked again.

COME ON! you were saying.

Just then, the ice beneath your feet rocked again. You and your master streamed forward a few dozen inches even as you stood there, motionless, on a piece of what had been your road. Or maybe it was a few feet of road? Rumbling, tumbling, it sank, it shook. You didn't have time to jump off, make a run for it. Everything was heaving. The whole Lena was lurching, crunching, shuddering. Around you, the other dogs were howling. The flow of the river itself was barking. Yes, Anubis, this was it—it was happening. You were in the midst of the whirlpool, unable to keep up with the pace of events. You felt things shifting: up becoming down, down becoming up. You were plunged into the water for seconds, then bobbed up again. You were drenched. You understood. THE PATH HAS BROKEN, THE PATH IS A RIVER, GET OUT OF THE RIVER, GET TO THE BANK!

THAT WAY!

You leapt from one unbroken part to the next, deciding in a split second which way to go. THAT WAY, THAT WAY! But your body felt heavy, weighed down. Everywhere you looked was shaking. Everything you saw was roiling wet. You lost your sense of balance. It was happening all around you, Anubis. This was it, but you weren't sure what it was, you couldn't grasp the details.

Still, you ran. You were running, that alone was sure. Your vision of the scene was riddled with holes, but somehow you crossed them, you reached the bank. The bank wasn't just a bank, it was a cliff jutting up at an angle of seventy or eighty degrees. A layer of Siberian permafrost. You climbed. Your body felt heavy. Because someone was clinging to you. An idiot human had his arms wrapped around your body. He was crying. *Oh, oh, oh,* he wailed. *Oh, oh, oh, oh, oh,* he wailed. SHUT UP! you thought. You managed to scramble up the bank despite the burden of him. You didn't slip. No, not you. You weren't the one who lost his footing and careened down a gaping crevice in the permafrost. It was him—your master. That idiot. And he took you with him. He kept his arms wrapped tightly around your body, your left leg, as he went, tumbling down into that cavernous hole that plunged like a tunnel into the permafrost.

You tumbled, your body at a diagonal.

You didn't climb up from the bank onto solid land. You went down. Underground.

You slid. You fell very, very fast.

Your body was bashed, abrasions everywhere.

You didn't lose consciousness, but your vision went black.

It was too deep. Too narrow. Your master, who had fallen first, was groaning. At intervals, even deeper down. You smelled death. A nasty scent that curled upward, another ominous sign marking all but certain doom for your master. It was cold. The earth was frozen all around you. The air eddying over your body was around 25 degrees Fahrenheit—not unbearably cold, but you were soaked. You began to feel the chill in your bones. In your cervical vertebrae, your lumbar vertebrae, your shoulder blades, your skull: you felt the cold seeping in, tightening its grip. You felt: I'M GOING TO FREEZE. And you thought: No. You thought: I WANT TO LIVE, I WANT TO LIVE, I WILL NOT DIE. You were determined. The cavern in the permafrost was tight, cramped, a natural tunnel, a world of perfect darkness. It was too dark. You were terrified. Yes, Anubis, you recognized the truth: I'M SCARED. The long night had come.

AM I GOING TO DIE?

Again and again, you asked yourself the same question.

AM I GOING TO DIE?

From time to time, you wriggled your hind legs to make sure you were still alive. You had no idea how you landed, there in the tunnel. You might be hanging from an outcropping of rock, or leaning on it. You tried not to doze. I DON'T WANT TO FREEZE, you thought, and struggled to stay awake. Only it was so dark in the tunnel that even with your eyes wide open, you felt as though you might be sleeping. You had been sleeping for a long, long, long time; so it seemed. Maybe it was real? Had you been asleep? Your vision had gone black, been black—and maybe that blackness had continued, now, for ages? You searched for sunlight. Of course. There in the depths of that long, long, long night, you yearned for some sign of a subterranean morning that would never come.

The cliff you had climbed, and from which you had fallen into the tunnel that plunged into the permafrost, was on the left of the Lena River, facing downstream. On the western bank. The cliff jutted up, almost vertical. The days were short at this time of the year, but the sun did rise. And when it did, the morning sunlight shone on that cliff. There came a moment when the light streamed in through a crack near the tunnel's entrance.

It shot in at an angle, and for ten or twenty minutes, no longer, there in the pure darkness, the faint glow filled you.

You started and came to.

Who knows, maybe you had been asleep.

You noticed the sunlight bleeding into the space you were in.

IT'S MORNING, you thought.

And then, the next moment, you stiffened, stunned. Because you had discovered something. Immediately overhead—though of course you had no idea how you had landed, what was up and what was down—was an eye. A mammal's eye. Enormous. Just one, one side of the head: an eyeball. It had to be a few times larger than your own, Anubis, or even bigger...maybe ten times bigger.

The eye stared down at you from directly overhead.

From within the ice.

You were face to face with a prehistoric animal encased in the permafrost.

Suspended along the edge of the tunnel, inches away. It had tusks. Long, curved tusks. A long nose. Its body was covered in long fur. It was over eleven feet tall. Alive, it would have weighed six tons. It was something like an elephant that had lived ten thousand years ago, even longer ago than that, and had evolved to live in the cold. An enormous mammal, given the name "mammoth" by a French scientist in the eighteenth century.

One of these extinct creatures had been preserved, frozen, in the tunnel. In the ground. In a layer of Siberian permafrost more than 160 feet thick. Without decaying.

And now, Anubis, its huge eye, more than ten thousand years old, stared down at you.

WHO ARE YOU? Anubis asked.

WHO ARE YOU? The question bounced off the ice.

I'M…I'M A DOG.

The eye in the ice was not, of course, a dog. So it didn't answer.

HAVE YOU BEEN THERE ALL ALONG? Anubis asked.

I'VE BEEN HERE ALL ALONG.

This time, the frozen earth answered. It transmitted the ice-packed mammoth's answer to the dog's mind: I'M FROZEN.

YOU'RE AN EYE. Anubis told the eye, very simply.

I'M AN EYE. The mammoth agreed, very simply.

YOU'RE LOOKING AT ME.

I'M LOOKING AT YOU.

AM I…ALIVE?

YOU'RE…ALIVE.

WILL I LIVE?

LIVE.

Anubis's final question, rebounding off the ice, was transformed into a command. Anubis interpreted what he had heard as a command. He realized that this enormous eye, no one else, was his true master. It was not a dog. The eye (and the creature whose eye it was) had not said it was a dog. But neither was it a human. Anubis realized, then, at that moment, that this thing was his Absolute.

Anubis had no word to express his discovery.

Perhaps a human might have called this thing the "Dog God."

And so Anubis, whose name itself means the "Dog God," acknowledged this "Dog God" as his true master, and awoke.

Anubis, Anubis, at last you have awoken.

You were not asleep.

Ten minutes, twenty minutes passed. The brief period during which the tunnel filled with the morning sun's faint glow was over. Once again pure darkness enclosed you. Your encounter with your true master had ended. What would you do? Obey the command you had been given, of course. The order. One simple word: LIVE. Already, you were trying. You had to break free. You twisted your body, twisted further. You moved. You slipped. You slid down the wall of the tunnel, you fell. But you weren't afraid. The tunnel did not injure you. You descended.

Into a *space*.

You searched for your old master.

You looked for that idiot human.

You found him, deep in the tunnel, barely breathing but alive. Too weak even to groan. You were hungry. You knew you would need to build up your strength if you were going to escape from this place. So you saw him as food. You gorged yourself. There was nothing wrong with this. It had happened once before…then too, you'd had no choice; you had sated yourself on your former master's corpse. You had been eleven months old, or maybe a year. It was the first time you had ever set foot on the Arctic Ocean, and you had almost died. You had eaten your master in order to survive, as if it were a sort of sacred rite. You had eaten that human, that former idiot. Then too. If there was a difference between this time and the last, it was that last time your "former master" had been wholly dead, whereas this master was still slightly… still breathing, barely. There was nothing wrong with that. You could stop his breathing.

Right?

RIGHT, you reply, to someone. To whoever it is that puts the collar on your moral sense. YES, THAT'S RIGHT, you said and put an end to it, and sated yourself on the flesh.

You wandered, step by step, slowly, through the bowels of the earth. The crevice in the permafrost was narrow, but it branched out in all directions, north and south and east and west, diagonally up and down, in shapes nature had determined. There were blind alleys, of course, and forks that led into loops. But you, Anubis, had a fine sense of smell. You had a dog's nose, and you sniffed the ground with it. You had an animal's persistence. You didn't mind trying and failing and trying again.

You made it out in two days.

So you lived. Because this was the command your true master had given you. You would not return to the Arctic Ocean. You understood: I'M NOT A DOG OF THE ARCTIC OCEAN, NOT NOW. It wasn't logic that told you this. You had once devoured the flesh of your dead master, the musher, in order to survive, to go out onto the Arctic Sea. Now, once again, you had eaten the flesh of your master, another sled driver—once again, you had performed the rite. The two rites formed a pair. I CAME HERE, AND NOW I WILL LEAVE. Yes, Anubis, by the time you made your way aboveground, you had already grasped the meaning of those two rites. In your heart, you understood. It wasn't a matter of logic. This time, you would head south.

Your talents as a hunter served you well. There on the Arctic Ocean, hunters living in polar regions kept you with them, and you learned to find prey, chase it down, attack it. You honed your fighting instincts, improved upon your natural abilities as a wolfdog. Here your prey were not musk oxen. You didn't hunt polar bears. But the procedure was essentially the same. It was practice. You learned to read the weather outside the Arctic Circle. And what did you like to eat, Anubis? Reindeer. Reindeer were abundant in the tundra far to the south of European Russia, and in that special variety of Siberian forest known as the taiga. Some were wild, some were domesticated. In spring and summer, you would encounter herds of several thousand in the wetlands bordering the Lena, property of the nearby *sovkhoz*. You attacked. You took the reindeer down with the greatest of ease. You gobbled their innards, and their stomachs were stuffed with moss—a kind of lichen known as "reindeer moss." Their stomachs were green. You smeared those bags with fresh red blood as if it were a sauce and savored the dish. Meat, blood, vegetable matter. The perfect combination of protein, minerals, and vitamins. The ultimate one-dish meal. When you had eaten your fill, you bayed. Your baying rang across the vast Siberian expanse. You might as well have been a pureblooded wolf.

A *pureblooded* wolf?

But you weren't. You were a half-breed.

You didn't care about that stuff.

Strength was everything. The resilience to go on living, living, living. As a dog. As a dog, but also as a family tree. Yes, Anubis, you were one dog, but you were also a lineage. Your line began with Kita, a Hokkaido dog, and then your "father," some nameless wolf roaming Alaska and the Arctic Circle, added his blood to the mix. That was how you were born. And your seed would grow the tree. You were an individual dog, but you were also a family tree.

I'LL MINGLE MY BLOOD WITH OTHERS! you proclaim.

I'LL MONGRELIZE MYSELF, AND THAT WILL MAKE ME STRONGER! I'LL BE THE STRONGEST DOG EVER! you determine, without the use of words. To LIVE, TO LIVE, TO GO ON LIVING!

You pay no heed to established "breeds" created by humans. You pursue your own ideal. You had come face to face with the Absolute, there in the permafrost. A mammoth that had lain there, frozen, for more than ten thousand years. An enormous mammal, now extinct. And what of you, Anubis? You were a member of the canine tribe, which had appeared around the same time that mammoth died, more than ten thousand years ago. Half the blood in your veins was lupine; in that sense you had reverted to an earlier stage in your evolution. You were *reliving* your own evolution. You had been given a chance, once again, to press ahead toward what dogs were originally meant to be. You understood. And so you said: I WILL NOT BECOME EXTINCT.

Only dogs can guide canine evolution. You, Anubis, had that desire.

You were awake.

Here, in this vast territory, you were what your name declared you.

Who could stop you from going south?

The short Siberian summer ended. A vaguely autumnal season passed, and winter came. The nights were long. A reindeer sled glided along the horizon, just within sight. The land was a field of snow now, and the reindeer on the *sovkhoz* could no longer nibble the lichen that was their main source of nourishment. Whenever people or dogs pissed in the snow, the reindeer would come and lick the stain. For the salt. The reindeer would stand there licking the guard dog's piss, and you, Anubis, would attack. You would never starve, not even in the winter. The Lena had frozen over again; here and there on its surface, people fished. They sawed holes in the ice and hooked fish through the holes. The fish bellies brimmed with eggs. Sometimes, having hoisted a fish up onto the ice, the stupid humans managed, incredibly enough, to let the creature escape, and you would grab it and scamper off. You would tear into the soft bellies of those river fish, gobble down the eggs. You left the Lena before spring came, pressed onward, walking in the caterpillar-tread marks an armored vehicle had printed in the snow. Once, you heard people operating a radio a few hundred yards away. They weren't members of the local ethnic minority, they were Slavs who had settled in this region less than a century and a half before. Another time you stood and stared at the white breath gusting from the nostrils of a Yakutian horse. This time too, you stayed a few hundred yards away. In the spring, you filled yourself with nutrients and your body tingled. You had been born in 1952, but your hormones raged, still got horny. Your sexual organs were fully functioning. You kept getting erections all spring and all summer, from summer into fall. You searched for bitches among the guard dogs on the reindeer farms, and when you found them, you had your way with them. You scouted the pets in villages and copulated with every good female you happened across. Still you weren't satisfied. Because none of them was strong enough. None of these bitches came close to answering the needs of your lineage. You had your way with them, planted your seed. But when it was over, you barked: I NEED MORE! THERE ARE BETTER DOGS! SOMEWHERE ON THE FACE OF THIS EARTH, THERE IS A PERFECT MATE FOR ME, I KNOW IT! Yes, Anubis, you were trying to evolve. That was why these erections came. You forced yourself on more bitches. When another dog interfered, you killed him. And you kept heading south. You were walking through a coniferous forest now. You encountered a hunting dog, and she was good, she was a superior dog, and so you took her.

Still you hadn't had enough. You needed wilder blood.

South. You wandered this way and that. You were laughing in a blizzard. Laughing a dog's hilarious laugh. Winter came, then spring. You caught a whiff of smoke—a mosquito repellent. You skirted human lands, keeping just outside the boundary, and then, every so often, casually, you would intrude. Some lands had been inhabited by humans once but were empty now. You passed the remains of one of Stalin's gulag. You trotted past gold and silver mines, now ghost towns, glancing curiously at the buildings. You discovered a hot spring bubbling up deep in the forest. You sniffed the water and barked. *Woof!* You noticed a silver coin from the Russian Empire imprinted with an image of a sable, lying in the garden of an abandoned hunting cabin. In the summer, after a long absence, you arrived once again on the banks of the Lena, whose waters were now five miles wide.

At night, the short summer unfurled a sky full of stars.

It was August.

August 1960.

Suddenly you were seized with an impulse. You had felt this before— this pressing urge to do something, *something*. This unnameable feeling had seized you, impelled you to lift your head to the heavens. You didn't know the date—you were a dog, you had no use for dates—but it was November 3, 1957. Yes, that was it. A day inscribed forever in the history of the canine tribe. It was year zero Anno Canis, so to speak: that sacred, epoch-making day when a bitch in an airtight chamber, on board a man-made satellite named Sputnik 2, gazed down from orbit at the earth. She had gazed down, that third day in November, on you, Anubis, and you had felt what others felt. Yes, you felt it, sensed a gaze sweeping over you from the vastness of the sky. SHE'S LOOKING AT ME. That dog was Laika. Laika, a space dog, a Russian laika named Laika, a bitch from the USSR, looking at you, gazing down upon you.

And now it was August 19, 1960.

Year 3 Anno Canis.

Another epoch-making day.

Two dogs were in space. One a male, one a bitch, both Soviet space dogs. They had been sent up earlier that day on Sputnik 5. They had been entrusted with a task. The space race was entering the next stage. The Eastern and Western camps (which was just another way of saying the Soviet Union and the United States) were each rushing ahead, desperate to be the first to send a manned spaceship into space. Each side was determined to beat the other in the race. The Americans had been devastated when Sputnik 1 went up, and the launch of Sputnik 2 had turned their devastation to shame. But then, c'mon, they just put *dogs* in space, right? Animals, that's the best they can do. The Yankees nodded to each other in satisfaction. There you had it, the limits of communism laid bare. And now it's our turn! Just watch, here in this free land of ours, we'll send a person into space! The Yankees were sure they could do it. The preparations were progressing surprisingly smoothly. They were selecting an astronaut. Working to create a manned spaceship, not some silly *dogged* spaceship. The space race had come to stand as a vehicle for a competition between ideologies, to demonstrate once and for all which of the two was superior. And how were things going in the USSR? How smoothly was its program progressing? The USSR didn't care about smoothness. It was pouring five percent of its national budget into the space program. As an actual figure, that was six times more than the US was investing. That's how committed the USSR was to beating the US. This time too, they would win. They would send what the Yankees called a "cosmonaut" (a term coined to describe the Soviet equivalent of the American astronaut) into space. In short, the Soviet Union was pressing ahead with its preparations, not exactly smoothly, no—insanely.

And before there could be cosmonauts, there had to be more space dogs.

When Sputnik 2 went up in year zero Anno Canis, Laika, the space dog, the Russian laika, had perished. Sputnik 2 had been an incredibly primitive artificial satellite: in fact, it had been designed so that it was impossible to bring it back to Earth. It was all but certain from the start that it would be destroyed upon reentering Earth's atmosphere; essentially Laika was fated to die. There was no hope that she would make it back alive. The situation was different for the two dogs who starred in the program in August 1960—year 3 Anno Canis. They were outfitted with pressurized suits. They had clear helmets that stuck out to accommodate their snouts, odd snaky tubes, brown protective skin. These suits had to be tested before the cosmonauts could fly. If dogs could be sent into outer space in these suits and make it back alive, then the same thing could be done with humans. This would prove that people could be launched into space and brought safely back to Earth.

That was the point of this mission.

Sputnik 5 blasted off on August 19. It circled the earth seventeen times in its planned orbit. And the following day, the two dogs returned to Earth alive.

These dogs had finally succeeded in a mission that did not result in inevitable death. One male dog and one bitch, each in a pressurized suit, had seen the earth from outer space and then returned. To the earth that had given birth to the canine tribe. Two dogs—two Soviet dogs. Their names—Belka and Strelka.

Belka and Strelka. They received a joyous welcome. They were Soviet heroes, these dogs, following in the footsteps of that other great hero, that dog among dogs, Laika.

Nikita Khrushchev was premier of the Soviet Union at the time. Having brushed aside various political enemies in the wake of Stalin's death, he had become both First Secretary of the Communist Party and Chairman of the Council of Ministers. He was the first to crack a smile upon being informed that the two dogs had accomplished their glorious mission. "Two more heroes are born! *Ura!*" he said, grinning. Once again Communism had overwhelmed the West in the areas of science and technology, demonstrating to the world that Communism would lead mankind forward! And we accomplished it with dogs! *Haha!* Those bastards must be quaking in their shoes, terrified to think that they're about to be overtaken yet again in the space race. And yes, yes, all their fear was occasioned by two little dogs.

Ura!

Khrushchev had particular cause for his somewhat childish glee. As it happened, that first Soviet hero, Laika, had become a hero largely as a result of his efforts. Which is to say, the whole thing had started out as a whim on his part. This isn't speculation, it's truth: Khrushchev created the space dog. At first, he had given the go-ahead to the rocket program because he recognized the potential military significance of the research, not because he was captivated by the romance of space exploration. So it came about that on August

21, 1957, the USSR succeeded in launching an R-7 rocket whose astonishing propulsive force derived from a pack of booster rockets. The rocket, the Soviet Union's first intercontinental ballistic missile, had a range of 4,350 miles. People called it by the affectionate nickname Semyorka. Sputnik 1, which was launched less than a month and a half later and became the first man-made satellite in the history of mankind, was essentially the same rocket, except that the Semyorka's cone had been fitted with a man-made satellite rather than the nuclear warhead it had originally been designed to carry. All of which is to say that Khrushchev hadn't had a whit of interest in or sympathy for his scientists' dreams. *People in space! The greatest adventure of the century! The spine-tingling thrill of science, of technology!* He didn't care. At first. But then, once they had actually launched the satellite, beating the US to the chase, he saw how stunned the entire world was. Those bastards in the West were quaking in their boots! Communism had opened the door to a new age for mankind, and they were flabbergasted! They were stunned!

This was very cool. Khrushchev grinned.

He even thought up a slogan. *Whoever conquers space wins the Cold War.*

At last, Khrushchev's perspective changed. This was in October 1957. The anniversary of the October Revolution was coming up soon, the very next month, on November 7, and as it happened this year they would be celebrating the Revolution's fortieth anniversary. Plans were being made for a grandiose ceremony. *This is perfect!* Khrushchev thought. If we had the Yankees trembling in their boots because we set a satellite in orbit around the earth, sending out little beeps, just imagine how humiliated they'll be when we do it again almost immediately! We'll turn their shock into shame.

Well then, let's hit 'em with a bang!

There's no time like the present, as they say, and so Khrushchev lost no time in arranging a meeting at the Kremlin with the people who had created Sputnik 1—the starry-eyed scientists who had been the driving force behind the rocket project. So, guys, how do you feel about sending up something flashy and doing it in time for the anniversary next month?

How do we feel about *what?* said the scientists.

Something that'll make the Yankees groan with shame.

With only a month to prepare, it seems…

What should it be, I wonder? Khrushchev went on, ignoring the scientists' befuddlement.

Something that would make them groan? You realize, of course, that we have certain plans of our own that…

Something flashy, Khrushchev told them, not even registering the consternation written on their faces.

Well, yes, Comrade Khrushchev, if you think that would…but what…

Something that'll makes their jaws drop, those bastards in the West, you know? *Bam!* Just like that. You get what I'm saying? We won't niggle about the budget, of course, it's there, the same as always. Whoever conquers space wins the Cold War. *Hahaha!*

He was demanding the impossible. What sort of project could they possibly develop from scratch in a month? Still, it was an order. And so Sputnik 2 was born. The basic structure was the same as Sputnik 1, except that it had suddenly grown much larger, and it was equipped for experiments on living subjects. And it would carry the very first mammal ever to travel in space. It would carry a dog.

A dog?

The scientists themselves were dumbstruck when it occurred to them.

But that was the decision they made, and that's how history unfolded. That's how the great Soviet hero Laika was born. Khrushchev deserved the credit. Khrushchev created the space dog. And so, in the year zero Anno Canis, Laika rocketed into the sky and died.

Gazing down, all along, at the earth.

Khrushchev deserved the credit.

And now Khrushchev was bellowing *Ura!* In August 1960, two dogs returned alive from space, and Khrushchev guffawed. Two more heroes had been born. A male dog named Belka and a bitch named Strelka. They had returned to Earth as the Soviet Union's great space dogs, Communism's space dogs. Now Khrushchev had a dream. It was a quest—a political, military adventure. It was totally stupid. The kind of dream scientists wouldn't care about at all.

The two dogs should mate. There was a need for their children to be born. The scientists were more than happy to go along with this part of the plan. They were gathering all sorts of data, everything they could think of relating to the effect of space flight on animals—on the animal, that is to say, as a living organism. Soon they would be sending a person up. They had to keep cranking out all kinds of experiments. Not just everything they could think of, even things they couldn't quite imagine. This, in particular, was crucial. They had already determined that dogs could live in space, but might their bodies have been damaged in some way invisible to the eye? For instance, were these dogs, having once rocketed into space, still capable of reproduction? Could their sojourn in weightlessness have stripped them of that ability? Or might the lack of gravity one day produce some irregularity in their genes as a side effect? The scientists, eager to test this possibility, gladly mated Belka and Strelka. In fact, they later did the same thing with their human cosmonauts. The first female cosmonaut, Valentina Tereshkova—who rode the Vostok 6 in June 1963, and whose call sign ya chaika, "I am a seagull," became famous around the world—was pressured by the Kremlin elite into marrying Andrian Nikolayev, who had ridden on the Vostok 3 in August 1962. Data about the couple, including their experiences leading up to Tereshkova's pregnancy and information relating to their daughter's physical development, were gathered and closely guarded as a state secret. Of course, in a sense this made sense: at the time, the USSR treated any data related in any way to space exploration as top-secret information.

But that's neither here nor there. We were talking about Khrushchev's dream. His proposal. The two returnee space dogs, reborn into the world in August 1960—August of year 3 Anno Canis—devoted themselves to their procreative activities under the scientists' round-the-clock watch, until at last they achieved their mission as the lab animals they now were. The bitch Strelka became pregnant by Belka and gave birth to a litter of six. For the next few weeks, the scientists monitored the six puppies' every movement. Veterinarians and animal ecologists were called in. There seemed to be nothing at all unusual about the pups. The scholars presented their results: all six of the heroes' children were in perfect health. They had entered their third month now and were growing like beanstalks. *Ura!* cried the scientists. We have approached a step nearer to launching a manned spacecraft! Khrushchev selected one of the six puppies, a bitch, and sent it as a gift to the leader of those bastards in the West. John F. Kennedy had been inaugurated as president of the United States in January 1961. Khrushchev had heard that the Kennedys were unusually fond of dogs, and so he sent the puppy with a card signed "From Khrushchev" to Kennedy's daughter Caroline. This present, however, had nothing to do with Khrushchev's dream. It bore no relationship to the political/military adventure he was fantasizing about. He was just rubbing it in. The young American president, leader of the capitalist bloc, oozed charm, and so Khrushchev had decided to send him a message, that was all. "Pretty cool, huh?" he was saying. "Here in the Soviet Union we've already bred a second generation of our space dogs! Not bad, eh? Yes sir, science and technology are pretty advanced here in the Communist bloc, if I do say so myself. Yes, yes, I know what you're thinking. We're screwed, you're thinking. How about it? Am I right, Kennedy, my boy?"

There went the first puppy.

There had been six, so now there were five. Five healthy Russian laika puppies. There they were. And Khrushchev had a dream. Or rather, he had a whim. He had created the space dogs, so now, he thought, he would create a platoon of dogs descended from those Soviet heroes! There was no telling when the Cold War might suddenly turn into a hot war. Proxy wars were brewing in the Third World even now. They could send this new platoon of dogs there, to the front lines. A meticulously trained, elite group led by the descendants of space dogs. *Yes! Yes!* Khrushchev groaned at the brilliance of his idea. What will happen if we succeed with these dogs? It will be the best possible propaganda within the Communist world, and with respect to the West it will have the combined effect of the first Sputnik flights—all that shock and shame balled up into one. And it will work! Just imagine! Mere animals, beasts, made special by the impossibly rare distinction of descent from the very dogs that expanded the USSR's territory into outer space, kicking the shit out of dippy little capitalist soldiers! *Wahahahahaha!*

It started as a joke. But Khrushchev's every word was a command. The enormous Soviet state had developed a rigid system of governance. Almost immediately, Khrushchev's dream was funneled through bureaucratic channels, transformed into stern directives. Power in the USSR was apportioned, essentially, to three separate organs. The party, the military, and the Committee for State Security, aka the KGB. The task of realizing Khrushchev's dream would fall to the third of these three pillars of the state. Because the KGB would be able to push the plan ahead most efficiently and with the greatest secrecy.

It wasn't a joke anymore.

Among the largest military organizations within the KGB was the Border Guard. Though it wasn't really part of the official Soviet military—it was not under the jurisdiction of the Ministry of Defense—it was sizeable. Usually its forces numbered two hundred thousand; in its heyday it was expanded to include some three hundred fifty thousand. Its forces were highly trained and its units were provided with the latest small arms, firearms, rockets, tanks, armored vehicles, armed helicopters, and military transport aircraft. Naval units, of course, had their own ships. Members of the KGB, as well as their families, were all part of a privileged class in the USSR. This was a necessary consequence of the KGB's status as an organization dedicated to preserving the peace by collecting intelligence about ordinary citizens. In addition, because the Border Guard's operations included suppressing anti-Soviet guerrilla activities, and crushing antigovernment minority movements—meaning all such movements, since all minority movements were so regarded—was a regular part of this, Russian applicants were given preferential treatment in hiring. Pure Slavic Russians. Slavs. That was the nature of the Border Guard. It was a privileged military elite.

Each individual defensive platoon in the Border Guard had its own team of guard dogs. A posse of war dogs, in other words. In emergency situations, of course, they used all manner of small arms, firearms, and attack vehicles, but they also used dogs to close the border.

At this point in history, in the vast Soviet state, troops of dogs, who had been fighting all along on the front lines, were active in this context as well.

The stern directives made their way down the chain of command.

And at the end of the chain, where Khrushchev's dream landed—stripped of its romance, reduced to an ordinary, utterly pragmatic order—was the handler.

He was a major in the Border Guard. A young commissioned officer, twenty-seven years old. Six months before the order was passed down, he had been assigned to head up the Committee for the Purchase and Rearing of Guard/War Dogs. Needless to say, he was a pureblooded Slav. Blond hair, white skin. Mild and yet somehow forbidding features. He had not, however, been born into a privileged class. He had made his way up in the world, but his father was a farmer. His parents worked on a *kolkhoz*. His blood was pure, but his Slavic lineage contained no trace of any aristocratic blood, no noble seed. He was a second son. After graduating with outstanding grades from a school that trained future military men, he applied to the KGB, eager to show his loyalty to the homeland in some more passionate way—actually, the KGB had first gotten in touch with him, though that was kept highly secret—and after two years spent on the European border as a candidate officer, he was assigned to a detachment that answered directly to the head office. Later, he successfully applied to a special forces training school. He spent a year and a half studying a curriculum centered on guerrilla warfare but which included various other topics, ranging from assassination and advanced firearm techniques to basic procedures for causing confusion behind enemy lines and their applications, methods of torture and how to resist them, medical techniques, the use of codes, and individual survival techniques. Many students found the regimen too demanding and dropped out. The last three months of training took place at a camp on the Arctic Ocean. There the students were housed three to a room—prior to this they had lived in a wide hall—and were encouraged to develop a sense of camaraderie. There were microphones buried in the walls, the floor, and the ceiling, and every conversation was recorded. Anyone who couldn't keep himself perfectly in control at all times was given the boot. A man needed nerves of steel to survive. If your roommates said, "Man, this is hell, isn't it?" you had to respond immediately, "Absolutely not." If they kept pressuring you to agree, saying, "C'mon, you know it is. We're all exhausted," you had to tell them right off, "I will either graduate from here, or I will quit the military. One or the other."

And the young officer did what he had to do.

A smile flickered across his face, faint but brutal. "The day I give up being a military man, I will start calling myself the Archbishop."

"Why?" his roommates asked.

"Because the only reason I would ever quit is if it was all over anyway—if the glorious promise of the revolution was squandered. And if that day comes, I will call myself the Archbishop. You had better kill me then. Assassinate me."

Under the Communist system, the Russian Orthodox Church was a symbol of conservative values. "Huh," the fellow students laughed, "so you'll take orders?" They laughed, but while they smiled, their expressions were stiff.

1958. After graduating first in his class from training school, he was assigned to the Chinese border. He was a captain now and led a defensive platoon. 1959. He created his own special forces unit and tried to control the conflicts breaking out in Central Asia—in Kazakhstan and eastern Kyrgyzstan, along the Sino-Soviet border. He revealed a talent for putting pressure on Islamic populations as well. 1960. He was promoted to become the head of the Committee for the Purchase and Rearing of Guard/War Dogs. He was a major now, twenty-six years and seven months old, and he took his position seriously. 1961. The directive was handed down. Yes, Comrade Khrushchev's dream. Here, in this environment, in the eyes of the man responsible for carrying out the directive, the dream was reduced to a realistic strategy, political and military. The adventure lost its sparkle.

1962.

No. Year 5 Anno Canis. I've focused too long on the human perspective. Dogs, where are you now? You, Anubis, closest to the origin of the new era. Where are you?

You were getting close. At last.

Yes, Anubis. You still had your erections. You were an old dog now, on the cusp of your tenth year, but your spirit, your vigor, was undaunted. MY DESTINY AWAITS ME, you barked. All along, you kept your nose to the ground, following the scent. The odor of that glorious bitch whose blood, coursing through her veins, was wilder and more powerful than the rest. It was there, you felt it. Your nose led you on. And so, Anubis, you kept heading south. You had faith in the impulses stirring within you, and you continued south. Or perhaps that's not quite right; it was less impulses in the plural than the lingering trace of a single impulse. Its echoes. That summer, you had felt something gazing down at you from the vastness of the sky. In year 3 Anno Canis. And you had understood. YES, you thought. I MUST PURSUE THAT GAZE.

Therein, you understood, lay the evolution of the canine tribe.

Woof! you barked.

I'LL SIRE THE STRONGEST BLOODLINE!

Your mind was made up; your penis was hard.

I WON'T DIE. MY SEED WON'T DIE. IT WILL LIVE…AND LIVE, FOREVER!

MY FUTURE WIFE! you barked.

Year 5 Anno Canis. At long last you arrived, your massive penis straight as a flagpole. Stirred by the sensation of that gaze from outer space, you had run to the very ends of the earth, and now here you were in the distant outliers of the Soviet Union. Here where the USSR hit up against South Siberia and Mongolia. You were in the west of the Tuvan Autonomous Soviet Socialist Republic. Grasslands and squat mountains as far as the eye could see. You emerged from a forest of white birches, and there you were.

The KGB Border Guard had set up its breeding grounds in these grasslands.

The facility, administered by the Committee for the Purchase and Rearing of Guard/War Dogs, was the largest anywhere in the USSR. It was outfitted with equipment for training inexperienced dogs before they were assigned to their units. During the past two years everything had been updated. Because there was a new man in charge. And because the five remaining children of those two dog heroes, Belka and Strelka, had been welcomed to the camp. They were no longer puppies. They were fully mature. Already they were creating the next generation. Getting pregnant, making others pregnant. The puppies were Russian laika, of course, but the facility head decided to mate them with different breeds. For the future—to create a corps of dogs loyal to the homeland. They would draw on these bloodlines, on the bloodlines of those five puppies' parents, to establish a corps of the mightiest dogs on the planet. They had gathered magnificent males, magnificent bitches. These dogs contributed the use of their wombs, their sperm. A third generation of heroes was being brought into the world, litter after litter.

The space dogs' grandchildren.

Woof! you barked.

I'VE ARRIVED! you announced.

Inside the breeding grounds, 213 dogs froze in their tracks. Dogs with standing ears raised their heads; dogs with floppy ears raised their tails. WHO HAS ARRIVED? they were saying. LISTEN TO HOW STRONG THAT VOICE IS! WHO IS IT WHO IS IT WHO IS IT? Each dog felt that the other dog, the one that barked, had been calling to her, or to him. YOU, YES YOU.

I'LL HAVE MY WAY WITH YOU! you barked.

I'LL MAKE YOU PREGNANT! you barked. You, Anubis, you barked.

TO LIVE!

And the dogs were afraid. Each time you barked in the breeding grounds, the dogs broke into a commotion. Some were struck with terror. Some suddenly went into heat. The bitches got wet between their legs, while the males leapt at their handlers' legs and waists, at nearby poles, and simulated intercourse. People hurried this way and that, unsure what was happening. *Woof!* you barked again. And again: *Woof!* At last, you were almost there! But you weren't yet inside. You were outside the fence. You stood three feet away. The fence was electrified. You had sensed that, of course. You were clever. You saw danger before it struck. You had made it this far, after all, from the Arctic Ocean. You had come, what's more, by way of Alaska. And you had another strength too: you could read the workings of destiny before it became manifest.

So you waited.

For something…SOMETHING.

Barking all the while.

Barking. And it came.

Riding a horse.

A human.

"So you're the one barking," he said in Russian.

Woof! you answered.

"You want to go inside?" he asked. "Caught the scent of our bitches?"

Woof! you answered.

"You're male?" he said, appraising you. "And I see you're erect," the young man who was in charge of the facility said, still atop his horse, impressed.

OF COURSE, you said.

The young man lowered his Kalashnikov automatic rifle, took aim.

But no gun was going to scare you off.

I'VE ARRIVED! you barked.

"You seem," the young man continued in Russian, speaking entirely seriously even though you were a dog, somehow maintaining his dignity as a commissioned officer, "to be saying that you're the dog, the breeder male, I've been waiting for. What confidence!"

I'VE ARRIVED! you barked.

"Is it true? Have you really come?"

IT'S TRUE! you barked.

"You're built a bit like a wolf," the young commissioned officer said. He had dismounted by now. You stood facing each other through the fence, which buzzed with electric current. "You've got wolf blood in you? Is that it? Did you know how close wolves are to German shepherds? You know about German shepherds? A breed created just sixty years ago, specifically to fight in war? They're war dogs through and through. People wanted the perfect build for war, and they made it. That's what a German shepherd is."

Woof!

"Are you a natural…ideal?"

Woof! you answered.

"If you want a bitch, I'll let you have one. She's good. Young animal from a good line. But she's not complete. She's missing something. She's not a soldier. You understand what I'm saying? I want a dog with a soldier's pride. I'm waiting for puppies that have that. How about it? I'll let you have her, see what happens. Shoot your sperm into her. I can see you're special. I see that erection of yours. All right."

The young commissioned officer had given you his permission.

It had happened.

"My passion brought you here. It's true, I can see that. Take them. The second generation of heroes, and the third. If the puppies you sire are as good as I expect, I'll name them as the true successors. The males will all be Belka, the bitches will be Strelka. That will be the mark of their legitimacy. The sign that I approved of them. The proof."

Woof!

"Come!"

You understood that command. You leapt the fence. Jumped right over. Just like that. And you became a Soviet dog.

"Woof!"

The Boss began by sending three "bullets." He shipped them off from Toyama Port on a fishing boat late one night, and from there they transferred mid-ocean to the cargo vessel that carried them to a port in the Primorsky Krai. After that, he sent seven more bullets. Trained assassins. Up to this point, they were all new recruits, youngsters. Show us what you can fucking do for the organization, boys, he'd told the new recruits, all barely in their twenties. Think of it as a sort of hustle. Go pop a few of them fuckhead Ruskies for me.

He had done well, he thought, put some fear into them. Can't have 'em fucking besmirching the old escutcheon now, can we? And in fact, the young guns had brought in a whopping sum. A cool forty million yen per head. Japanese yen. Even when you factored in "transport fees" for illegal entry and the various other little presents they had to distribute, and even if you offered the bullets—or their families, in some cases—a reward for seeing their jobs through to a successful conclusion, the profits that came streaming into the organization were still unfuckingbelievable. And of course, the Boss mused, it wasn't just that nice cash reward; I also set it up so they could spend the eve of the attack whooping it up with beautiful white chicks. Sexy Slavic sisters.

Blond-haired blue-eyed supermodel-class hotties, fuck yeah. Some harem. Bet they knocked themselves out, lucky pricks. Then I had 'em batten the hatches with vodka and caviar. Very nice indeed. Shows what a fucking ten-derhearted yakuza daddy I've been.

The man—the Boss as they called him—cast his thoughts back, agony written all over his face. The thing was, the bullets were just that. Bullets. They went out and didn't come back. In the beginning, they'd had better than a fifty percent survival rate, but now it had sagged below twenty percent. Only one in five made it back alive, in other words. If that. But what choice did he have? He had to keep sending the poor fuckers in. Stormtroopers. He hunted around for hit men who wouldn't just follow the money, going through one of his "brothers" from his time in the clink. He located four, trained 'em to do their work as bullets, and sent 'em off on a Russian transport vessel, this time from Niigata Port. He snuck 'em in without dicking around, no stupid paperwork. Next he picked up some fucking traitors. Dickheads who'd betrayed their gang and were lying low under aliases, trying to keep from getting caught in the wide net their old bosses cast. He sent off eight of them, one after another. Gave 'em good tools. A nice cache of pistols: Tokarevs; Makarovs; Italian-made automatics; M-16s that had found their way out of American bases, now equipped with 40mm grenade launchers; Uzis; and last but not least twenty-three hand grenades and seventeen sticks of dynamite. Plus some other stuff.

These "soldiers" kept getting more flashy all the time, putting more bang into their work. One guy had gone into a nightclub the police ran jointly with the Russian mafia and shot the hell out of the place with a submachine gun. Miraculously the attacker managed to get out of the club alive, not that it mattered—they found his body in Nakhodka Port. Others had taken aim at two successive chiefs of police, both times bringing about a change in person-nel. They slaughtered executives in a bank the mafia controlled. After the organization started using yakuza from outside, though, the bullets' survival rate sank below ten percent. Soon, no doubt, it'd be grazing zero. Still, this little hustle had already brought in more than six hundred million yen in pure profit. How the hell could this be? the Boss wondered. What was going on?

he asked himself. He didn't know the answer. And he had no choice, he had to keep sending these fucking stormtroopers in. How could he refuse? They had his daughter.

The client had his daughter.

It doesn't fucking make sense, the Boss moaned. How many months had his stomach been hurting like this? Sure, I expect to be threatened, used. But why are the fuck are they paying us these fees? He knew the Russian market. You could hire a hit man, some guy with no fear of death, for a lot less; you could take a zero or two off the figure they were paying him, even if the target was a policeman or a kingpin type. And you could do it domestically. What the hell was this client thinking? The Boss had lost twenty pounds over the past few months. He'd grown thin. Skinny, even. He couldn't make sense of the situation. He had no idea what effect these dramatic attacks were having on the local population. No idea how a certain paper—a dissident tabloid specializing in yellow journalism—was fanning the flames. He didn't even know where all this cash was coming from. Who was behind the client, funding him?

Someone, he was sure, was behind the client.

Shooting pain in his stomach. Blood in his urine.

His daughter had been taken hostage.

The Boss sent over three more bullets. The client kept making demands. ELIMINATE THE TARGET. I mean, what the hell? The Boss clutched his stomach with both hands. What's the plan here, what the fuck are you trying to do? The information the client sent regarding the targets' location, routine, and protection was always precise, detailed, and up-to-date. It's better than a damned spy flick, for fuck's sake! And the second we pop the target, the money comes through, wired into one of the organization's underground bank accounts. What are we, businessmen? the Boss asks. Speaking to himself, of course, since there was no one else to ask. It's just another kind of business. How many fucking ulcers have I got in my stomach now? Already the supply of yakuza-on-the-run was drying up; he was having to rely on non-yakuza. Fuckheads who had been drummed out of the criminal world forever by their own groups. And he had to hire these guys as bullets. Totally fucking against the rules. I'm no underworld daddy, not anymore. Forget underworld, this is just plain old hell. But who the fuck cares. I can't fucking let it bother me. After all, the Boss thinks, becoming defiant, this is the best hustle ever!

Until then, what little income the organization brought in had consisted of protection money from bars and restaurants, betting on baseball, underground casinos, black-market lending, various degrees of blackmail, ranging in size from tall to venti. They didn't deal much in speed. The key, fuckers, is how much money you can launder, the Boss was always saying. Use your heads and fucking rake the shit in. The twenty-first century is right around the corner, and then it'll all be business! Business! That's what we're aiming for with this Russo-Japanese joint venture!

Only…was *this* the kind of business they'd wanted? No, no. The Boss had chosen defiance—that was the way to go. Just think how much his men had suffered trying to gather the fees they had to send to the main branch. How much fucking pointless suffering they had been through. This business was his reward for all that, as their underworld daddy.

Or rather, their hell daddy.

Shit. Hell…hell. Whatever.

He tried to reason his way out of the dilemma. His stomach twitched. It hurt like fuck. He had diarrhea too. The client was using him, it was clear. That was one way of looking at it. He was just a piece in someone else's game, a pawn, the king of the pawns. You could look at it that way. ELIMINATE THE TARGET. ELIMINATE. ELIMINATE. The three bullets he'd just sent over brought in more than a hundred million yen. Again. Business. What am I supposed to do, my daughter's been taken hostage! My fucking hands are tied.

I just have to keep sending over more bullets.

He would send another.

Recruiting even non-yakuza wasn't easy anymore. Still he demanded that arrangements be made. Arrangements couldn't *not* be made. They had his daughter. Though he realized, in some shadowy corner of his heart, that maybe this was just an excuse. Maybe all the spiritual agonies he was suffering, the blistering pain in his stomach, the boys the organization had sacrificed… maybe none of it had anything to do with his daughter.

He clutched his stomach. Fuck, have I gotten skinny.

Losing my imposing presence.

He had a bad feeling about all this. And his instinct was right. The main branch registered its displeasure. They were scraping the bottom of the barrel, and they hadn't yet found a taker. One of the main branch's advisers came as a messenger. He implied, without actually saying so, that the Boss was guilty of actions at odds with the Way of the Yakuza. It was perfectly clear what the problem was. Perhaps, the Boss thought, he'd gone overboard in trying to find his bullets. The messenger told him of various other unpleasant rumors.

Then, finally, he cut to the chase. "So you mean to start a war in Russia?"

The Boss gaped. Had someone ratted on him?

You're sending hit men over, aren't you? the adviser shouted. The main branch *will not* stand for out-of-control violence of that sort! He went on bellowing. It dawned on the Boss that they must have heard about the cash flowing in from the far side of the Japan Sea. Aha, he thought. So that's it. They noticed how well we're doing, so they did some poking around....We made a bit *too* much, I guess.

The messenger's next statement confirmed his suspicions. "The main branch is considering your expulsion. Your territory would go right to the Chief. They're ready to replace you. If you want to put things back in order, it'll cost five hundred million. You've got the money, I'm sure. You've been making it hand over fist in Russia."

"Five hundred...million?"

"That's what the main branch wants."

They did their homework, the Boss thought. With our fucking coffers as larded as they are, we could send 'em five hundred million in a flash. And they want us to hand it over, just like that? Pay our dues? You must be fucking kidding, the Boss thought. The man they called the Boss, who had just been threatened with the loss of that title. My boys *died* for that money. The first guys I sent over as bullets were my own, you know, official members of this organization! They laid their lives on the line, all for my little darling. And you're telling me to fucking cough up *that money*? Cash I got at the price of my boys' lives?

No boss would agree to that.

Not even a hell boss.

The messenger gazed coolly at the Boss. As if to say, So, what's it going to be? You dick, the Boss thought. You think you've got me by the balls, and you're laughing inside. You're fucking chuckling. Messenger from the main branch, my ass. Think you can give me advice, do me the favor of sharing your great wisdom? Just trying to get your bit, you fuckhead. No sooner had this thought flashed into his mind than he put his hand behind his back, lifting his suit jacket. He kept a Beretta tucked into his belt for protection. He whipped it out. He fired. The gun. At the fuckhead.

Three shots.

No, four shots.

Then, without so much as a glance at the body, he grabbed his stomach and moaned.

The incident had taken place in a closed room. The Boss's office at headquarters was totally soundproof, bulletproof, constructed so that it would be safe even if people smashed their way into the building—or, conversely, even if his boys were working some bastard over, torturing him. The Boss took three or four small bottles of medicine out of a cabinet, grabbing at them like straws, and gulped them down. Digestive tonics. He rocked his head back and forth a few times, trying to reset himself. He rubbed his hands down his front where the esophagus was, to make sure the medicine was on its way. *Phew*, he sighed. The gastric acid in his breath stung, but not so much he couldn't bear it.

He dropped himself into a leather chair.

He picked up the remote control on the table. This one worked both the TV and the video deck. The TV was positioned in front of him. He turned it on. The screen flashed white for a second, then faded to black. The video player was already going. There was already a tape in the deck. He rewound it for a while, then pressed PLAY.

His daughter appeared.

My darling.

She sat in a cold-looking room with a dog, glaring into the camera. Glaring, that is, through the screen at him. At the man they called the Boss, her father, him, himself. A fucking hostage video. The client in Russia sent them at regular intervals. This was the latest. Nothing had changed. The girl still cursed at her father. The same foul-mouthed harangue. "Fucking dick," she spat. The only thing that had changed was the dog. The dog looked like he was guarding her. He'd been a puppy the first time he appeared in a video, but in no time he had grown into an adolescent, and now he could have been called a young dog. The dog, too, glared into the camera.

A girl and a dog, staring, unblinking, straight at the lens.

Fact is, they looked creepy.

They looked heartless.

C'mon, the dog too? the Boss thought. Even the dog looks at me like that! What, are you sizing me up? Seeing how much weight I carry?

Darling, the man thought again. My darling by my first wife. Fucking little brat. He stared at the screen, transfixed, unable to tear his eyes away. He remained slumped in the leather chair as if in a trance. "All the shit I've been through for this brat…" he said, aloud this time. All the men I've sacrificed, he continued voicelessly, in his mind. Then, once again, he spoke aloud. "My child…my own child. You think I fucking love you? Damn you!"

The second he'd said those words, the floodgates broke. Okay, it's true, it was my fault. I'm the one who forged that fucking parasite's death certificate to make it look like she'd been sick. I would never have married that dumb bitch if my uncle hadn't forced me. What was I gonna do, he would have made me chop off a finger. Besides, I needed someone like her if I was gonna set up my own organization, starting so late in the game, in my thirties already. Except that she was fucking useless. She was a totally hard-core fucking stupid dumbass bitch. So I popped her. Dirtied my fucking hands with her. That was good, though, because that way I was able to make my woman official, make her *my* woman. The Boss's second wife was only twenty-three. She was tough. She looked after the young guys in the organization real well. The boys. They looked up to her, the Boss's woman. They called her Big Sister. She gave me a daughter too, another daughter, bound to me by blood. A year-and-a-half old. The half sister of *that* one there…*that one.*

I hate her. The Boss admitted it. He hated that darling in the videos. But even I couldn't bring myself to pop my own daughter. We're father and daughter, after all, so I let you live, as if I had no alternative. Even after I killed that stupid bitch mother, which I could do because she was nothing to me. And just look what happened! The way she glares at me, that girl. The way she glares at her stepmother. Who did she think she was? And then she started swelling, getting so fat it was like someone put a hex on her. As if her dead mother's deadweight shifted to her. Her face got pudgy. She was in elementary school, but you could hardly believe it. Her wrists bulged, bulged more. My god, I thought, she looks like a fucking fat infant! What, is she fucking imitating her newborn sister…her half sister? Man, is she creepy. And ugly. And the way she looks at me, revulsion in her eyes. And demanding. I want this, that, that. I WANT IT! She screamed, and I bought the shit. Bought everything, no matter what. Everyone has it, so buy me one! That was never her game. She told me, *ordered* me, to buy things no one had. Forced me.

Buy me Gucci so people don't fucking piss around with me.

Tokyo Disneyland is for middle-class fucks. Take me to Florida.

I felt like I was being tested, so I did everything she asked. It got so I thought she was always silently asking me, You wouldn't, by any chance, happen to have popped my mother?

She couldn't have guessed, there was no way. And yet…

It's just my imagination.

And every time I gave her anything, the brat got fatter. Creepily obese.

And then, finally, when I was going to Russia for a business talk, she ordered me to take her along, take her where ordinary fucks, laymen, couldn't go. And we were attacked, and she was taken hostage.

By the client.

"I've had enough," the Boss said. "I'm gonna end this with my own hands."

He stopped the video. He stood up. For the first time, he looked long and hard at the body of the messenger from the main branch, this new Buddha, lying in the corner. Oh shit, he said. But his tone was cheery. How old am I? Thirty-…nine, that's right. Still in my prime. Pecker's still in working order. If you think I'm gonna be a pawn in someone else's game, fucking think again. He pushed open the door to his office. Walked out into the hall. Went in to say hi to the boys in the main office. His expression was bright, relaxed.

"Gather the soldiers," he said. "All of 'em."

You mean…all of them? they asked.

"Yup. We're crossing the Japan Sea. It's war."

What the hell, why not set up an organization in Russia? Take over Siberia, maybe, the Boss thought with a chuckle. A hacking sort of chuckle: *Kekh kekh kekh kekh.* He hadn't noticed, but his stomach wasn't hurting anywhere near as bad. He briefly explained the situation to the guy in charge of the boys and gave instructions for disposing of the body, told him to find someone to take care of the slime, say some hothead got out of control or something, find a way to buy some time.

But, uh, Boss…what are we going to do then? someone asked.

"Hmm? We're gonna pray. Pray for the fucking main branch once it's fucking dead. But first, we're gonna take some Russian mafia heads to the Chechens as a souvenir."

After that, the Boss flew to the Primorsky Krai, taking twenty-seven men along. He set up an unmarked office in the city there, in the Russian Far East, at a cost of about twenty million yen. Japanese yen. There was no longer any need to scramble searching for non-yakuza recruits. Because he had ditched the middleman: he and his men were the bullets now. They were the storm-troopers. Two days after they arrived in Siberia, they had already killed the target, acting on information from the client, and confirmed with the local police that he had indeed been a bigwig in the Russian mafia. It had cost about five hundred thousand yen to establish a pipeline to a certain faction within the police. He blew another two hundred thousand yen on the cover-up, to make sure the attack wouldn't be traced to them. They went to pay their respects to the Chechen mafia, taking along the bigwig's head and a gift of thirty thousand dollars. US dollars.

Things were going even better than the Boss had expected. And for good reason: the bullets he had been sending in, one after the other, had turned the region into a sort of fucked-up war zone. The Chechens and the Russians were both weakened. The two main organizations were practically bleeding each other to death, and the power vacuum this had created attracted all sorts of little dipshit crime rings from the rest of the country. And the local underworld was internationalizing too. Heroin was streaming in from the Korean continent. Rumor was the North Korean secret service was bringing it in with help from the Koryo-saram—common knowledge among the criminal class. Amphetamines and a nice selection of coca-derived drugs were shipped in from China. And there was traffic in the other direction too: Russian prostitutes sent off to Macao, Beijing, Shanghai. The Triad had a monopoly over this "trade." At the same time, mafia organizations based in Central Asian countries of the Commonwealth of Independent States were trying to grab a slice of the pie by providing higher quality drugs. Minor interorganizational battles were popping up.

The Boss was puzzled by the situation on the ground. Can the bullets I've been sending be responsible for all this shit? As it happened, the penetration of various East Asian criminal organizations had rendered the Japanese bullets' presence much less noticeable. They had draped the bullets in a cloak of invisibility, as it were.

And to top it all off, the yakuza's killing of Russian mafia bigwigs and others with vested interests in their doings had been rather fancifully interpreted as an expression of the honorable Yakuza Way. Everyone knew that members of a Japanese organization had visited this city for important business talks with the Russian mafia, only to suffer a fatal attack at a hotel restaurant. Immediately after that, the yakuza had cut all ties with the Russians. And then the assassinations began. No doubt that's how they do things, those yakuza. So people imagined. Yakuza don't listen to excuses, they adhere absolutely to…something. It was revenge, with rage thrown in for good measure. Honorable conduct, in other words. So people believed, mistakenly. The rest of the criminal underworld found the yakuza kind of creepy. Not that they couldn't understand their point of view. Their method of gaining satisfaction was, after all, not unlike the Chechen's *krovnaya mest*, blood revenge.

So when the Boss showed up on the Chechen mafia's doorstep with the head of an enemy boss and thirty thousand dollars as an icebreaker, they were willing to form an alliance. They responded right away to the yakuza's money and strength. Even if it was a creepy kamikaze sort of strength. The

Boss wasn't entirely pleased by their success, though. No repeat performance of that hacking laugh: *Kekh kekh kekh kekh.* Things were only tilted to their advantage now because someone was running the game. That was why the Chechens were so eager to jump at any cash that came their way, because this constant battle was wearing them down.

Yeah. All this shit, it was all the client's doing. He was orchestrating it all. I'm going to smash that fucker, the Boss thought. He'd made up his mind. He shelled out seven hundred thousand yen to develop a relationship with a group of retired veterans of the Soviet-Afghan War. This got him a free pass to a market where you could get all kinds of old Soviet firearms. You could buy anything there, dirt cheap, even antiaircraft missiles. In three days, all twenty-seven of his boys were heavily armed. It cost him about sixty thousand yen per man. Cheap. He expended another 1.4 million yen on weaponry for his own use, including four trench mortars and cases of cartridges. He had the Chechens introduce him to a "launderer" free of charge. He had the guy figure out the stops the last payment made after the client wired it, for popping the bigwig, backtracking from the unlicensed bank in Japan where it ended up. The money had only been wired the day before, so there were still plenty of clues to go by. He told the launderer he'd cover unlimited expenses and give him a bonus of five million yen if he succeeded. Two days later, the launderer requested that he bring in a micro-organization specializing in technocrime. The Boss had to pay that group three hundred thousand yen just to get acquainted.

Russia produced the best hackers in the world. It kept the twentieth-century international underworld well stocked with sophisticated techies. For two million yen the Boss got the undivided attention of a rare specialist in the illegal use of computer systems for a half day. That night, he ended up paying the launderer a total of 7.5 million yen, but he had the tracks he was after. They led to the city's old Communist Party headquarters—to a particular room in the building, in fact. They led to a statue of Lenin that had somehow remained standing, and to a secret meeting that had taken place at its base. The Boss then got in touch with four former KGB officers whom he hired for between five hundred thousand to six hundred thousand yen each to assemble the last few pieces of the puzzle.

See there? the Boss said. Just like the movies. You want pounded rice? Buy it at the fucking pounded-rice store.

When I've grabbed the tiger's tail, I don't let go.

He spent 1.9 million yen on a covered military truck. This wasn't from the black market. It had been sold off by a private company, and he bought it more or less legally. All twenty-eight of the yakuza, including the Boss, piled inside. Four men sat up front; everyone else went in the rear. They wore fur coats and felt boots, and were armed not only with guns but also with items that seemed appropriate for an interorganizational war. They left the city at daybreak, heading west. Grasslands sailed by the windows. Then wetlands. Then grasslands again, and a graveyard for old cars. The heaped-up bodies had been stripped of their parts, left as mere shells. After that came a stretch of houses. A suburban farming town, apparently. They kept pigs. The grasslands changed into plowed fields. It wasn't clear what they were growing, but whatever it was there was a lot of it. The roads had been sprinkled with sand. Plenty of sand, to keep the pavement from icing over. Clouds of sand billowed in the truck's wake like smoke from a signal fire. Once again they plunged into an expanse of uncultivated grasslands, and then, four hours after they had set out, they caught sight of the dense dark taiga ahead, outlined against the horizon.

Up ahead, the Boss saw. He gripped a map in his hands. A map on which the location of a town that wasn't on any map had been drawn in, precisely, by hand. The map had cost him twelve million yen. There it was. A closed city, left over from the Soviet era. There *he* was. The client. All of a sudden, the Boss felt like he might, at last, be able to laugh again. You want pounded rice? Buy it at the fucking pounded-rice store indeed, he laughed. No one beats us yakuza when it comes to a scrap.

Man-made structures came into view over the taiga, in silhouette, high above the treetops. Observation towers. Not one, not two, but four. Set at intervals. Then a sliver of land belonging to the town, enclosed by a concrete wall. We're here, at long last, the end of the road, the Boss thought. Beyond it, a world within walls.

"Looks like a prison," the Boss said. Fucking jaily sort of place, isn't it? he thought with a chuckle.

"We'll fucking make this day go down in history," he said. "Fucking Independence Day."

The truck stopped a hundred yards short of the wall. A young yakuza sprang out of the covered cargo bay. He carried a mortar, pre-loaded with a 51mm high-explosive grenade. He squatted down close to the ground and hoisted the weapon up. He wasn't using the angled aiming device, he just fired straight in, level with the ground. Straight into the doors. The gate, the entrance, the way into the town unmarked on any map.

In a flash, the two doors were destroyed. Blown to hell by a force ten times stronger than a hand grenade. The next second, the truck was moving again. Charging in. The young guy who had fired the mortar jumped in as it passed. And on they went, into the world they had forcibly opened—liberated. They raced ahead a few dozen meters. Paved roads divided the town into fairly regular blocks. There were a lot of potholes, though. Big depressions. One of back wheels slammed down into a hole and the truck ground to a halt.

The Boss and his twenty-seven men, giddy with the excitement of war, immediately jumped out of the truck, all at once, even though no one had given any sort of signal. A total of twenty-eight yakuza, armed to the teeth with three million yen worth of firearms. They scattered. A few held back, staying near the truck to manage the mortars, which they aimed out in four directions. They had the whole town in their sights. The Boss wasn't one of them. He had no intention of staying in the safety zone, giving the others orders while the youngsters protected him with the mortars. He dashed out with a new-model Kalashnikov in his hand. He was in this too! He felt something snap in his head. *YESSSSS!* he thought. I'm fuckin' over the game! He had a young yakuza on either side, watching out for him, but he felt like he'd come out punching, ready to kick ass, all on his own.

"In fifteen minutes sharp, I want to know the lay of this place!" he yelled. "Take anyone you can. Don't hesitate. Kill. Go!" he ordered. The Boss was raging, wild. He barreled past a cluster of white buildings, bellowing something that sounded like *Ghuuuoogh!* Things weren't yet heating up, though, in terms of actual military action. Because there was no one there. The town kind of looked abandoned. In fact, it *was* abandoned. The official residents were gone. As for unofficial residents…well, there were perhaps some…just a few…

Then, suddenly, something was coming.

Dogs.

Here they came. And a little more than ten minutes later it was all over. Things didn't go quite the way the Boss had imagined. First, he heard three shrieks. Then he heard seven more. For the first few minutes he had no idea what was going on. Because the dogs didn't bark. Fifty dogs had fanned out around them, and not one so much as whined. Silence, too, was a weapon. The dogs attacked. Killed without a sound. They moved in formation. Two dogs would take aim at each yakuza, tear into his throat—their victims left with gaping holes under their chins—and then run off with his submachine gun, automatic rifle, or pistol. Six highly trained members of the posse attacked the truck, with its four-mortar guard. It fell in no time. The mortars had been aimed out in four directions, yes, but there were six dogs, and none of them was running less than forty miles per hour. Two of the mortars did go off, but randomly; one grenade plowed into the ground and the other ended up hitting an observation tower. Which was half-destroyed. The tower tilted, toppled, creaked, fell. It exploded onto the ground with a mighty *whabang*. That, it seemed, was taken by some to be a sign. Shots were fired into the air throughout the town, in different areas. Some yakuza shot out of fear, some didn't shoot but screamed "I'll fucking blast you! I'll fucking blast you!" It wasn't clear how effective shouting at the dogs in Japanese was. They were clearly unfazed by gunfire. They kept calm.

Still, some of the dogs did die. One fell victim to an out-of-control machine-gun burst of fire. Another three died. *Gnyaarhf!* they uttered as they went down. *Hhuunn,* they whined as they died. The other forty-six decided, at this point, that the battle had progressed to the second stage, and started barking messages back and forth. Finally the Boss understood. Dogs? he asked himself. Finally he realized that the town wasn't abandoned, because there were dogs. He began to grasp what was happening. Are the dogs attacking my boys? Is that it? Taking down the young guns? *Whatwhatwhatwhatwhat-*

thefuckisgoingon—dogs? Why dogs? I'm looking for the client! What is this? Meanwhile, the dogs had moved into the "mopping up" stage. They had been conscious from the start that THIS IS NOT PRACTICE, but the loss of their comrades—they had communicated the fact of their deaths to one another by warning barks—made the forty-six dogs wildly, fiercely calm. They cornered people. They chased two yakuza into a four-story building, killed one on the stairs, on the landing, drove the other off the roof. THERE'S NOWHERE TO RUN, THIS IS OUR TOWN, OUR TERRITORY! YOU SHOULD KNOW THAT, THIS IS THE DEAD TOWN! TOWN OF THE DEAD! TOWN OF DEATH! Not surprisingly, some unfortunate mistakes were made in this, the first real battle they had fought. These dogs were absolute pros when it came to fighting, but they weren't invincible. Another two died. Another one. But the yakuza were being weeded out even faster. The twenty-second died. The twenty-third bit the dust. The Boss had a sense of what was happening. He suspected the horrible turn things had taken; he saw the evidence, heard it, felt it in his spine. A kind of sixth sense told him, a quaking in his vertebrae. You fucks! *Whatareyouwhatareyouwhatareyoufuckingdoing*...what are you...to my boys! Risking their lives for the organization! Whenever a dog came into view, he immediately fired at it. He glared furiously around him, his eyes practically emitting death rays. You fucking assholes! he screamed, and killed more dogs.

The two young yakuza at his side were still alive.

Protected by the Boss's intuition, that quaking in his vertebrae.

Someone's going to die. Now.

A large dog leapt out of his blind spot, tore into the throat of the man on the Boss's right, then, camouflaged by the spraying blood, wriggled across the ground and took aim at the man on the Boss's left, his leg. He attacked. Took him down. Rolled, bit, killed him. This dog was not a member of the posse. Not a dog in active service, not a current fighter. But before age took its toll, he had been perfect. Even now he had a dignified aura that told you he was not a dog to be trifled with. Gravitas. He had a terrifying sense of gravitas. You could feel it now that he had reared himself to his full height. The Boss, standing face to face with him, could feel it.

Face to face. That wasn't a blind spot.

The dog opened his blood-smeared mouth and barked.

Bang.

The Boss watched the dog tumble, dead, to the ground. He lowered the barrel of his new-model Kalashnikov, but he stayed there, motionless. He didn't take a single step. He hardly even shifted his gaze. He was looking, now, at the first non-dog resident of this town unmarked on any map. The first human. Here, to this field of battle, his darling had come.

You killed Belka, she said.

In Japanese.

Hey there, hostage, the Boss said. Haven't lost any weight, I see.

You killed Belka, his darling said again.

The Boss called her by her name. Her Japanese name. The name he had given his darling. The name he had given her *because he was her father.* She didn't reply. She continued glaring at him. Ah, the Boss thought, just like in the videos. So, he asked, ready to break jail?

"Think again," he said without waiting for her answer. "I came to end this," he said.

"I'm talking about *you,*" the Boss continued.

"You're a pain in my ass. Fucking brat," her father continued.

He had raised the barrel of his new-model Kalashnikov.

His daughter didn't flinch, didn't avert her eyes for a second, not even as she spoke. Said something. Issued a command. In Russian. Instantly the shadows sprang into motion, darting from a cluster of trees along a road, from behind a building, from a second-floor window. Dogs. Seven dogs. Still too young to be called adults. KILL, his darling was saying in Russian. ATTACK. ALL OF YOU. AND YOU, FORTY-SEVEN, FINISH HIM. Six dogs in a cluster. First one of them snatched the Kalashnikov in its mouth, flung it away. The weapon clattered as it hit the ground. The target's arms and legs were splayed, as if he were being crucified—the dogs were tugging on his felt boots, biting into his bare palms and the sleeves of his coat, pulling. He stood there, almost upright. And then one more dog, number 47, came running. Thirty-eight miles an hour. He leapt. Bared his fangs. Sank them into the soft, fleshy throat. Twisted. Took him. Finished him.

He was finished.

He tumbled forward, spouting blood.

The Boss. The man they called the Boss. Her father.

And there was his daughter.

There was the girl, seven dogs, already done with their prey, gathering at her feet.

For a few minutes, none of them moved.

They stayed there, perfectly still. The girl and the dogs.

Then the girl turned around.

She had noticed that someone was there.

The old man.

She said only a few words to him. In Japanese. "Hey, Old Fuck, I just earned the name. I'm Strelka now."

Her voice was shaking. Tears brimmed in her eyes.

1963-1989

Dogs, dogs, where are you now?

Everywhere. You scattered. You increased without limit. Naturally, some of you bore puppies and some didn't. Bloodlines extended, ended, became intricately intertwined. Thus were you born, one dog at a time, and thus did you die. One dog at a time. Your lives had limits. Your family trees, however, kept growing.

It had begun on the western tip of the Aleutian Islands, and it continued. All across the globe.

You would never go extinct.

But you were toyed with, exploited. Why? Because this was the twentieth century. A century of war. A century, too, of military dogs.

Two great wars were fought during the twentieth century on the chessboard of the world. In the first half of the century, that is. In the second half, two more wars were fought, both alike in many respects. Both were limited wars. Both were offshoots of the Cold War, and both were played out in Asian nations. In the first, American soldiers shed their blood; in the second, Soviet soldiers shed theirs. The first unfolded in Southeast Asia; the second in Central Asia.

One war on the Indochinese peninsula, one war in Afghanistan.

Each lasted a decade.

America first sent combat forces into Vietnam on March 8, 1965. The Vietnam War lasted until 1975.

The Soviet Union sent its forces across the border into Afghanistan on December 25, 1979. The Soviet-Afghan War lasted until 1989.

The Vietnam War and the Soviet-Afghan War. A quagmire for each nation. Each a product of the Cold War, each a decade long from the point of direct intervention to the end. Similar indeed. Dogs, dogs, how you were toyed with, exploited, in the name of these two catastrophes! And it wasn't only the United States and the USSR that left their mark on your family trees. It wasn't only these two nations that pruned and spliced, made your destiny grow.

There was also China.

Red China, the third player.

1963. Mao Zedong despised Khrushchev.

At that time, in that year, every dog in the PLA Military Dog Platoon was descended from Jubilee. The platoon was not permanently stationed in any military region; it was assigned instead to the highly mobile field army—the army's main force, which went wherever strategy demanded.

1963. America was operating under a misapprehension. In its eyes, the globe was still a page in a coloring book that two ideologies were rushing to fill in. It was, so to speak, a geographical contest. Needless to say, communist states were red. This much of the American interpretation was correct. Even America wasn't always wrong. And yet…and yet…it had it wrong. America had failed to understand that the red patches in the book were by no means all the same tint of red. Or perhaps the Americans understood that fact but decided to ignore it, intentionally chose to be color blind and narrow-minded. America's political decisions were all based in a sweeping, simplistic judgment that red is red, even when the crayons were, in reality, of quite different hue.

1963. The USSR and China were both red, but those two reds were nothing at all alike in brightness or saturation. America's decision to overlook that distinction would prove politically fatal.

But America clung to that fatal vision.

What were the roots of this altogether inflexible approach? It began in February 1950, with the signing of the Sino-Soviet Treaty of Friendship, Alliance, and Mutual Assistance. At this point, America decided that Red China was essentially a satellite of the Soviet Union, and it adhered steadfastly to this view. As part of its anticommunist stance, it continued to treat Chiang Kai-shek–led Taiwan—which is to say the Kuomintang and the Republic of China—as China's true representative. The Sino-Soviet Treaty of Friendship, Alliance, and Mutual Assistance had been signed, however, by Mao Zedong and Joseph Stalin. Mao had trusted Stalin. But Mao did not trust Khrushchev, who had taken over after Stalin and criticized Stalin at the Party Congress in 1956.

Here, in a nutshell, were the dynamics of the Sino-Soviet opposition. America didn't recognize this, though. America failed to see that it all hinged on the *personal relationship* between Mao and Khrushchev. This was the season of Mao's hatred of Khrushchev. Khrushchev, for his part, was wary of Mao. History is moved, rolled this way and that, so simply. The twentieth century was a pawn. As were the dogs.

America had succumbed to narrow-mindedness. America was color blind. In 1963, China was anything but a satellite of the Soviet Union, but America didn't see that.

Perhaps it would have, had it lowered its gaze to the level of the dogs. Yes, the dogs. The PLA Military Dog Platoon. If America had paid attention to that platoon, it would have seen that China and the Soviet Union were gradually drifting apart.

It was unmistakable.

First there was the Korean War. China dispatched the Chinese People's Volunteer Army. This was in October 1950, eight months after the Sino-Soviet Treaty of Friendship, Alliance, and Mutual Assistance. Chinese forces had some military backing from the Soviet Union, but it wasn't enough to make up for the poverty of their munitions, and during the Fourth and Fifth Campaigns they were repeatedly overwhelmed by the superior power of the UN forces, which had largely been provided by the American military. The UN forces' "superior power" came from the fact that they had modern weaponry, modern military strategy. Up to this point, the Chinese had relied on human-wave tactics and had been trained to fight guerrilla wars; now they had to confront the inadequacy of these techniques for an army dedicated to national defense. It took five million soldiers deployed to the Korean Peninsula to learn this lesson. Then, in July 1953, a truce was called. Predictably, the Chinese military took advantage of this opportunity to shift its strategy, to begin preparing its troops to fight a modern war.

And the dogs?

Three had been captured and incorporated into the PLA. Jubilee was the only bitch. The two males were News News (aka E Venture) and Ogre. All three had formerly been American dogs, but now they were Chinese. Purebred German shepherds. When Mao announced the establishment of the People's Republic of China, the military had no military dogs. Now, in the wake of the Korean War, it had become focused on "modernization." Twentieth-century war. War in a century of war. The modern military dog was the symbol of it all.

Dogs on the front lines.

So China created its Military Dog Platoon. First the American dogs were taken as prisoner-dogs-of-war on the battlefields of the Korean Peninsula. Then, after the fighting ended, these three elite supporting combatants were given Chinese citizenship, as it were. They were incorporated into the PLA's first military dog platoon, right from the get-go. All three: Jubilee, News News (E Venture), and Ogre. Making a platoon of thirty-two dogs. At that time, in 1953, China was still on good terms with the USSR, so the platoon was based largely on the Soviet model. Most of the dogs were Russian laikas. Modern military dogs had first entered Soviet military history, incidentally, as early as the 1920s. The military had dogs, that is, even before the USSR itself existed. By the time the Great Patriotic War against Nazi Germany started on June 22, 1941—a Sunday—ten thousand military dogs had been trained. And so the PLA decided to follow the Soviet model. Military officials contacted the Central Military School of Working Dogs in Moscow and received a gift of twenty-nine Russian laikas. This was one of the many ways in which the Soviet Union provided China with military support.

In this sense, the composition of China's first military dog platoon, with its heavy slant to the East—twenty-nine Russian laikas and only three German shepherds—symbolized the Sino-Soviet honeymoon. Alternatively, you might say the symbolism lay in the special weight China's military placed on Russian history. The three German shepherds, Jubilee, News News (E Venture), and Ogre, were valued as extraordinarily capable dogs—the most modern of the modern—but they were excluded from the breeding program.

What happened, as a result, to the dogs?

In the winter of 1953, the males were castrated. The bitch was carefully kept away from any lusty males in the platoon.

The bitch. That means you, Jubilee.

You were kept away from the males, but still you harbored the potential for growth. There were times when you hungered for a male. But you weren't allowed to mate. When you let your eagerness show too long, they whipped you. *No sex for you, Yankee dog!*

This situation continued until 1956. Then, in February, first secretary of the Communist Party Khrushchev delivered his speech "The Personality Cult and its Consequences" in a closed session at the Twentieth Congress of the Communist Party of the Soviet Union. It was a "secret speech" in which he presented a thorough critique of Stalin. He had given no indication that anything like this was in the wings. The other communist nations could have been consulted, but they were not. China, above all, had been ignored. The content of the speech became public almost immediately, and when Mao learned the details, he was dumbstruck. *What! Stalin...a despot?*

What are we Chinese supposed to do when Khrushchev takes a stance like that, when we've been working so hard to realize an ideal state modeled on Stalin's USSR?

Hey, Khrushchev! Hey, Nikita...Nikita Sergeyevich!

We've got everyone worshiping Chairman Mao over here! Do you realize the mess you're causing?

And so, starting in 1956, signs of a mutual antagonism between Mao and Khrushchev began to appear. The effects of this friction were reflected on the Chinese side in two areas of its military strategy: its nuclear policy and its dogs. First, the dogs. That means you, Jubilee. At last you were released from the prohibition on mating. Sex was fine now, you were told that summer. No longer, it was decided, would the PLA Military Dog Platoon be based exclusively on the Eastern model, in terms of its structure or future breeding plans.

It was German shepherd season now.

Twenty-two males were purchased, all purebred German shepherds, all bursting with youth, and you, the only bitch in the platoon, became the object of their affection. On the grounds of the camp. They had decided to make the most of your lineage as an American elite.

And you, Jubilee—you were hungry.

Who were you, after all? Do you remember? Do you recall, for instance, your sister? Sumer was her name. You were separated six months after you were born. Sumer hadn't made it as a military dog; she was recognized, instead, for the perfect beauty of her form and bought by a breeder. She entered the dog-show world. She remained in America, on the mainland. She gave birth to any number of puppies and was eventually subjected to a peculiar fate. She suckled seven pups that were not her own. And what about you?

ME?

You were across the Pacific. You had not participated in planned breeding. You yearned to mate but weren't allowed. You wanted to get pregnant, but that was forbidden. You understand what that means? You were starved for a male. You: Jubilee.

ME?

Yes, you.

Woof! you barked.

You didn't get pregnant in 1956. You didn't go into heat in spring 1957. You were getting old, so they fed you specially prepared food. Your coat regained its youthful shine. But still you didn't get pregnant. They prepared traditional Chinese medicines to make you go into heat. They even fed you human milk. *Multiply, multiply!* But summer came, and still there was no sign that you were pregnant. Then it was autumn. November. Early in the month, something happened. You raised your head to the heavens. You didn't know why, it was just an impulse that came over you. SOMEONE'S LOOKING AT ME,

FROM ABOVE. IT'S A DOG, A DOG'S GAZE. You lifted your head and peered up into the vastness of the sky.

You thought you had seen a star there, shooting by.

Not falling, but shooting.

You realized how starved you were. Your procreational abilities came one hundred percent back on track. They were turbo-charged. And you gave birth, Jubilee, in 1958—not once, but twice. You bore fifteen puppies in total. You gave birth twice more in 1959. Twelve more puppies. Then, in 1960, you managed to give birth one last time in what could only be considered a *super*-advanced-age pregnancy. At the same time, in the vast lands up north, on the same continent—in another communist state by the name of the USSR—a wolfdog named Anubis with an erection strong beyond *his* years kept forcing it into bitches, planting his seed. He was a father beyond his years. You, Jubilee, were a mother beyond your years. This time you gave birth to four puppies. When all was said and done you had brought thirty-one puppies into the world.

In winter 1958, your first litter gave birth to another generation.

In spring 1959, your second litter gave birth to another generation.

By autumn 1959, the children of the dogs in your first litter were themselves getting it on. Their numbers increased. Your bloodline thrived. And over time your descendants proved the superiority of your lineage, its wonderfully *modern* superiority, and they were urged, males and bitches both, to get raunchy. Finally, in 1963, the day came when the entire platoon was composed of dogs belonging to your family tree. Their number: 801.

And how was Mao's China doing?

It becomes necessary to touch on the nuclear issue. China's strategic vision required that it possess nuclear capability. The decision had been made. This was a perfectly natural stance for Red China to take; it was, after all, the third player in the game, along with America and the Soviet Union. In 1958, a telling incident took place: the so-called "Second Taiwan Strait Crisis." In August, China, under Mao's direction, initiated a large-scale shelling of the small island Quemoy that belonged to Taiwan. Quemoy was located in Amoy Bay, off the coast of Fujian Province, and the Kuomintang had stationed members of its regular army there. Chiang Kai-shek's forces intended to use it as the base for their counteroffensive against China. At the time, the only China America recognized as a state was the Republic of China on Taiwan, led by Chiang Kai-shek's forces and the Kuomintang government. Obviously America couldn't allow this reckless violence. Mao's China was *red*. If Red China were to expand, red patches would start bleeding onto the rest of the Asian page in that ideological coloring book. *Warning! Beware of Mao Zedong!* The situation became critical. From summer to autumn, the United States considered the possibility of using nuclear weapons. The American military had spread nuclear arms across the entire Pacific. Bases on Guam, Okinawa, and Taiwan had been outfitted with secure installations to handle them. All right, then, why don't we use these things? To contain Maoist China! America had boiled the complex situation down to a simplistic vision of "communism vs. capitalism," and if nuclear weapons were what it would take, well, gosh darn it America was ready to do it. Mao, on the other hand, had summed up the situation in his own simplistic way: "Chinese socialism vs. American imperialism."

That, basically, was how Sino-American relations stood.

In the end, actual conflict was avoided. But Mao had learned his lesson: fight nuclear with nuclear. There was simply no other way to push back against the American menace. And there was more. In an earlier age, when China had been on good terms with the USSR, it had been solidly protected by the Soviet Union's "nuclear umbrella." Yes—it had been a satellite nation. But now?

Can't rely on 'em, Mao thought.

In fact, my dear Khrushchev, Mao thought. Nikita…your nuclear bombs are a menace from behind!

Khrushchev, for his part, wondered what Mao was getting all worked up about.

What'll you do if nuclear war actually breaks out? What then? Man, this guy's unbelievable. Here I am *blahblahblahing* about "US-USSR cooperation" to make sure we don't end up stumbling into a full-scale war, and look at you. Idiot.

Look, Khrushchev thought—though he never voiced his thoughts. Look.

Just leave world domination to us and the Americans. You can just chill, okay?

Khrushchev may not have said anything, but his actions showed very clearly what he was thinking. How wary he was of Mao. As a matter of fact, in 1956, China had already made up its mind to develop nuclear weapons. In 1957, the Soviet Union had at least outwardly projected a willingness to support China's nuclear program by signing the "Sino-Soviet Agreement on New Technology for National Defense." But the Second Taiwan Strait Crisis had made Khrushchev apprehensive about Mao. I mean, look at this guy, he's actually doing this stuff! It's dangerous. In 1959, Khrushchev scrapped the Sino-Soviet Agreement on New Technology for National Defense. The next year, he recalled the USSR's nuclear specialists from China.

He completely cut off all nuclear technological support. If that led to a split between China and the Soviet Union, well, so be it. You can't have everything.

Sorry, Mao.

Then, in 1963, something happened that brought about a definitive change in the situation. Astonishingly, the three nuclear powers—the United States, Great Britain, and the Soviet Union—signed the Partial Test Ban Treaty. The point of this action was to impress upon the rest of the world that that was it, no one else was going to get these things. And that was the last straw. Mao blew his top. China reacted by releasing a statement explicitly criticizing the Soviet state.

1964.

Two pieces of good news made China giddy. First, on October 14, Khrushchev was ousted. Mao howled with glee. Hah, serves you right, Nikita! Second, just two days later, on October 16, China's first nuclear test was a success. We did this on our own! Mao cried. Eat our dust, losers!

Now China was a superpower too.

As soon as Mao's relationship with Khrushchev came to an end—and as fraught as it was, it was still a relationship—he formed another, and this one, too, moved history. Mao developed a personal connection with Ho Chi Minh. This one wasn't bad. Mao had been Ho's only supporter during the First Indochina War, when Vietnam, which is to say the Democratic Republic of

Vietnam, founded in 1945, battled for its independence from France. "Down with Imperialism!" Red China shouted, and made the Vietnamese army a present of 160,000 small arms. It trained some fifteen thousand Vietnamese to fight, turning them into professional guerrillas. It did Ho some other favors too. Ho remained grateful for this until the end of his life. He continued throughout to show his respect for Mao.

Naturally, the warm personal bond between these men affected Sino-Vietnamese relations, and this in turn had an effect on Sino-American and Sino-Soviet relations.

So what happened?

The chaos of the Vietnam War, aka the Second Indochina War.

Yes, at last we come to the Vietnam War. The infamous Vietnam War. A limited war fought on the Indochina peninsula: America's quagmire. In 1964, John F. Kennedy was no longer the American president. He had been assassinated in Texas on November 22 of the previous year, almost a year before Khrushchev exited the stage. There was a crack, turbulence in the air, and he was gone from the world. Kennedy had been disinclined to get into a full-scale war, but not Johnson. Not Lyndon B. Johnson, former thirty-seventh vice president of the United States, now thirty-sixth president of the United States. On August 2, the Tonkin Gulf Incident took place. An American destroyer, claiming to have been attacked by the North Vietnamese Navy, which was part of the communist Democratic Republic of Vietnam's military and was thus led by Ho Chi Minh, conducted a retaliatory strike. In fact, the original attack had been fabricated by the Americans.

1965. On February 7, the American military began bombing North Vietnam. As the bombing continued, the targets moved progressively farther and farther north…

So what happened?

Naturally, Mao-led China grew suspicious. What, ultimately, was America's goal?

Where did it really want to end up?

What's just above Vietnam to the north?

We are.

That was it. Mao decided that America was taking aim at China. American encirclement all over again. Ho sent out the SOS. On March 22, the National Front for the Liberation of South Vietnam, popularly known as the Vietcong—short for Vietnamese Communists—announced that it was "prepared to accept aid from its friends around the world."

Mao was Ho's friend.

And so the policy of "support Vietnam, resist America" was established. Mao had made up his mind. We'll push back against America's war of imperialist aggression, put people on the ground in support of North Vietnam. Some thirty-five hundred US Marines had begun landing near Da Nang on March 8, so the land war was already under way. They had moved ahead into "direct intervention." Warning! they yelled in Beijing. Beware of the US! This war could easily expand into mainland China!

Send in the PLA!

And so it happened. On June 9, 1965, a substantial support force from China crossed the border. The soldiers marched through Friendship Pass onto the Indochina peninsula and into Ho's Vietnam. Only the main forces of the People's Liberation Army, the true elites, had been called to serve. Prior to deployment, they underwent two months of special training.

These efforts to support Vietnam were conducted in total secrecy. Still, by the second half of 1965, more than a hundred thousand troops had been shipped off to the peninsula to "support Vietnam, resist America."

Humans. And dogs too. Seventy-five dogs from the Military Dog Platoon had been sent over the border as an extremely modern and practical fighting force. All were descended from Jubilee. They moved south, down the peninsula.

Southward…southward…

Had America noticed?

Of course. The US had, by and large, figured out what was happening. It was the leading power in the West, and it had the best, maybe the second best, information-gathering network in the world. But the US kept silent. Johnson's administration had learned of China's covert intervention in the conflict, but it kept this knowledge secret. Because it was kind of at a loss. What the hell is China doing? it wondered. Are they trying to turn our limited war into a total war? They seem to see things sort of differently from Moscow, but…is this, like, a trap or something? Washington, in other words, was stymied by its own insistence on viewing two different shades of red, Soviet and Chinese, as though they were the same. And its provisional solution to the problem was to battle secrecy with more secrecy. As long as both sides didn't make what was happening public, China and the US wouldn't yet be at war.

The important thing, Washington decided, was to avoid direct confrontation.

The Indochina peninsula was split into North and South. The line was drawn at the seventeenth parallel north, along a buffer zone created by the Geneva Accords, which had ended the First Indochina War in 1954. This region was known as the Demilitarized Zone, the DMZ. In 1967, Quang Tri Province, which abutted the DMZ on the south, was the scene of a series of ferocious battles between the American military and the joint forces of the North Vietnamese Army and the Vietcong.

In summer, the direct confrontation with China that the US had been trying to avoid finally broke out in Quang Tri.

The participants in the battle were not human.

You were the soldiers.

Yes, you were the ones battling it out. Dogs vs. dogs.

Among the American dogs who came to Vietnam, shipped over from mainland America, was one named DED. In November 1963, President John F. Kennedy, JFK, exited the scene. In March 1968, Lyndon B. Johnson announced in his State of the Union address that he would not be running for president in the next election, and he, too, left. Goodbye LBJ. And hello DED. The dog was sent to the front in the summer of 1967 and kept fighting there for a year, until he himself left in summer 1968.

JFK, LBJ, DED. That, from a dog-historical perspective, was the progression. And so there you were.

ME?

Yes, you.

Woof.

DED barked.

June 1967. You had crossed the Pacific, but you weren't yet in Vietnam. You were on Okinawa, about to be separated from your sister. That's why you barked. You had both passed a screening test at Marine Corps Base Camp Pendleton, in California, and then they had shipped you off to this distant island. You had undergone six weeks of special training. You were siblings by different mothers, born of the same seed. The difference between your ages was two years and four months. You were descended on your father's side, some seven generations earlier, from Bad News. Five generations back, your great-great-great-grandfather had had, as his aunts and uncle, Jubilee, Sumer, and Gospel.

What kind of training did you undergo on Okinawa? Your handlers took advantage of the extreme similarity of the Okinawan environment to that of the Indochina peninsula to teach you specialized techniques for fighting against the Vietcong. First you had to get used to the jungle, with its oppressive heat and humidity. Then you had to learn to find hidden tunnels. Because the elusive communist guerrillas hid out, generally, in a vast network of underground passageways they had constructed. You had to hone your ability to navigate minefields. You had to be able to detect ambushes before they happened and respond to surprise attacks.

That's what these six weeks were for. To turn members of the American military dog elite into Vietnam War professionals.

Specialists.

Ten dogs in addition to DED and his sister had been brought in from the mainland, along with another forty-six from a base in the Philippines and twenty-nine specially selected from a platoon at a base in Korea. Unfortunately, seventeen out of the total of eighty-seven dogs were unable to become fully capable specialists. DED's sister was among these. And so, DED, you barked. Because while you would be sent off to the Indochina peninsula, your sister would be shipped back to Oahu, Hawaii.

You sensed, somehow, that you would never see her again. That you would never again be able to play with her. And so, DED, you barked.

Your sister's name was Goodnight. Though she had failed the screening test on Okinawa and was shipped off to a military installation on Oahu to serve as a sentry dog, she was still an outstanding dog—they wouldn't have used her if she wasn't—and in time, she would have her own rather complicated role to play in your history. For now, we will set her story aside.

To focus on you, DED.

ME?

Yes, you.

Think of your name. DED was an acronym for "dog-eat-dog," and it had been given to you in the hope that you would become a tough fighter worthy of the phrase. Do you get what that means, DED? Giving you a name like that was in poor taste, yes, but there was more to it than that. And as it happened, in the end, your name suggested your destiny.

You would consume canine flesh.

And soon.

That was the fate that awaited you.

MINE?

Yes, yours.

Woof!

Seven days later you were prepared to ship off to Vietnam. This was still June 1967. You and your sixty-nine fellow specialist anti-Vietcong dogs departed Okinawa and landed on the Indochina peninsula. One by one, the dogs were assigned to their new units. None was assigned to the IV Corps Tactical Zone, which was farthest south. Forty-four were assigned to the III Corps Tactical Zone. Half that number were assigned to Tay Ninh Province in the west, along the border with Cambodia. Four dogs were assigned to the II Corps Tactical Zone, and the rest—twenty-two in all—were assigned to the I Corps Tactical Zone, up north. Of the latter, eight went to Quang Ngai Province, four to Thua Thien-Hue Province, and ten to Quang Tri Province, all the way up north.

July 1967. DED was among the ten dogs sent to Quang Tri.

They went by helicopter.

They swooped down from the sky into a landing zone that had been cleared in the forest, into the thick of war.

The northern border of Quang Tri butted up against the seventeenth parallel. Against the DMZ. That summer, the DMZ was far from demilitarized—it was the site of intense fighting. The American Joint Chiefs of Staff had given permission to start shelling the DMZ a year earlier, though naturally this fact had not been made public. The Americans had one simple slogan in the border area, where the two states and the two sides in the conflict met: "Keep the Commies Out!" Seven months earlier, permission had been granted to return fire across the DMZ. Shooting back could be considered a form of invasion. Five months earlier, permission had been granted to carry out preemptive strikes. This was…well, obviously a form of invasion. They were doing all this and still had no results to show for it. Then, three months earlier, they started constructing a defensive wall. This time they were going to try closing off South Vietnam. This was the beginning of the "McNamara line," which required an incredible investment of manpower and involved the use of all kinds of equipment: barbed wire, mines, observation towers, searchlights, and so on. They carried all this stuff in using CH-54 heavy-lift helicopters, commonly known as sky cranes, and conducted frequent flyovers to protect the project.

Did the wall work? Was it impermeable?

It was not.

At all.

True, they were still building it, but this was kind of ridiculous. Not infrequently the enemy would actually slip past the McNamara line and turn up *behind* the US forces. And then they would run around doing whatever the hell they felt like, launching surprise attacks on the Marine Corps advance base, demolishing the McNamara line even as it was being constructed.

Clearly something was going very wrong.

The reason for this lay underground in that highly developed network of tunnels. Vietnam had begun preparing for an all-out war of resistance in March 1965, and in the major cities all the crucial facilities had already been moved underground. Underground passages and shelters had been dug early on, and the digging had continued ever since. Naturally the DMZ was no exception. Over the course of the two years previous, an extremely intricate system of tunnels had come into being below the seventeenth parallel.

To make matters worse, the North Vietnamese Army had the help of a corps of supporting combatants with superhuman powers who could lead them across the DMZ to South Vietnam, and do so even through the pitch-black of night.

Dogs.

Chinese dogs whose presence in Vietnam was a closely guarded secret. Their collars, which bore the emblem of the PLA, had been removed.

The dogs had been doing their thing for quite a while already. When the US Army's anti-guerrilla special forces, the Green Berets, secretly entered Laos, organized a Civilian Irregular Defense Group, CIDG, and started threatening the DMZ's western border, it was the dogs who, by summer 1967, forced this strategy to a halt. "Resist America!" the red dogs (that's just a metaphor) barked as their showdown with the CIDG in the mountains began.

Over the course of the summer, the red dogs' numbers dwindled to twenty, of which only eleven were assigned to the area around the seventeenth parallel, but they remained North Vietnam's most powerful ally on the ground.

They remained a symbol of Mao Zedong and Ho Chi Minh's friendship.

This was the situation in the DMZ and in Quang Tri. This was how matters stood in the northernmost reaches of the I Corps Tactical Zone. Offensive and defensive maneuvers were conducted aboveground; all kinds of other things went on belowground. The US military was determined to build the McNamara line, and the North Vietnamese Army just kept smashing it to pieces. It was almost as if the wall were being built expressly to be destroyed. Naturally the Vietcong were everywhere in the south, west, and east of the province, and they kept plugging along with their war of attrition. In essence, the US military had erected, here in this Buddhist land, to no good purpose, a hell whose flames the military itself was burning in.

And you were sent into those flames. You, DED, were given the command. Your ultimate goal was the complete and utter annihilation of the communists; the first step was to track them down. That was your mission. Yours, and the other nine dogs'. A specialized elite. You were told to keep track of the Vietcong as they slipped quietly into invisibility in the jungle, to search out the North Vietnamese special forces, and to follow them at a distance *without attacking*. As long as they could figure out where the bastards kept bubbling up from, they could get this chaos under control. And that was the whole purpose of your special training on Okinawa, right?

YES.

Well, then, show us what you can do.

Woof!

You were already accustomed to the environment. To the tropical terrain, the climate. And so, DED, they set you loose—you and your fellows. But...it was different. These thunderous explosions, the horrific smells, the artificial blasts of fire...Was this some kind of show?

You had been set loose. Ten of you. Into the faint miasma of tear gas sprayed somewhere in the distance, eddying through the air. A droning close by that assaulted your ears. Rockets and grenades whizzing overhead, the stuttering of machine guns, bullets sweeping over the ground, shrapnel, flying gunships. Ghastly odors. And there, infiltrators, commies—you'd found them. You pulled back fifty yards. One hundred yards. But you never, not for a moment, let them leave your sight. You pursued them. You kept going. Ten dogs heading, now, in ten different directions, each discovering a camouflaged entrance to the subterranean network of tunnels.

But were they real?

Each of you, one after another, poked your head in to see.

And here everything happened at once. You, DED, and each of three of your fellows, were suddenly approached from behind by another dog. These four new dogs weren't wearing collars. They didn't have tags. But they weren't wild. They simply weren't revealing their affiliations. They were red dogs with a terrible wealth of experience fighting real battles in the jungles of the Indochina peninsula. Yes, there behind each of you was another dog. Those other dogs attacked.

You were all driven into the holes.

You were anti-Vietcong specialists, yes, but you weren't fighting dogs. You knew how to deal with people and minefields, but no one had taught you what to do if you were set upon by another animal like this. And these weren't ordinary animals; these were creatures of the twentieth century, these were weapons. *Modern* weapons. And they were like you. Members of the *Carnivora* order and the *Canidae* family. Dogs.

You were driven down, underground.

As were your three fellows.

An officer in the North Vietnamese Army stood and watched through a pair of binoculars. Two dogs sat at his feet. Waiting, ready to go. Glancing down from the eyepiece, the officer gave the dogs a sign. "Lure them into the fourth layer! Or under the tiger trap!" he commanded. The two dogs, set loose, immediately dove into the well-hidden holes underground.

What of the other six dogs? Three were skewered with bamboo spears by commie sentries waiting inside the entrances to the tunnels and died instantly. Their bodies tumbled belowground, as if they had simply rolled into a deep, straight hole, disappearing as suddenly as the Vietcong themselves. One of the remaining three fell victim to an identical bamboo-spear attack but didn't die—was, rather, unable to die—and simply lay there yelping. Three minutes later its lungs filled with blood. It lay there wheezing. Each of the American dogs had been accompanied by an American soldier. Two of these soldiers were panicking. A second before, the dogs had been walking along a few dozen meters ahead—the soldiers usually watched their dogs through binoculars—and now all of a sudden they had disappeared, just like that, or in the case of the fourth dog, been transformed into a wheezer who lay writhing on the ground. Shit, they thought, they're here! Vietcong nests!

They put in a request for an air sweep to neutralize Vietcong forces.

Two dogs to go.

THESE LOOK LIKE VIETCONG HOLES, the dogs decided, and waited nearby. They stretched out on the ground as a sign to the soldiers following them that they had found something. And they listened to the earth. They heard a sound. Their fellows were being pursued. Their friends, down beneath the ground—BELOWGROUND? BUT HOW? HOW?—were being attacked.

And then the explosions came. One after the other, four grenades landed nearby. They had nothing whatsoever to do with the mission the ten dogs were engaged in—with their pursuit of the commies. But the shock inspired a split-second reaction. The two dogs instinctively leapt down into the holes they had discovered, into the network of tunnels.

A fighter aircraft appeared on the horizon. It was flying extremely low, dropping bombs with minute precision from under its wings. Air-to-surface missiles, ordinary bombs. This jet's bombing really was marvelously precise— excellent support. Only the areas in the sights, visible in the plane as the coordinates on a map, erupted into a spectacular display. Showtime! The earth crumbled, erupted, heaved, crashed. Fragments of bombs flew, scattered, mixed with ruthlessly torn-up clods of dirt that somersaulted through the air. And the burial began. The underground passageways caved in. The "Vietcong holes," targeted in a manner intended to cause minimal damage to the sur- roundings, were sealed off with almost unerring precision.

You were underground then, in the fourth layer.

You, DED, felt the first layer collapse.

Overhead.

For a moment, you lost consciousness. You and the red dogs—there had only been one in the beginning, but somewhere along the way a second had joined the chase—who had pursued you down from the second layer to the third, then finally to the fourth, slammed your heads against the tunnel's hard rock floor and earthen walls as the jolt of the explosion rocked it. This wasn't part of the limited bombing that had been requested. This was a separate battle that had started at the same time, and the offensive and defensive maneuvers associated with it would continue for three hours without rest on the ground, over a range of four thousand feet above and below the McNamara line. Two observation towers still under construction were toppled. More than seven hundred sandbags were catapulted into the air. An electrified fence, torn in places, zipped and zapped. Some thirty-three thousand cartridge cases were scattered. Soldiers' limbs were airborne, then dotted the ground. It was impos- sible to judge how many humans had been wounded, because of course there were left and right arms, and right and left legs. The earth itself was a wave transporting an unusual sort of surfer: the McNamara line, with the wooden barriers that had been built to conceal it as its surfboard.

Part of the earth, that is. A tidal wave.

The world crumbled.

And then, eventually, you awoke.

You had lost consciousness for only a moment, but the past was severed from the present. Did you know what had happened, DED? You'd been buried inside the earth. The entrance—which is to say, from your perspective, the exit—had been closed. Not all the entrances/exits to the vast network of underground tunnels, of course, but all the entrances/exits to the fourth layer, where you were. Just a few moments ago, there had been two vertical openings through which you could drop down into, or climb up out of, the fourth layer. Only two. Now there were none.

Part of the first layer had crumbled. This caused the collapse of the second and the third. And then.

The vertical openings were closed. Lost.

So three dogs were buried alive in the ground in the general area of the seventeenth parallel north, the DMZ, in the fourth layer.

Not just in the ground, but under it.

Three dogs, not just you. That fact would soon become clear.

You awoke.

In the beginning, there was darkness. AM I BLIND? You had just suffered a concussion and your judgment was unsound, you became anxious. But no, DED, you weren't blind. You were in a place that rendered your eyes useless. Pain wracked your body. You had been bashed, you were covered with scrapes. OH, IT HURTS, IT HURTS, you whimpered. And your whimpering echoed off the rock floor and the hard walls of packed earth. OOOHHH, it echoed. IIT HHUURRTTSS, IIT HHUURRTTSS. You had no way of knowing this at the time, but over the next few weeks you would acquire more and more of these bruises. WHERE AM I? you thought. WHAT AM I?

IIIT HHHUUURRRTTTSSS! your echo said.

After that, you kept quiet.

There were enemies.

In the beginning there was darkness, and then there were your enemies. I'M UNDERGROUND, you recalled. AND I'M AN AMERICAN DOG. AN ELITE. I'M PROUD OF WHAT I AM.

Your enemies, too, kept quiet.

You caught a whiff of something awful. Your eyes might be useless, but you were still a dog. Your nose rendered you omniscient. After all, you weren't just any dog, you came from a special line of German shepherds that was the pride of the US military, and you had gone through a rigorous screening process in California, and then again on Okinawa. I'M A TOP-CLASS MILITARY DOG! I'M THE PRIDE OF AMERICA! Something stank. Two enemy dogs.

IT'S THEM.

THE SAME KIND. GERMAN SHEPHERDS.

Two of them.

Something stank. You knew what it was. One of them was injured. One of them. And the other…was frightened? But it wasn't simply frightened of you. The evolving situation itself had stunned that red dog. But such excuses were meaningless. The point was that from that moment on, the two dogs dropped into the weaker position. And you, as a result, ascended to the anti-weak position.

You had power now.

Their fear empowered you. You: DED.

You bristled with a murderous strength. They moaned. Both of them.

Incapable of enduring the silence any longer, they started barking. ARE YOU FRIGHTENED?

YOU…ANTI-AMERICAN DOGS.

Next you attacked them. You did it in a flash, with no warning. In no time at all you had closed the distance between you and them, taken aim at the wounded dog, buried the deadly weapons in your jaw into its flesh. The other dog scampered away, crouched in a posture that made a counterattack unthinkable, its tail literally between its legs. You didn't pursue. This was a strategic decision. You were unaccustomed to this darkness. This closed network of tunnels was a whole new world. You mustn't be rash.

EXPLORE, you told yourself. FIGURE THIS PLACE OUT.

Unsteadily, uncertainly, you began. This world had only just been born.

A step forward. Ten steps forward. Three forks in the tunnel. It took an hour to get that far. You returned to where you had started. The dog you had toppled wasn't yet completely dead. It was teetering at the edge of death, but still breathing.

You lay down beside it to rest.

And then?

Two hours had passed, and you were worn out. You were getting hungry. There was nothing to eat. Where was the food?

There.

You could eat that, right?

You tore into the red dog's stomach. You made that last breath he had taken his last breath. In the beginning there was darkness, and then there were your enemies. And then you were hungry. And so you did it.

This was a world with new rules. You became a moral being. Yes, DED. You consumed the body. Flesh of your flesh. You couldn't have grasped it, but that meat was…a distant relative. A pure German shepherd that traced its ancestry back to Bad News.

And so you lived, and you had one less enemy.

You hadn't yet noticed that five of your fellows had ended up underground as well. They, too, had no way out. And more enemy dogs as well: six in all, including the two the officer in the North Vietnamese Army had ordered into the tunnels. Except that now one of those red dogs was gone.

Six vs. five.

What's going on here? What is this?

Sino-American conflict. The direct confrontation that both sides had been avoiding was now taking place, here on the Indochina peninsula. Happening on the ground—indeed, not just on the ground but under it, several layers down. A Vietnam War of the dogs.

The next day—although there was really no basis for speaking of one day or the next as there was nothing to mark the passage of time—you discovered one of your fellows. She was dead. She had stumbled into a tiger trap. This was a brutal sort of contraption consisting of sharp bamboo spears angled up from the bottom of a hole, meant to kill "American imperialists." There were a few in the fourth layer that targeted the US military's underground combat specialists, so-called "tunnel rats," who would be lured in and disposed of.

Five vs. five.

You inspected the tiger trap. Not by sight, since you could hardly see anything. By sniffing and touching. And then you hauled your fellow's body up out of the trap, one chunk at a time, and ate it.

Over the course of the next year, the remaining dogs dedicated themselves to a slow process of subtraction. Four vs. five. Four vs. three. Two vs. two. On average, one dog died every two months. In the second week, DED, you and your fellows came together to form a pack. Your enemies did the same. Some dogs were able to adapt to this sunless new world, and some dogs were not. The red dogs, the Chinese dogs whose affiliation had been concealed, had already acquired a close familiarity with the network of tunnels—they remembered its structure; carried, as it were, a mental map in their heads—and so they realized that the entrances/exits to the fourth layer had been closed off, and they despaired. Or else they were thrown into confusion by the shock of what had happened. THE MAIN TUNNEL THAT HEADS OFF TO THE RIGHT HAS COL-LAPSED! AND SUDDENLY A BRANCH...THERE'S A NEW BRANCH HEADING OFF TO THE LEFT! You and your fellows knew nothing of this loss. You were not tormented by the anguish that consumed your enemies. You knew it: THERE IS THE FIRST STEP. ALWAYS, ALWAYS. Again and again you pounded this instinct into your brain. You took one step at a time, and before you knew it you had taken ten steps, a hundred steps. YOU UNDERSTAND? you asked your fellows. GO ON, BUT GO CAREFULLY, you commanded your fellows.

And fairly early on, you discovered a storeroom. Preserved food the com-mies had stashed away. The cave held enough to keep you alive for a few weeks down there, underground—besieged, as it were. Enough, perhaps, for a few dogs to survive for a few weeks. But how many? The North Vietnamese Army and the Vietcong, incidentally, had left the fourth layer untouched for almost a year, ever since the attack the previous summer, assuming it was beyond salvage. And intense combat continued along the McNamara line, rendering it impossible to dig down again. As long as the first and second lay-ers remained functional, they decided, thinking strategically, those two layers would have to suffice. And this strategy affected the dogs too, as they fought their own Vietnam War. The supplies hadn't been gathered in one place in the fourth layer, of course; they were dispersed. There were a few of these caves. And just as you, DED, and your fellows had found a storeroom, so too had the enemy pack. Right around the same time. So you were even. You had equal portions. And so a territorial dispute began.

How did you mark off your realms of influence?

You were dogs, so you claimed space with your scents.

The front lines were the areas covered with your piss and shit. And through the process of marking the ground, you created your own canine military map. Here, in this still new world, in the fourth layer, deep underground, coordinates were organized in terms, not of latitudes and longitudes, but of shititudes and pissitudes. In those terms—carefully, ever so carefully—you grasped the contours of a place that rendered vision useless. Scent spoke eloquently, telling you, for instance, that war had been declared. Or that the enemy was constrained. It was all on the map. An ambush was planned at a certain location. And then there was the canine version of a search-and-destroy mission. The deadly struggle continued. How many bruises did you acquire? Not only from your explorations, but from grappling with the enemy, and from overhead, the repeated cave-ins. You kept adapting, though. Your right front leg was bent, yes—you had broken a bone and there were no splints down here. So WHAT? You had power. Your enemies' fear had empowered you, and you had been emboldened ever since. Needless to say, you were the leader of your pack. BEAT THEM BACK! you shouted. KILL THE ANTI-AMERICAN DOGS!

Attack. Defend. Strengthen defenses. Turn danger to victory. Attack and win.

A canine Vietnam War.

Pure subtraction.

You acquired a sixth sense, suited to the new world in which you lived. It can't be named. The point is that you adapted. Not all your fellows could. Not all your enemies could. One dog turned to skin and bones. Another went mad at seven o'clock on the seventh day of the seventh week. He barked ferociously, endlessly, and was mauled by the other dogs, had both his eyes gouged out and one ear and his tail torn off, yet he managed to survive seventeen more weeks. You lapped water from a pool, listening to him howl hoarsely in a very distant sector of the map. There were springs. In the floor, in the walls. In the deepest regions of certain paths. You had been aware of the underground stream's rumbling for a long time. Your nose caught the faintest whiff, almost an illusion, of the South China Sea. No, it wasn't your nose, it was that unnameable sixth sense. You sensed the motion of the tide. There was water and disease. One dog came down with scabies. There was diarrhea. Colds. Avitaminosis. There were all kinds of worms and insects and parasites, and though some could cause illness—one of the parasites had caused the scabies—some of those creatures that came wriggling out of the earth were rare delicacies. They were fresher than the preserved foods. Naturally, DED, you took the initiative in trying them. To LIVE, you told yourself. LIVE, you told your fellows. DIE, you told your enemies.

Sometimes you waited motionless for moles and mice to emerge from their holes.

A few times, your new world was visited by catastrophe brought on by the human Vietnam War raging aboveground. One day a storehouse in the second layer, crammed full of munitions the North Vietnamese Army and the Vietcong shared, caught fire and exploded. This changed the terrain of your world. Made it even more complex, into a labyrinth of new branches. This happened once, then again, a third time.

But you, DED, you were alive.

The subtraction continued until, a year later, it was one vs. one.

You had no way of knowing the time or the season, living underground, but it was summer. Summer 1968.

And suddenly, subtraction became addition.

There came a point when you realized that all your fellows were gone, and simultaneously that only one of your enemies was left. A moment later, you were prepared to shift gears, to make the switch to addition. Yes, you grasped what had happened, didn't you? You did indeed. Here in this new world, which was no longer new—here in the fourth layer, underground, in the general area of the seventeenth parallel north, on the border between North and South Vietnam, only two dogs remained. One was you, and the other…? That smell…that odor?

A bitch.

In the beginning there was darkness, and then there were your enemies.

Then came hunger. You killed your enemies, ate them, became the embodiment of your name. And then…you were seized by desire.

You lusted. The new world was populated by one male and one bitch. And you knew what was happening. I HAVE TO LIVE, you thought. To live. What did that mean? It was a matter of lineage, its continuation. Your…family tree. So your instinct for self-preservation kicked in, issued a command. DED, get hard.

The underground war was over. It was time to take the bitch.

Don't kill her.

There was food. Enough for two dogs, now that there were only two, to survive at least a few months. You began sending signals. Signs in shit and piss, barks, whispers. COME TO ME, you said. COME, THE WAR IS OVER.

This is the reconciliation, you announced.

And she felt the difference. You, in turn, understood, by means of your unnameable sixth sense, that she had understood.

You came together. In your storeroom. On your—American—territory. I'M THE ONLY MALE LEFT, you barked. THERE'S ENOUGH FOOD, WE HAVE WHAT WE NEED, you barked. THE TIME HAS COME TO MATE.

WE WILL BE THE ORIGIN OF THIS WORLD.

Did she understand your words?

Three days later, the red dog was wet, in heat. For the first time, this "anti-American dog" as you had thought of her, last among her fellows, grew wet between her legs. She had eaten her fill in the storeroom on your—American—territory, running in, rooting around, sleeping, waking, and running in again, spreading food around with her nose as she gobbled it down, sleeping, waking, making a mess, and then, finally, she was ready, she assumed the position. You were ready, you were hard. You straddled her. You were on top of her, panting, shaking your butt.

Not once.

Twice.

A third time.

The bitch was obedient.

Your sperm dribbled from between her legs. Your seed.

You were calm again.

And then, five days after you and the bitch met up, late at night—late at night aboveground, that is, and in Vietnam—you were murdered in your sleep. You had your testicles bitten off and your throat ripped open.

You died.

Just like that.

Yes, DED, you were dead.

From here on out, it was the bitch's story. She wouldn't let the body of a fellow dog go to waste. She tore into it with her fangs. It was warm. She gobbled down the liver, the spleen. She took mouthfuls of the meat. She lapped the still uncoagulated blood. Because she required it. She needed the nutrition. Lots of it—vitamins, minerals, proteins, everything. Because she had a litter of puppies growing inside her.

The bitch knew by some unnameable sixth sense. That she was pregnant. She had to prepare. She readied herself to give birth.

Nine weeks passed. Thumps came from overhead, from the layer above, even though it was supposedly closed off. She ignored them. The North Vietnamese Army and the Vietcong had begun redeveloping the network of tunnels. The bitch kept silent, however, so that her former masters wouldn't find her. She wasn't a red dog anymore, she was a mother. A mother dog preparing to give birth for the first time. Her instincts told her everything to do. Find a quiet place and hide. Ignore the humans, all you need is food. Forget the humans. Turn your back on humanity.

The mother dog obeyed these commands.

She kept a low profile, there underground.

Labor pains began. Then, at last, the delivery. A slimy, half-transparent bag slithered out as she pushed. Then a second, a third, a fourth, a fifth, a sixth. One after another, slowly. Three of the pups were dead. The bitch ate the afterbirth, as all mother dogs do, and she ate her dead children too.

Three puppies had been born alive.

She began raising them. But she had problems suckling them. She didn't have much milk. Two of the puppies grew weak. Again the mother's instincts kicked in. She didn't hesitate at all. She bit into the weaker puppies, killing them.

And ate their bodies.

One puppy.

He sucked powerfully at her teats.

He lived. He was healthy, strong. He, DED, was your child. A male with no name. He did not inherit your name, and he would not eat the flesh of his flesh. Even when his mother died. This was in February 1969. The puppy was no longer suckling. He didn't eat the body. Instead he imitated his mother's actions when she had been alive. He ate the food she had brought to the cave where he had been born, their nest.

His mother's body rotted, stank.

AWFUL, the nameless puppy thought. The stench grew worse with every passing day until at last it drove him away. He would go. You see, DED, how clever your son is? He wandered quietly, secretly, through the fourth layer. There was a need for secrecy—he knew this from his mother's actions, he had figured it out. It wouldn't come as a surprise to you, DED, even on the other side, to learn that the labyrinth of tunnels and branches had been completely transformed. There were new passageways, and others that had been closed off. All the paths too narrow for humans to pass through had been abandoned. But if you were a puppy? Could they be used? Yes, they could. And so the fourth layer was now connected to the third, and so to the second, and to the first.

You would have been impressed by your son's intimate knowledge of the map's coordinates. He had grasped it all. He appeared and vanished without warning in this "new new world," faster even than the humans.

Yes, he was fine.

Relax, no need to worry.

You need not linger.

Spring came and the nameless puppy was growing healthily. He was an orphan, but he had never suffered from hunger. He knew well where in the network of tunnels he could find food, and what it was safe to take. He knew everything. Everything relating to this world, that is. But he wasn't satisfied with this…this routine, with no aim beyond survival. At this early stage in life, he placed no stock in omniscience. He wanted the unknown.

It was this, the things he had never experienced, that called to him. And so, even as he surpassed the humans, he spied on their doings. Explored the new munitions storeroom they had dug. The cave next to the underground kitchen, where they kept live chickens that began laying eggs day after day. When an operating room was added to the underground hospital after a medical unit was sent down from Hanoi, he tried to get as close as possible to the astonishing thing they had in there: a light bulb powered by a bicycle-powered generator that the surgeons used when they operated. He was doing all kinds of things, seeing all kinds of things.

Early summer.

The nameless puppy began encountering difficulties. He was growing healthily…in fact, he was now fully grown. He was no longer a puppy, and he was no longer the size of a puppy. His body had filled out remarkably. But this bewildered him: how could the world have shrunk so? The narrow paths that led in and out of the fourth layer were now impassable.

WHAT'S HAPPENED? the nameless dog asked himself in his frustration.

He shouted, IT'S TOO TIGHT! EVERYTHING IS TOO CLOSE!

This circumscribed world didn't satisfy him. It wasn't enough. He didn't feel fulfilled. And he started losing track of his coordinates, which made it difficult to keep hidden. Everything had changed, his measurements were all wrong! He was no longer omniscient, he realized that. So what was he to do? *What?*

He was approaching an answer.

First there was the fourth layer. Then there was the third. Then he found the second and finally the first. He kept probing the network of tunnels for things he didn't know. And at last…at last…

Summer. He was crawling through the first tunnel. It stank. It stank. He crawled. He kept crawling and crawling. He forgot all the coordinates he had carried in his head. WHO CARES, he thought. WHO CARES ANYWAY! His body tingled with a heightened sensitivity. An unnameable sense growled within him. He was biting through to something new. Which way had he come, which branches had he chosen? Which forks in which paths had he entered? It didn't matter, he was being led on. By a voice. You, nameless dog.

A nameless sense dispensed its commands to you, a nameless dog. The voice spoke to you. And you heard it, didn't you?

To live. Live. Live at the edge of starvation. Hunger to live.

YES, you replied. YES, YES, YES.

Woof!

At last, nameless dog, you, too, barked.

Unsatisfied, you set out, beyond the confines of the world you knew by smell. You sniffed, inhaled the odors, searching for the unfamiliar. Finally, you crawled out aboveground. Your fixation on the unknown had made it happen. The smell of grass, undergrowth, moss on a stone, a dangling vine. It was hot. That's what it was like up there. On the Indochina peninsula, in the tropics, just above the seventeenth parallel north. You had emerged into North Vietnamese territory, outside the DMZ. The exit from the network of tunnels, incidentally, was a camouflaged wooden trap door of the same sort used at crucial junctures underground, so you knew how it worked. You scratched at it, broke through. There was no sentry on guard. You pressed forward over a terrain devoid of humans, devoid of any trace of humanity, and you were out. You stood there, dazed.

WHAT IS ALL THIS? EVEN THE SOIL SMELLS DIFFERENT?

IT'S ALL SO DIFFERENT!

You were moved. The scent in your nostrils was the earth baked by the sun. But it wasn't daytime now. When you emerged from that cramped world, it was the dead of night.

July 1969.

The moon was out. You turned to look at it. It was dazzling. This was nothing else, only moonlight, but for you, born and raised underground, it might as well have been as bright as the sun. You had seen the Vietnamese doctor's light in the tunnels, so your eyes were familiar with illumination. They had been educated by the bulb in the operating room, and they had felt awed by its vivid round glow. But the moon hovering up there in the sky... this was different. The shock of it was altogether different. You were moon-struck. Any number of stars twinkled in the sky along with the moon, but it was the moon that got you. An American reconnaissance plane carrying an infrared camera flew by, but you were enchanted by the moon.

That summer, humans, too, found their gazes drawn to the same celestial body. The whole world was focused on the moon that season, because the US National Aeronautics and Space Administration had launched Apollo 11 and, for the first time in human history, landed a man on the moon. That was the human world, though, not the dog world. Dogs had been the ones to open the door to space travel, but now the man-made satellite Sputnik 2 was all but forgotten. Twelve years had passed since then.

The human twentieth century continued, that summer, as though Anno Canis didn't exist.

You cried.

Nameless, gazing straight up at the moon, you were pained. Your eyes hurt. You had been born underground, where vision was useless, and the moonlight was too strong for you. Tears welled in your eyes. Tears fell. But you didn't look away.

You kept staring up at the moon, overwhelmed.

You sensed something behind you.

You turned around. Your eyesight still blurred by tears.

It was a human. He held a night vision device in one hand and a military map in the other. He was different from all the other humans you had seen… spied on…so far. There was a difference in race—in build, in odor—but of course that meant nothing to a dog like you. You were on the edge of a firebase to the north of the DMZ, an area that was on the front lines but which had been cleared of North Vietnamese soldiers.

You were unsure how to react.

Because instinct told you there was no need to run.

WHAT IS…WHAT…?

You, nameless dog, were at a loss. How could a human do what he was doing, stand there opposite you as he was, in the darkness?

The human spoke: "Are you crying?"

His voice sounded like a dog's whine. It radiated through your body with the same warmth as the commands the unnameable sense issued. You had no way of knowing, of course, but the language the man spoke was not

Vietnamese. Neither was it Chinese. Or English.

WHAT IS IT, HUMAN?

"I saw you," the human said. Then, holding up the night vision device, "I saw you with this. Crawling up out of the ground. Like the earth was giving birth to you. You were looking up at the moon."

ARE YOU A GUIDE? you thought, your vision clouded with tears. A GUIDE TO THIS OTHER WORLD?

"You're the opposite of those dogs who returned from outer space. But not unrelated. And look at that physique of yours...you're purebred, huh? Purebred German shepherd? You don't look that old either. Young, in fact. You've just graduated from puppyhood."

HEY, HUMAN, you say. THIS IS A GREAT, MYSTERIOUS WORLD.

"Strange...are you an American dog?"

I CAME ABOVEGROUND.

"They set you loose in the tunnels to explore them in secret, and you got lost—is that it? No, it can't be. You don't have that kind of attitude at all. Are you Chinese, then? One of the dogs in that platoon they talk about, the one they say the PLA sent in four years ago? No...that's not right either."

YOU WERE HERE.

"Anyway, I was here, and then you turned up," the human said. He spoke the same words, dog, nameless dog, that you yourself had just said. Not in Vietnamese, or in Chinese, or even in English. In Russian.

"Come. I'll take you with me. Can your children be the next Belka, the next Strelka?"

The KGB officer held out his hands, and you barked. *Woof!*

In March 1969, the Sino-Soviet split finally escalated into armed conflict. The two armies exchanged serious gunfire in the area around Zhenbao, aka Damansky Island, in the Ussuri River, on the border between the nations. In June a similar border dispute broke out along the edge of Xinjiang Province, and in July the same thing happened around Bacha Island, aka Gol'dinskii, in the Heilong River. The participants in the conflicts were always border guard troops. The tension had been building for some time. In 1967, as China was pressing ahead with the Great Cultural Revolution, the Red Guard attacked the Russian Embassy in Beijing. They set fire to effigies of Soviet leaders. A more offensive demonstration would not have been possible. And did this shift in Sino-Soviet relations have an effect on the Vietnam War? Of course. As if the Vietnam War weren't already chaotic enough. In June 1965, the USSR and the Democratic Republic of Vietnam signed two agreements concerning "free Soviet aid in the development of the national economy of the DRV" and "strengthening the DRV's defensive capabilities." Just one month after the PLA marched through Friendship Pass to provide secret aid to Ho Chi Minh's Vietnam, the Soviet Union and Vietnam were building a new relationship. Ho's health went into a decline that year, and the party secretary took control. The USSR exploited this shift to try, in a variety of ways, to chip away at the Sino-Vietnamese friendship. During the first half of the Vietnam war—America's quagmire—the world's two great communist powers were in fact engaged in a tug-of-war, each trying to attract that small communist country, North Vietnam, to their side. In the end, Vietnam chose the USSR.

History revealed itself almost prophetically. On September 3, 1969, Ho Chi Minh died. Just like that, the personal relationship he and Mao Zedong had cherished was over. And by then Vietnam had already made its move. It chose to leave China, move closer to the USSR. Fully fifty percent of the aid that poured into North Vietnam from communist countries in 1968 came from the Soviet Union. This aid didn't only take the form of weapons; the USSR actually put feet on the ground. It sent military advisors to the Indochina peninsula, to the front. The series of "Sino-Soviet conflicts" in March and June 1969 led the Soviets to include a large number of officers from the Border Guard among these specialists. The men on the ground weren't only specialists in fighting, they were specialists in fighting and maneuvering against China.

And so a certain Russian KGB officer found his way, that summer, to that spot.

Or could it be…that it was *your* history, dogs, that called him there?

Could it be?

Dogs, dogs, where will you bark next?

Woof, woof!

1975: one dog was in Hawaii, one was in Mexico. To be precise: one bitch was on the island of Oahu, at the twenty-first parallel north, and one male was in Mexico City, at the twentieth parallel north. Their names were Goodnight and Cabron. Goodnight was a purebred German shepherd; Cabron was a mongrel whose father had been a purebred boxer—who had sprung, that is to say, from boxer seed. Goodnight's origins have already been discussed. Her brother, DED, died in 1968, underground, on the Indochina peninsula, at the seventeenth parallel north. His neck had been torn open by a dog belonging to the PLA Military Dog Platoon, a dog descended from Jubilee. Jubilee had been the aunt of Goodnight and DED's great-great-great-grandfather, five generations earlier. Okay. What of Cabron, the mutt in Mexico City? Where did he spring from?

It's complicated.

Cabron wasn't descended from Bad News. But if you were to trace his line back through his mother's side, you would find that, in a way, he was directly descended from Bad News. Four generations earlier, Cabron's great-great-grandmother had had six maternal aunts and uncles. Cabron's great-great-grandmother's mother and her six siblings—a litter of seven in total, each dog entirely different in appearance from the rest—had basked in the love of two mothers. The first was their birth mother. She had suckled them for the first half month of their lives. Their second mother was the one who raised them. She, too, had suckled them for a few weeks, until the time came for them to be weaned off her milk. Their birth mother's pregnancy with them had been her fourth. Her name was Ice; her father had been a Hokkaido dog, her mother was a Siberian husky, and one of her grandmothers had been a Samoyed. The Hokkaido dog was Kita, of course. Their adoptive mother had given birth several times before she took charge of the seven puppies, but after that she never gave birth again. She was a lovely purebred German shepherd, and her name was Sumer. She was Bad News's child.

And she was Jubilee's sister.

Sumer became the mother of the seven puppies Ice had given birth to in

1957. Year zero Anno Canis. In October of that year, the mother and her children had entered the area around the Mexican-American border. They had been brought in to serve as guard dogs on the property of a certain prominent Mexican-American who ran an orchard there. That wasn't all this man ran, though: the Don, as they called him, was the head of a family with another, secret face. He was the boss of a criminal organization that specialized in smuggling. His partners in business all lived on the other side the border, to the south...in Mexico. Or at least they did in the 1950s. Time passed. By now the Don was the old Don, and Sumer had lived out her allotted years. What happened to the prominent family's secret trade? And what happened to the dogs?

First, their trade. In the 1970s, the old-style mafia, with its ideal of "rustic chivalry," was in the process of collapse. A new generation of underworld organizations was coming to the fore, attempting to supplant their predecessors, and among these the most prominent were those that dealt in "dirty" businesses such as the drug trade. The prominent Mexican-American family, having itself experienced a changing of the guard, rode that wave. The new Don was a man of the new generation. He had thoroughly revised the family's business operations, identifying drugs as the principal source of their future income. By 1975, he had grown the organization's total business dealings to a figure eight times what it had been two decades before. They controlled about half the inflow of drugs from south of the border. Indeed, it was the enormous investment of capital this family had made during the 1960s that had allowed the Mexican drug cartels to expand in the first place.

They were known in the underworld as Texas's "La Familia."

Next, the dogs. The dogs were used as tokens to strengthen the bonds between members of La Familia. The first eight—Sumer and her seven puppies—had understood this from the moment they were presented to the old Don. They had to shine as guard dogs and to pledge their unfailing loyalty to the Don. Their old owner, the man with the boxcar in the switchyard where Sumer had made their nest, the man who sent them off to work in La Familia's orchard, had commanded them to do their best, and they had. The Don was pleased to see how seriously they took their work, how loyal they were. This was the kind of dog La Familia needed. And so he treasured them. He didn't let them mate with just any dog. He only "wed" them to purebred Dobermans, collies, Airedale terriers—proven animals, with personalities, looks, and the skill set a good guard dog needed. The seven siblings had looked completely different from one another to begin with, and as they continued to mate they produced a monstrous elite. Dogs have, on occasion, been referred to as "shape-shifters" because the various breeds look so different, and the dogs in this lineage pushed that potential to the limit. Not all of them were involved in this, however. Even as a few of the dogs were carefully mated with the cream of the crop—with Dobermans, collies, and Airedale terriers who could accurately be described as "totally the best, Don"—a few others remained under strict guard, a sort of birth control.

Why?

Because, as has already been said, the dogs had a role to play in strengthening the bonds among members of La Familia. For the most part, they remained within the boundaries of the orchard. But whenever a new member "joined the family," so to speak—joined the Texas-based criminal organization La Familia—he would be presented with a dog. This living gift had become the custom in the 1950s with the old Don, and the current Don inherited it. Only the men who had been granted one of the dogs from this special line belonged to La Familia's inner circle. Only they had been recognized by the Don as "family."

The dogs were the evidence of this.

The dogs showed that La Familia was as tight as family.

And here we come to Cabron. A male dog, great-great-great-grandson of one of the seven dogs Sumer had adopted. He was living, now, far from La Familia's orchard on the Mexican-American border, far to the south of La Familia's territory, in Mexico City.

One dog on the twentieth parallel north.

One dog in Mexico.

And the other, on the twenty-first parallel north.

Goodnight. What were you up to?

You never went to the Indochina peninsula, to the seventeenth parallel north. Having done a fine job during his six weeks of special training on Okinawa, your brother DED was sent into the midst of the Southeast Asian conflict as a specialist anti-Vietcong fighter. You, however, had failed to make the cut. You had been judged unfit for service on the front lines of the Vietnam War, and in June 1967, you left Okinawa for Hawaii. At the time, incidentally, Okinawa was under the administration of the US government. The Hawaiian Islands, for their part, had been annexed in 1898 and were elevated to the status of a full-fledged state in 1959. These historical developments meant nothing at all to you, Goodnight, but the point is this: you were born on the American mainland, in California, and you were raised and had lived your life until then as an American military dog, moving from place to place within the vast expanse of "America." You had never passed beyond its borders. Not yet. You had been sent to Oahu, where you worked at Wheeler Air Force Base as a sentry dog for approximately eight years. In all that time, you had been exposed to real stress on only one occasion: the day you had come face to face with a spy of unknown provenance, and you were shot. The bullet passed right through you, and you completely healed in three weeks. You had, however, saved a human life, and so you came away from the trauma with the canine version of two medals: a purple heart and a silver star. This meant you were assured a lifetime pension (money for food) even after your retirement. The man whose life you saved was a lieutenant on security patrol; you had taken the bullet trying to protect him.

After that, you were respected by everyone on the base, not only the humans but the other dogs as well—you did have two medals, after all—and your life as a sentry dog became even more relaxed than it had been.

That was how you passed the eight years since June 1967.

And then it was *the year*. 1975. It began in February. At long last, you were released from your position as a military dog. You were retired. A family had volunteered to take you in. They lived in the suburbs of Honolulu. The father was a retired officer—the very man whose life you had saved. That same lieutenant. Or rather, that same former lieutenant. He himself had retired from military duties when he turned forty—just six months earlier— and now worked in tourism. He was originally a mainland *haole*, but during his time on Wheeler Base he had fallen in love with Hawaii and decided to settle permanently on Oahu. He would start out fresh here—it would be a whole new life. He moved his elderly parents from Ohio to live with him. They had kept a young dog as a pet, a bitch. Naturally, she made the move from Ohio as well. Then, finally, he had brought you in. You completed the picture.

"Here we are," the former lieutenant said. "This is your family."

MY FAMILY? you thought. Looking up, you saw four faces: a human, a human, a human, and a dog.

The other dog was a beagle. She had a compact build and an extremely mild disposition. She sensed immediately that your master felt indebted to you and didn't try to challenge you.

Yes, you were the dog that had saved your master's life. And for that reason, your old age, your retirement, should have been as placid and peaceful as it gets. One hundred percent stress-free. You had no title, you were just an old German shepherd. But although you were nine years old, you were still vigorous. Your family played with you a lot. You did a lot of sightseeing. The former lieutenant, thinking to repay you for what you had done, took you all over Oahu. You walked through Waikiki with your aloha-shirted master. From the beach into town. From the backstreets to the canal. The scents of Chinatown bewildered you. All those Asian spices, the mounds of Chinese medicines in the market. You climbed to the tip of Diamond Head crater, 232 meters above sea level. You visited Pearl Harbor. And you saw something. You gazed at the chalk-white memorial. It was out in the harbor, just over the remains of the USS *Arizona*, submerged twelve meters in the muck. The battleship had been sunk by a Japanese plane on December 7, 1941. That had inaugurated the Pacific War. A surprise attack by the Japanese military. To this day, the bodies of 948 men lie sleeping within the body of that battleship on the sea floor. The boat is a grave. You gazed at the grave, Goodnight, at the sea that was a grave, and you felt nothing. You were staring out at the place from which your history, the history of your tribe, had begun. But you felt nothing.

It never occurred to you that it was all on account of the battleships that sank there that three Japanese military dogs and one American military dog had been thrown together on the Aleutian Islands, in the Arctic regions of the Pacific.

You were near the middle of the Pacific now.

And all you thought, there on an island located at the twenty-first parallel north, was How BEAUTIFUL THE OCEAN IS.

You liked the sea.

You liked the beach.

You were always frolicking at the water's edge.

In April, something changed in your family. It emerged that the young beagle was pregnant. She had been knocked up somewhere, probably in that holy land of doggie free sex: the leash-less park. In May, the beagle gave birth to four healthy pups. And you, Goodnight, found the sight incredibly moving. You had never had puppies of your own, but still you found the little ones irresistible. You helped the beagle raise them, as if you and she were sisters, maybe cousins. Naturally, you were careful not to go too far, to do anything that would be too much for their mother. But they were adorable! Your maternal instincts cried out within you: How CUTE! How ADORABLE!

Beagle puppies milling about their beagle mother's teats.

You couldn't nurse them yourself since you had no milk, but you were enthralled.

When you weren't helping to look after the puppies, you played on the beach. In July, you discovered something unusual on the one you frequented most often. A boat. A double canoe. It had two masts, two sails, and it was a little less than twenty meters long. It was totally different from an ordinary canoe.

Humans, both haole and pure Hawaiians, had clustered around the double vessel and were learning how to operate it. They came back the next day and the day after that, and since the beach had essentially become part of your territory, you watched them as they worked. You mingled with the people, wandering among them. When a man patted you on the head, you licked his hand. Good dog, he said. Good dog, they said, again and again. They remembered you, just as you had remembered them.

"You know what I heard," one haole announced to the party in English. "Seems this guy was a military dog! Heard it from his owner. Could have knocked me over with a feather! He's got two medals. Real medals! He had a showdown with a spy, and the spy shot him, and he didn't even flinch. Incredible, huh?"

Wow! Cool! the humans cried. In recognition of your distinguished career, they let you onto the boat. The view from there was amazing. You stood at the prow.

The people could see you liked it.

Then one day in September, one of the crew members, excited, called out, "C'mon, girl!" He was inviting you to accompany them on a short practice sail, just forty or fifty minutes. The time had come. *Woof!* you barked. And you jumped up with them.

You weren't at all afraid.

Indeed, you were excited to see another face of the sea.

You didn't get seasick.

The peculiar double canoe was the embodiment of a dream. An embodiment of the thrill of the Hawaiian renaissance and its effort to revive ancient Hawaiian culture. The West had its first encounter with the Hawaiian Islands in 1778 when the explorer James Cook landed there in the course of one of his voyages, and from that point people puzzled over the question of how humans could possibly have reached the islands, which were completely isolated—set down plop in the middle of the Pacific Ocean, near no continent. And when Cook arrived, the Hawaiians didn't have the technology necessary to set out on long trips across the sea. What they had was a legend, an old chant that said, "Our ancestors came from Tahiti."

Tahiti was south of the equator.

Far, far away, in the South Pacific.

Could this be true?

A group of people decided to try and find out. Decided to demonstrate that before it was polluted and degraded by the influx of Western civilization, in its very earliest years, Hawaii had possessed a sophisticated culture of its own. The Polynesian Voyaging Society was founded in Hawaii in 1973. Its goal was to build a replica of a prehistoric Hawaiian voyaging canoe, and to sail it all the way to Tahiti. The project was intended as a sort of experimental archaeology. It was also an adventure. They would set out for the South

Pacific relying only on ancient navigation techniques, reading the position of the constellations, the wind, the tides.

In Hawaii, the Polynesian Voyaging Society project was made part of the US's bicentennial celebrations.

The boat you rode on its trial run, Goodnight, was not, however, the replica the Polynesian Voyaging Society had created.

It was a replica of the replica.

Secretly built in California, it had been transported to Oahu in July. The humans had gotten into a dispute. Since the techniques for navigating long sea voyages had not survived in Hawaii, a Micronesian—a man from Satawal, an atoll of the Central Caroline Islands—had been brought in to steer the vessel. There was a faction who disapproved. The first project was being led by a California-born surfer and professor of anthropology, but he had a competitor: a researcher who was jealous of him. Who was, in addition, a wealthy brat. At the same time, another navigator turned up asking to be chosen. He was a Polynesian from Rarotonga, one of the Cook Islands, and all he wanted was the fame.

Thus, a group of people angry with the Polynesian Voyaging Society made up their minds to break away, to try and beat the original adventurers at their own game.

Indeed, the wealthy researcher decided that he would go a step further and outdo the professor who made him insanely jealous. To crush him once and for all. Long ago, when the first sea voyagers immigrated en masse to Hawaii, they had taken twenty or thirty plant species along with them for cultivation. They had also taken pigs, intentionally, and rats, unintentionally. And chickens. And dogs.

At the time, the oldest dog fossils that had been unearthed on the Hawaiian Islands dated from sixteen hundred years earlier.

That was exactly when the ancient Polynesians were thought to have immigrated.

Well then, why not include that element in the experiment—in this essay in experimental archaeology? That would really prove that it could be done!

Yes, the wealthy researcher thought, stunned by the brilliance of his idea.

A *dog.*

Hey, dog!

This time you didn't bark in response to the call, you just cocked your head.

The wealthy researcher was moved, now, by the engine of his ambition. He knew a dog that wouldn't be afraid to cross the sea in a canoe. And the dog was a strong, healthy, purebred German shepherd. And it had gotten friendly with everyone on the project, the entire crew. And…and…

Your owner immediately agreed to let him have you. The negotiations occurred in October. "Are you serious? That's quite a promotion," the former lieutenant said. "He's really going to be an important player in this project, part of the great Hawaiian Renaissance?" The researcher assured him you would with a terse, "He will have that honor." And that was all it took to sell the former lieutenant. "Oh my god! Oh my god oh my god I can't believe it!" he yelled. "The honor! The glory! I was a military man, you know, and so was she! Well, she was a military dog. Honor above everything! Right? Isn't that right, girl?" he asked you. "Besides, she really likes to go out and enjoy the ocean. I'm sure she'll love it, I'm happy to let her go. What an adventure! Go out and bring us something back to show for it!" he told you. "A third medal! You know what I'm saying? You understand?"

Though your master didn't mention this, his family had grown too large. There were too many of you. The beagle's pregnancy had been entirely unexpected, and in the past six months the four puppies had grown almost into adult dogs. The family had been unable to find anyone to take them. That, ultimately, was what mattered. You were a burden, so he got rid of you. He didn't have to feel guilty, and he got a $500 reward to boot.

"I hear in Tahiti," your master told you at the end, "they're going to welcome you as a hero, back after 1,600 years, and you'll live out the rest of your life as a canine king."

October 11. You set out from Oahu. A crew of sixteen men and a dog sitting in the double canoe. You were riding the great, wide sea. You, Goodnight, were no longer a dog of the twenty-first parallel north. You were headed south of the equator. But the Polynesian navigator you were all counting on was, it turned out, a fraud who had only joined the crew to get his name in the newspapers. "If worst comes to worst," he thought, "someone will rescue us with whatever modern equipment they've got." He hadn't totally mastered the traditional navigation techniques, which were by then being passed down in Polynesia only in secret, to a select few. He was all bluster, just like the researcher. Still, when night fell the sixteen human members of the crew gazed up at the sky. They read the stars. During the day, they watched which way the birds flew. You, Goodnight, didn't look up at the blue sky; you kept your gaze trained rigidly on the flat horizon. By October 12, you were already growing homesick. You missed the little beagles. Those four puppies you had mothered, and whom you had kept caring for even after they were grown. Your teats tingled. Five pairs of teats that had never lactated.

1975. And the other dog—the male on the twentieth parallel north? Cabron, in Mexico City. He had acquired an alter ego. An alter ego that was simultaneously human and canine. But only when his face was covered; then, and only then, was this man transformed into a dogman. He was thirty years old, a *mestizo*, and they called him the Hellhound. That, at any rate, was the name he used in the ring. The Hellhound was a *luchador*.

The Hellhound was active in entertainment wrestling, known as *lucha libre*, "free fighting," a sport that had been practiced in Mexico since 1933.

Of course, he donned a dog mask in the ring and fought as a dogman. His special maneuvers were the Dog-Hold and the Dog-Bite, the latter delivered to the top of his opponent's head. He also did a torpedo kick called the St. Bernard.

The numeral two had a special meaning for the Hellhound. He had two faces, for instance: his outer and his inner face. In the 1970s, there were approximately two thousand *luchadores* in Mexico, seventy percent of whom wore masks. A certain number of these wrestlers maintained a policy of total secrecy and lived without revealing their true names or places of birth. The Hellhound was one of these. From the time of his debut, he had paid the company that created his mask a huge sum to keep all information regarding his countenance, his unmasked face, under wraps. Two faces: one outer, one inner. The vast majority of luchadores, eighty percent of whom also had other jobs, treated their everyday, unmasked faces as their public faces; the masks were the hidden identities they assumed only in the ring. The Hellhound was different. For him, the masked self, the dogman, was the public self.

The reason for this was obvious: he appeared without his mask, his ordinary face exposed, whenever he had underworld dealings. He had a position in one of the two cartels competing for domination in Mexico. And not just any position—the Hellhound was the boss. He had a special token to prove it. A dog. The dog on the twentieth parallel north. Yes, that's right, the mongrel Cabron was his. The Hellhound, in other words, was Cabron's alter ego. The Hellhound looked after Cabron—he owned Cabron, he was owned by Cabron—and so, for precisely that reason, he was acknowledged throughout the underworld, from North America all the way down into Central America, as an official member of La Familia. Texas's La Familia. *The family.*

Once again, two. Having an alter ego, being an alter ego.

What's more, the Hellhound was the second generation in his family to work in this business. He had taken over from his father, who had changed the course of his life. His father had been the first to initiate a relationship with La Familia, and he'd had his own dog. A mongrel the Don had given him. The dog's father—his seed, that is to say—had been a giant St. Bernard, incredibly brave, fabled throughout the region for having saved no fewer than seven lives. The Hellhound had been born in 1945; his father's dog joined the household in 1949. Almost as far back as the Hellhound could remember, the dog had been there. The Hellhound had loved to pet the dog, and he would ride him—he had gone in for dog-riding, you might say, not horse-riding— and he would sleep with his head pillowed on the dog's fluffy, roly-poly stomach, tug on his ears, and pet him some more. The Hellhound had hardly any childhood memories in which this dog did not figure. When he grew older, he used to grapple with the dog, pretending to fight. It was a sort of pseudo-wrestling and also a sort of pseudo-dogfighting. Dogfighting, incidentally, was big in Mexico too. As a boy, the Hellhound had never once managed to get the upper hand on his mongrel opponent. Of course not. The mongrel was a master. On the night of his seventh birthday, frisking around with the dog on the patio, he realized that he would never win. He shed tears of humiliation at his weakness, but at the same time he felt a new respect for the dog welling up within him. From now on, he decided, the dog really would be *his* master. *Master!*

Ever since he was a boy, the Hellhound had tended to run with his passions. If he wasn't as good as the dog, he would learn from the dog. And so his relationship with the mongrel La Familia had given his father deepened; the dog became his family, his teacher, his closest friend. It was during those days that he perfected his killer St. Bernard Kick. The Hellhound had always been an outstandingly physical child, ever since he was born, and he was always landing flying kicks in his classmates' stomachs at school whenever he flew into a rage. He'd been doing this since almost the first day, even attacking the older tough-guy types.

At the same time, going to school introduced a new worry into his life. Until then, he always assumed his family's business was perfectly above board, but now it began to dawn on him that the activities they were involved in were criminal. His classmates' parents weren't involved in organized crime. What? You mean we're doing *illegal* things? Drug dealing and stuff? Killing people? But…isn't that…isn't that *bad?* The boy began to be tormented by moral qualms. Then it was 1957. The year the dog died. The boy's family, teacher, and closest friend—gone. The boy was twelve, and it hit him hard. He felt as if a hole had opened up in his heart. He visited the local Catholic church every day to pray for the repose of the dog's soul. Then one Sunday three months after the dog's death, something happened. During the sermon. The pastor, as it happened, had spent the previous night with a cousin who had come up to the city from their hometown, and since the two men hadn't seen each other for four-and-a-half years, the pastor imbibed a bit too much tequila. So he wasn't doing too well. His voice, as he stood declaiming from the pulpit, was so toneless that most of the congregation started nodding off. The boy, too, felt himself falling under a sort of spell, as if he were succumbing to hypnosis. Only in his case, it wasn't hypnotism of the *You're getting very, very sleepy* type. He was having an actual hallucination. Hearing a mysterious message. First, he heard a voice. A male voice: "Hello? Hello? Hel-*low!*" It was an adult voice. What? Who is that? The boy glanced around the church, then froze. Up there behind the priest, a little to his right, at the rear of the pulpit, the statue of the crucified Christ was moving its lips. Their gazes met. And *BAM*, a bolt of spiritual lightning slammed through his body.

"Hey!" Jesus Christ's voice bellowed in his brain. "Don't you think you've got some things to take care of before you come here to pray for a dog? What about all this immorality you're part of? You gotta make amends for that stuff first!"

All at once, just like that, the boy felt the hole the dog's death had left in his heart close up, plugged by the wisdom he had been granted.

Whoosh. In it went, just like that.

Bear in mind that the Hellhound had always been unusually passionate. He was particularly susceptible to hallucinations. Physically prepared, you might say, to receive the word of God.

Age fourteen. The young man made his first appearance in the ring. He was a luchador now. He had spent the last two years training four hours daily, and expectations were high for this newcomer able to pull off impeccable high-flying moves. In Mexico, fourteen was not considered a young age to debut as a wrestler. And of course lucha libre was the preeminent form of popular entertainment. People watched, captivated, as the struggle between good and evil played itself out in the ring. Cheering for (or jeering at) the luchador who stood for goodness and jeering at (or cheering) the luchador who stood for evil offered a means of letting out the stress that accumulated in day-to-day life. Wrestling was a world of fantasy. And so the boy entered the ring. *Watch me. Be happy!*

This was his solution to the moral dilemma that plagued him.

His family's business was evil. Well then, he would serve the public by becoming a luchador, showing his audiences a good time!

Thus he assuaged the prickings of his conscience.

His ring name was the Hellhound. He had chosen a dogman as his character, obviously, out of respect for his father's dog—his family, teacher, and close friend. The various techniques he had picked up horsing around with the dog as a child played an important role in his fighting, albeit in more refined forms. That was how, at the age of fourteen, the Hellhound became the Hellhound. He was transformed from an ordinary human into a human capable of turning, at any moment, into a dogman.

The Hellhound was never, however, exclusively a wrestler. He continued attending school until he turned sixteen, and then he started helping his father. By then he had already found his way out of his moral quandary. He was doing good as a luchador, so even if he was involved in organized crime, and organized crime was evil, that was okay. By giving himself over to these two different aspects of his life, he achieved a kind of balance.

Once again, two.

The public face, the hidden face.

His father was assassinated by a competing organization in the winter of the Hellhound's twenty-second year. The Hellhound took over the leadership of the cartel. Of course, even then he didn't retire from the ring; the Hellhound remained his public face. *Two.* He was now the second man in his family to run the cartel. For two years, he struggled to keep things going, both in public and behind the scenes. By then everyone he worked with as a luchador—from his manager to his handlers, his drivers, everyone else— belonged to the organization. They made certain that security at stadium entrances was very strict and took extra precautions to prevent information relating to the Hellhound's true identity from being leaked. The Hellhound's underworld doings kept him so busy early on, when he first took over, that he competed in matches only in Mexico City and the small cities nearby. Even so, he managed to appear in 150 matches a year. At the same time, he worked hard to keep his other business thriving as it had when his father ran the organization. He found ways, little by little, to get in with corrupt state police officers and buy off tax officials, gaining a reputation as a promising newcomer in the world of North and Central American drug trafficking.

All this in order to be recognized by La Familia.

To convince the Don to give him a dog like the one his father had received.

That, ultimately, was his dream. That was the future he could hardly wait to make real. *Then I'll be just like you, right, Dad?* He heard no answer from heaven, but he knew that if only he could get that dog, he would be number two. The second leader, a powerful presence in the underworld with a dog, an alter ego, as a symbol of his status.

He turned twenty-four. At last, he was presented with a dog. The Don sent the Hellhound a male pup, three months old. The dog's father—his seed—was a boxer, and something about his features brought to mind a bulldog. Young as he was, he had incredible fighting instincts. When you got him going he would rear up on his hind legs, looking as if he were really getting ready to box. At the same time, he obviously had more than boxer blood; the traces of his mongrelization were unmistakable. Traces, that is, of everything he had inherited from his mother. That dog was you, Cabron. You.

The dog on the twentieth parallel north. *You.*

Here you were at last. You had made your way south from Texas to Mexico City. As a pup, you weren't known by the name Cabron. When you lived on your family's original territory, on the Mexican-American border, people had called you by a different name. The Hellhound had used that same name until you were a year and three months old. But then he renamed you. He christened you Cabron.

Cabron meaning "male goat." Not, of course, that he would have preferred your being a goat or anything like that. In Spanish, the word *cabron* was used as slang in various senses, all negative. You could call someone *cabron* when you wanted to point out that he was a fucking shit, or a pathetic loser, or to ridicule him for letting another man sleep with his woman. This last meaning was the meaning the Hellhound had in mind. You were the cuckold. Not that anyone had slept with your wife. That had happened, not to you, but to your master.

La Familia was impressed with your master. They anticipated that in time, he would become an even more capable boss than his father. So they invested in him. In his future, his promise—his youth. When La Familia presented a man with a dog, as it had presented you to your master, it showed that he had been recognized as "one of the family." Your master got more than just you, however. The Don also sent your twenty-four-year-old master his eighteen-year-old second daughter. You and his new bride had both come down from Texas at the same time, to Mexico City, to the twentieth parallel north. Naturally, the Hellhound was delirious with joy. Now he and La Familia really were family! The Don was his dad, and the Don's wife was his mom! And to top it all off, his new wife was a pretty piece of work—not exactly the slim big-breasted type he usually preferred, but he certainly had no complaints.

The Hellhound was happy. He threw himself more wholeheartedly than ever into his work—his secret work, that is—and into his wrestling. His new wife couldn't believe it. She had been looking forward to immersing herself in the delicious, melting joy of newlywed life, and instead just look at this guy! What was he thinking, going off and leaving her like this, packing whatever time was left after he finished dealing with business into that silly pro wrestling, and taking it so seriously? His new wife was Mexican-American, not a true Mexican, and she had no sense of the significance of *lucha libre*. Her husband's side of their double bed was often empty, and so naturally she began bringing in a lover to share it with her. This had been going on for a year when her husband found out.

The new wife left the compound. The Hellhound couldn't just rub out the jerk she'd slept with because she had the upper hand. "Listen," she told him, "if you kill my lover, I'm going to have my great-uncle cut you out of La Familia's business." And so, in an instant, the Hellhound was plunged into despair. That was when he decided, rather masochistically, to rename his dog Cabron. Your master was fond of you, Cabron. He kept you constantly in his presence. And he took a sort of bitter, self-mocking pleasure in talking to you, addressing you by your new name. *Hey, cuckold, how about it, cuckold? Don't you agree, cuckold?* At the same time, the Hellhound wasn't the sort of simple young man to do this simply to vent his emotions; the new name was the result of careful thought. If someone in the business ever happened to call *him* "cabron," even as a joke, he might fly into a rage and shoot the guy dead before he even realized what he was doing. That would be really bad.

But what if that word were also the name of his constant companion, this dog?

What, your master thought, if it were *your* name?

"It's okay," he could tell himself then, "he's just talking to my dog."

And so you became Cabron. Three months into your second year. Your master was twenty-five. He was still emotionally malleable. Day after day, as he talked to you, called you by your name—*Cabron! Cabron!*—he began to forget his pain. Hey, what's the big deal? It's a dog's name. And though his wife had now run off with another man, he remained as tight as ever with La Familia. *No, please,* the Don said, *call me Dad, just like before.* Your master had been "bought," as it were, as a promising young leader in the business, and his position in La Familia didn't change. He was still free to come and go as he pleased in the orchard in Texas. He was family. And there was someone there who tried to comfort him as best she could. "I'm sorry my sister was such a bonehead," the girl said. She was the Don's third daughter. Thirteen years old. "Don't let it get you down. I think you're great."

Huh? Me? You do?

Six months later, he had recovered.

So that was your master's story. The melodrama of your alter ego's life until 1971. But you, Cabron, you were living your own melodrama. From the time you turned eight months old and spilled seed for the first time, you rarely had a problem getting it. Who could resist you? As long as your alter ego had his private face on, no bitch's owner would ever refuse to let you have her. And when he wore his public face, they let you have their bitches because of the love and desire they themselves felt for the Hellhound—they were more than happy to let the Hellhound's dog knock up their pets. And then there were the strays who knelt for you, overwhelmed. You mated with this bitch, took that one, littered all of Mexico City with your progeny. You…you betrayed your name. You were no cuckold; you were a lady-killer. But then, toward the end of 1974, everything changed. You fell in love.

Love. Melodrama.

Your master had gotten involved in something big. His bodyguard had brought him the lead. The bodyguard was a huge dude from American Samoa, upward of six foot two and a champion underground boxer. He had an astonishingly thick neck, fat arms, and a massive stomach. Samoans and Tongans were legendary among professional boxers. Lucha libre wasn't real fighting, of course, but this only gave the Hellhound greater respect for true strength. He was still a fighter, he told himself, even if he wasn't much of one. And what point was there in being protected by bodyguards weaker than he was? He had first been introduced to this guy, whose arms and torso and thighs were covered with traditional Samoan tattoos, by the nephew of the Don's wife, a producer. The introduction alone wasn't enough to convince him to hire the Samoan. If the bodyguard was going to be with him all the time, he had to be totally sure he was trustworthy. The Samoan had two other characteristics that made him attractive. One was that this towering giant, who spoke Spanish with a Samoan-English accent, was a twin. "You mean you've got a brother *exactly* like you?" "That's right, man. An identical twin." "That's so *cool*! It's like having a fucking alter ego!" It turned out, furthermore, that the older twin—the bodyguard—was also a devout Christian. "Are you kidding? The Samoan Islands are Catholic?" "Sure, man. The first missionaries came to Samoa in 1830, so what do you expect? Sometimes when I hear a hymn I get teary." "That's terrific!" "My brother, though, he's Muslim." "He's a…but why?" "Lives in Asia. Went there to work. Does the same kind of shit I do, in Indonesia I think it is. Or maybe it's Pakistan? He swore to obey the Koran in order to get in good with the people there." "That's awesome! That's the kind of dedication I like to see in this line a work!"

So the Hellhound hired the Samoan hulk—who was simultaneously an older twin and a championship underground boxer—as his bodyguard, and the two survived several bloodbaths together, and the Hellhound came to see that he could trust the Samoan absolutely, and then to regard him as his right-hand man. In 1974, this right-hand bodyguard was one of the main movers in a major incident: he helped lead the Hellhound to attack an officer in the Mexican Federal Police. "This dude's *bad*, man," the Samoan had muttered. "And I mean *bad*." "Is he?" the Hellhound asked. "He's building his own secret organization, Boss. Fixing it so he has access to all the confiscated drugs, building ties with the Colombians, putting all the department heads in Customs in his pocket." "What the hell? Are you kidding? That *is* bad. I was thinking the paperwork guys in Customs seemed kind of unfriendly lately—so it's this guy's doing, huh?" "It is, Boss." "How'd you figure this out? Who snitched? One of the little guys in the state police?" "No one *snitched*, Boss. More like I got him to talk. Gave him a hook to the jaw, smashed the bone. *Brraahahahahah!* It's hard work getting these guys to talk, Boss." "Hilarious. *Hahahahah.*" "You know that business we got going on in Cabo San Lucas, dropping drugs from the sky? I got wind someone was trying to interfere, so I had 'em tie him up and bring him to me. And let me tell you, when that guy started talking, boy did he start talking." "So what's this plan you got for me?"

This officer in the Federal Police lived in a port city on the Gulf of Mexico, and that was where he had his storehouse. They attacked the storehouse. The officer had been put in charge of all the confiscated drugs, and he often went out on busts himself. He had commandeered the best drug dog in the force, a member of a true super-elite, essentially turning her into his own private dog; no one tried to stop him. He would take her to airports and up to the border and have her sniff out only the purest drugs, which he would seize. It would have been hard to find a worse instance of a man abusing the authority of his position. And once he had the drugs, he would sell them back at very steep prices to the Colombians. "You go too far," the Hellhound told him. "You're *too* bad." He punched him, kicked him (with his torpedo St. Bernard Kick), put him in his mighty Dog-Hold. He got all the information he needed and then, just like that, had his bodyguard kill him. They cleaned out every last packet of shit in the storehouse. They'd brought a four-ton truck for that purpose. No one interfered as they carted the stuff out, but there was this dog barking its head off. A Labrador retriever. A bitch. The officer's drug dog. "Well, look what we have here," the Hellhound said. "Want me to shut her up, Boss?" the Samoan asked. "No, no, no. You should never kill unless you have to, not when it's a dog. Besides, this bitch is the force's number one drug dog, right? The one everyone talks about? She'll come in handy. She can sniff our shit, tell us how good it is." "Nice thinking, Boss. Very nice."

So they ended up taking the Labrador retriever.

And where did they take her? To the twentieth parallel north. To the estate in Mexico City. And there you were. It was December 1974, when your master brought her in and introduced her to you, Cabron. "Hey there, boy," he said, beaming. "Look who's come to visit. The best *perro policia* in all of Mexico." What did you feel then? Nothing, at first. You weren't hot for her then, it wasn't the season, and besides you had all the bitches you could want. So you just glanced at her and thought, HMM? A NEW FACE? The fact was, she was a very beautiful dog. A purebred Labrador retriever, only two years old, with an iridescent, jet black coat and a nice muscular ass. Before long, Cabron, you would be creeping around, whining up a storm, pining with desire for that ass—but for now, you barely noticed her. A NEW BLACK FACE? you thought, and that was it. You watched as your master tested her, had her sniff a bunch of drugs and pick out the heroin, cocaine, crack, marijuana, speed, and all kinds of other shit, and tell him how pure they were. WHAT KIND OF TRICK IS THAT? you wondered. Two days later, though, the situation changed. All of a sudden, things were different. The Hellhound was in a fight with a Colombian cartel. That business with the officer had deprived the cartel of one of its transport routes, and they were pissed. A gang of South American hit men turned up in Mexico. Your master realized right away what was up. He said, "This isn't good." "Sure isn't," replied the Samoan.

"We're at war."

In next to no time, the estate in Mexico City was transformed into a fortress. Preparations were made so that when the hit men came for the Hellhound, they'd be ready. And you, Cabron, were holed up in the fortress with your master. You held the fort together. Your master, by the way, had had to give up on his wrestling for the time being. This meant you no longer had the pleasure of traveling from one arena to the next, going from city to city, growling and glaring at your master's trading partners. You no longer even got taken out for walks. Someone might kidnap you and use you to get at your master. You were your master's alter ego, so if he was going to be stuck in one place for a few months, so would you. There was a difference, though, because while your master could always bring in women from outside to satisfy his sexual urges, you didn't have that option. No matter how horny you got. And you got very horny. You were frustrated, the frustration built up, until you wanted to explode. You noticed that bitch in the fort. That drug dog, the Labrador retriever with the firm round butt. But she gave you the cold shoulder. You, Cabron, were supposed to be a lady-killer, and yet she was ignoring you. You put the moves on her, turned on the charm, to no avail. It was worse than that: she used her police-dog training to tell you to go to hell. *Buzz off, mutt!* She knew how to fight—in fact, she was at least as good as your master, with his surefire moves like the Top-of-the-Head-Dog-Bite. You'd yelp and retreat, instantly. But you were still horny. WHAT AM I SUPPOSED TO DO? C'MON, you pleaded. LET ME DO YOU. Again and again, you pleaded. I WON'T SPLIT AS SOON AS WE DO IT, I PROMISE, I WANT TO HAVE KIDS WITH YOU, I WANT TO MAKE YOU MY WIFE!

Uuuuuuurrrr…wooooof! you barked sadly.

It was love. Melodrama. What's up, Cabron? your master asked, laughing. Can't get her in bed? What the hell happened to you, stud? He didn't even try to help. So what did you do? You followed her around, trying to make her like you. You groped for a solution to the problem. You tried hard to seem interested in the things that interested her. You didn't see the point, but you tried. OKAY, I'LL LEARN TO DO THE SAME TRICKS!

There in that closed fortress, you poured all your energy into realizing a dream. You were absolutely determined to have sex with that bitch.

Three months later, your master was staring wide-eyed, calling his bodyguard over. "Hey! Look at that! Just look!" "What's up, Boss?…Huh? Wait a sec, he's…isn't he?" "I know! It's incredible! Cabron actually found the marijuana—just look at him, scratching the bag like that with his paws!" "Like a real police dog, huh?" "Seriously." "He can tell the difference…that it's not cocaine." "Wow." "That's that trick magazine with the drugs in it, right? And he found them with no problem!" "Wow, he's totally turned—" "Into a drug dog."

Ah, the power of love. Love had helped you memorize the scents of different drugs. You taught yourself, and you made it to the more advanced stages. You could differentiate among various levels of purity, to a limited extent. Generally speaking, in order to be employed as a professional by the police or any other organization, a dog had to have started specialized training between its fourth and seventh months. Once you got to be an adult, it was too late. So the trainers said. But you proved them wrong. You, Cabron, had pulled off the impossible. It was quite a trick. All on account of love. Finally even the Labrador retriever was moved by your attentions and stopped snubbing you.

CAN WE DO IT NOW? you asked.

She proffered her rear.

In June 1975, as the siege continued, the Labrador retriever gave birth in the basement of the estate-turned-fortress. You had recognized her as your official wife, and you watched over her as she bore your puppies. It took hours, testing your powers of endurance. More than half the day, in fact. Why? Because the litter was astonishingly large. Eleven puppies, each one different from the others. Their father's mongrel blood had shown what it could do. Your master was stunned when he saw how many pups there were. "Man, Cabron, your sperm must be like jelly, huh?" he said. "He hadn't done it for a while, Boss," the Samoan said. "I saw some, actually, and it was yellow, not white." The Samoan named one of the pups. Overall his coat was brown, but he had six narrow black lines on his left side and a black spot on his haunch that made him look vaguely like a stringed instrument. His appearance made him stand out from the rest. The Samoan called him Guitar.

MY CHILDREN, you thought.

MY LINEAGE, MY CHILDREN.

Right from the start, the next generation was faced with a problem. There were eleven pups. Dogs have only ten teats. Worse still, the top two don't produce milk. The bitch could only raise seven or at most eight puppies, so inevitably there was competition for her teats. "Man, I know it's great to have lots of kids, Cabron," your master grumbled, "but this is ridiculous." Still, he had a servant prepare bottles of milk, and he and the bodyguard fed the puppies that had been left at loose ends, as it were. "Shit, just look at this little cutie-pie," said the towering Samoan as he cradled a pup in his arms. Your master went so far as to consult a veterinarian. On her advice, he mixed powdered milk with cow's milk to thicken it so it would be better suited for puppies. The two men couldn't look after those loose-enders twenty-four hours a day, though, and during the first two weeks of July two pups dropped out of the game. They couldn't survive.

Another died in the last week of July, as the bitch started weaning her puppies. The lack of adequate milk in the first days had taken its toll.

Then it was August 3, the first Sabbath of the month. Men armed with light machine guns and howitzers forced their way into the fortress where you and your master were holed up, shattering the peace of the Catholic world. Obviously these were the hit men the Colombian cartel had hired. Expecting the situation to come to a head soon, your master had tripled the number of guards stationed around the estate since the previous year. Each guard had an automatic rifle. The shoot-out began. Sometime later, your master would describe this day to his second wife as "Bloody Sunday." The blood was not only human. You and your wife and your children—the eight surviving puppies—were holed up in the estate as well. Ten dogs in total. Of those ten, only one shed blood. Your wife. Because your wife, Cabron, was a police dog. She had been trained to respond to gunfire—to burn with righteous anger. It was tantamount to suicide to react that way. She dashed up out of the basement, eager to find the villains, and ended up caught in the gunfire, shot through.

Intruders stomped on two of the puppies.

When the shooting ended, seven dogs were left. You, the father, and your kids.

Guitar was alive. Guitar had made it through the first test—the competition for his mother's teats—managing to live because the Samoan had kept an eye on him, encouraging the mother to let him suckle or giving him a bottle if he was pushed out of the circle. Then there was "Bloody Sunday," which Guitar survived by staying put, not scampering this way and that through the landscape of hell which the estate had been transformed into. He didn't lose his wits in the sudden explosion of violence—or rather he had, but he didn't let his terror lure him into making the same mistake as his siblings, who ran around in a panic, barking their heads off. Instead, he hid in a kitchen cabinet until the noise stopped and only then ventured out in search of his mom. He found her immediately. A bullet had left two holes in her body: one at the top of her skull where it entered, the other in her neck where it exited. There she was, sprawled in the hallway that led into the living room. His mother's corpse. Blood had pooled around her. Red blood, starting to congeal. Maybe Guitar understood something as he inhaled the smell of that blood; maybe he didn't. He whined, nudged her stomach with his little nose.

He felt how cold she was.

How stiff.

He sensed that he was losing her.

Guitar was too old to drink his mother's milk now, but he groped for her teats, nuzzling them one by one. One, two, three, four, five, six, seven, eight, nine, ten. The last two had never meant anything. But now, even when he sucked the others, no milk streamed forth. There was no warmth.

He sucked furiously.

Twenty minutes later, Cabron, you stumbled upon the scene. There, in a corner of the hall surrounded by the tumult of an estate still in chaos, was your wife, the bitch whose ass you had pursued with such passion, stretched out in the solemnity of death, with one of your children, a puppy with stripes like a guitar, beside her—beside her body, trying to suck her teats. You stood stunned, you hung your head. Soon another of your children padded over, and a second, then three more. They all, one after the other, followed Guitar's lead, clustering around their cold mother's teats, to suck.

The third trial continued through the rest of August and into September. Slowly your children began to die. The reason was simple: their mother was gone. The shock of her sudden death was more than they could bear. By the last week in September, only two puppies were alive. It wasn't as though you weren't trying to help—you were doing everything you could. Ever since "Bloody Sunday" you were spending all your time looking after the puppies. You were unbelievably careful. You never let them out of your sight, you kept watch over them twenty-four hours a day. You had, in fact, started raising them yourself. Even though you were a male dog, not a bitch.

My children, you thought.

My rightful descendants.

Live. Stay alive. Live.

Of course, you weren't tending to them in the right way. You couldn't call on your "motherly instincts" because you didn't have any. Half of what you did was just horsing around. Though even then you were serious. The other half was education. That's okay, you can do that, don't do this, remember. You did all you could. And what sort of education did you pour most of your energy into? Into the very same trick you had devoted most of your energies to learning. In order to impress their mother. That, naturally, you *had* to teach them. You gave them an elite education. Your children, still under three months old.

Learn to smell the difference between these drugs.

Learn to identify their purity.

You taught them all the tricks a drug-sniffing dog needed to know. Almost as though you were engraving their mother's memory onto their minds.

In November, the last two puppies were alive and well. Guitar was one of the two. One day, the Samoan shouted to your master, his eyes wide with surprise. "Hey, Boss! Boss!" The Hellhound, your master, practically shrieked when he realized what was happening. "What the hell are you hollering for… huh? Wait a sec, he's…*OH MY GOD!*" "Amazing, huh, Boss? Look at Guitar there, scratching at the shoe with the marijuana hidden inside, just like his old man, Cabron." "Looks like a real police dog, huh?" "Seriously. And look, his brother is doing it too!" "He…he can tell the difference between the marijuana and cocaine!" "They've totally turned into drug dogs!"

Your master turned and stared at you. He was moved. "Incredible…raising them all on your own, without their mother…and you taught them to do this?"

You sensed that he was praising you. You barked confidently.

Woof!

In the human world too, the same amount of time had passed since that first Sabbath in August. Three months. During that period, as the two puppies had learned how to be drug dogs, similarly momentous changes had occurred in the two-legged world as well. First of all, the conflict with the Colombians was over. So much blood had been shed on "Bloody Sunday" that one of the bosses in Panama, unwilling to stand by and watch the carnage, stepped in to mediate. The conditions of the truce weren't bad. So a bargain was struck. For the first time in ages, the Hellhound's Mexico City estate went back to being just that—an ordinary organized crime boss's compound, not a fort. The security detail was reduced to a few men, though they still carried light machine guns and ammunition belts at all times. Now that there was no need to man the fort, the Hellhound lost no time in flying off to Texas. He wanted to pay his respects to the Don. "I'm real sorry, Dad. Quite a commotion I caused." "You idiot! You idiot! You idiot!" the Don said, berating him a touch too dramatically. "You sure as hell caused a commotion! You gotta be sharper than that, right? Listen, I want you to remember this. World War II is long over. This is 1975, there are no 'gangsters' anymore, not like they used to have 'em in the old days. You're part of the new generation. I invested in you, right? You're part of the new guard in this business. So you gotta learn to be a businessman. Wise up. Learn to make it look legal, okay? *Look* legal." This exchange with the Don left the Hellhound feeling kind of blue. He hadn't just been told off, of course—the Don had been trying to impart some serious knowledge—but he hadn't expected to be bawled out. Not at all. Maybe I'm just not cut out for this, he thought glumly as he stood in the courtyard of La Familia's compound, chucking bread to the dozen ducks bobbing on the pond. Just then, he heard a bright voice at his back. "Hey, it's my favorite brother-in-law! Long time no see!" It was his ex-wife's younger sister, the Don's third daughter. She was eighteen now. He hadn't seen her for three years because she had been sent to get an education in Vienna when she was fifteen. The Hellhound gasped. She had grown into quite a woman. A real beauty. A beauty of the slim, big-breasted type.

"Uh…yeah…long time no see."

"What's wrong? Feeling blue again?"

"No, no. Just…feeding the ducks."

"The ducks?"

"Yeah. Bread, see?"

"Bread?"

Soon they were embroiled in a heated discussion concerning the most appropriate food for ducks. Then they left the courtyard to take a stroll through the orchard, and two hours later they were kissing passionately. The Hellhound had fallen in love with the young woman at first sight—though technically this was the second time he'd encountered her—and the Don's third daughter, then in the throes of puberty, had a megacrush on the Hellhound. They started going on dates. North of the border, south of the border. The Hellhound had gotten back into his work as a luchador by this time, and the young woman actually came to see him in the ring. His ex had never once done that. The Hellhound was so bowled over he devised a brand new killer move that he called the "Love Love Dog-Drop." They were both sure of their feelings, so in the last week of November the Hellhound broached the matter with the Don. "I'd like to ask for your daughter's hand in marriage," he said.

"Yeah, I guess my other daughter turned out to be a loser, huh."

"No, no! That's not the point. I'm really serious about her, and I—"

"Sure."

"What!"

"With one condition. This is going to be the second time I've given you a daughter, so I want you to expand your operations a bit for me, all right? Think of it as a wedding present to La Familia."

Nothing wrong with that. And so, once again, twos came into play. The Hellhound had to start running around, east and west, trying to rummage up some big new game he could bag for his second wife. As it happened, the biggest tip of all came from a source very close to home: his bodyguard. "I've got a good route, Boss." "Hmm, I don't know. Where does it lead? I've had enough of these South American connections." "You can trust this one, Boss. It's my brother." "What? You mean your twin brother?" "I told you he's in the same business, right?" "Come to think of it, you did." "He's in Asia. Works for the head of an organization that deals drugs. He's the guy's *secretary*." "His secretary? You mean his bodyguard?" "You got it, Boss. *Brraahahahahah!* And this organization, seems they've got some fields out in Pakistan, out in the middle of nowhere." "Fields growing…poppy seeds?" "Bingo." "I seem to recall that your brother's a Muslim?" "Sure is. It's all *Allah, Allah,* every day. Anyway, this organization…" "All right, I hear you."

Plans were laid for a corporate tie-up. The Samoan twins (the *two* of them) were very much part of their respective organizations, and their bosses trusted them implicitly. With the two (*two*) of them acting as middlemen, might it be possible to bring even two (*two*) organizations as profoundly distinct as these—one operated in America, one in Asia; one boss was a Catholic, one was a Muslim—together? The twins considered the question and delivered their verdict: Yes, we can! Samoan culture placed great importance on family, by the way, and maintained a social structure based in extremely large families. The ties among relatives were very strong. The twins suggested that since the two bosses would have to talk, maybe they should meet up somewhere in the middle. In between America and Asia was…the Pacific Ocean. Well, then, why not arrange a summit in our hometown?

Sounded good.

Thus, in the middle of December, the two groups arrived in American Samoa, disguised as tourists, and met up in a hotel. The Hellhound decided to take his alter ego along —his second self, his dog, Cabron. "We'll scare the bejeezus out of 'em," he'd said before they left. "Show 'em that with this dog we've got, we'll sniff out any funny business, diluting shit down and stuff. Sniff it out in a second. We'll show 'em what we can do!" "Nice. I like it, Boss," the Samoan said. "The only worry is—do you think Cabron will leave the puppies?" "Hmm…good point. He's been fawning over them nonstop, it's true. How about this, then? They're six months old now, right? Why not take the little buggers along?" There were only two of them. (*Two.*) The Hellhound decided this was the best solution. Besides, just imagine the look on those Asian faces when they see those two roly-poly dumplings zipping around, trying to outdo each other in ferreting out carefully concealed heroine, marijuana, and speed! Hats off to the *Nuevo Mundo*!

"You can have a whole roast pig, Boss," said the Samoan. The older one, the Hellhound's bodyguard. The younger twin's group flew from Melbourne by way of Fiji and landed in Samoa, formerly known as Western Samoa, then moved on to the final destination. The older twin's group—including the Hellhound and the three dogs—flew first to Hawaii. They changed planes in Honolulu and headed for the South Pacific.

It was December 9, 1975, when Cabron left Mexico City. He and his alter ego. He was no longer a dog of the twentieth parallel north. He passed over Oahu, over the twenty-first parallel north. But Goodnight wasn't there anymore. The bitch of the twenty-first parallel north was no longer living on that island.

You, dog—you, Goodnight, who no longer reside on the twenty-first parallel north. Where are you now?

You were riding in a double canoe. Taking part in a glorious adventure, heading for Tahiti using ancient maritime navigation techniques. If this magnificent project, part of the Hawaiian Renaissance, was a success, you had been told, you would be awarded a third medal to add to the Purple Heart and the Silver Star you received during your days as a military dog. Your master was the one who told you this. The former lieutenant who had taken you into his family when you retired from the military, then let you go when the family beagle had children—not your master, then, strictly speaking, but your *former* master. Well, you would never get that third medal. A month after the canoe set out, on November 11, 1975, you were starving. The canoe was adrift. Swept this way and that on the vast sea. Once, earlier, the humans had tried to kill you, to turn you into food. Canine cuisine. Fortunately, however, you had no master now. No new master had appeared. As far as you could see, the boat was populated with idiots.

Do you really think you can sacrifice me? Are you fools crazy? That was your answer to them. And so you revolted. You sank your teeth deep into one man's biceps, tore off the hands of two others at the wrists, and that was that—you had beaten them back. All your years as a military dog came back to you, erupted within you. You ate the body parts you had taken. Then you sucked the bones. You had been starving since the second week of the voyage. The Polynesian navigator had revealed himself as a useless, run-of-the-mill fraud. Unable to read the stars in unfamiliar seas. The Hawaiian Islands and the Cook Islands were part of the same Polynesian cultural sphere, it was true, but they were just too far apart. The navigator was from Rarotonga Island, and the ocean here was nothing like the ocean there. This was too far north. To make matters worse, he couldn't see what was happening with the waves. He wasn't sensitive to his surroundings. By the third day, the canoe had started moving off course. You heard the humans quarreling.

"Secret techniques my ass!" the wealthy researcher shouted. "Where's this fucking 'wisdom of the ancients' you were talking about, you fucking bluffer!" As it happened, the researcher's insults were right on target: the navigator had been bluffing his way through life for years. And he didn't stop now. "I swear to you, sir, that I will carry us onward to Tahiti using the traditional techniques I have inherited. I would be grateful if you would address me more politely. That's the problem with these academics…" His voice trailed off into muttering. The researcher was so incensed at this that he took out the precision watch, sextant, and radio he had brought in case of emergency and threw them all overboard. "All right, then, great! We didn't need those, right?

That's what you're telling me? *Ha ha ha!*" He howled. From then on, the trip no longer felt like an adventure. The canoe was heavy with despair. The direness of the situation became apparent when they entered the doldrums. They had reached the equator, at least, but now they weren't going anywhere: not east, not west, not north, and not south. The humans tried desperately to catch fish, to capture seabirds. Then one morning, two of them were dead. Starved to death. That was the day the others attacked you, right around noon.

At the hour when the sun beat down most ferociously, fourteen members of the crew held a meeting—you were part of the crew too, but they didn't invite you to participate—in which it was decided that if they couldn't get any fish or any birds, they had no choice but to eat the dog. They chased you to the prow of the canoe. And then you attacked. You owed them no loyalty. Isn't that right, Goodnight? You…you were merely exercising your basic rights. You had as much right to live as those humans did. So you made it clear that if you couldn't get any fish or any birds, you had no choice but to eat the humans. You demonstrated this beyond any doubt by devouring the hands of the two crew members you had beaten back. And you didn't just devour them, you *relished* them. They could see that. You showed them, too, that there was no point in holding meetings. That evening and later that night, one, two, then three died. The two men whose hands you had torn off and the one whose biceps you had bitten. They had lost too much blood, and they were already on the edge of death anyway. The survivors didn't dump the bodies overboard. They converted them into "food." You observed them from your position at the prow. One of the haole crew members was so unnerved by the steely glitter in your eyes that he tossed you his companions' livers. Also their penises and testicles, which the survivors found somehow unappetizing. You devoured it all. It was tasty.

Morning came. You were still sitting at the prow. Naturally, the humans ended up clustered at the stern. There were eleven left, but they had split up into three factions. There was no point trying to reach a universal consensus: it went without saying that the haole, the pure Hawaiians, and the Rarotongan would each form their own groups. No one attacked you anymore. The secret fighting techniques you had acquired during your time in the military protected you. There was a ritual now, starting that morning. When one of the fatigued crew members finally died, only the humans in his faction would share the "food." Cut it up, divvy it up. They always tossed the dead man's raw liver, as well as his penis and testicles, up to the prow. To you. As an offering, so to speak. This had become the custom. As long as they did this, they believed, that terrifying dog wouldn't attack them in their sleep. They didn't need to fear being attacked, that is to say, by you.

The most dangerous thing they could do, they decided, was let you starve.

The humans had come to regard you as a ferocious, wild beast.

Soon the three factions became two. The Polynesian navigator died, and the others fought over his body. They battled for the "food." The haole faction gave you the penis and testicles as an offering; the pure Hawaiians gave you the liver as theirs. The death of the single member of the Rarotongan faction meant that they had lost the only person with any experience navigating the open ocean, even if he had wildly exaggerated his abilities, but the other two factions didn't mind. The wealthy researcher died the next day, as if he couldn't stand to have been beaten by the navigator. You took your time gnawing on the usual parts. Now the canoe had no leader.

Still you remained at the prow, and the humans at the stern.

Two factions became one. Only three humans remained, all pure Hawaiians.

You had passed through the doldrums. But where were you? No one manned the rudder. You had drifted off course, yes, but in which direction? East? West? North? South?

Who knew?

November 11. You were starving.

The double canoe was still adrift.

Still being swept this way and that on the endless sea.

You sat at the prow, gazing, not up at the sky, but at the level horizon.

The Hawaiians caught a few fish every day. They gave you the innards. Tossed the offering to you at the prow.

You didn't attack the humans. Why would you? You weren't a wild, ferocious beast—you never had been. You would never have gone for them the way you did if they hadn't tried to kill you, to turn you into food. So you sat there at the prow, starving.

Starving.

You were still starving on November 12, and on the thirteenth, and on the fourteenth. Your body felt oddly light. You couldn't feel your weight. You were becoming invisible, you thought.

I'M INVISIBLE.

I'M AN INVISIBLE BITCH.

The fifteenth. You were almost dead. Dehydrated. You faded in and out of consciousness. But your eyes were open. The horizon. More horizon. More horizon. Finally, you became delirious. You thought of your family on Oahu. Back on that island on the twenty-first parallel north, the beagles. Four puppies. SO ADORABLE! SO CUTE! You hadn't given birth to them yourself, true. But at that moment, in that muddled mental state, you floundered in the fantasy of being their mother. You were suckling them. Giving your teats to those four tiny pups to suck. MY DARLING CHILDREN! you shouted. FRUIT OF MY WOMB! You were growling. *Uuuuurrr*. And the mistaken memory was burning itself into your mind.

The sixteenth.

The seventeenth.

You felt the ocean. Yes, you could feel it. Surging beneath you. The canoe was your cradle. The Pacific Ocean occupies fully one third of the earth's surface. You sensed its enormity. The double canoe had now drifted way off to the west of the planned route. It had passed south of the equator, but if it kept going in this direction, it would never reach Tahiti. If it kept going in this direction...it wouldn't reach Tahiti or any of the Society Islands. It was heading for another island group. As it happened, another boat traveled regularly along more or less the same course. A cargo ship. You noticed it, way off on the horizon. AM I INVISIBLE? you asked yourself. You watched the silhouette as it grew progressively larger. AM I AN INVISIBLE BITCH?

No, you told yourself. I'M NOT.

No, I'M A MOTHER, you told yourself. Mistakenly.

The mistaken memory that had burned itself into your mind was what brought you to your feet, your teats aching with a mother's love.

You stood up.

You sent out an SOS. *Woof! Woof! Woof!*

At three o'clock on November 17, 1975, local time, having crossed to the east of the international date line, the cargo ship picked you up. When you started barking at the prow, the sound brought the Hawaiians at the stern back to their senses—they, too, had been driven by extreme hunger into a state of delirium. For a moment they had simply gaped at the sight of *hope* moving across the ocean, there, right in front of them, and then they had started whistling, waving their arms. You didn't wave, but you did wag your tail. The ship's crew noticed you, and your thirty-eight-day nightmare voyage came to an end.

It was over. And where, Goodnight, were you now?

The cargo ship was on its way from the American mainland to a point on the fourteenth parallel south that was itself one of the United State's unincorporated territories. The ship was headed for American Samoa. It would be taking on a large shipment of canned tuna on Tutuila, the main island in the archipelago. Approximately thirty percent of the American Samoan labor force worked in the canneries, packing and sending can after can of South Pacific tuna to the mainland. Shortly before the date changed from November 17 to November 18, the three men, now identified in the ship records as "survivors," were taken ashore at Tutuila, after the ship docked in Pago Pago Harbor. The records noted, too, the presence of one dog, also a "survivor." She was a German shepherd. You, Goodnight. You looked like a bag of bones. You were exhausted, both physically and spiritually. You were a dog of the fourteenth parallel south now, though it would take a few weeks for you to realize this. For the time being, you still had the illusion that you were adrift in that canoe on the wide, wide sea, exiled from Oahu island, exiled from your home on the twenty-first parallel north. But you weren't. You had become a Tutuilan dog. A dog of the fourteenth parallel south. From the American state of Hawaii to the central island in the American territory of Samoa. The two islands were separated by a distance of 2,610 miles, and even so you had simply moved from one place to another within "America."

Even after thirty-eight days adrift on the ocean.

The three survivors didn't discuss the details of what they had endured. Those three pure Hawaiians would not divulge the inside story of their thirty-eight days at sea. They had violated various taboos. They had hallucinated. What were they supposed to say? And so, in the end…they said very little. It was a hellish trip, they said, and fell silent. One man added that he'd never get in a canoe again. Then they boarded a plane at Pago Pago International Airport and flew back to Hawaii.

They did. But not you.

They intentionally left you behind. The Hawaiians were terrified of you and insisted there was no need to take you back. They looked at you with horror in their eyes, as if you yourself were the embodiment of a taboo, and they abandoned you. You made no effort to follow them. Those three men who had lived until the end, gathered at the stern of the canoe, were not your masters. If anything, they had been serving you, because that was the ritual. Because the livers, the penises, the testicles had become the custom. And then, later, the innards of the fish they caught. You had no master, no new master appeared, and all you had to show for the horror you had endured was a mistaken memory. MY PUPPIES! FRUIT OF MY WOMB! And now here you were, and here you stayed, from November to December 1975.

The fourteenth parallel south. Tutuila Island.

No one took you in as a pet, and yet you were fed. Days passed. At first they kept you on the grounds of the government office. You still resembled a bag of bones. "Hey, dog! You're alive! Eat!" the Samoans who worked for the local government called to you, tossing you scraps of taro and fish. More offerings…the same custom, you thought. You began to put on weight, but you were still living in a daze. You stood out on this island, a single pure German shepherd among a Tutuilan population made up entirely of mongrels. You had style. The local dogs felt it. And so they avoided you. You went out on the beach. You gazed at the ocean. At the horizon. The horizon, the horizon, more horizon. I'M ADRIFT, I'M LOST, THIS IS A CANOE IN THE FORM OF AN ISLAND. You felt it. Coconut crabs scuttled on the shore. Slowly you grew accustomed to the stench of rotting coconut. An island. You felt it. From the second week of December, you began to understand that the island was an island. THIS PLACE IS...AN ISLAND? You were incapable of understanding that this island lay on the fourteenth parallel south. The island had been home to an American naval base until 1951, and as a dog who had served as a sentry until just ten months earlier, you could sense that history, sense the lingering base-ness of the place like a scent buried just under the surface of the earth, and it confused you. There was too much rain here for it to be that other island on the twenty-first parallel north.

You took shelter from the rain in the shade of a banyan tree.

You were facing the road.

You watched the road.

You stared at it as you had stared at the horizon. Your eyes were blank. You weren't looking at anything in particular.

The road had two sides: a far side and a near side. Your empty gaze lingered on three dogs standing on the far side. A father and his children. You were new to the island; so were they.

The three dogs were about to cross the road, from that side to this side. To cut across it at an angle. The road was narrow. It wasn't a highway. But still it had two sides, a near side and a far side, and to get from one to the other one had to cross it, like a river.

Seconds before your listless gaze took in the car, your ears had picked up the roaring of its engine. Then the car itself entered your field of vision. It was an expensive car: a Jaguar. The first sports car on the island. The driver, and owner, was a thirty-seven-year-old man who had made it big in the United Arab Emirates. He had paid for the car in US dollars and brought it ashore the day before, and now he was driving it in as flamboyant a manner as possible, showing off. Right now, he was pushing seventy miles per hour. Driving like a nut. You saw what was coming. Those three dogs were about to be run over. The father and his children. Three dogs, just like you.

Suddenly you were up and running.

Your premonition was confirmed by a noise. A shift in the sound of the engine. A sudden slamming of the brakes.

Something was moving you. CH...you were thinking. CH...CHILDREN!

The father was hit. So was one of the puppies. The two dogs were thrown together six feet into the air. The third dog was dangling by his neck from your mouth. You were on the far side of the road; you had run, and you had made it. You had…you had saved the puppy. You had been taught how to survive on a battlefield. You had almost been sent to the front lines in Southeast Asia, to fight the Vietcong. You had been awarded two medals for your outstanding service as a military dog: a Purple Heart and a Silver Star. The puppy you saved was smaller than his dad, but at six months old he was heavy enough. But you had saved him. An instant later, he would have been dead meat.

You shuddered. Somewhere inside, Goodnight, you were barking your pride.

There on the far side of the road, you set the puppy on the ground.

He was less a puppy, really, than a young dog. He was an odd-looking thing. His coat was brown, but he had six thin black stripes on one side and a black spot on his haunch. He looked a bit like a guitar. He was paralyzed with fear by the sudden catastrophe. But then he started walking. Gingerly, unsteadily. His father's body, and his brother's, lay sprawled on the asphalt. The Jaguar was long gone, of course. The driver didn't hang around to pay his respects to the two dogs he had killed. He didn't come to apologize to the child he had orphaned. Soon enough the dogs' owner and his bodyguard would track him down and beat him half to death. But that was still several hours off. The time for that hadn't yet arrived.

Right now, it was just the young dog who looked like a guitar peering down at two dead bodies. Tragedy. Trickling blood. It had happened so suddenly, this…death. The shock of it. The guitar dog had been through this once before. Only this time around, the number of dead had increased—doubled. This time it wasn't just one dog stretched out on the ground, it was one plus one. It was two.

He backed away.

He sensed that he was losing them. He was scared. Terrified. He was being pushed back to his earliest memory, his first experience of fear.

He stepped back off the road. Onto the ground.

And there you were. You, Goodnight, were waiting. As the guitar dog backed away step by step from the bodies, he pushed slowly up against your warm body. Your fur was short, and under it was your skin. It was warm. Soft. The young dog was afraid of things that were cold and hard. And there you were.

He collapsed into you. *Bam*, just like that. He cuddled desperately against you. He needed to feel safe...truly safe. He nuzzled for your teats. He had responded in the same way to his mother's body, but this time the infantile impulse was even stronger. You had teats. Five pairs of them, ten in all. They had never produced milk. But as he moved from the first to the second, the third, the fourth...each teat he tried exuded warmth. Living warmth.

So he pressed desperately against you and kept sucking.

And you understood.

I'M A MOTHER.

You felt it.

I'M SUCKLING HIM. HE IS MY CHILD.

Destiny was doing its work, and you were confused, you were reconstructing your memory. You had given birth to this child with the guitar-like stripes—he was yours. That was how you remembered it now. And so you told him: GO ON, SUCK. You gazed down at this mongrel who looked nothing like you, a purebred German shepherd, and you told him: GO ON, YES, DRINK MY MILK. In 1957, on the American mainland, another dog in the same situation had spoken those same words. At the edge of a highway in Wisconsin, another German shepherd had told seven mongrel puppies, monstrosity embodied, the same thing. You had no idea of this. No knowledge of that fact, no ability to grasp the connection.

You understood. MY CHILD HAS COME TO ME.

This scene took place in December 1975. Soon 1975 turned into 1976, which turned into 1977, which turned into 1978, which turned into 1979. And in December 1979, we come to the other big event. The second of the two strikingly similar wars that took place in the second half of the twentieth century. In April 1975, Saigon fell. That's what had happened in Southeast Asia. The capital of South Vietnam was taken. The United States gave up supporting South Vietnam. And so, that same year, the first of the two limited wars, the one that has come to be known as the Vietnam War, came to an end. And so we move to Central Asia. December 1979: the USSR sent its army into Afghanistan. It decided to initiate "direct intervention" in a nation torn by civil war. The Soviet Union's own ten-year quagmire had begun.

The Afghan War.

The fuse blew on December 25, 1979.

Another limited war, another offshoot of the Cold War. Obviously.

War number two.

And so, dogs—mother and child, as you had now become, incognizant incarnations of the circularity of time—where were you, four years later?

Woof, woof, woof!

A bright red, gaudily painted truck barreled along the highway that headed west out of Peshawar, the old capital of the North-West Frontier Province. It was a mile out of the city, then two, three, four, five miles. A gate appeared. A checkpoint. This was not a national border. Through this gate lay the Federally Administered Tribal Areas (FATA). Administered by the Pashtuns, the Tribal Areas were home to two and a half million people belonging to a number of tribes, each of which lived in accordance with its own Pashtunwali, an ethical code prescribing notions of warfare, loyalty, bravery, revenge, hospitality, the isolation of women, and so on. The land was populated by men with beards and veiled women. It was a region of steep hills whose major industries were the manufacture of weapons, smuggling, and farming illegal drugs. The truck drove into a village. It stopped. A dog leapt down from the bed. A second followed.

The first dog was about twenty-six inches tall with sinewy muscles and a fierce glitter in his eyes. His thick, short coat was brown, and he had a striking guitar-like pattern of stripes on one side. He had inherited the texture of his hair from his mother, a purebred Labrador retriever. His father's father had been a purebred boxer. He himself belonged to no one breed, however. His blood was so mixed that all one could really say about him was that he was a mutt. Still, he had an air of tough, masculine power. Of unity…the odd sense of balance one feels when confronted with a monstrosity. Indeed, this dog had more than one mother. There was the mother who had given birth to him, and the mother who raised him. The dog who had jumped down out of the truck after him was his second mother.

She was a purebred German shepherd. She was twenty-two inches tall and already thirteen years old. Not that you could tell it from looking at her. Her coat had lost its luster, but that was about it. She was steady on her legs. She looked at the world calmly. She had dignity. And, above all, she had love.

The first dog was Guitar.

The second was Goodnight.

Two men got out of the truck. One was the Hellhound. Another was a Samoan. This was not, however, *that* Samoan—not the Hellhound's body-guard and right-hand man. He was a towering giant, six foot two, but he wasn't *that* towering giant. He had the same face, but the tattoos on his arms, torso, and thighs were a little different. This Samoan was a devout Muslim who prayed five times each day without fail and spoke English with a Samoan accent and Urdu and Pashto with an English-Samoan accent. He had never once stepped into the boxing ring, but he was American Samoa's top wrestler. He had even been invited to join a sumo stable in Japan. This Samoan was the number two, as it were, of *that* Samoan. The other Samoan's alter ego. His twin brother. He was here in Central Asia serving as the Hellhound's body-guard, just as his older brother had. His older brother had stayed in Mexico to run the business while the boss was away. The Hellhound had expanded his operations into Asia. The summit in Samoa had been a success, and four years earlier the Hellhound had teamed up with the organization over here. Then, without any warning, the Asian organization's boss died. It had happened two years earlier: one day, he got into a rage about some disagreement with a Chinese-Malaysian organization and he suffered a heart attack, and that was that. The Hellhound had pretty much taken charge of the dead boss's territory—he had mollified the Chinese-Malaysians by helping them make some very profitable connections in the *Nuevo Mundo*. It was inevitable that the Samoan—the younger brother, of course—would become his local representative. And so the Hellhound had two right-hand men, both more or less identical in appearance: one to the west and one to the east of the Pacific

Ocean. Two men. Two places. The past four years had seen other additions to the *two* theme as well. When the Hellhound succeeded in expanding his operations, La Familia's Don sent him a second beautiful wife. A slim woman with very large breasts.

And there was more.

The Hellhound had a new dog as his alter ego. The second generation.

The exchange would be taking place at the village meeting place. A group of Pashtuns, none of them Pakistani citizens, was waiting there for the Hellhound and his associates. And for the dog. They were holding automatic rifles and a sample of the product. The latter wasn't out in plain view, it was inside a metal briefcase. The dog would be able to evaluate the quality of the drugs through the metal. The Pashtuns hadn't believed the rumors until they actually saw the dog do its stuff. They had lived all their lives in the hills, and the only dogs they were familiar with were strays and half-pets that they treated like strays. As far as they were concerned, dogs were unclean. It was as simple as that. But not this one. This dog had huge power over their livelihoods. When he growled, he might as well have been speaking in dog language: THIS IS INFERIOR, WE CAN'T BUY SHIT LIKE THIS. He had never once made a mistake. He noted the slightest decline in purity, whether it was an intentional effort to play fast and loose with the Hellhound and his group or not. He noted it and pointed it out.

In dog language.

They had learned their lesson. You couldn't fool this dog's nose.

The Hellhound greeted the Pashtuns. The Samoan greeted the Pashtuns. He was interpreting for the Hellhound. The men sat down in a circle in the meeting place, and the Samoan conveyed his boss's words to the Pashtuns. An old Pashtun whose beard was going white nodded.

Guitar padded over to the briefcase and sniffed it.

Four years earlier, on Tutuila Island, the Hellhound had lost his first alter ego. Cabron, the mongrel the Don had given him as proof of his status as a member of La Familia. He had lost the dog, but not his mongrel seed. Cabron's six-month-old son had survived. He had emerged unscathed from the accident that instantly killed both his father and his brother. The Hellhound hadn't been on the scene of the accident. He had sent the dogs out on their own to get a bit of fresh air after the successful conclusion of the summit. "Go on, boys," he said. "You were the stars of the show. Take a break." He thought they might like to go to the beach and horse around, a father and his two sons doing the "dog family taking it easy in the South Seas" thing—what a scene, just like a postcard. But it had ended in tragedy. Fortunately, there had been a witness, so he was able to learn in detail what had happened. The Hellhound rushed to the scene and burst out wailing. At least one dog had been saved, though—that moved him profoundly. It was a miracle: according to the witness, a German shepherd that had been wandering around in the area had sprinted over and saved Cabron's son in a manner that was all but suicidal. The German shepherd had recently been rescued. She'd come from Oahu, up in the North Pacific, and ended up adrift on the ocean…The puppy and the dog who saved him were still there at the scene of the accident—or rather just beside it, at the side of the road. The puppy, the son of now-dead Cabron, was pressed against his savior's stomach, and the German shepherd was letting him suck on her teats. *Oooaaoo, aaoooooh,* the Hellhound moaned. The scene tugged almost violently at his heartstrings. It was a miracle, a true miracle. He was convinced of it. A dog who had drifted across the sea from Hawaii had saved the child of his alter ego, here in Samoa? Without realizing what he was doing, he was kneeling on the ground before the German shepherd, crossing himself. "I swear to you I'll never forget this!" he cried. "So long as I live!" And he kept his promise.

On December 21, 1975, the German shepherd entered Mexico. She arrived in Mexico City and became a dog of the twentieth parallel north. Yes, her: Goodnight.

Finally she had left that enormous space called "America."

Two months and ten days had passed since she had stopped being a dog of the twenty-first parallel north.

And then there was the other dog, Cabron's child, who had also returned alive to Mexico City. Yes, Guitar.

Guitar knew. He understood that Goodnight was his second mother.

And the Hellhound knew. He understood that he should keep the two dogs together, treat them as mother and son.

Guitar had lost his true mother, lost his father, and acquired a second mother. There on a roadside on Tutuila Island he had regressed into an infantile state, lost all memory of his first six months. He believed his second mother had suckled him, and she, too, believed that he was her true child, the true fruit of her womb. It had seemed unlikely, given the shocks Guitar had endured—two sudden deaths in just six months—that the profound psychological wounds he had suffered would ever heal, but they did. The love of mother number two, pure and overflowing, enabled him to forget those two traumas. Two minus two equals zero. At the same time, Guitar never did forget the special ability he had learned. That ability, that *power*, had been pounded into him, and he clung to it. It was his father who taught him that, his father Cabron—no longer of this world, no longer present even in Guitar's memory—who had himself acquired the ability as a sort of trick only because of his fixation on a certain bitch. The bitch, a Labrador retriever who belonged to the Mexican Federal Police, and whose talents as a drug-sniffing dog were without peer. How sad to think of that poor bitch, her life snuffed out on the first Sabbath of August 1975, then erased as well from Guitar's memory. And yet that *power* of hers lived on.

Guitar didn't just keep this power, he honed it. There was no surprise in that. All sorts of drugs—marijuana, heroine, cocaine, speed, and various new products—were constantly being carted into the estate and then whisked back out. Guitar smelled them all as a matter of course. And identified them. Because the custom was the same at home: Guitar would smell the drugs, tell the pure from the impure, and when he was right his master would praise him.

His master. The Hellhound.

So Guitar became *two*. The Hellhound's second alter ego. Cabron's son, a drug-sniffing dog like his father. His talent in this department was an undeniable sign of his *twoness*. And as it happened, *two* was better than *one*—in very little time, he had surpassed his father. Indeed, he even surpassed his true mother. 1976. Guitar was the Hellhound's alter ego, and the Hellhound was Guitar's alter ego.

The Hellhound's business was growing. First, things started happening with his associates. The Asian organization, whose boss the younger of the Samoan twins was still serving as a "secretary," was active across Indonesia, Malaysia, and Pakistan. Its operations were based in the so-called "Islamic world." But of course not all Islamic countries were brothers. Far from it. Take Pakistan, for instance. Pakistan's western border ran up against Afghanistan. The line had been drawn by the British in 1893, splitting the traditional homeland of the Pashtuns in two. The British had completely ignored the history and distribution of local ethnic groups. So Afghanistan insisted that the rest of the Pashtun area, in Pakistan, was really Afghan territory as well, and this led to all kinds of disputes. Pakistan was first established—after its independence from Britain—in 1947, and within two years the countries had broken off diplomatic relations. The fact that both nations were Islamic didn't help anything. Something else thawed the ice, though: in 1973, Afghanistan ended its monarchy and emerged as the Republic of Afghanistan.

Early on, the new republic's foreign policy aligned closely with the USS.R, but within two years it began drifting away. At the time the international situation was very complex. The Cold War, between the USSR and the US, was playing itself out. At the same time, relations had grown tense between the USSR and China. In 1969, these two states engaged in armed conflict. China and India were enemies. They fought in the Himalayas in 1962. India and Pakistan were in a state of constant tension, and in 1971 the third Indo-Pakistani War broke out, leading to Pakistan's defeat—for the third time. Having India as a common enemy brought China and Pakistan together. Since Afghanistan had been moving toward the USSR, the US decided it would be good strategy to get in with Pakistan. Pakistan, which was now friendly with both China and the US, necessarily came to view the USSR as an enemy. Then, in 1976, as the Republic of Afghanistan distanced itself from the USSR, the president reached out to the prime minister of Pakistan to explore the possibility of improving relations. He ended the border dispute—the argument over the line dividing the Pashtuns' lands, that is. From that point on, Afghanistan and Pakistan began having all sorts of interactions. The most visible were those between the president and the prime minister; the least visible were those related to the drug trade. Poppy fields and purification plants across Afghanistan were "opened" to the population east of the national border. All at once. Huge quantities of high-quality hashish started flooding across as well. Previously the largest drug-producing region in Asia had been the so-called Golden Triangle on the border of Burma, Thailand, and Laos. The situation was different now. The criminal center, as it were, had shifted from Southeast Asia to Central Asia. And the organization the Hellhound had become tied up with was getting in on the game. In 1976 alone, the traffic didn't merely double—and even that would have been incredible—it quadrupled. *Bam*, just like that. And so, again, in 1976, Guitar was the Hellhound's alter ego, and the Hellhound was Guitar's alter ego.

Guitar checked twice as much drugs, four times as much drugs. He took all the experience he'd accumulated so far and multiplied it by two, then multiplied it by two again. He became the best drug-sniffing dog the world had ever known.

Then in 1977, the boss of the Asian organization suddenly passed away, and the Hellhound took over the organization's territory. The younger of the two Samoan twins became his local representative—in essence, he had been promoted, becoming the organization's next Muslim boss. And so the Hellhound had two Samoan right-hand men: one to the west and one to the east of the Pacific Ocean. Two places, two men. The Hellhound supervised the two regions with equal care. In that one year, he made more than ten trips among Mexico City, Karachi, and Islamabad.

As did his alter ego.

Guitar, that is, flying with his master.

You, Guitar.

Me?

That's right—you turned one, and then two, and in 1978 you turned three, and in 1979 you turned four. Isn't that right?

That's right.

Your mother accompanied you on those trips across the Pacific, from that side to this side and back again. Your alter ego, the Hellhound, was a true dogman. He understood how your mother felt (he understood her feelings as a dog, as a dog who was also a mother), so he never separated you. The

Hellhound, who was your alter ego and also your master, all but worshipped your mother, Goodnight. She was his Madonna. And so there you were. You and your mother, flying over the Pacific, from this side to that side and back again—and again, and again. Your mother told you, didn't she? I KNOW THE SIZE OF THIS OCEAN, she said. I HAVE FELT THE TRUE IMMENSITY OF THIS OCEAN. She spoke the truth. In the entire history of the twentieth century, there was only one dog who, having survived an inconceivably hellish period adrift on its waters, ever grasped the vast reality of the Pacific Ocean itself.

Listen, Guitar, in all humility.

OF COURSE.

Do you promise?

Woof! you bark.

And so you and your mother became dogs of both sides of the Pacific. Your sense of smell, Guitar, and your ability to use it to sniff out and appraise drugs, grew more sensitive with every day you spent on the front lines, where deals were struck and where the drugs were produced, and more sensitive with every year. In 1978, a coup d'état toppled the anti-Soviet Republic of Afghanistan and a new communist Democratic Republic of Afghanistan was created in its place. This political change did surprisingly little damage to your alter ego's affairs. Why? Because the Democratic Republic of Afghanistan went overboard. For example, the previous flag had been heavy on green, the color of Islam, but now, all of a sudden, it was changed to a solid field of red, the symbol of communism. It was a bit too much. This "democratic republic" started oppressing antigovernment elements. Anticommunist members of the previous government, intellectuals, religious leaders—huge numbers were thrown in jail, executed. This was way too much. Armed rebellion broke out all over Afghanistan. The rebels declared that they were engaged in an Islamic jihad. They referred to themselves as *mujahideen*. Often these antigovernment organizations established their bases in neighboring countries…in Pakistan, say. And often they funded their activities with drug production and smuggling. As a result, from 1978 to 1979 your master doubled the quantity he trafficked once again. The mujahideen organizations began using him to funnel drugs from all over Afghanistan out of the country.

You gained twice as much experience as the year before. Two times two times two.

Day by day, month by month, the front lines, the territory where you worked, shifted further to the west, toward Afghanistan's border with Pakistan.

And at last, Guitar, we come to the fourth year. Exactly four years had passed. December 1979. Four years since you and Goodnight had become mother and child. You and your mother, and of course your alter ego, the Hellhound, and the alter ego of the Hellhound's right-hand man in Mexico, the younger of the two Samoan twins, left the North-West Frontier Province to come even further west, to the FATA. To the region the Pashtuns administered themselves. You would never forget this land. You would never forget the FATA's hilly terrain.

Because this was where your mother would die.

Goodnight.

Listen. Looking back, you can see how fickle your mother's fate had been. In 1967, she had been denied the chance to go and fight on the battlefields of the Indochina peninsula with her brother DED. She played no role in the Vietnam War. Southeast Asia had nothing to do with her life. Now, in 1979, here you both were in Central Asia. You and your mother were standing in the Pashtuns' traditional homeland. A line just like the one that had split Vietnam into North and South had divided the Pashtuns. You and your mother were on the front lines. Your mother was about to be swept up in the Afghan Wars.

To die in the Afghan Wars.

A little more Afghan political history. The few months leading up to December 1979. All of Afghanistan had plunged into civil war. The confusion the mujahideen had bred was exacerbated by power struggles within the communist government itself. The president placed great faith in the Soviet Union, but the second in command—the deputy prime minister—was more of a nationalist. A nationalist communist. He was focused on the potential negative effects of reforms carried out too suddenly and decided it would be advisable to loosen restrictions on religious freedom—restrictions, that is, that had been placed on Afghanistan's traditional, local forms of Islam. Hoping to establish Afghanistan's independence from the Soviet Union, he secretly initiated communications with the United States Embassy in Kabul. The president, working with members of the Soviet intelligence team, plotted to assassinate him. The plot was put in action on September 14, but the deputy prime minister struck back with help from the Afghan army and intelligence agency. The president was taken prisoner. On September 16, his resignation was announced, and the deputy prime minister became the president. A few days later, the former president was "taken care of." And so the elimination of the pro-Soviet faction within the government began.

A purge.

Yet another purge.

And once again, adrift from the USSR.

Far from ending the civil war, this actually worsened it. December 1979. You, Guitar, were on the Pakistan side of the Pashtun homeland. You had come with your mother and your alter ego and your alter ego's bodyguard's alter ego. A first transaction took place, then a second. On December 25, the Soviet army moved south at a number of different points over the twelve-hundred-mile border with Afghanistan. It invaded Afghanistan's territory. This was actually the start of the Afghan War, although it took some time for that information to radiate around the country. That same day, you participated in a third transaction. In the days leading up to the war, a few different mujahideen organizations had hosted your master. On December 27, Soviet special forces attacked the Tajbeg Presidential Palace in Kabul. The Afghan president was killed. The USSR immediately established a puppet government. It installed a new leader to replace the old one. On the afternoon of December 29, Kabul fell. Antigovernment forces had been laying their own plans since before the USSR began its "direct intervention," and the Soviet occupation gave them, in effect, the go sign. At the same time, Guitar, you watched as your master entered into negotiations with a powerful commandant from a mujahideen group, a member of the Ghilzai tribe—also part of the Pashtun confederacy. That was a very busy day. The commandant kept getting calls on his radio. In the end, he and your master decided to arrange another meeting in a remote region even further west in the FATA, almost

on the border with Afghanistan. There were four opium purification factories there, disguised as ordinary brick houses, belonging to the commandant.
And so the next evening, that's where you were. Your mother too. And your
master—your alter ego. The Samoan had some business to take care of and
hadn't come. He had gone to a smuggling base near Peshawar the day before
and would be joining up with you again the next day.

So the Hellhound, your master and alter ego, had no bodyguard.

And so it happened.

Go on, you tell it.

ME?

Sure.

I SAW IT.

You saw it?

I SAW IT. I SAW MY MOTHER DIE. SAW THAT VILLAGE ON THE BORDER BECOME
THE PLACE WHERE MY MOTHER DIED. I SAW IT.

What did you see first?

A…CAR.

That's right. It was a truck, actually, with a canvas tarp. It arrived that
evening in the village near the western border of the FATA. That evening—
the evening of December 30, 1979. The word TOYOTA was printed on the
back. Not that you could read it.

I COULDN'T READ IT. BUT I HATED IT.

You hated the Toyota?

YES.

As well you should have. Because, Guitar, the man who would shoot
your mother was soon to emerge from it. At first, everyone assumed it was just
another transport truck. They thought it was one of theirs. As a matter of fact,
the truck itself was being used by the commandant of the mujahideen organization your master was currently negotiating with. It was supposed to be full of
freshly harvested poppy fruit and hashish. The commandant wanted to show
your master, the Hellhound, what they could produce. You were going to be
part of that scene too. You would smell the raw materials, then accompany
them to the factory, where you would smell the finished products…

I NEVER GOT TO DO ANYTHING.

No, you didn't.

PEOPLE JUMPED OUT OF THE TRUCK. THEY HAD GUNS.

Soviet-made guns. Kalashnikovs. About a dozen men leapt out of the canvas-covered back of the truck, each one carrying a Kalashnikov. They were Pashtuns, but they weren't from this area. Neither were they part of the organization the commandant ran, with this village as one of his bases. They were Pashtuns in the Afghan army, obeying top-secret orders from the new government—a government that was, of course, no more than a Soviet puppet. The USSR believed it was essential to maintain stability in Afghanistan, now that it had taken control, and that meant thoroughly clamping down on the movements of all antigovernment forces. It meant crushing the mujahideen. Crushing the jihad. They had a list. Twenty-three leading figures in four organizations were named. The third from the top was the commandant. The list included his true name and seven aliases.

SO THAT WAS IT?

That was it.

THAT'S WHY THEY CAME?

That's why they came. And they came quickly. They had been ordered to execute their man before the new year. Ordered by the new government—by those who stood behind the new government. These Pashtuns, members of the Afghan government's army, had formed an assassination squad, and then, on the Afghanistan-Pakistan border, they had seized that Toyota you hated. And now here they were, in the village.

I SAW THEM. THEY HAD GUNS.

That's right. And whom were they aiming them at? The commandant, standing dumbstruck, taken completely by surprise…yes, the commandant of the mujahideen organization. But not only him. Also your master.

AND ME.

And your mother.

YES! MY MOTHER! MY MOTHER!

And who protected the Hellhound at that crucial instant, in the absence of his bodyguard? Your mother. Who, if you could split that first second into a hundred fleeting snippets of time, was the first to respond to the eruption from the truck of that group armed with Kalashnikovs? Your mother. Goodnight. A bitch with an eight-year career as a military dog behind her, and actual battle experience. A dog who had successfully seen missions to a successful conclusion even as shells rained down around her. Yes, your mother—the German shepherd who was your mother—was quicker to see what was happening, moved faster than anyone into combat mode. Just as you could instantly distinguish all sorts of drugs by smelling them, so your mother instantaneously recognized the scent of war. No sooner had she detected it in the air than she was acting, reacting, pure reflex. Your mother gave no thought to her age. She threw herself courageously at those men, went on the attack. She leapt at the Kalashnikov group, one man after the other, to take them down. There were no rules. She made it up as she went along.

ONE MAN DOWN!

You saw it.

ANOTHER MAN DOWN!

You saw it.

BUT...BUT...BUT!

You barked. And then your alter ego barked. The Hellhound was shouting. He realized what was happening, saw it unfolding in slow motion before him. Saw who had stepped up to protect him. He understood. He understood her bravery as she flew in the face of all those guns. He was watching it happen. She flew at the Afghan government's troop of assassins, she threw herself at them, she leapt at them, she was shot. A lurid spray of red blood burst from one of her shoulders, she was thrown almost two feet, she crumpled to the ground. She got up. Once again, she leapt. Once again, she was shot. But she didn't stop. And then one of the assassins shot another of the assassins. And then...and then.

The Hellhound was shouting.

And you were shouting.

Aaaaah! you both shouted.

Your mother died, and the commandant of the mujahideen organization didn't die, and neither did the Hellhound. The Kalashnikov attackers' surprise attack had failed. Because there was a dog, and the dog had confused them, gotten the better of them—they had missed their chance at carrying out the assassination. Finally, the commandant's men responded. Seven minutes later the men with the Kalashnikovs had been killed. Every last one. But...but your mother was gone and wouldn't be coming back.

She had died.

Even her corpse had dignity.

This, Guitar, was the second to last turning point in your destiny. Yes, because things were changing. Even before you realized it, Guitar, your alter ego—your second self—was switching from one track to another, changing the course of destiny. The Hellhound was kneeling before Goodnight's corpse. Kneeling low, almost bowing, crossing himself. You'd seen him do this once before. The Hellhound was moaning. *Oooaaoo, aaoooooh.* I swear...I swear I'll never forget this...the second time you've risked your life...I'll never forget! he cried. I swear on my life, I'll get them for this!

A bolt of spiritual lightning slammed through the Hellhound's body.

1980. The Hellhound would get his revenge. What did that mean? It meant he had declared war on the Afghan government's army and on the new Afghan government that supported the army, and on the Soviet Union that stood behind them both. The Hellhound was himself a mujahideen now. He abandoned his Catholic faith and recited the Shahada before witnesses, thereby officially converting to Islam. The choice came naturally. He had been given a sign. My dog lay down her life to protect me—how could I not honor her by...how could I...how could I! So he pressed the switch, changed course. He gave up being a luchador. He was too old now anyway. It was too much of a drain now, getting up there in the ring. But he still needed a second face, needed to serve the people somehow, or he couldn't deal with the moral dilemma that faced him. And so, with absolutely perfect timing, ever so easily, the Hellhound converted. He was reborn. Devoting himself to jihad as a member of the mujahideen was good. That was it: for the benefit of the Afghan people, he would "Destroy the Soviet Union!" as he cried in his Mexican Spanish–accented Pashto, and this would make up for the negative effect of his immoral activities. This would balance out the evil of his work as a criminal. An outer face and an inner face. And so, even as he managed the cartel, he trafficked drugs from Afghanistan on a global scale and used the profits to support mujahideen organizations and often went out onto the battlefields himself.

As did you, Guitar.

Just as your alter ego's destiny had changed, so had yours. Naturally, you accompanied the Hellhound onto the battlefields. You yourself desired this. You had seen it—seen your mother, Goodnight, doing her stuff as a military dog, putting up a fight. Fighting to the death. The sight of her valiance was seared into your mind: how she had hurled herself at the attackers without flinching and struggled against them, bitten them, killed them. The image was there, indelible. SHE SHOWED ME WHAT TO DO! you thought. MY MOTHER DIED TO SHOW ME!

I'LL FIGHT!

And so, in 1980, you lived a new life, acted out a new role, as a mujahideen military dog. You went into battle in Afghanistan. Like your alter ego, you possessed two faces. An outer face and an inner face. You were a drug-sniffing dog and a military dog.

It was a huge transformation.

But this was still only the second to the last.

You, dogs, dogs whose bloodlines were channeled by the twentieth century, by a century of war, a century of military dogs, you who were scattered over the face of the earth, increasing your numbers, where, in the end, would the branches of your great family tree converge?

What was your destiny?

The Afghan War devolved into a quagmire. For the USSR. All sorts of miscalculations were made, right from the start. Kabul had immediately been brought under control, and yet people refused to recognize the Soviet-backed puppet government. Any number of rebellions and riots broke out. The situation remained grave. Far from being worn down, the mujahideen organizations grew stronger by the day, month after month, year after year. New anti-Soviet factions kept popping up, and by spring 1981 the USSR had surpassed what was supposed to be the upper limit of one hundred thousand soldiers stationed in Afghanistan. This was all a miscalculation, of course. They still couldn't crush the rebellions. They had bungled it.

In 1981, efforts to suppress the jihad made no headway.

No headway was made in 1982, either.

Afghanistan could not be kept stable. The country was being destroyed. The miscalculations continued.

Clearly this war (this "conflict," from the Soviet perspective) was going to be long. Clearly it was going to be a quagmire.

As the Afghan War continued, the Soviet Union itself began undergoing changes. The most obvious was the drama that surrounded the change in leadership. It wasn't a coup. On November 10, 1982, Leonid Brezhnev (General Secretary of the Communist Party, Marshal of the Soviet Union, Chairman of the Presidium of the Supreme Soviet) died. He was seventy-six and died of illness. He was succeeded as general secretary by Yuri Andropov, who had previously served for fifteen years as the director of the KGB. Andropov was sixty-eight. He called on the resources of his old haunt in order to solidify his grasp on power. He named the chairman of the KGB, a confidant, as interior minister and named the Azerbaijan KGB chief as deputy premier. He tried, in other words, to remove everyone in the Brezhnev faction from government. And his reliance on the KGB didn't stop with personnel matters of this sort— he realized its potential usefulness in bringing all sorts of problems under control. If General Secretary Andropov said "Do it!" every bureau in the KGB snapped into action. For instance, it was occasionally possible to dilute the criticisms that were being leveled against the USSR and that had been growing shrill in the wake of its invasion of Afghanistan, by spreading information about arms reductions and the abolition of nuclear weapons, and it was the job of the KGB First Chief Directorate, which handled everything relating to foreign operations and intelligence, to spread (quietly) this information (or misinformation). The First Chief Directorate was made up of ten departments that handled espionage operations in various geographical regions. The third department, for instance, was in charge of the United Kingdom, Australia, New Zealand, and Scandinavia; the sixth department was in charge of China, Vietnam, and North Korea; and so on. Andropov fully exploited the potential of these ten departments and did so by granting himself vast authority of a sort that would never have been permitted when Brezhnev was general secretary. Naturally, he also decided to use the KGB to improve—from the Soviet perspective—the situation in Afghanistan. And so it came about that *they* were sent in. It happened in summer 1983: the most highly classified unit under the administration of KGB Border Guard Headquarters set foot on Afghan soil. It was known by the code name "S," or sometimes "Department S." On June 16, Andropov had been chosen as the new Chairman of the Presidium of the Supreme Soviet, so he now had control over everything—the party, the KBG, and the army. He had climbed his way to the top both in name and in fact, and was both the leader of and the most powerful person in the entire Soviet Union. This was how "S" got permission to carry out independent operations, free from army supervision—an unprecedented level of authority. "S" had no need to be in contact with the Main Intelligence Directorate, or GRU, despite the fact that the GRU oversaw all the special forces in the USSR.

"S" was in charge of all special operations within the KGB. The KGB Border Guards as a whole had more combat experience than any of the Soviet Union's other military organizations, having been active since the Great Patriotic War (World War II). And within the Border Guards, "S" was special. It specialized in unconventional warfare.

"S" rapidly adapted itself to the battle against the mujahideen.

Its fighters made use of the difficult, hilly terrain. They learned how to counter the special tactics of the Afghan jihadists.

Even then "S" hadn't realized its full potential. The Soviet Union itself was still changing. The drama surrounding its leadership continued. On February 9, 1984, General Secretary Andropov suddenly passed away after fifteen months in office. His successor was Konstantin Chernenko, a man who had been born, astonishingly enough, in 1911. He was way too old to be doing this. The only reason he could take over from Andropov was that he had been a loyal follower and right-hand man to Brezhnev. The old faction Andropov had struggled to crush was back. General Secretary Chernenko died on March 10, 1985, however, also of sickness.

Too old.

"S" found its fortunes changing, then changing again. If Andropov had remained general secretary, "S" might have managed to turn the quagmire of the Afghan War into something closer to a pond, at least, with relatively clear waters. "S" probably could have calmed the situation. But that wasn't what happened. Because the Soviet leaders kept popping in and out so fast, one after the other. General Secretary Brezhnev was replaced by General Secretary Andropov, General Secretary Andropov was replaced by General Secretary Chernenko. Three deaths from sickness, one sudden. But these three men weren't the only ones to have an effect on the fortunes of "S." The unit—the most highly guarded secret at KGB Border Guard Headquarters—had been created by the man who preceded General Secretary Brezhnev. The previous general secretary...except that he wasn't general secretary. Until April 1966, the party had put a moratorium on the use of this title, going instead with "first secretary"—a title that Brezhnev had used for his first year and a half in the position. First Secretary of the Central Committee of the Communist Party. Why had "general secretary" been abandoned? Because that was the title Stalin had used. And who had decided to abandon the title? Which forces? Forces critical of Stalin, obviously. Who was first secretary before First Secretary Brezhnev? The man who had declared that Stalin was a despot. The man who had delivered a searing critique of Stalin in 1956 in a closed session at the Twentieth Congress of the Communist Party. Nikita Khrushchev.

The man Red China's leader, Mao Zedong, hated.

Khrushchev had had a dream. He dreamed of a day—sometime, somewhere—when the Cold War would turn hot. Perhaps the magma would come spurting up in the form of a proxy war somewhere in the Third World. And just imagine how cool it would be if, when that day came, the USSR could dispatch to the front lines of that regional conflict a unit so unlike any other that it would take people's breath away—imagine the value that would have as propaganda! Incomparable! He had that dream. And so he gave the order, almost as a joke. And when it reached the end of the long chain of command, having made its way through that rigid bureaucratic system, the order was rigorously enacted. All the romance of the dream died, and it was turned into something utterly pragmatic and real. Two former communist space dogs were the raw material from which the new reality was fashioned. Two Soviet heroes. A male dog named Belka and a bitch named Strelka.

It had all started with them.

And it was continuing with them.

In 1982. A dog and a bitch, heirs to the same names.

And in 1983.

And in 1984.

And in 1985.

Their line continued, unbroken.

A unit of killers who would fight the anticapitalist war, training in the very real Arctic.

In short, "S" had its origins in Khrushchev's dream. Years later, reality had chipped its way through the shell of that dream, picked at the edges of the hole, and then shaken the last pieces off so that it stood fully revealed, a monstrous "unit" with a life of its own. But Brezhnev had a memory. He had been part of the group that brought Khrushchev down. He himself had pushed Khrushchev out in October 1964 and taken his place as first secretary. He wanted to expunge all trace of Khrushchev's administration. And so he offered a reappraisal of Stalin's legacy and changed his title from "first secretary" to "general secretary." And so, in April 1966, General Secretary Brezhnev was born. And so, years later, when the situation in Afghanistan became impossible, Brezhnev chose not to call on "S" to make things right. The KGB suggested bringing "S" in, but Brezhnev refused. The whole idea… it sort of had that Khrushchev smell to it.

Then Andropov became general secretary, and he used "S."

But he died.

Then Chernenko became general secretary, and as an old geezer who had once been the late Brezhnev's right-hand man, he thought this whole "S" thing stank of Khrushchev. He couldn't pinpoint the source of the effluvium because he was so old, his sense of smell going. But he intuited it. Brezhnev had always made a point of that, back when he'd been boss. *Don't give Khrushchev anything. Not a thimbleful of cat food.*

Chernenko steered clear of "S."

In the end, "S" only had seven months to show what it could do. It never had a chance to play a significant role in the first half of the Afghan War.

Only a little more than seven months. A very short time.

And yet, even so, something happened.

An epoch-making event. For dogs.

In the second week of December 1983, "S" was in a valley amidst the hills of northeastern Afghanistan, having been led there by a general known as the Director—the Director of Department S. In this area the main road to the capital was subject to frequent targeted attacks from a mujahideen organization hoping to steal Soviet supplies. "S" launched a targeted attack of its own against the mujahideen organization, which excelled in guerrilla techniques. "S" used the same sort of guerrilla techniques. But while the jihadists really were guerrilla fighters—in the sense that they were "irregulars"—"S" was a regular army unit. The difference between the two was enormous in terms of their structures for communicating orders, their discipline, and the refinement of their land war tactics. "S" was a regular guerrilla unit, so to speak. Its fighters were consummate professionals, but they conducted only surprise and sneak attacks. The mujahideen had no idea the Soviet army had units like this, so "S" had no trouble penetrating their defenses. "S" didn't rely on MiG fighters, after all, and didn't ride in on T-64 tanks, and didn't even send in attack helicopters. It had some auto-cannons to intimidate the enemy, but heavy firearms were not its main weapons. It used another kind of weapon.

Military dogs.

The unit's special nature allowed it to catch the mujahideen off guard.

Ever so easily. From behind.

And then it happened.

The scene was set. Ninety-one men lying on the ground. Ninety-one bodies, that is. Dead. Eighty-eight were mujahideen. Former jihadists. Their weapons had not been particularly up-to-date. They had a rocket launcher, but that was their only heavy firearm. Other than that it was all automatic rifles and pistols for self-protection. A few of the men had even had matchlocks. Most of the mujahideen were Pashtuns. Farther north there were armed groups made up largely of Tajiks, but in this more rugged region the bands tended to be composed of Pashtuns, and of Pashtuns known for their Islamic fundamentalism. There was one casualty among the mujahideen who was not a Pashtun, however. One among eighty-eight. He was a Mexican. He had a beard, and his blondish *mestizo* hair had been dyed black. His once-brawny physique had no strength in it now, all his life having flowed out onto the sand around him.

The wind sighed pointlessly over the desolate valley.

Apart from that, it was quiet.

And then you growled.

You, Guitar. The Mexican lay at your feet, two cartridge belts slung across his chest, dressed in the manner of the Muslims of this particular region. He was your master. He was dead. Your master, your alter ego, your second self, the Hellhound. He was dead.

You were alive.

The single survivor on the mujahideen side.

You were surrounded.

By countless dogs. Military dogs belonging to "S." Four strategic divisions, subset of "S," were operating together that day, in that place. Each one was composed of four humans and twelve dogs. So there were, in fact, forty-eight dogs in all. That was the exact number, though you couldn't count them. There should have been sixteen people, but in fact there were only thirteen. The other three were bodies. Corpses. You had killed them.

You had taken them down, trying to protect your master.

You, a mongrel. You had watched your mother, Goodnight, and then... all on your own, you had learned, turned yourself into a military dog. You had guarded him as best you could.

But your master died.

Your second self died.

You were surrounded. Because you were the only survivor. The humans were standing on the outskirts of the circle, and all you could see were dogs.

You didn't bark.

You growled.

The dogs watched you.

Then suddenly one barked. *Woof!*

Another barked. *Woof!*

And another. *Woof!*

Woof!

Woof!

Woof!

You stopped growling, though you didn't realize it. You were overwhelmed. Swept up in the phenomenon that had suddenly blossomed around you. For a moment you felt as if you were listening to a chorus. You were enclosed, and the enclosure was singing. Not loudly—the melody was, if anything, tranquility itself. So it seemed to you. Unable to look your enemy in the eye, because the enemy was all around you, three hundred sixty degrees, you lowered your gaze, stared down at your feet. That, you felt, was all you could do. The Hellhound was dead. Yeah, I'm dead, he was saying to you. You...YOU'RE DEAD? YOU'RE MY ALTER EGO, AND YOU'RE DEAD? And you listened to the song. All around you, three hundred sixty degrees of singing.

Woof!

Woof!

Woof!

Woof!

Woof!

You raised your eyes again.

You didn't growl. You barked. *Woof!*

Forty-eight dogs fell silent. Then one stepped toward you. A male. A fairly large dog. His stride was dignified, leisurely.

He stood in front of you.

This is it, Guitar. This is the moment. This is the place where your destiny changes course again, one last time. Your alter ego was gone, and now only one being in the entire world had the right to flip the switch, to turn your destiny from one track to the other, and that was you. You. Two had become one. You felt a bolt of spiritual lightning slam through your body. You felt a sign. But that sign wouldn't turn you into a devout Christian or a devout Muslim. You...you would be a dog. That was all. The dog standing in front of you spoke to you, first with his eyes, and then by speaking to you.

ARE YOU A MONGREL? he asked. A DOG WHO MONGRELIZES?

I'M ME, you answered. I'M ONE.

YOU WANT TO LIVE?

TO LIVE... YES, I'LL LIVE! I'LL NEVER DIE!

COME, THEN.

AM I A PRISONER?

NO.

NO?

YOU'VE COME.

I HAVE?

YOU CAME TO US. SO WE CAME TO GET YOU.

You shuddered when you heard those words, and then you pressed the switch. You would make the great change.

The dogs spoke among themselves in dog language; the humans spoke Russian. A man in camouflage with no epaulettes was making a report over the radio. He was asking for a truck to come get them, and soon a six-wheel-drive vehicle arrived on the scene. The scene changed: now there were forty-eight dogs plus one, ninety-one bodies, thirteen people, and a six-wheel truck—an "S" rapid-deployment vehicle—carrying heavy machine guns and mortars. An officer dressed in an ordinary army uniform hopped out. The wind was still whipping wildly over the valley. The man who had spoken Russian over the radio had conveyed the dogs' wishes, not his own, and the officer who had come was neither a company nor a battalion commander; he was a general. He was the man known as the Director.

The thirteen living men saluted the general crisply with one motion.

As he approached, the circle of dogs, the enclosure, broke.

"You've accepted him?" the general asked.

Two dogs stood before the general within the ring of "S" dogs: the mujahideen survivor and the male dog who had taken up a position opposite him. The general had addressed the latter. His gaze, however, was fixed on the survivor.

Woof! said the male dog.

"All right, then, Belka," said the general. "He looks a bit rough around the edges, but you think it'd be a waste to kill him, huh? He's got what it takes, I guess…he was born with it. Or maybe he's got some amazing story too? I bet he does. You, boy, here in Afghanistan, serving the mujahideen." The general was addressing the new dog now. "I believe it. Belka accepted you. You were chosen. Your blood is good enough, you can join the line. You are accepted. Come."

That's what happened on the battlefields of Afghanistan in the second week of December 1983.

An epoch-making event in dog history.

Woof, woof, woof, woof!

The Afghan War continued, but "S" pulled out. For the time being, that is. Because General Secretary Chernenko had stripped it of much of its authority, steered clear of it. Then, in March 1985, General Secretary Chernenko himself pulled out—of Soviet politics, of the world. And the fifty-four-year-old Mikhail Gorbachev was chosen as the next general secretary. Gorbachev was much, much younger than his predecessor, Chernenko, and than Chernenko's predecessor Andropov, and than Andropov's predecessor Brezhnev. Party personnel at other levels began changing too, as one generation gave way to the next.

General Secretary Gorbachev insisted that reform was necessary.

Under General Secretary Gorbachev, the Communist Party leadership announced one new policy after the next.

He made *perestroika* his slogan. "Restructuring."

The Afghan War continued. It wasn't over yet. Of course not. It was a ten-year quagmire, after all.

In July 1986, Gorbachev declared in a speech that he "would equate the word *perestroika* with revolution." He stated explicitly that he was aiming to reform the USSR fundamentally. But how could this be? Hadn't the Soviet leadership always regarded as absolutes the bourgeois revolution of February 1917 and the socialist revolution in October the same year? So there were those who voiced their doubts. And there were others who had doubts but kept them to themselves, became confused. And there were those who declared, smiles playing on their faces, that only the revolutions of 1917 could ever have real meaning for the homeland.

Those, for instance, who belonged to "S." The humans, of course, not the dogs.

The general of "S," the Director, had pounded this into their heads.

The Director himself had taught them how to fight without weapons, how to kill without a sound, how to survive. And he had filled their minds with rigid, unyielding ideas. We will not allow the counter-revolutionaries to take control; we must defend the achievements of socialism at home and abroad; Marxism-Leninism alone is strong, legitimate. If you can't be a true believer, you might as well be a priest. Indeed, when new members were inducted into "S" they were required to sign a document pledging their loyalty to the unit—any member who betrayed the unit would be killed. So even if they had wanted to, it would have been impossible for anyone to start having doubts about their ideology—to abandon their faith in the Revolution—and go back to the Russian Orthodox Church. If you changed your mind, if you had a change of heart, you would be executed. It was as simple as that. Though in actual practice, this was never a problem. Once a man entered "S," no one from the general on down ever had the slightest doubt about the legitimacy of his work. The men were fervent in their belief. The unit's insignia proved their legitimacy.

Their insignia featured a skull.

Not a human skull. An animal skull. A dog's skull.

A dog's skull with the earth in the background.

That was the badge "S" used.

The earth was angled so that the north of the Eurasian continent was visible. So that this part of the globe faced the viewer, so that it was the front.

Every member of the unit had seen the skull on which the insignia was modeled. Once or twice, maybe three times, they had been granted an audience. There, in the room known as the Director's Office, they had trembled with emotion at the sight. The real thing was preserved in a sort of casket shaped like the earth. In a globe specially constructed for that purpose. It was burned, blackened, little scraps of flesh clinging to it, hanging from it, here and there. Those were the traces that had been left when it was immolated on its reentry into Earth's atmosphere, when the man-made satellite began to burn, to disintegrate. This was the skull of the first living creature from Earth to look down at the planet from outer space. These were the remains, in other words, of the space dog, the Russian laika, that had extended the reach of Soviet territory, of the homeland, into outer space.

"We will wage war against the counter-revolutionary movement and fight with the power of heroes—and of this hero! We are the embodiment of legitimacy!" The words reverberated through the Director's Office.

It was never made clear how exactly the skull of this dog—once both a hero of the state and a popular idol—found its way into the Director's hands. Because all information, even the most trivial, relating to the space dogs was classified as top secret. But the man who created "S" was closer than anyone else to those secrets. He had control of the space dogs' bloodline. And he determined that nothing as insignificant as Khrushchev's fall from power would derail the project, now that his posse at the breeding ground in South Siberia was unquestionably approaching the ideal. This project could not be allowed to die...this lineage could not be allowed to die. These dogs. This was where a master spy showed his true value as a master spy. And so, at the age of twenty-six and seven months, this young man who was expected to go far, who had been promoted within the KGB to the rank of lieutenant, responded to nonexistent expectations by contacting various branches of the KGB, trying this and that, working to realize a plan of his own. For the dogs... to guarantee their survival.

And one day a door opened, and out came the skull of the first space dog.

Someone told him Sputnik 2 wasn't designed for recovery, so it had broken to pieces when it entered the atmosphere on May 14, 1958. Someone else insisted that the date had been April 4, not May 14, and the satellite burned up. One document, however, indicated that the wreckage of Sputnik 2 had in fact been recovered. The real thing, the secret document itself, remains in some KGB office. A copy is held, as well, in the secret vaults of the Council for the Memorial Museum of Cosmonautics. They may have been there from the beginning, or perhaps they found their way in at some later date. Either way, the documents are there.

And the door opened. The same door that opened to admit the wrecked cockpit of the MiG fighter Yuri Gagarin—the first human to fly in outer space, on the Vostok 1 in April 1961, known for his famous comment "The earth is blue"—had been riding in when he was killed in a mysterious crash in 1968. It opened, and out came the skull.

It was a real laika skull, from a mid-sized dog.

Documents proved that this was *her* skull.

"S" came into existence toward the end of the 1960s. It was a code-named unit under the administration of the KGB Border Guard Headquarters, but with its own authority. "S" had been inspired by Khrushchev's dreamy romanticism, but the cheesiness of its origins had been eliminated, and it now had a rational basis for its existence. The involvement of that dog, the bitch who demonstrated to the world the greatness of the Soviet homeland, proved that we, "S," were not just some group of renegades.

We were born of that event, on November 3, 1957—Marxism-Leninism's single greatest achievement. We are its progeny.

"We are a corps centered on dogs, and it is our job to support our dogs," the creator of "S" told his men. "We ourselves are the progeny of the bitch named Laika."

So their legitimacy could never be in doubt.

And so, he said, pledge allegiance to the "S" insignia!

The men pledged their allegiance. They saluted the skull in its globe.

And so, when Gorbachev declared that perestroika was revolution in July 1986, the members of "S" could deny this without batting an eye, smiles on their faces. The revolution had already happened, in 1917, and we were its progeny—we, the members of "S." Gorbachev's statement was a joke. They knew it. But sometimes even words mumbled in sleep can alter the course of history. It doesn't matter who is legitimate, who is the renegade.

The Afghan War continued. The two sides were in a stalemate, to put it simply, and it was slowly becoming apparent how closely this Central Asian

quagmire resembled those ten years of war that America had initiated…
America's Southeast Asian quagmire. First there was the massive scale of the
two conflicts—endless wars of attrition fought against guerrillas. Then there
were all the other, smaller similarities. Young Soviet conscripts were destroying themselves with drugs. They smoked hashish the way young American
conscripts had used LSD, heroin, and marijuana during the Vietnam War.
Indiscriminant massacres were committed because it was impossible to tell
civilians from guerrillas. During the Vietnam War, unspeakable tragedies
had unfolded in villages the Americans regarded as Vietcong strongholds—
everyone in these villages was slaughtered, from infants to the elderly; even
domestic animals were shot; and naturally the women were raped—and now,
in the same manner, villages the Soviets regarded as mujahideen strongholds
were completely wiped out. Everyone in these villages was slaughtered, from
infants to the elderly, even domestic animals were shot, and naturally the
women were raped, gang-raped. Limited use was made of chemical weapons,
albeit in secret. In the Vietnam War, the American army had done the same
thing, in secret.

The Soviets were confronted with the fact that the Afghan War was "our
Vietnam."

And there was Gorbachev. There was Gorbachev, singing his slogan: *Perestroika! Perestroika!* He initiated a completely new foreign policy. Relations
with the West would now be aimed at fostering dialogue, guided by the notion
of "new thinking" diplomacy. Gorbachev was trying to change the direction
of the Soviet-American arms race. The Soviet economy was stagnating. It
had been subsiding into stagnation for some time, but Gorbachev was the first
to acknowledge this. In fact, the USSR was on the verge of bankruptcy. He
admitted it. And their enormous military expenditures were putting the most
pressure on the treasury. One aim of Gorbachev's "new thinking" diplomacy
was to make it possible to cut the military budget. He pushed ahead with
negotiations concerning nuclear non-proliferation, and finally he was able to
improve relations not only with America, Britain, and France, but even with
China. Red China—the third player in the Cold War. The whole shift was
described by the term *détente*.

Something was changing.

Something was speeding up.

And then Gorbachev made the announcement: "Withdrawing troops from Afghanistan is also perestroika."

The United Nations had gotten involved in peace negotiations relating to the Afghanistan problem in 1982 but had failed to make any progress. In April 1988, with this statement by Gorbachev, everything happened in a flash: a peace accord was signed. Now it was settled. The Soviet army would withdraw from Afghanistan.

The withdrawal began officially in May 1988 and was completed in February 1989.

On February 25. But did the Afghan War really end on that day? No, it did not. Because the Afghan government was still communist, and it was still friendly with the USSR, and it was still at odds with the mujahideen. And to make matters worse, the mujahideen organizations were at odds with each other as well, divided by all sorts of factors: were they composed largely of Pashtuns or non-Pashtuns, were they Sunni or Shi'a, and so on. Obviously the country was bound to descend into civil war. The USSR decided, first of all, that it would be unprofitable to allow Kabul's pro-Soviet communist government to collapse; second, that since the Soviet Union shared a twelve-hundred-mile border with Afghanistan, any exacerbation of the situation within Afghanistan would pose a threat to the safety of the border regions; and third, that if the current government were to fall and be replaced by an Islamic government, the ensuing confusion was bound to spread to the Central Asian members of the USSR, including Tajikistan, Uzbekistan, and the other Islamic autonomous republics.

So the USSR continued to supply the communist, pro-Soviet Afghan government with vast quantities of aid, both financial and in the form of weapons.

And then something else happened.

This was just before the last of the one hundred thousand occupying soldiers withdrew.

On January 24, 1989, a meeting of the Politburo of the Central Committee of the Communist Party of the Soviet Union ratified a top-secret report that gave permission to the KGB Border Guards, then stationed in the north of Afghanistan, to carry out a certain strategic mission.

Needless to say, this was in violation of the peace accord.

The USSR's quagmire, the Afghan War, wasn't over yet. The Soviet Union itself refused to let it end. It kept going until the end of the year. But only in secret. The KGB took control, and only units that knew how to keep their activities secret were involved. Once again "S" was called in. Its fighters were special operations professionals, and they would keep quiet about their achievements in battle. Its fighters were the most powerful unconventional troops in the entire Border Guard. As for Gorbachev...Gorbachev was content to let this happen, as long as the Afghan "problem" was settled, as long as it didn't cause any disruption domestically. He wasn't concerned that the plan "stank of Khrushchev," as Chernenko and Brezhnev had been. Indeed, as far as he was concerned "S" was just another useful organization—he wasn't even aware that it had originated in Khrushchev's time. And so once again "S" was granted authority to carry out illegal assignments in secret. It eliminated targets marked for elimination. In public, Gorbachev continued shouting his slogan as before: *Perestroika! Perestroika!* And in December 1989, he finally pushed his "new thinking" diplomacy to the limit. A Soviet-American summit was held off the shore of Malta, on a Soviet missile cruiser named *Slava*. Gorbachev welcomed American President George H. W. Bush with a smile. He announced that the Soviet Union and the United States were now friends. The Cold War was over. Lasting peace had been achieved between the two states. A press conference attended by reporters from all around the world was held on December 3. All across the globe, people stared at their television screens. This was a day that would go down in the history of the twentieth century. In human history. And as for dog history...dog history...

On that same day, December 3, a secret order was issued.

"Destroy all the evidence," read the order, which had come by way of Moscow. "Leave no trace of the top-secret operations in Afghanistan. There is no Cold War. Kill the dogs."

"This is not 1991."

And then the street fighting began.

This was not a rehearsal. This was no simulation in the life-sized model of an abandoned city. Eighty-two people died the first day. Among them were seven bosses in the two largest criminal organizations. Three from the Russian mafia, four from the Chechen mafia. No one was paying attention anymore to whether the bloodshed was balanced. Then there were casualties among the various criminal organizations that had started streaming into the city from all across Russia, all over Asia. Many, many casualties.

The dogs began by paying house calls. There were groups on the move with lists of the members of the mafia organizations, photographs affixed. Three or four of them. One of the groups comprised an old Slavic woman with thick glasses who was built like a barrel, a Japanese girl still in her early teens, and seven dogs. Their list had the names and addresses of the mafia headquarters, affiliated facilities, and businesses, and the names and home addresses of their leaders, along with other details. The old lady led the dogs on a leash. The girl wore a *shapka*, pulled down low over her forehead against the cold; her face, as she walked, wore no expression at all. She looked, somehow, like the old lady's granddaughter. She was obese. Obese in a combative sort of way. A cold glitter shone in her eyes. She was Japanese, but not in the usual way. She was Japanese like a Hokkaido dog is Japanese. Yes, indeed: she wasn't a person, she was a dog.

Why? Because she had a dog name.

Given to her as a sign of her legitimacy: Strelka.

House calls. They'd finish one, then go on to the next. The old lady managed the gun, the dog-girl handled the dogs. Their first target lived in a luxury apartment complex. They could make him open the door himself, or they could blast it open with the gun. The girl-dog gave the commands, sometimes in Russian, sometimes in a dog language made up solely of gestures. The dogs dashed in. Keeping low, keeping out of sight. Seven dogs entered, one in charge. He was a male. The dog that was once known as number 47, the dog the girl-dog used to call Forty-seven. He went by a different name now.

Now he was Belka. His dad had died, so he had graduated from a number to a name.

Belka sprang, killed. Fell into formation with the other six dogs, leapt instantly at the target, and it was over. Just like that.

At the same time, in another place, on the grounds of a grand estate, a guard dog was killed. Teeth ripped silently into his throat. First the dogs killed their brethren, then they killed the target's guards, then they killed the target. In some locations the target knew immediately that he was under attack and tried to escape in his car. But the surrounding roads had been closed. By dogs. They ringed the expensive car with its bulletproof windows, leapt at it, caused the target to panic, to err—to die.

They led him to kill himself.

It was a canine rebellion. On the first day, no one noticed how many mafiosos had been killed. Aside from the mafia themselves, that is, and the authorities and the company executives the mafia had bought.

Then, late at night, the city caught fire. *That* people noticed…And there was rioting. That same night, an old man surrounded by dogs read coordinates from a military map. To the dogs. And then into a radio handset.

1991. Moscow in the summer. In the early hours of the day, before dawn, the government declared a state of emergency. Now it was the afternoon. Already more than five hundred tanks were positioned at various points around the city. The man who had been elected the first president of the Soviet Union in March of the previous year had suddenly been removed from power. A conservative coup d'état was underway. The ringleaders included the defense minister, the head of the KGB, and the vice president. The troops in the tanks were prepared to conduct a mass arrest of everyone in the reformers' camp. Television was censored, and the radio played the "Declaration of the Soviet Leadership" again and again. Nevertheless, the people were out in the streets. Gathered before the Russian Parliament, the reformist faction's base. They linked arms to form a human chain, tried to keep the tanks and armored cars from entering. They built barricades—barricades behind barricades, barricades behind barricades behind barricades. Already several thousand demonstrators had converged in the square.

The old man was among them.

All beard and moustache.

He listened to the cheering crowds. The man emerged from the building. The reformists' standard-bearer, the man who stood with the people, who had come to office just two months earlier as the first president of the Russian Federation…of a new Russia that was no longer Soviet—no longer the homeland. His last name began with the letter E.

In the English- and Spanish-speaking worlds, the E became a Y. In German, it became J. It was a J in Dutch as well. In French it remained an E.

This man could change everything, even his initials.

E climbed up onto a T-72 tank stranded among the crowds. The old man watched him, then glanced down at his watch. It was 1:15. The old man watched as E exchanged a few words with the lieutenant in the tank. He read the two men's lips. *Did you come to kill me?* E asked. And the lieutenant replied, *No.*

E was smiling.

The cheering reached a crescendo. The square shook with the chanting: *Ura! Ura!* Only the old man spoke a different word. "Awful," he said, "awful."

With only the slightest of gestures, E urged the crowd to be silent and listen. The people understood his body language and, like well-trained dogs, obeyed. The old man, all beard and moustache, kept muttering to himself. "Awful, awful." E lambasted the reactionary right. E called upon the people to resist. From up there on the tank—rubbing his boots on the tank. The old man glanced at his watch. Soviet time, the homeland's time, had stopped. It was 1:21 now, but only in Russia.

The old man kept grumbling under his breath. "Awful, awful, awful—the whole thing." He could see what was coming. Four months down the road. There would be no Soviet Union. E would have destroyed it. He wouldn't be picky about how he accomplished this, anything would suit him as long as the Union was destroyed. And it wasn't only the Union. At the same time, E would have brought something else, something much larger, to an end.

The dogs set fires. The fires were a trap. They forced the police to disperse, fan out to different areas of the city. A second area was burning, then a third, then a fourth. The police converged on each of these locations. They searched for the arsonists but couldn't find them. The arsonists had vanished into the darkness, leaving no traces. Or perhaps they had left footprints, but no one noticed, because they weren't human. The pads of dog feet, front and back. No one even saw them. Sometimes the dogs remained on the scene, as if they had nothing to do with what had happened, as if they were someone's pets. Others left and wandered the streets, pretending to be wild dogs. Acting the part of a dumb animal was all it took—people were deceived. The dogs climbed trees, if there were any nearby, and hid in the foliage. The arsonists' targets were bases for organized crime, so when the fires started, members of the gangs would come running out, ready to fight. *Who did this? Who's responsible? What group is it?* Reports had been flying back and forth since shortly after noon, so they were ready to give chase. They set out to catch whoever it was. And then the dogs, concealed in the leaves of the trees, would leap down on them, and the men would die. By the time the fourth blaze had been brought under control, people were panicking over the sixth. All the fire engines were out on call.

Attacks were launched simultaneously on all the casinos.

The banks were targeted. Sirens wailed endlessly late at night. You could hear them outside, echoing down the streets. Until the police arrived. Or until the mafia who secretly backed the financial institutions got there. Or until dawn broke.

When morning came, the city was enveloped in clouds of black smoke that announced the collapse of order. Arsonists had struck in seventy-two locations; the temperature across the city had risen a full two degrees.

A two-seated motorcycle was driving along the otherwise empty highway. The speedometer remained fixed at forty miles per hour. Two middle-aged women were riding it. The one gripping the handlebars looked just like the one sitting behind her. The two Slavic sisters that Strelka called WO and WT.

A large posse ran behind the motorcycle.

Down the highway. Incredibly fast.

Eight o'clock in the morning. Before people headed to work. The dogs following the motorcycle split into two groups, one going right and the other left. Then they spilt into four, one for each direction.

Also at 8:00 AM: Strelka woke up.

As she stirred, the seven dogs around her lifted their heads. They had been sleeping in the garage of a mafia estate they had taken. The old lady wasn't there. She was inside, in the kitchen. Making breakfast for Strelka and the seven dogs.

Did you sleep? Strelka asked her dogs.

WE SLEPT, they answered.

DID YOU DREAM? Strelka asked Belka.

No, Belka replied.

I FEEL LIKE I DID. I WAS X YEARS OLD, I THINK, AND HUMAN. FUNNY TO DREAM THAT, SINCE I'M A DOG.

TIRED, HUH? Belka licked Strelka's face. His tongue was soft.

WE'LL ERASE HUMAN TIME, Strelka said. ERASE IT, AND MAKE IT...MAKE THIS...

WHAT? Belka asked.

WHAT YEAR WILL IT BE? the other six dogs asked.

"A year for dogs. The year nineteen-ninety...X," Strelka said. "For starters."

LET'S DO IT! barked Belka.

He barked. Already Strelka and the six other dogs were on their feet. They sensed something. But it was over. By then a sort of *phut* had sounded— a gun with a silencer. Outside the garage. A mafia fighter lay on the ground. Moaning. Twice more: *phut, phut.* And then the old lady appeared in the door to the garage, gun in hand.

"Breakfast is ready," she said. In Russian.

Strelka's face remained blank for a moment; then, slowly, slowly, she began to smile.

"You meant 'breakfast'?" she said in Japanese. "For us."

1991. Moscow in the autumn. The old man was crazy. He listened intently to the military radio transmissions he intercepted. He played with money. He killed. Russians, Armenians, Georgians, Chechens. He fooled around with mounds of banknotes: rubles, US dollars. He was living in an abandoned building. It stood on the outskirts of Moscow, near a garbage dump. For some reason, people were throwing away huge quantities of meat and vegetables. In secret. To control how much went to market. The dump was a sort of graveyard, suspended between the controlled economy and the free-market economy.

The old man stared down at the dump from a paneless window. Sometimes he'd stare at it all day long. People came to pick over the trash. Housewives plowed through it, collecting cabbages. Ignoring the rotting meat. Meat on the verge of rotting...they grabbed. There were old men too, and people out of work, and alcoholics. They took bars of soap. They took empty bottles, which they exchanged for two or three rubles at the recycle center. They picked up old clothes to sell on the black market. The old man watched a man dig up a tattered red flag someone had thrown away, then throw it away again.

In the eyes of the scavengers that autumn, the old man hovering by the window of the abandoned building looked like a ghost. His beard and moustache had been left to grow until his cheeks, his chin, his upper lip were buried in white. Look at him—he is a ghost, lower than the scavengers themselves.

So they ignored him.

Earlier, near the end of summer, someone noticed him.

A burglar had broken into his apartment and tried to steal the only thing he had left in his possession. *Fucking stinks in here*, the burglar said as he scanned the room. He went over and reached out to it. The globe. A second later he was dead. The old man had killed him. The burglar had brought a knife. The knife was stuck in the burglar's heart.

"Even the bones?" the old man had asked the corpse. "The skull? You would go that far?"

And the corpse answered, *Yes*.

So the old man began working for cash.

He killed a punk with a tattoo on his right arm that glorified America. He killed a prostitute with a pro-democratic slogan tattooed on her left arm. People asked him to do it, and he did it. He killed bureaucrats. He killed police officers. Sometimes he charged one hundred rubles, sometimes he charged one hundred dollars. When he returned to his apartment at night, he talked to the globe. I will protect you, he said. Because you're the perfect match for me, he said, I will protect you. Yes, I am talking to you, the skull of a dog whose destiny it was to die in space, sent up with no hope that she would return, sent up to be killed, to continue wheeling around the earth, in orbit, you, skull of a murdered hero.

Who will protect you? I am the only one. I will protect you.

One day, the old man had a guest. An invited guest. The first guest this apartment had seen. A Slavic man, his head balding. He stroked the globe, humming some sort of melody.

A military march? the old man asked.

The middle-aged man looked up. Ah, the song. I didn't realize.

How is your mother?

She's fine. She's still grateful to you, Director. For those...splendid last days.

I am no longer the Director.

Sorry. We're so used to calling you that at home. My father, and me. Both my men.

The only ones in the unit. Father and son, wearing the same insignia.

And how are your sisters?

They're fine too. They've started speaking a bit, two or three words a year.

Your family…did not dissolve.

I beg your pardon?

The Soviet Family Code predicted the dissolution of the family. In 1926.

As far as we're concerned, you're our father now.

Even though we are not related?

That's right.

That is a good family. Except that…I am gone.

You're gone?

The old mad nodded, then asked one last question.

And how are the dogs?

The dogs are well, the guest answered.

That afternoon, the tension that had been building between the mafia organizations throughout the city finally erupted. According to the radio. The television reported that the gangs had declared war on each other. The authorities issued a statement calling for residents of the city to remain indoors. Newspaper reporters rushed hither and yon. The two news agencies, Interfax News and the Russia News Service, transmitted up-to-the-minute reports to every corner of the Eurasian continent. And to the New World. The extraordinary number of dogs on the streets that day was not considered newsworthy. Reports of abnormal sightings were treated as mere blather, vaguely occult in nature, and ignored. Ordinarily one would have expected the tabloids to jump at this kind of thing, but they didn't that day, or the next, or later on. This, too, had been carefully factored into the calculations—the kinds of stories the mass media inevitably focus on, their blind spots. Elaborate preparations had been under way for months in this city, laid on the foundations of hundreds of casualties.

The dogs were rebelling, but their rebellion was invisible.

Ordinary citizens noticed the disorder but assumed it was just the usual gang violence, nothing they should be concerned about.

It helped to have the chaos noticed. Because the media fanned the flames.

And when the flames had been fanned hard enough, people snapped. Finally, the incident expanded to encompass the entire nation.

Certain functions of the city were paralyzed, but the mass transit system was still in order, more or less. The airports were fine. The trains were running. The planes and trains carried "support troops" to the Russian Far East. Naturally, these newcomers got into arguments with the police at the entrance to the city. Not the dogs, though. By afternoon, the dogs were already lying low.

The dogs were guerrillas. They served no government. But they did have rules. Their fighting techniques were as refined as those of any regular army.

But they were guerrillas. They conducted only surprise attacks.

The dogs seized control of several areas. Areas dotted with mafia facilities, the scenes of deaths as yet unknown to the authorities. A printing house that produced counterfeit dollars. A vast underground factory that manufactured counterfeit brand items. A warehouse holding mountains of drugs (these were real, not counterfeit). Another warehouse full of contraband antiquities. Yet another warehouse holding concentrated uranium and disassembled nuclear warheads destined to be smuggled out of the country. The dogs were waiting. Because sooner or later, someone would come to steal these items back. Or some new players would come to make off with them, make them their own. Or maybe someone would simply come looking.

Pretty much anyone who came along was killed.

Four PM. A middle-aged man was directing the dogs. A balding Slavic man. He gave signals to the dogs, eliminated everyone who approached. The dogs' unusual fighting techniques had been used before, in the 1980s, somewhere in Afghanistan. They had been used, as well, west of the line that divided Europe, to assassinate a senior NATO officer. The middle-aged man hummed loudly as he led his lightning squad into battle. He had a submachine gun that he used to cover the dogs' tails, as it were, very precisely. He was the man Strelka called Opera.

At 4:30 PM, still humming, he mowed down four mafia fighters without bothering to send in the dogs. A bit of rapid-fire action was all it took.

The sun had already sunk well below the horizon.

The dogs remained invisible to human eyes.

Other dogs saw them, however. There was barking in the distance. Distant barks answered by distant barks—a conversation. Someone had been cutting the chains on pet dogs' collars. In the forests outside the city, hunters' dogs disappeared. Wild dogs ran through the city streets as if gone mad. Slowly, little by little, something was happening. Little by little, one by one, the dogs were being freed. Various mafia were heading by land toward the Russian Far East. To join the conflict—to enlist in a war that was, they still believed, with other mafia. To steal the drugs that had been left behind, to play their part in what they still believed was a tug-of-war among different criminal organizations.

Mafia all across Russia watched the city very closely.

Here and there, gates were opened. Whole trains were bought. They would screech to a halt a mile short of the station, and dozens of men would descend. Counterfeit papers worked their magic in airports. Police squads that had set up inspection stations on the highway saluted as their old buddies, the mafia kingpins, passed in their motorcades: *Welcome to the Far East!*

Around midnight, the nature of the street fighting changed as a new strategy was introduced. Now the dogs were taking hostages. They no longer lunged at the throats of their targets but brought them back alive, as they had been commanded to do. They brought the hostages back, presented them to the old man.

First one.

Then another.

And another.

All night long.

Barks echoed back and forth across the city.

"I can prepare a table for us to negotiate at," the old man said.

What is all this? the other man said. What the hell are these dogs?

"You remember 1812?" the old man asked.

Who are you? the other man asked. The head of their tribe?

"The Napoleonic Wars. You remember? You are a Russian, right? Or rather, you are a former Soviet? You must have learned your history. How that stupid French emperor marched into Moscow in 1812 with an enormous army, 110,000-men strong—marched into the capital, which the Russian army had decided, strategically, to give him. You remember what happened then?"

What the hell?

"They let the city be destroyed so that Russia would survive. Moscow's residents abandoned the city. Napoleon's army marched into a capital that was all but empty. That night, Moscow burned. It was set on fire. By the Russians. The city burned for a week, two-thirds of it reduced to rubble. And the French...they occupied the rubble and starved. All 110,000 men died of starvation. They ate crows. They ate cats. And still they did not last a month. And what is happening now?"—the old man asked, speaking now to himself, and then answering himself—"This is not 1812. This is not 1991. That is your explanation. You understand? We, the dogs, we condemn Russia! There is your answer."

The hostage's face was deathly white.

1991. Moscow in the winter. The temperature was below five degrees Fahrenheit. Sunset was still a ways off. A blizzard. The old man was walking. He saw three hundred people lined up outside the US Embassy. He stared at the snaking line of visa applicants. People standing without talking, exhaling clouds of white breath. Snow dusted their hats, their hair. The line progressed hardly at all.

It was decided. The end of a state so huge it covered one-sixth of the earth's landmass. Soon, the white-, blue-, and red-striped Russian flag would be hoisted up the pole in front of the Kremlin. Four months had passed since those summer days, and during that time a handful of men who acted in secret had won, and the Soviet Union was finished. Dead.

The old man reached his destination. A closed kiosk on the corner, a large umbrella in a stand in front. A man in an Italian designer suit, his features instantly branding him Caucasian, from the Caucasus, stood waiting. He was young. In his late twenties, perhaps—no older than thirty-one or thirty-two.

"That business this morning," the young man said. "Truly professional."

The old man grinned. "Who did you have following me?" he asked. "And why did you want to see me? Was the guy I killed one of your associates?"

"No, no," the young man said. "He was an enemy. You did me a favor. You know, having a real professional out there…"

"A professional?" the old man said. "You mean me?"

"Yeah. Having a professional like you running around…unchecked… don't know if I like it. Seems dangerous, to tell the truth."

"You want to kill me?"

"No, the opposite," the young man said. "I want to give you what you deserve."

"You want to give me a job, you mean? In your organization?"

"Exactly. Is that against your policy?"

"No," the old man said. I have no policy, his eyes said, twinkling.

Twinkling with scorn…for history.

"Well then, shall we discuss terms? Contract period, benefits, compensation…by the way, I was wondering, what should I call you?"

"My name, you mean?"

"Yes, your name."

"Listen."

"Hmm?"

Silence. Two seconds later, a bell began chiming. It hung in the belfry of a church that had been destroyed long ago, in pre-perestroika times, whose restoration began in the late 1980s. It rang and rang as the snow skittered lightly in random patterns over Moscow.

"Call me the Archbishop," the old man said.

One morning, Strelka awoke to a smell in the air, all over the city—it was the scent of the dogs. One morning, Strelka noticed that the temperature in the city had risen. Hot, isn't it? she said to the dogs. Are we actually killing that fucking cold Russian winter? she asked Belka. *Winterwinterwinterwinterwinterwinter, the fucking billion-year-long Russian winter is finally ending!* she sang to herself, again and again. She lifted her face to the sky, looked once more at the billowing black smoke. She was about to blow up a mafia weapons storehouse she had been guarding until a few minutes ago. She'd watched the old lady making explosives with TNT. You old bag, you're *good*, she had said. And then she had listened to the old lady talking to her—You have no way of knowing this, of course, darling, but my husband was a commissioned officer in the special forces, and so was my son, and I myself used to look after the dogs in the breeding facility, and part of my job was to set up explosives in the training grounds. I know what I'm doing. Since the old lady was speaking in Russian, she didn't understand a word, but she nodded. When someone died, the old lady continued, the Director always took care of the family left behind. Strelka listened, then replied: You're half dog yourself, aren't you? Not that I'm one to speak—I'm *all* dog. She said that in Japanese. Strelka knew that last night, WO and WT had gone around cutting the chains on pet dogs, setting them loose, and agitating the wild dogs. She knew that when WO and WT breathed, their breath smelled like a dog's breath. I'm a dog, so I can tell. They're half dogs too.

I'm a dog. They won't kill me.

With all this street fighting going on, we're invisible.

Belka protected Strelka. He carried out her commands immediately. He was the older brother, watching over the others—and more. There was also the name. He had become the next Belka, so the other dogs acknowledged him, acknowledged that one day, at some point in the future, he would lead them all. Belka slept, awoke, ran. Belka slept stretched out beside Strelka, awoke, ran. Belka lay low, watching passively as gangsters had shootouts in the streets in the early morning, as black cars with tinted windows were blown into the air with rocket launchers. Belka understood. He knew the humans didn't realize that the flames of this war they were fighting were being fanned by dog guerrillas. He knew the humans were looking for human enemies, so they wouldn't suddenly start shooting dogs, or Strelka for that matter, because Strelka was a dog, and because in human eyes she looked like a defenseless human girl. So, Belka said, they'll let Strelka kill them, they'll be killed, and even as they die they won't understand what's happening, and all along, all throughout the town, the dogs…we dogs…*we* will multiply. Belka could feel it happening. He didn't think it, he felt it—all across the Eurasian continent, his brethren, the other dogs…they were setting out, heading for this land, the

Russian Far East, a massive migration.

The humans had it all wrong.

The city was full of dogs loitering, hanging around. So they thought.

They allowed the dogs to remain invisible. Even the dogs who had been trained, thoroughly trained, in the deadly art of street fighting.

All morning, the barking continued back and forth in the distance. Echoing. The dogs were on their way. The dogs were coming. The dogs were getting closer. From the taiga beyond the city, from enclaves in the mountains dozens of miles away, from across the Amur River, from the lands where Russian aristocrats were exiled in the nineteenth century. Gradually, little by little, their numbers increased as they converged on the city. In reality, however, three planes contributed the most to the great migration. Three planes owned by private companies that took off one after the other from Moscow, then landed together in the city. Dogs obeyed their own instincts. When a dog barked somewhere far off, they responded. And humans too... mafia members, too, acted in accordance with instincts they could not disobey. When an organization began to lose its grip on an area, competitors moved in to gobble it up. The three planes brought in 220 members of the most powerful criminal organization in Russia: a far-reaching international gang whose operations extended as far as the old Eastern Bloc, come now to overwhelm the city by force of numbers. The organization could display its power by taking control. We don't need you little guys diddling around—we control the Russian underworld. That was the message. The mass media had been waiting, they were ready to spread the news across the Eurasian continent. They had been primed for two days now.

The timing was perfect.

That afternoon, there were two hours of hell. Hell for the mafia. Then an hour of rest. Rest for the dogs. Intermittent gunshots continued into the evening, but that was all—it was a scene, peaceful in a way, of ordinary mafia warfare. Then, suddenly, the situation changed. First there were Strelka, Belka, and six other dogs; ten minutes later there were Strelka and Belka and five other dogs. Number 114, a bitch, had died. Belka's sister. So there were Strelka and Belka and five other dogs, and then, two minutes later, there were Strelka and Belka and three other dogs. Number 46 and number 113 had died. Belka's brother and sister. Strelka barked. The old lady was yelling frantically in Russian. *Pull back! Pull back!* One minute later Strelka and Belka and three other dogs had become Strelka and Belka and one other dog. Number 44 and number 45 had died, been killed, and Strelka was still barking, and Belka was watching.

The enemy had changed.

The enemy had noticed the canine rebellion.

The dogs in this city were no longer invisible.

All of a sudden, the humans began shooting them.

Belka stared. At the equipment of a group of a dozen men who had joined the fray. They were not mafia. They wore bulletproof helmets that fighter pilots wear and camouflage uniforms, and they had assault rifles with folding stock. They looked nothing like gangsters. Belka stared as number 48 was shot, yelping; Belka heard the yelp, he had to protect Strelka, the dogs are visible, and so Strelka is visible; the enemy will not hesitate to eliminate her. Belka recognized their smell. Not their biological, animal scent, but the smell of their group. Belka felt it. And he was right. The enemy was a special unit belonging to the Russian Federal Security Service, the new Russian secret police, successor to the Soviet KGB. The unit was in charge of domestic security. It was in charge of fighting terrorism. The unit would destroy. The dogs. Their revolution. Officials at the highest levels of the Federal Security Service had realized, during a committee meeting with KGB veterans, that many of the dogs that had turned up in the city were using the same combat techniques "S" had cultivated. The special forces unit was briefed, and arriving on the scene, they killed the dogs very quickly. In fewer than fourteen minutes, Strelka and Belka found themselves alone, with zero other dogs.

At the same moment, in another part of town, a second special forces unit leapt out of an eight-wheel-drive armored truck and started firing at dogs, killing them. None of these extraordinarily talented dogs were allowed to survive. They brought in the truck, jumped out, did their work quickly. Another human ran into the crowd of special forces. Humming as he ran. Opera had bombs strapped to his stomach. He put his finger on the switch.

Singing, now, at the top of his voice, he pressed the switch.

Two hours earlier. The old man said: *These are my terms.*

An hour earlier.

All right, the old man said, I have just injected two different chemicals into you: the first is a truth serum, and the second—you may be surprised to hear—is a rabies virus. It is a biological weapon, actually, he explained kindly, developed during Soviet times. I have got to say it again and again to make the hypnosis work, so I will keep repeating it as often as you like: now that I have captured you, I have finally got what I was after. Now that you have come to this city with 220 of your soldiers, you have finally given me the card I need to negotiate successfully. You volunteered to take charge of this raid because you wanted to put yourself forward. You wanted to be noticed. What are you, number three? Or is it number four? You are the treasurer, right? Yes, it is very nice to rely on your mafia instincts, the old man said to the hostage. I know, you wanted to do something big, he went on. I have been waiting for you, you know, stupid thugs colluding with the government. Here, look, this is a serum that kills the rabies virus, see? The incubation period for rabies may last thirty days, but when you get sick, you will get sick, there is no escape: you will feel uneasy, then terrified, you will have delusions, hallucinations, and then your whole body will go numb and you will die, the old man told the hostage kindly. All I want are the documents that show how the money moves, that is all I ask for, the old man said. All I want to do is stir up a little scandal in the office of the president. That is all, the old man said.

Ten minutes earlier.

That is all I need, that is enough to topple the eight leading figures in the government. With this information I could do it tomorrow, the old man said. I have prepared channels to pass the information along to the Western media—a little international pressure is all it takes in these cases, am I right? Then the whole system will collapse. This is a real revolution, my friend, not like that stuff they pulled in Moscow in the summer of 1991, that was no revolution. Not bad, this, huh? A revolution carried out entirely by dogs, the old man said. The problem is, dogs cannot disappear in Moscow, it is too urban, too much of a national capital, you know what I mean? But out here in the Far East! A *kak zhe?* I am sure you have guessed this already, my friend, but I have totally lost my mind.

One minute earlier.

The old man had trapped his prey in a room in a thirteen-story hotel. The commander of a force of 220 mafia fighters in a room on the twelfth floor. The room had windows, but the shades were drawn. You could hear things, though, from outside. Even through the thick soundproofed glass he could hear the roar of military helicopters hovering over the city. He stood up.

The window exploded. A spray of bullets shattered the glass, shredded the curtains. Quick work, the old man thought. They are fast, faster than I thought, if only by a...he thought. But he never finished his thought.

Now.

The old man's body danced as the bullets pounded it.

1990

Dogs, dogs, where are you now?

Early in 1990, you lay sprawled on the ground at an execution site. You lay in a sea of blood. You had been part of the unit before, part of "S," but now, with one exception, you had been eradicated. The one survivor was looking up, devotion in his eyes. Peering up at the man who stood at the top of the chain of command. At the man known as the Director, the General, and by various other names.

The man had aged.

Our own homeland, he said. To the dog. The Soviet issued the command, he said. That we be eliminated. They ordered it. We are the evidence, they say, that must never be discovered. And so we must be destroyed.

The old man raised his gun, aimed it at the dog.

The dog did not flinch. He listened.

All around the man and the dog a terrible stench hung in the air. The smell of countless deaths, of so much spilled blood.

The old man gazed at the dog.

The dog's name, this dog's name, was Belka.

The unit has disbanded, the old man said. Do you understand that?

Belka listened. He heard. And he answered: *Woof!*

Tears spilled from the old man's eyes. His right hand, gripping the pistol, trembled. I just, he said, I just...I just, I just...

Woof! the old man cried.

"I am going to lose my mind," he told Belka. "And you, you are going to live."

"Belka, why don't you bark?"

Dogs, dogs, here you are.

You penetrated the military's encirclement of the city. Strelka, Belka, the old lady, WO and WT, and a dozen dogs managed to escape. By the next morning, however, WO, WT, and their motorcycle were blown to smithereens. Orders were issued in cities throughout the Russian Far East that dogs were to be hunted down and killed, and as a consequence four thousand dogs died, including many unrelated to the rebellion. Three days after they fled, Strelka's band was reduced to Strelka, who would disguise herself, depending on the situation, as a Chinese-Russian, a Korean-Russian, or a Mongolian-Russian; Belka, who disguised himself as an ordinary pet; and the old lady. It was easier this way; they had greater freedom of movement. Though they did have one bulky bit of luggage. They had the globe. The old lady had presented it to Strelka in an abandoned cabin, in a region midway between the taiga and the wetlands. Strelka accepted it, she pondered its meaning. She decided the old lady was asking her where they should go. She spun the globe.

They had to get out of Russia.

Out, off the Eurasian continent altogether.

For a moment she thought to point at Japan, but then she reconsidered. Like I'd fucking go back there. She moved the tip of her finger up to Sakhalin, then up over the Sea of Okhotsk to the Kamchatka Peninsula. East. They'd keep heading east, off the continent, beyond. But not as far as North America—too fucking *worldly* to go to a fucking English-speaking country, she decided. She jabbed her finger down randomly to the east of the Kamchatka Peninsula.

On an archipelago sandwiched between the Bering Sea and the Pacific Ocean.

The old lady understood.

She got them on a train, which took them to the ocean. They crossed the ocean. The old man's bank account hadn't been frozen yet, so funds were not a problem. They flew in an eight-seat charter plane from Sakhalin to the Kamchatka Peninsula.

Three weeks later, they crossed to another island in the Pacific, though they still hadn't left Russian territory. The crossing took twenty or thirty minutes on a fishing boat that set out from a small coastal village on the southeast edge of the peninsula. They got off the boat, went ashore. The island was unpopulated, but there were a few old wooden buildings. A factory that had all but rotted away. A seafood processing plant run by Japanese capital in the wake of the Russo-Japanese War; it had, apparently, produced canned crab and salmon and had been the base of the North Atlantic fishing industry. You stayed there, preparing, for three months.

You. Three of you. First: Strelka. You watched as the old lady did this and that, working toward the goal. You watched, trusting her. You obtained fake identities, fake pasts, and still you remained there, on the uninhabited island, biding your time. The old lady made trips to the village on the peninsula to buy food and eventually a boat. You and Belka went to the village a few times and learned that sled dogs were kept there, and that there were puppies, four or five months old. The old lady chose seven puppies, bought them.

Little by little, you were getting ready to set sail.

It would happen in secret.

And I ask you: Where will you go? And you answer: We'll leave the world behind, we'll go to Dog Heaven. Who are you? I ask. And you answer: I'm me, fucking asshole.

And then there's you. The other you.

You stand on the beach on the island's eastern shore, gazing out over the vastness of the ocean, beyond the fog. You hear the other dog talking to you, in Japanese. Asking you, "Belka, why don't you bark?"

Soon you will cross the ocean together. And you will kill the twentieth century. You will build a heaven for dogs, only dogs, on that island within the fog, and from there you will declare war on the twenty-first century.

WHAT IS HAIKASORU

?

SPACE OPERA.

DARK FANTASY.

HARD SCIENCE.

With a small, elite list of award-winners, classics, and new work by the hottest young writers, **Haikasoru** is the first imprint dedicated to bringing Japanese science fiction to America and beyond. Featuring the action of anime and the thoughtfulness of the best speculative fiction, Haikasoru aims to truly be the "**high castle**" of science fiction and fantasy.

HAIKASORU
THE FUTURE IS JAPANESE

METAL GEAR SOLID: GUNS OF THE PATRIOTS
—PROJECT ITOH

From the legendary video game franchise! Solid Snake is a soldier and part of a worldwide nanotechnology network known as the Sons of the Patriots System. Time is running out for Snake as, thanks to the deadly FOXDIE virus, he has been transformed into a walking biological weapon. Not only is the clock ticking for Snake, nearly everyone he encounters becomes infected. Snake turns to the SOP System for help, only to find that it has been hacked by the SOP's old enemy Liquid Ocelot—and whoever controls the SOP System controls the world.

GENOCIDAL ORGAN
—PROJECT ITOH

The war on terror exploded, literally, the day Sarajevo was destroyed by a homemade nuclear device. The leading democracies transformed into total surveillance states, and the developing world has drowned under a wave of genocides. The mysterious American John Paul seems to be behind the collapse of the world system, and it's up to intelligence agent Clavis Shepherd to track John Paul across the wreckage of civilizations and to find the true heart of darkness— a genocidal organ.

THE FUTURE IS JAPANESE
—EDITED BY NICK MAMATAS AND MASUMI WASHINGTON

A web browser that threatens to conquer the world. The longest, loneliest railroad on Earth. A North Korean nuke hitting Tokyo, a hollow asteroid full of automated rice paddies, and a specialist in breaking up virtual marriages. And yes, giant robots. These thirteen stories from and about the Land of the Rising Sun run the gamut from fantasy to cyberpunk and will leave you knowing that the future is Japanese!

VIRUS: THE DAY OF RESURRECTION
—SAKYO KOMATSU

In this classic of Japanese SF, American astronauts on a space mission discover a strange virus and bring it to Earth, where rogue scientists transform it into a fatal version of the flu. After the virulent virus is released, nearly all human life on Earth is wiped out save for fewer than one thousand men and a handful of women living in research stations in Antarctica. Then one of the researchers realizes that a major earthquake in the now-depopulated United States may lead to nuclear Armageddon…

SELF-REFERENCE ENGINE
—TOH ENJOE

Toh EnJoe's prize-winning fiction crosses the streams—from hardcore science fiction to bizarre surrealism—and has found an audience across the genre divide. *Self-Reference ENGINE* is a puzzle of a book, where vignette and story and philosophy combine to create a novel designed like a concept album.

THE OUROBOROS WAVE
—JYOUJI HAYASHI

Ninety years from now, a satellite detects a nearby black hole scientists dub Kali for the Hindu goddess of destruction. Humanity embarks on a generations-long project to tap the energy of the black hole and establish colonies on planets across the solar system. Earth and Mars and the moons Europa (Jupiter) and Titania (Uranus) develop radically different societies, with only Kali, that swirling vortex of destruction and creation, and the hated but crucial Artificial Accretion Disk Development association (AADD) in common.

THE NAVIDAD INCIDENT: THE DOWNFALL OF MATÍAS GUILI
—NATSUKI IKEZAWA

In this sweeping magical-realist epic set in the fictional south sea island republic of Navidad, Ikezawa gives his imagination free rein to reinvent the myths of the twentieth-century Japan. The story takes off as a delegation of Japanese war veterans pays an official visit to the ex-World War II colony, only to see the Japanese flag burst into flames. The following day, the tour bus, and its passengers, simply vanish. The locals exchange absurd rumors— the bus was last seen attending Catholic mass, the bus must have skipped across the lagoon— but the president suspects a covert guerrilla organization is trying to undermine his connections with Japan. Can the real answers to the mystery be found, or will the president have to be content with the surreal answers?

HARMONY
—PROJECT ITOH

In the future, Utopia has finally been achieved thanks to medical nanotechnology and a powerful ethic of social welfare and mutual consideration. This perfect world isn't that perfect though, and three young girls stand up to totalitarian kindness and super-medicine by attempting suicide via starvation. It doesn't work, but one of the girls—Tuan Kirie—grows up to be a member of the World Health Organization. As a crisis threatens the harmony of the new world, Tuan rediscovers another member of her suicide pact, and together they must help save the planet…from itself.

YUKIKAZE
—CHŌHEI KAMBAYASHI

More than thirty years ago a hyper-dimensional passageway suddenly appeared… the first stage of an attempted invasion by an enigmatic alien host. Humanity managed to push the invaders back through the passageway to the strange planet nicknamed "Faery." Now, Second Lieutenant Rei Fukai carries out his missions in the skies over Faery. His only constant companion in this lonely task is his fighter plane, the sentient FFR-31 Super Sylph, call sign: YUKIKAZE.

GOOD LUCK, YUKIKAZE
—CHŌHEI KAMBAYASHI

The alien JAM have been at war with humanity for over thirty years…or have they? Rei Fukai of the FAF's Special Air Force and his intelligent tactical reconnaissance fighter plane Yukikaze have seen endless battles, but after declaring "Humans are unnecessary now," and forcibly ejecting Fukai, Yukikaze is on its own. Is the target of the JAM's hostility really Earth's machines?

LOUPS-GAROUS
—NATSUHIKO KYOGOKU

In the near future, humans will communicate almost exclusively through online networks—face-to-face meetings are rare and the surveillance state nearly all-powerful. So when a serial killer starts slaughtering junior high students, the crackdown is harsh. The killer's latest victim turns out to have been in contact with three young girls: Mio Tsuzuki, a certified prodigy; Hazuki Makino, a quiet but opinionated classmate; and Ayumi Kono, her best friend. And as the girls get caught up in trying to find the killer—who just might be a werewolf—Hazuki learns that there is much more to their monitored communications than meets the eye.

TEN BILLION DAYS AND ONE HUNDRED BILLION NIGHTS
—RYU MITSUSE

Ten billion days—that is how long it will take the philosopher Plato to determine the true systems of the world. One hundred billion nights—that is how far into the future Jesus of Nazareth, Siddhartha, and the demigod Asura will travel to witness the end of all worlds. Named the greatest Japanese science fiction novel of all time, *Ten Billion Days and One Hundred Billion Nights* is an epic eons in the making. Originally published in 1967, the novel was revised by the author in later years and republished in 1973.

THE BOOK OF HEROES
—MIYUKI MIYABE

When her brother Hiroki disappears after a violent altercation with school bullies, Yuriko finds a magical book in his room. The book leads her to another world where she learns that Hiroki has been possessed by a spirit from The Book of Heroes, and that every story ever told has some truth to it and some horrible lie. With the help of the monk Sky, the dictionary-turned-mouse Aju, and the mysterious Man of Ash, Yuriko has to piece together the mystery of her vanished brother and save the world from the evil King in Yellow.

BRAVE STORY
—MIYUKI MIYABE

Young Wataru flees his messed-up life to navigate the magical world of Vision, a land filled with creatures both fierce and friendly. His ultimate destination is the Tower of Destiny where a goddess of fate awaits. Only when he has finished his journey and collected five elusive gemstones will he possess the Demon's Bane—the key that will grant him his most heartfelt wish…the wish to bring his family back together again!

ICO: CASTLE IN THE MIST
—MIYUKI MIYABE

A boy with horns, marked for death. A girl who sleeps in a cage of iron. The Castle in the Mist has called for its sacrifice: a horned child, born once a generation. When, on a single night in his thirteenth year, Ico's horns grow long and curved, he knows his time has come. But why does the Castle in the Mist demand this offering, and what will Ico do with the girl imprisoned within the Castle's walls? Delve into the mysteries of Miyuki Miyabe's grand achievement of imagination, inspired by the award-winning game for the PlayStation® 2 computer entertainment system, now remastered for PlayStation® 3.

ROCKET GIRLS
—HOUSUKE NOJIRI

Yukari Morita is a high school girl on a quest to find her missing father. While searching for him in the Solomon Islands, she receives the offer of a lifetime—she'll get the help she needs to find her father, and all she need do in return is become the world's youngest, lightest astronaut. Yukari and her sister Matsuri, both petite, are the perfect crew for the Solomon Space Association's launches, or will be once they complete their rigorous and sometimes dangerous training.

ROCKET GIRLS: THE LAST PLANET
—HOUSUKE NOJIRI

When the Rocket Girls accidentally splash down in the pond of Yukari Morita's old school, it looks as though their experiment is ruined. Luckily, the geeky Akane is there to save the day. Fitting the profile—she's intelligent, enthusiastic, and petite—Akane is soon recruited by the Solomon Space Association. Yukari and Akane are then given the biggest Rocket Girl mission yet: to do what NASA astronauts cannot and save a probe headed to the minor planet Pluto and the very edge of the solar system.

USURPER OF THE SUN
—HOUSUKE NOJIRI

Aki Shiraishi is a high school student working in the astronomy club and one of the few witnesses to an amazing event—someone is building a tower on the planet Mercury. Soon, the enigmatic Builders have constructed a ring around the sun, and the ecology of Earth is threatened by its immense shadow. Aki is inspired to pursue a career in science, and the truth. She must determine the purpose of the ring and the plans of its creators, as the survival of both species—humanity and the alien Builders—hangs in the balance.

THE LORD OF THE SANDS OF TIME
—ISSUI OGAWA

Sixty-two years after human life on Earth was annihilated by rampaging alien invaders, the enigmatic Messenger O is sent back in time with a mission to unite humanity of past eras—during the Second World War, in ancient Japan, and at the dawn of humanity—to defeat the invasion before it begins. However, in a future shredded by love and genocide, love waits for O. Will O save humanity only to doom himself?

THE NEXT CONTINENT
—ISSUI OGAWA

The year is 2025 and Gotoba General Construction—a firm that has built structures to survive the Antarctic and the Sahara—has received its most daunting challenge yet. Sennosuke Touenji, the chairman of one of the world's largest leisure conglomerates, wants a moon base fit for civilian use, and he wants his granddaughter Taé to be his eyes and ears on the harsh lunar surface. Taé and Gotoba engineer Aomine head to the moon where adventure, trouble, and perhaps romance await.

DRAGON SWORD AND WIND CHILD
—NORIKO OGIWARA

The God of Light and the Goddess of Darkness have waged a ruthless war across the land of Toyoashihara for generations. But for fifteen-year-old Saya, the war is far away—until the day she discovers that she is the reincarnation of the Water Maiden and a princess of the Children of the Dark. Raised to love the Light and detest the Dark, Saya must come to terms with her heritage even as the Light and Dark both seek to claim her, for she is the only mortal who can awaken the legendary Dragon Sword, the weapon destined to bring an end to the war. Can Saya make the choice between the Light and Dark, or is she doomed—like all the Water Maidens who came before her...?

MIRROR SWORD AND SHADOW PRINCE
—NORIKO OGIWARA

When the heir to the empire comes to Mino, the lives of young Oguna and Toko change forever. Oguna is drafted to become a shadow prince, a double trained to take the place of the hunted royal. But soon Oguna is given the Mirror Sword, and his power to wield it threatens the entire nation. Only Toko can stop him, but to do so she needs to gather four magatama, beads with magical powers that can be strung together to form the Misumaru of Death. Toko's journey is one of both adventure and self-discovery, and also brings her face to face with the tragic truth behind Oguna's transformation. A story of two parallel quests, of a pure love tried by the power of fate, the second volume of Tales of the Magatama is as thrilling as *Dragon Sword and Wind Child*.

SUMMER, FIREWORKS AND MY CORPSE
—OTSUICHI

Two short novels, including the title story and *Black Fairy Tale*, plus a bonus short story. *Summer* is a simple story of a nine-year-old girl who dies while on summer vacation. While her youthful killers try to hide her body, she tells us the story—from the point of view of her dead body—of the children's attempt to get away with murder. *Black Fairy Tale* is classic J-horror: a young girl loses an eye in an accident, but receives a transplant. Now she can see again, but what she sees out of her new left eye is the experiences and memories of its previous owner. Its previous *deceased* owner.

ZOO
–OTSUICHI

A man receives a photo of his girlfriend every day in the mail…so that he can keep track of her body's decomposition. A deathtrap that takes a week to kill its victims. Haunted parks and airplanes held in the sky by the power of belief. These are just a few of the stories by Otsuichi, Japan's master of dark fantasy.

ALL YOU NEED IS KILL
–HIROSHI SAKURAZAKA

When the alien Mimics invade, Keiji Kiriya is just one of many recruits shoved into a suit of battle armor called a Jacket and sent out to kill. Keiji dies on the battlefield, only to be reborn each morning to fight and die again and again. On his 158th iteration, he gets a message from a mysterious ally—the female soldier known as the Full Metal Bitch. Is she the key to Keiji's escape or his final death?

SLUM ONLINE
–HIROSHI SAKURAZAKA

Etsuro Sakagami is a college freshman who feels uncomfortable in reality, but when he logs onto the combat MMO *Versus Town*, he becomes "Tetsuo," a karate champ on his way to becoming the most powerful martial artist around. While his relationship with new classmate Fumiko goes nowhere, Etsuro spends his days and nights online in search of the invincible fighter Ganker Jack. Drifting between the virtual and the real, will Etsuro ever be ready to face his most formidable opponent?

BATTLE ROYALE: THE NOVEL
–KOUSHUN TAKAMI

Koushun Takami's notorious high-octane thriller envisions a nightmare scenario: a class of junior high school students is taken to a deserted island where, as part of a ruthless authoritarian program, they are provided arms and forced to kill until only one survivor is left standing. Criticized as violent exploitation when first published in Japan—where it became a runaway best seller—*Battle Royale* is a *Lord of the Flies* for the twenty-first century, a potent allegory of what it means to be young and (barely) alive in a dog-eat-dog world.

MARDOCK SCRAMBLE
–TOW UBUKATA

Why me? It was to be the last thought a young prostitute, Rune-Balot, would ever have…as a human anyway. Taken in by a devious gambler named Shell, she became a slave to his cruel desires and would have been killed by his hand if not for the self-aware Universal Tool (and little yellow mouse) known as Oeufcoque. Now a cyborg, Balot is not only nigh invulnerable, but has the ability to disrupt electrical systems of all sorts. But even these powers may not be enough for Balot to deal with Shell, who offloads his memories to remain above the law, the immense assassin Dimsdale-Boiled, or the neon-noir streets of Mardock City itself.

THE CAGE OF ZEUS
-SAYURI UEDA

The Rounds are humans with the sex organs of both genders. Artificially created to test the limits of the human body in space, they are now a minority, despised and hunted by the terrorist group the Vessel of Life. Aboard Jupiter-I, a space station orbiting the gas giant that shares its name, the Rounds have created their own society with a radically different view of gender and of life itself. Security chief Shirosaki keeps the peace between the Rounds and the typically gendered "Monaurals," but when a terrorist strike hits the station, the balance of power is at risk...and an entire people is targeted for genocide.

MM9
-HIROSHI YAMAMOTO

Japan is beset by natural disasters all the time: typhoons, earthquakes, and...giant monster attacks. A special anti-monster unit called the Meteorological Agency Monsterological Measures Department (MMD) has been formed to deal with natural disasters of high "monster magnitude." The work is challenging, the public is hostile, and the monsters are hungry, but the MMD crew has science, teamwork...and a legendary secret weapon on their side. Together, they can save Japan, and the universe!

THE STORY OF IBIS
-HIROSHI YAMAMOTO

In a world where humans are a minority and androids have created their own civilization, a wandering storyteller meets the beautiful android Ibis. She tells him seven stories of human/android interaction in order to reveal the secret behind humanity's fall. The tales that Ibis tells are science fiction stories about the events surrounding the development of artificial intelligence (AI) in the twentieth and twenty-first centuries. At a glance, these stories do not appear to have any sort of connection, but what is the true meaning behind them? What are Ibis's real intentions?

VISIT US AT WWW.HAIKASORU.COM